HOUSE OF SKIN

TIM CURRAN

WWW.COMETPRESS.US

A Comet Press Book

First Comet Press Trade Paperback Edition
November 2013

Cover illustration by Amy Wilkins

ISBN 13: 978-1-936964-39-0

Visit Comet Press on the web at: www.cometpress.us

Tim Curran hails from Michigan's Upper Peninsula. He is the author of the novels *Skin Medicine, Hive, Dead Sea, Resurrection, Hag Night, The Devil Next Door, Long Black Coffin, Graveworm,* and *Biohazard*. His short stories have been collected in *Bone Marrow Stew* and *Zombie Pulp*. His novellas include *Fear Me, The Underdwelling, The Corpse King, Puppet Graveyard, Sow,* and *Worm*. His short stories have appeared in such magazines as *City Slab, Flesh&Blood, Book of Dark Wisdom,* and *Inhuman*, as well as anthologies such as *Flesh Feast, Shivers IV, High Seas Cthulhu,* and *Vile Things*. Find him on the web at: www.corpseking.com

BLOOD RED CHERRY

Although there were any number of beginnings to what came to pass, Lisa would later be certain that it began the night she left Chowchilla and picked up a rider.

It was one of those nights cribbed from a Gothic novel: a whipping, wind-driven rain was falling from the black, lonesome sky and lightning flashed on the horizon, limning the prison buildings in ghostly, strobing phosphorescence. Thunder roared and the wind screamed. She had felt the storm coming all day as she could feel her period sneaking up on her late in the month sometimes. This was Mother Nature's menstrual cycle; this was how she cleansed herself. Not with a flow of blood but with an acrid fall of rain, an ozone stink of lightning, and a roar of thunder. Out with the bad and in with the good.

"Christ in Heaven," Lisa said under her breath.

It was a bad one.

That was just great.

She had a big day ahead of her tomorrow and if the storm raged through the night, she'd get no sleep. It was an affliction she'd suffered with since childhood: a mortal fear of storms. Rain and wind filled her with a creeping sense of foreboding that was completely inexplicable. When a storm raged, she'd cower on the sofa, stare blindly at the Weather Channel, hoping for a sign of relief, an indication that the tempest would pass quickly. When it didn't, she would start drinking cognac, the only liquor she could stomach for some reason. At first just in a glass with ice. Then, as her nerves frayed with every boom and flash and her reserve went to pieces with them, straight from the bottle.

Storms.

Thunder. Wind.

She thought: I can't take another night of it. I'll lose my mind this time.

She climbed behind the wheel of her SUV and drove to the gates. The guard waved her through. The storm was gathering quickly, intent on destroying her peace of mind. She had to get home as quickly as possible.

The traffic was heavy, of course. Every idiot with a set of wheels was out on the streets tonight. It would take a good thirty minutes, if not more, to get home to the relative safety that awaited her there. Her knuckles were white as she gripped the wheel for dear life. Perspiration was running down her temples. A stink of fear came off her skin—salty and hot.

It took her no less than three-quarters of an hour to make it to her lonely little house outside Modesto. By that time the rain was cascading down in sheets, the night world shuddering with the rumble of thunder. Lightning flashed at regular intervals, the countryside exploding with blinding light. The wind lashed at the car, trying to force it into the ditch.

Not far now, she told herself, just hang on.

Finally, her driveway. She pulled in and killed the engine. Her fingers trembled so badly, she dropped her keys. It took two hands to pick them up: one to steady the other.

The wind slammed into the car.

She reached for the door handle and something shifted behind her.

Someone's in the back seat—

But she never finished that thought. There was a blur of motion and then a loop of wire encircled her throat. Tightly, but not tight enough to kill. Not yet. Her heart thudded in her chest, her breath rasping in her lungs.

So dark, so terribly dark. She could see nothing in the rearview mirror, just a black shape. Her hands were clutched on those that held the wire. They felt cool, damp even, but feminine.

"Who are you?" she managed.

There was a smacking sound. Someone licking their lips.

"Please. Who are you? What do you want?" she gasped. "I . . . I have money."

"It's not enough, Dr. Lisa," the voice answered.

Lightning flashed and the car was flooded with light. She saw her attacker. It was one of the patients from the prison hospital. Cherry Hill. *Cherry,* of all possible inmates. There were a lot of bad ones at Chowchilla, but Cherry was somehow worse. During one of their sessions, Cherry had told her that she could smell death on herself, that it clung to her like a sewer stink clings to a buried pipe. It could not be sanitized or washed away, she claimed, because it oozed from her pores like sweat. It was on her skin, it was in her hair, she could smell it on her fingers and taste it on her tongue. Every morning in Ad-Seg, solitary, she tried to cleanse herself of it: she stood in the hot shower soaping herself with foam and gel and body wash, she scrubbed and scrubbed until her skin was red and hurting. She washed her hair again and again until it smelled like green apples and it was so clean it squeaked.

It was a psychosis, of course. Cherry had murdered many people, even members of her own family, so it wasn't that surprising.

As difficult as it was, Lisa tried to keep her composure. "Cherry. Listen to me. Can you do that? Will you listen to my words?"

"No." Flat denial. When she was in that mood, there was no talking to her. It was best to keep quiet and let her begin, if she would begin at all.

Cherry had many obsessions as most killers did, but her favorite was *evil*. The nature of it, the politics of it, the way it contaminated minds like some toxic contagion. She considered it a natural force like wind or rain. Evil (she had said) not only turned minds black with hate and turned cities into graveyards, but it spread like a virus, jumping body to body in a ceaseless, remorseless circle of infection. Evil existed to destroy the human race. Its goal was to strip you bare at your most primal level. It did this by invading your body until your body was no longer your own, but a vessel for itself. Once it had you, it would kill and maim everything you loved, it would rape your soul and enslave your mind and force you into the most diabolic acts, shitting on your morals and ethics and pissing all over your belief system until you could only believe in evil itself and nothing more.

"Death is leaking from me, Dr. Lisa. Can you smell it?" she said.

The insane thing was for just a moment, Lisa almost could.

"Cherry?"

"Cherry's dead." The voice was flat, emotionless.

"Please, Cherry . . . please . . ."

"That's what they always say, isn't it?" the voice said. *"Please."*

"What do you want?"

But she wouldn't say.

Cherry believed not only that evil was a force of nature, an elemental, but that death itself was a parasite. It entered you in the larval stage when you were weakened from abuse and despair. Then it crawled up your spine and attached itself to your brain stem where it grew, lengthening and thickening, filling itself with eggs until it was ready to burst with spawn.

"That's when you kill," she had said during one of the sessions. "It controls your mind and makes you. Do you know why?"

"Why, Cherry?"

"Because . . . that is its life cycle. When you kill, it plants its eggs in your victim and infests other hosts."

Lisa gasped as the wire cut a bit deeper.

She knew Cherry was expert with it. The *garrote*. She'd killed several people with it out in society and murdered an inmate at Chowchilla, nearly taking her head off. Lisa could not have been in a more dangerous situation. Cherry was deluded, paranoid, schizophrenic, and psychotic. She was housed in the criminally insane wing of the hospital. How she had gotten out was open to conjecture. The fact remained: she *was* out.

The wire constricted and Lisa's eyes bulged like egg yolks. Her fingers fought and tore at the wire, but it was hopeless. The wire had severed her skin now, cutting into meat, going deeper where no fingers could find it. Her head pounded and her lungs ached, but it was her throat that knew the real pain. She started to wish she'd left the hospital at a normal time, came home and stretched out the sofa. A glass of wine, a little TV . . .

The thoughts in her mind were spiraling now from lack of oxygen. They were spinning around and around, faster and faster. There was no focus or cohesion. She trembled on the edge of consciousness.

She opened her eyes. She had blacked out, but just for a moment or two. The wire was still around her throat. Cherry had her face very close. Lisa could feel her hot breath in her ear. *"I love your hair, Dr. Lisa. It's soft. It's the color of wheat. I want to shave your head. I want to wear your scalp and dance in the rain."*

The wire had loosened. "What do you want, Cherry?" Lisa said, her voice dry and gritty. "Tell me."

The wire tightened and tightened.

A thousand thoughts and memories converged on her drifting, oxygen-starved mind as she saw static, gray glittering specks, and everything was washed away and she fell into darkness.

And a coo of a voice said, "Not yet, Doctor. It won't be that easy for you . . ."

THE CONFESSIONS OF DR. BLOOD-AND-BONES (1)

There are places death goes.

A multitude of dead-ends and vacant quarters that it inhabits and calls its own. Abandoned cemeteries and forgotten crossroads where the night winds play and whisper in the tongues of lost souls. Dusty crematoria and dank crypt, prison, madhouse, and morgue. Cancer wards and slaughterhouses where the reek and scream of tortured life cling like grave mold or a child's echoing cry. Death lives on the razored edges of knives and surgical equipment. On the tips of fingers and tongues, in concentration camps and marriage beds, in cribs and mausoleums alike. Death is everywhere, sewn into the tattered, unwoven fabric of reality.

There is nowhere Death doesn't go, no hole too deep or altar too sanctified. And it is most at home in the twisted dreams and anguished thoughts of men and women.

It has a special place here.

It moves without check, in places where the living and dead mingle. Where the insane and the sane wear the same brooding faces. It lives in the dreamscapes where men deflower a thousand lovers, their children, and ultimately themselves. Where women mate and kill and destroy everything but their own vanity.

And sometimes death visits the same houses and buildings and thoroughfares that these same men and women call their own. This time it chose an old and crumbling house of filthy brick and here it looked for answers.

The aura of decay and depravity and human suffering was nearly overwhelming. Droplets of rain entered through the sagging, patched roof and fell into the attic. The air was pungent with the stink of rotting plaster and mice-gnawed wallpaper, the windows grimy, the floors uneven, and the walls bowed.

Death had heard things about this place, tales of madness and horror. Stories of unspeakable atrocities and blatant perversities committed behind these graying, powdery walls. So it came, hungry to learn more, looking for something, anything to call its own in this lifeless place that was untenanted by even rats or spiders or termites or silverfish.

Within the walls, reality and unreality were evenly balanced, like light and shadow at twilight or madness and sanity in the mind of a desperate man.

There are places death goes.

I know these places, for they are mine.

BLOOD BATH

The house stood high above the others on the street, set on a lurching hill covered with stunted grasses and denuded trees. Its neighbors crowded in to either side, dwarfed by the rambling, gothic monolith. It was desolate and weathered a uniform gray. Black turrets and crooked spires jutted from its sagging roof into a sky of rolling, moon-washed clouds.

Eddy stood before it, head bowed.

If houses had voices, then this one was calling to him. It went far beyond what he'd heard of the place—those were tales, true maybe, but just tales and this was reality. He didn't go in alone. He took Cassandra along. She had a hunger for heroin and sexual excess. She was a whore and a junkie and that's why he loved her. Like him, she was not whole. She was damaged and he understood damaged.

Holding hands, Cassandra and Eddy went in.

He wasn't sure what he expected. Perhaps a rush of demon wind; a rattling chandelier; clanking chains or ghostly laughter. None of these things were in evidence. Instead, there was singular neutrality suspended in the air like a flat and distant memory. To some, it would have been nothing—merely a feeling of desolation and destitution common to all old and empty houses; but to the truly sensitive, it was a huge and morose sound, a scream of nothingness, a chorus from the void.

Eddy heard it and stopped dead in his tracks, a feeling of elation and rumbling confusion in his head.

"Why so many mirrors?" Cassandra said.

Eddy shrugged. He wondered this himself. There were mirrors of every size and shape crowding the walls. Many were broken, many were not. All were covered in grime and dust.

He cocked his head as if he were listening.

"What is it?" Cassandra asked. She was used to his sensing things that she could not.

"Did you hear it?"

She shook her head.

He thought as much. Sometimes he wondered if he wasn't as disturbed as all those doctors said, hearing the things he did. But no, there was a rhyme and reason for everything and the sounds and voices he heard also fit into that pattern. All he had to do was make sense of it all, fit together the puzzle.

He and Cassandra had been together for six weeks now and he supposed it was the longest he'd ever spent with one woman. But she wasn't like the others. She understood why he had to find his father even if, at times, he didn't.

She gladly, willingly traveled from city to city with him, through ghetto and slum and desperation, as he searched, listened for the faint psychic echo that would lead him to the man who'd fathered him. Their travels had brought them here, to a desolate and shunned section at the edge of the Excelsior District. To this house in particular. A house his father had once called his own.

They moved quietly from room to room as Eddy smoked and listened to the wall of indecipherable noise he encountered everywhere. Close, so very close. They went upstairs and the noise thinned.

Cassandra was nervous. Was she, too, beginning to feel something? Or was it just her imagination toying with her? She decided it was probably neither and nothing that a syringe couldn't fix up.

*   *   *

"Anything?" she said after a time. She was beginning to sweat.

"He's been here," Eddy said in a breathless voice.

"Recently?"

"Yes."

Her eyes were bright and expectant. She was shaking and wiping her nose almost continually.

Eddy turned to her, stroking her cheek. "You don't look well. Do you need a little something?"

Cassandra nodded. "Yes, just a little."

He slipped a plastic bag into her hand. "Take as much as you like. Only go downstairs and do it. I need to be alone."

She thanked him and left.

Eddy listened to the thud of her feet on the stairs until she was gone.

Then he fell to his knees. He was alone in this crowded room. He had to think, to make sense of it all, to keep in mind that he was the catalyst here and without him, nothing would or could happen. He stared off through the dust and grime and tried to empty his mind, tried to let the quiet noise of the voices fill his head.

Just let it happen, he told himself.

But it wasn't that easy.

He kept seeing his father in his mind. The man he remembered from boyhood, a gaunt, hollow-eyed man who rarely spoke. A man who spent his days locked in a room full of books, his nights out on the streets practicing his art. William Zero considered himself an artist, they said, and his canvas was the human body. His admirers were few. It took a special mind to appreciate what he did to human flesh with his knives. Yet, an artist he was. And his son, Eddy, never saw him as anything else.

He'd been gone twenty years now. Twenty years in which his son's only contact with him was through yellowing articles his mother had clipped methodically from newspapers. Articles she had clipped and pasted into a scrap book. It was her hope, Eddy supposed, that by rubbing his face in his father's crimes he would be saved from the same life of derangement and violent delusion. But it hadn't worked. He never saw his father as the bogeyman she'd hoped, but as a complex individual he could never hope to understand, but wanted to.

A man he spent his teens and twenties fantasizing about.

A man he wanted to meet.

A man he needed to become if he ever hoped to find him.

Eddy stood and leaned against the wall. It was here, he knew that much, that special psychic odor he needed. His father's trail began here. But where? Where was the clue he needed to begin the hunt?

Think, he told himself, think.

Just let it come to you.

And what happened then, he wasn't sure. Thoughts cavorted through his mind, meaningless little ditties that were flat and lifeless. His respiration increased, his heart hammered in his chest, his blood flowed with a rushing din that was like thunder.

My God, what is this?

But questions weren't to be answered. He'd come seeking truths and now, in ways known only to the house itself, those truths were coming. It was like the delicate fabric of reality itself was beginning to open up, slit by razored fingers, insane, whispered secrets pouring forth. Everything he needed to know, or at least a good deal of it, was filling the air around him. His head was raging with a high, discordant buzzing. It was only a matter of deciphering it. The answers were here, all around him. The answers to what his father was and where he'd gone.

The ceiling seemed to be coming down on him . . . something dark as oil was seeping from it in a swirling, fighting cloud of blackness. And it was alive with squirming, worming, wanting life and it had secrets to tell.

And Eddy was listening.

He saw his father as a boy plucking the wings from insects. There were well over a dozen in a cardboard box on his knees. He was attempting to reattach them as if his fingers were blessed with impossible surgical gifts. But no, they wouldn't go back on. He was angry. He dumped the box out and squashed the pitiful things under his shoe. He was angry that he couldn't take them apart and then put them back together.

Eddy was grinning.

And here was another scene planted in his head. His father as a young man stooped over a corpse in an anatomy lab, picking and prodding at it with a knife, willing it to do something. Trying to breathe life into it, to make it overcome its cold simplicity.

Now here were answers, indications of the man and how he'd finally chosen his life's calling. But it was all so purposely vague, so terribly ambiguous. Eddy needed more to go on.

The shadows were gathering around him now, whispering in his ears, taunting him, teasing him, telling him things he couldn't understand, didn't want to know, but had to. He could feel pressure against him, an avalanche of being, of need, of want, of love, of hate. Oh yes, he was the catalyst here. They'd been waiting for him, waiting for this moment of moments and now it had come. They danced and played and clutched and clawed at him, these shadows that were not shadows at all. They had him now and if he was sorry he'd come, it was far too late. The darkness became a black, greased womb, a palpitating orifice that opened wide and spilled a flood of crawling, creeping things that swarmed over him: lice and maggots, rats and pale crabs, undulant leeches and blind squirming roaches. They covered him, buried him, encased him, physical representations of the shifting shadows themselves. He felt them feed in through his ears, his mouth, his nose, his ass, crowding in him, showing him the sights and sounds of broken lives and pain without end. He tried to speak, but they were in his throat, black and mulling, suffocating him with their ideas, their dreams. He tried to think, but they flooded his brain, pushing his thoughts aside, forcing their needs and wants and desires on him.

He was helpless.

They pulled him from the room, dragging him over the cold and dusty floor, peeling his clothing free, screaming in his ears, kissing his will away. They made him creep about, a naked and deranged thing. They led him to the attic door and pushed him through, up the dirty stairs and into the vaultlike space above where . . . where—

Where he could finally see what they were so desperate to show him.

Skins.

Yes, the multitude patchwork of skins tacked to the sloping walls like grim tapestries—the graying pelts of men and women, of dogs and cats and rats and even apes. All of them peeled free in a single sheet from their respective anatomies with the utmost surgical precision by a man who was a highly skilled dissector, a skinner of no little talent, who fitted them all into a great puzzlework of hides upon the walls. A gruesome work of art. Eddy stared around him at skins with faces and scalps, even fingers and toes completely intact.

It was his father's work. Here were the membranes of all his victims and the animals he had experimented upon before them. Each had been meticulously divorced of their skin, what lay beneath dissected and reduced to basal anatomy—skeletal systems, nervous systems, vascular systems. It was the work of a diabolical genius, some had said after the house was entered by the police, a demented medico, an insane surgeon . . . but they hadn't understood the purpose, the technique, the ritual.

Eddy blinked his eyes and it was all gone.

His father's workshop was just a series of dusty attic rooms and alcoves now. There was nothing left but a single antique mirror whose surface was thick with grime. The shadows had shown him what he wanted to see, hinted at the dark path he must soon follow.

He licked his lips, tried to swallow. "I don't understand," he managed. "What does it mean . . . what . . ."

They all seemed to rage in his head at once, screaming and shrieking. Not only the voices of men and women, but the whimpering of dogs and the pained mewling of cats, the squeal of rats and the shrilling of vivisected apes. It filled his head in a cacophony of noise.

Yet, through it all, he heard the voice coming up the stairs.

"Eddy?"

He couldn't hope to answer.

"Eddy? What are you doing up there?"

Cassandra. Jesus, he shouldn't have brought her! This place was too dangerous, too alive, too undead for her. She could never understand this. The touch of the shadows would drive her insane.

There was a jolt of electricity in them, a raw and pungent stink of ozone and he knew they wanted her just as his father had wanted them. He knew that he was the vessel with which they would get her.

His brain rioting with their lust and rage and insanity, he crawled down the steps until he lay gasping in the dust of the second floor, trying to breathe, trying to reason, trying to do anything but what he was doing: curled-up mindlessly in a fetal position, his thighs wet with his own piss and his mouth tasting of his own vomit.

Cassandra, Cassandra . . .

This was all his doing. Maybe he brought her here on purpose and not by accident, knowing, somehow, that an innocent would be needed. Her blood and life would be needed. Maybe this vague psychic trail he'd been following had demanded it. And now the trail ended here and in ending would only begin anew.

But what were these shadows that knew so much of his father as if they'd been witness to his every action, his every misdeed? They were more than shadows, more than bits of enfolding ghosting darkness, they were his victims. The parts of them that could never leave this plane. The anger, the shock, the need, the wanting of life, of living, the shattered minds and residual hate of the human condition. Yes, they were all around him and they wanted much more. If he wanted to know what path his father had taken, then they were the only ones who could show him, because they knew, they had to know. And the price of their services wouldn't be cheap, for only the negativity of what they'd once been was left behind in these cloying shadows. They were killers now, deranged and hateful bloodsuckers and soul-eaters. Sadists and perverts and abusers. A roll call of the damned.

"Eddy?"

They rushed towards her voice with him in tow.

"Please . . ." he whispered.

(you want answers we need something in return . . .)

A knife was pressed into his hand.

* * *

Cassandra was coming up the steps now.

She'd heard something from above—voices, whispers—she wasn't sure. It could've just been Eddy talking to himself again. Yet, she didn't think so. And in this awful place, she would take no chances. Her head was bright, her nerves at peace. Heroin could do such things for you. She felt she could take on the world and best it without so much as panting.

"Eddy? What are you doing up there?"

No answer. Did he need help?

"You all right?" She was standing at the top of the steps now.

Eddy was coming at her, rushing at her like the wind, enveloped in a mist of starving blackness. And he was coming for her . . . with a knife.

She tried to cry out, but the blade had already opened her throat and she went down, tumbling down the steps and landing in a bleeding heap. She stared up at the monster coming for her with eyes mirroring confusion and no little amusement.

I'm cut, she found herself thinking. *I'm fucking cut.*

Her head was so fogged with narcotic delights, she couldn't be sure of anything. Maybe it was a game. If it hadn't been for the spreading wetness at her throat, she might have believed it.

"I'm sorry," Eddy said. "I'm so sorry."

Cassandra's lips opened and closed, but no words came forth, only blood.

Eddy took the knife up again and let it dance over her flesh, watching her secrets, red and ripe, spill out over the floor in a wash of death until he was drenched in her wine. He grew hard at the feel and the smell of the blood. His heart was hammering, his breath gasping from his lungs.

He let out a scream.

"*They* made me do it," he explained to her staring face as the shadows soared and screamed about him. "They wouldn't tell me anymore without sacrifice. You understand that, don't you, my love? They're so hungry, my God, they're ravenous. But with blood . . . oh, then they'll talk, then they'll tell me . . ."

Cassandra didn't seem to mind.

Her lips were silent, her thoughts quiet, her pain and addiction finally at an end. She lay there, wrapped in a cloak of red dreams, cooling slowly to nothingness.

Eddy kissed her wet lips and ran his fingers over her like he used to as the red milk of death pooled around them. He eased her into stillness and soothed her life away as she'd done so many times with his worries and frustrations. Even in death, he supposed, she understood, she knew and still loved him the way only real lovers can. Never really dying, never really fading away.

But there was no more time for talk or sweet nothings or tender postmortem embraces. The shadows were starving. They demanded to be fed.

In a frenzy, Eddy gave them what they desired, hacking at Cassandra and bathing in her blood, swimming in it like a hungry fluke, orchestrating her mutilation like a conductor with a red dripping baton until the cold meat concerto was complete, until he was collapsed on top of her, welded to her with drying blood and entrails.

The shadows wove around him, heavy, drunken, and sated. There were no more screams or laughter or demands. They were bloated now, their death-bellies full of the seed of life.

Eddy lay over the violated corpse of Cassandra, muttering prayers and remembering something that he was certain was not his own memory: a clown. *A clown? I never knew any clowns.* But the memory persisted. A clown that came into his room at night, an obscene thing in yellow silk pantaloons and an orange ruffled shirt with pom-poms down the front. The clown's face was painted white, the eyes black holes, the mouth thick-lipped and smeared with red lipstick. It danced around the room before it covered him with its weight as he was doing to Cassandra now. The clown's breath stank of whiskey. Its fingers were cold. It smelled of sweat and filth and pig semen.

No, no, no, no, not that—

He shook it from his head. It seemed real, yet it was not his memory. And if it wasn't his that meant it belonged to—

Don't think it. Don't ever think it.

He sighed. The memory was gone.

The shadows. They would help him find his father, they would lead him there, they would take him home like a lost child by the hand. Together they would travel those same dark and enlightening roads as his father had and ultimately, they would be with him, in soul, spirit, and flesh.

"So tell me," he urged them later when Cassandra's corpse was cool, drying, and sticky. "Tell me what I need to know."

The shadows encircled him sluggishly, ready to tell tales and point the way. They began to speak and Eddy Zero, the boy who'd sprang from the loins of a deranged and delusive man, listened and learned. They told stories in voices like the wind, the stars.

When they were finished, the stink of old blood permeating the air, they fell back and began to dream.

And out on the street before that desolate and disturbed house, a wicked and depraved laughter fell like rain on the walks.

"AHA-HA-HA-HA-HA-HA-HA-HA-HA-HA-HA—"

And whether it came from Eddy or the crumbling pipes of that sullen house, it was anyone's guess.

*   *   *

It had to start somewhere, so it started here. Like winter starts with a few flakes of snow or spring with a few drops of rain, it began. Eddy knew the way, he knew the dark byways he would travel, through what gutters and boneyards and theaters of suffering his search would take him.

And he went willingly.

MEMOIRS OF THE TEMPLAR SOCIETY (1)

In the days of his youth, James Stadtler sought out the underbelly of society. He kept the company of criminals, perverts, fetishists, and prostitutes. All those who had sampled life's darker pleasures and lived to tell the tale. It was in this way he met Zero and Grimes. They were both older than he—professional men, it turned out—and equally as jaded by the experiences life and ready cash had brought them. There had to be a better way.

And together, they would find it.

*　　*　　*

He met them quite by accident in a Chinatown brothel. They had just finished with their evening's amusement and were hanging about the bar, drinking and talking in low tones. Stadtler paid them little mind. He was waiting for his oriental flower and wouldn't leave until he sampled her wares.

They sidled up next to him and sat quietly for a time.

"Haven't seen you here before," one said. "Name's Grimes. This is my associate Dr. Zero."

"What of it?" Stadtler said.

"And you're . . ."

"Stadtler. Jim Stadtler. Again, what of it?"

The two men looked to each other and laughed. Grimes was short and stout, balding with twinkling blue eyes. Zero was tall and thin, dark-eyed, with an immaculately trimmed beard. They both wore business suits and overcoats.

"Is there something funny about that?" Stadtler asked.

"We find your manner . . . refreshing," Zero told him.

"Do you?"

"Oh yes."

Grimes ordered more drinks for them all. Stadtler didn't mind; he barely had enough money to cover his whore, let alone all the booze he was sucking down. If these two queers wanted to pay, so be it. He'd gladly talk with them if they covered expenses.

"Do you have any favorites here?" Grimes asked.

"The Asian women," he told them. "Particularly Lee Chang. I've been through the rest. Whites, blacks, Indians. I'm tired of them all. Even Lee is getting boring. But what else is there?"

"Yes, what else?" Grimes said.

He and Zero exchanged another of their secretive looks.

Stadtler was waiting for the inevitable proposition he was certain was coming. Hopefully, they'd buy him more drinks before he had to turn them down. He figured Grimes was at least fifty; Zero somewhere in his forties. It was a novel approach they'd developed, he thought, hanging around whorehouses and trying to pick up men. It all seemed rather absurd when there were dozens of places males of all ages could be had for a price or for free.

"We know of your plight," Zero assured him. "There isn't a house of pleasure in this damn town we haven't milked dry for entertainment."

Grimes nodded. "A man reaches a point where he needs something new."

Here it comes, Stadtler thought.

"Before you bother going any farther," he said, "I should tell you I'm not interested."

"In what?" Grimes asked. He looked slyly amused.

"This isn't a proposition," Zero said.

"Isn't it?"

"If it was a young man we wanted, sir, the city's full of better pickings than you, I dare say."

Stadtler felt terribly foolish. He'd as much as insulted them and all on the part of an over-inflated ego. "My apologies," he said. "I thought—"

"Think nothing of it."

"What do you do for a living?" Grimes inquired, ordering more drinks.

"Private security," Stadtler said. "You're a doctor, I take it?"

Zero smiled. "I hold that degree, but I'm not in practice. I sometimes lecture in anatomy at UCSF."

"If it pleases him," Grimes said.

Stadtler studied Zero. His clothes were tailored, his nails manicured. Everything about him spoke of money. A man, apparently, who only worked when it pleased him. A dream life.

"And you?" he said to Grimes.

"I teach mathematical theory at the university."

"And you get together from time to time to enjoy certain pleasures?"

"Weekly."

Zero added, "But it seems there's less and less to be had. Our little circle of two is growing tiresome. We need fresh blood."

"New thoughts on the nature of experience."

"And you want me to join?"

"Maybe."

"And what do we call our little group?" Stadtler asked.

Grimes and Zero locked eyes again.

"The Templar Society," Zero said.

"As in the knights of history?"

"As in the way they were *reputed* to be," he explained, "not as they truly were."

"Interesting."

A silence passed between the three as each debated this possible partnership.

"I'm game, if you still want me," Stadtler said.

"What do you think?" Grimes asked.

"He'll do nicely."

Stadtler smiled. "A toast, then? To the Society of three?"

They swallowed down their drinks and Grimes ordered more. Stadtler was getting drunk and it seemed appropriate to celebrate.

"But first," Zero said, "will your profession stop you from indulging in anything considered immoral?"

"Or illegal?" Grimes wondered.

Stadtler thought about what he was getting into. He didn't give a damn. "Of course not. I'm game for anything."

They drank again and began talking about the women they'd had and what they'd bullied them into doing. They laughed and joked and confided like old friends. And through it all, Stadtler couldn't help feeling that it was the beginning of the end somehow.

*   *   *

"I'm glad you waited," Lee Chang said, coming up behind Stadtler and licking his ear. She was dressed out in silk and lace, her legs long and sensuous, her breasts high and full. Her eyes promised a thousand ecstasies.

"At last," Stadtler moaned, running his hand between her legs. "These are my friends. They'll be joining us tonight."

Zero and Grimes looked pleased.

Lee licked her lips with lecherous delight. "I'll do my best to amuse them."

The foursome went up the stairs to the chambers above.

*   *   *

And this is how it all came together.

They met more often in the weeks that passed, the games taking on a new and practiced urgency.

And by that time, there was no looking back.

DOCTOR OF DEMENTIA

The thing that bothered Lisa the worst was that she'd let Eddy Zero slip through her hands. It hadn't been her decision, of course; she'd been a junior member of staff at Coalinga State Hospital. The others—doctors Quillan, Reeves, Staidmyer—had the final decision. And after some five years, they'd decided to let Eddy go. Whether they actually believed his lies of being cured or it had more to do with overcrowding or budget cuts, she was never sure. Probably all three.

"We have to release him," Dr. Staidmyer told her one evening.

"With all due respect, sir, you can't be serious."

His face reddened. He didn't like being challenged. "And why not, Dr. Lochmere?"

"Eddy Zero is dangerous. You know that as well as I. He's a textbook sexual psychopath."

Staidmyer had smiled curtly, as if she, barely out of internship and a woman to boot, couldn't possibly know what she was talking about. "I disagree completely. He's compulsive, yes, but hardly a maniac."

"He has a history of psychosexual deviation. He raped two women."

"And has been rehabilitated."

"You can't be serious."

"I am. Before he came here, he was repressed and hateful, but he's come around nicely. I can't possibly keep him here any longer."

Lisa just stood there, feeling helpless and awkward in the male-dominated hierarchy of Coalinga. *Rehabilitated? He isn't goddamn rehabilitated. He's still a dangerous felon! If you think he's come around nicely, give him a few hours alone with your wife.* Of course, she didn't say any of that because it wouldn't have been professional and they liked their shrinks professional at Coalinga, a.k.a. Hotel California.

Regardless, that was that. Eddy Zero slipped through her hands. Oh, she could've told Staidmyer things only she knew. Like how Eddy admitted to her that Staidmyer and the rest were doddering old fools, how he'd lied to them, worked them like putty in his fingers. Made them believe they'd affected a cure on him. But she remained silent. She could've told them how he tried to rape her with an orderly just outside the door. But they'd made their decision.

And Eddy slipped away.

But she never forgot.

She never would.

The possibility that he was out there, even now, stalking innocents, is what really bothered her. Because of three naïve men who called themselves psychiatrists, a monster had been unleashed on the world. Maybe at the time of his release he'd been little more than a twisted sexual predator with aspirations of psychotic mania, but she knew that would change. A man who fed on suffering like he did could only grow more evil with time.

According to the law, Eddy wasn't insane. Insane individuals do not plot, do not plan like she knew Eddy did. But the law was wrong. He'd told her many things he hadn't dared whisper to the senior members of the Coalinga staff . . . and only when not being recorded. He was no fool. He planned to find his father one day, he'd said. The infamous Dr. Blood-and-Bones. And the only way he could do that, Eddy was certain, was to follow in dear old dad's footsteps.

A few months after Eddy had gone, Lisa resigned from Coalinga and found a job as a prison psychiatrist. The pay was poor, but she made her own decisions as to the sanity of certain individuals and her advice was usually followed. And that in itself made it all worth while.

But she was never happy. She quit the prison a year later.

There was no explanation for what followed. At least, none she wanted to think about. Suffice to say, she'd pulled herself up from the darkness and tried to forget.

There was little else she could do. Her own ambition had caused her to do things that completely went against the codes of her profession.

And she never stopped thinking about Eddy and what he was doing.

Pure psychopaths are a rare thing. Most psychiatrists would cut off a limb for a chance to work with one and she was no different. There was a book in Eddy. The son of a serial killer suffering from advanced multiple personality disorder who wanted to recreate dad's crimes. My God, it was positively unique. It could've been a big book, but it would be nothing unless she could find Eddy.

And she had every intention of doing just that.

She hired a private investigator. It took him several months to locate Eddy. He moved around a great deal. He found him in Chicago first, then in Detroit, and finally in San Francisco. And there the trail went cold.

But that wouldn't be the end of it.

He'd last been seen in San Fran and this is where she began her hunt.

For Eddy and perhaps for his father as well. If there was an answer to the madness that ate away at her life these many years, it lay with those two men.

CONFESSIONS OF DR. BLOOD-AND-BONES (2)

Can a man love a city?

Can he reach out and embrace it like a woman, make love to it and be loved by it? I'd lived in San Francisco for less than half of my life and it was only in those last precious years that I fell in love with it. And it fell in love with me. Together, we shared things in the dreaming, hot night. We whispered to one another of woes and hopes and nightmares.

I knew the charmless concrete and pavement like a lover's body. I knew its boulevards and avenues and dead ends and cul-de-sacs. I knew where to find life in the city. And death.

I loved it. But did it truly love me?

Or did it just tempt me, stealing away my innocence with whispers of love, allusions of a midnight seduction? Was it just a taker? A user? A cold and loveless thing that made away with my sanity in the dead of night?

There was no way to know.

No way at all.

But if nothing else, the city showed me itself like it had to no other. It was open to me, with me, showing me its depravity and lust and hatred of anything approaching order. After all, it was little more than a confused tumble of crowded streets and monolithic buildings parading as an orderly, modern city. And in its black, hungry heart, it hated those who had built it originally and those that resurrected it after the 1906 earthquake, breathing an ugly semblance of life into its diseased carcass. So if you happened to be one practicing certain atrocities upon its unwelcome tenants, the city would show you new and obscene vistas of pain.

Because it loved agony.

And it lived on human suffering.

It took me under its wing, under the guise of a lover, and by the time I was hopelessly infatuated with its decadent ways and profane means, it revealed to me that I was little more than a tool to it, an instrument to act out its criminal appetites.

But none of that bothered me by then.

Love of steel and stone, exploited humanity and nameless perversion had captured my heart. For that was the city. I loved it and I wanted to be used.

And was.

The city had dreams and so did I. And together we merged, flesh and concrete, thought and hopelessness.

We were lovers, host and parasite, needing and taking and giving no quarter. We were one.

EDDY IN THE SHADOWS

During the next few weeks after Cassandra's death, Eddy was busy. He searched and inquired and always the Shadows were nearby, hiding in alley and corner, throwing out bits of the puzzle to him.

But they were vague clues, always terribly so, but he took them like a starving man gladly takes a few meager crusts of bread.

The police had found Cassandra's body, led there by unknown means. The papers spoke endlessly of it, approaching the crime from every conceivable angle. They theorized that some new and vicious maniac was on the loose. After a week, then two, and no more murders, the subject became tired and any further discussion was relegated to the back pages. A two-week old murder, regardless of how brutal, was soon forgotten by the public as fresh crimes reared their grim heads.

Yet, the murder and its mysterious qualities—the unknown victim, the unknown assailant—had captured the imagination of a certain sector of the populace. They waited for the faceless killer to strike again, for surely he would. Eddy picked up bits of gossip in coffee houses and taverns. Tales concerning the killer's identity, previous crimes, and fresher atrocities the police were covering up. Some even suggested that Dr. Blood-and-Bones had returned from hiding to vent his hunger. If nothing else, Eddy realized, the public at large had a wonderful sense of drama where dreadful crimes were concerned. Horror stories never go out of fashion and the bloodier, the better.

And while these tales were told and quietly grew tiresome, he prowled the midnight streets of the city with the Shadows in tow, looking for signs of his father. It was an aimless search, but Eddy let his senses guide him. That and the Shadows that constantly led him into darker and more depraved sectors of the city.

He haunted the very worst neighborhoods by night—Bayview, the Tenderloin, Market Street, the Western Addition, Chinatown, all the places the wary avoided after dark, probing ever deeper into the diseased, gangrenous carcass of San Francisco. At ground level in the urban graveyard, the city looked like a defoliated forest, a jungle poisoned black to its hoary roots, nothing left but dead trees and stumps which were the crowded, crumbling buildings and rotting hovels around him. And everywhere he asked the same question: Did anyone know William Zero or even hear of him? Most said they didn't; a few said the name was familiar. But as to whether that was because of personal knowledge or a memory of the crimes twenty years past, it was hard to tell.

Eddy continued his search and became more frustrated than ever.

At a bondage house on Geary Boulevard, he met a man named Gulliver. He was a former Evangelical minister who had gone the way of sin. But he seemed happy. After a few drinks, Eddy asked the inevitable question.

"Zero," Gulliver said, mulling it over.

"Yes."

"William Zero?"

"That's right."

Gulliver looked thoughtful. "Now why is that name so damn familiar? I think I knew someone by that name. Parishioner? Could that be it? Or was it since then?"

Eddy waited.

"Can't place him."

"Maybe you read about him?"

"Zero . . . could be . . . I'm not sure."

"He was in the newspapers some time ago."

"Oh, I think I remember now. Politician wasn't he? Yes, you'd be surprised how many of our leading citizens come down here for fun and games. Councilman, was he?"

"No, you're thinking of someone else. This Zero was no one like that."

"You're sure? I seem to remember one of the mayor's aides. Had a fetish for lacey underthings and hot water bottles, I believe."

"No, that's not him."

Gulliver shrugged. "Sorry, love. Wish I could help."

Eddy fell into a somber mood. Maybe this was all just some insane quest and he was every bit as crazy as the doctors claimed. He'd done some things in his time. Brutal, vicious things. But until Cassandra, he'd never killed anyone.

"What did you think of that murder, Eddy? Nasty stuff, eh?"

Nasty? Yes, he supposed it was. To someone who didn't understand. "I guess."

"Cut the poor girl up like meat, I hear. No blood left in the body. Fucking vampire on the loose." Gulliver took a good belt from his Beefeater and tonic. "Not that it surprises me. The types we get down here . . . though blood's not usually what they want to suck."

Eddy smiled.

"But we were talking about this Zero character. Why are you after him?"

"He was my dad. He disappeared in this town a long time ago."

"Too bad. A boy needs his dad. Not that mine has any use for me anymore." Gulliver was laughing. "Did I tell you my old man's a minister, too?

Very straight-laced. That was my problem. I didn't like it straight. Not that I mind lace . . ."

"I don't suppose I'll find him."

"Don't give up hope," Gulliver said, putting an arm around him. "There's always hope."

"Sure."

"If you want to find him, you have to do what the cops do, love. You have to *become* him. You have to think like he does and act like him and then you'll know where he went and why. Simple."

Eddy leered at him, his eyes terribly dark and vacant.

Gulliver removed his arm. "Sorry. Didn't mean anything by that. Just a friendly gesture."

Eddy grinned and slipped on a pair of mirrored sunglasses. "And would I be here if such things bothered me?"

Gulliver shrugged, sipping his drink. It was amateur night and a couple of transsexuals were up on stage doing a B & D version of *Romeo and Juliet,* switching genders and roles at the drop of a hat. It was all quite amusing, if not somewhat confusing.

"About your father. What did he do to get in the newspapers?"

"Killed a few people."

"Terrible. Just killed them?"

"The citizens in general found the way he did it quite shocking."

Gulliver smiled. He wasn't sure if he liked this Eddy or not. "I know a guy who's into shit like that. An acquaintance, really. Strange boy. Maybe he could help you out."

"When could I meet him? It would be worth a try."

Gulliver checked his watch. "Sun should be set by now. He'll be up. We could go over there now, if you like."

"Let's, then."

Gulliver finished his drink and off they went.

*   *   *

They walked for some blocks, hand in hand. Eddy insisted upon it. Normally, Gulliver would've been intoxicated at the idea of escorting around a handsome young thing like Eddy. But that wasn't the case now. Despite his mysterious, dark boyish looks and lithe body, Eddy was somehow menacing. There was an aura of dread about him, a quiet and lethal desperation.

They traveled down deserted avenues, avoiding crazed homeless people who threw bottles at them and shrieked. They could hear sobs and moans and curses from the darkness around them. A pregnant whore offered them a good time. Faces leered from doorways. People injected drugs on stoops and stairways. They stepped around a man who was pissing on the sidewalk.

"When we get there, you're on your own," Gulliver said. "I like you and all, but this guy—Spider, they call him—is one weird freak. He's spooky."

"Just show me the way." Eddy seemed anxious.

Gulliver wanted to tell him to be careful around Spider, but he was beginning to think they were two of kind. He didn't like the idea.

They went into an alley and Gulliver stopped before a peeling door festooned with graffiti. "This is it," he said, knocking lightly on the door. He tried the latch and it was open.

"The lair of the spider, eh?" Eddy cackled.

Gulliver tried to smile. Too bad. Eddy was so attractive. His long dark hair and fine, almost feminine features. Lovely. His skin was flawless, his lips full. With the mirrored sunglasses, motorcycle jacket, and baggy black jeans he was indeed an object of mystery and desire in Gulliver's eyes.

"Eddy," Gulliver said. "This Spider . . . he's crazy. I think he might be dangerous."

"Don't worry."

"I can't help it."

"Ssshhh," Eddy told him. "It's all right."

"But . . ."

"You're trembling."

Gulliver knew he was. He felt a terrible, uncanny cabalism taking shape around him, a diabolic chemistry as if bringing together Spider and Eddy in this city was like bringing together the ingredients of a high explosive near flame. Eddy held his hands. Gulliver felt himself calming by the inch, practically swooning, as he felt Eddy's long, almost feminine fingers in his own. So perfect, so tapering, the skin so smooth.

Eddy went in and Gulliver closed the door behind him, shaking again. Then he got the hell out of there before some explosion ripped open the guts of the neighborhood.

*   *   *

Eddy found himself in a dark corridor studded with doorways. He could hear movement somewhere, but he couldn't pinpoint it. Then he heard a voice.

"The pain," it said. "Oh, God, the pain . . ."

Eddy followed the sound of the voice down the corridor and into a room. A single naked bulb was suspended from the ceiling. There were candles everywhere, but only a few were lit. There was a sagging bed shoved in the corner and debris everywhere. Books were stacked on the floor. A thin man wearing a dark, dingy overcoat with no shirt beneath was crouched on his knees. His hair was long, separated into a variety of braids. He wore rings, bracelets, and all manner of beads around his throat.

Eddy stood before him. "Gulliver sent me," he said, hoping that would explain all.

The man looked up at him. Blood ran from the corners of his mouth. His torso was crowded with tattoos. He held a razor in one hand and as Eddy watched he cut a slit in his gums and spat blood onto the floor.

"Are you Spider?" Eddy inquired. "Gulliver said you'd be here."

"Who the fuck's Gulliver?" the man insisted. He was apparently trying to work loose one of his teeth. "I don't know any Gulliver."

Eddy said, "Gulliver. I met him at Maxie's."

"Oh, that one. And what are you, one of his fags?"

"No, I'm just someone looking for information."

"There's none to be had." He began to cackle and finally cough more blood. "People like you are always looking for something. What are you? A cop? Are you undercover or are you just another faggot?"

"Are you Spider or not?"

"Yes. Do you have any drugs, *fag?* Something for the pain?"

"No, nothing." He'd given the last of his coke to Cassandra. He supposed it was sort of a going away present.

"Shit. What good are you?"

"I came for answers."

"So? What do I look like? A fucking librarian?"

"Gulliver said you knew things. That you could help me."

Spider shook his head. "I don't know anything. Who are you?"

"Eddy."

"Eddy? I thought you faggots preferred more colorful names?"

"I wouldn't know."

"No, I don't suppose you would. So you came here and you want information and you've brought no drugs." Spider laughed. "Dick-sucker."

Eddy studied him. What he saw before him was probably nothing more than some pathetic masochist. Yet, there was something about him, something that alluded to bigger things.

"I have money, if that interests you," Eddy told him.

"Money," Spider spat. "Tell me what you want."

"I'm looking for my father. Gulliver thought you might know of him."

"Does he have a name?"

"William Zero."

Spider's eyes went wide. He crawled to Eddy's feet, grasping his legs.

"The Doctor? You're the *Doctor's* son?"

"That's right. Do you know something of him?"

"I know what he did, what he claimed he'd *do,*" Spider told him. "He's a legend of sorts in this city. But I'm sure you know that. Oh, the media made him into some sort of monster, just another serial killer taking life without any true reason but dementia. But that wasn't true."

Eddy helped him to his feet. "Wasn't it?"

"You're his son and you can ask that?" Spider shook his head and wiped blood from his lips with the sleeve of his coat.

"He left when I was a boy," Eddy explained. "All that I know of him comes from books, newspapers, and my mother. None of them very accurate sources, I would think."

"That's too bad. Have you something to smoke? A cigarette even?"

Eddy handed him his pack. He watched Spider tease one out with trembling fingers. He was truly excited at the prospect of meeting the Doctor's son and that in itself was something. It gave Eddy hope. Maybe this search of his wasn't as crazy as he was beginning to think. Maybe Spider knew. Maybe he knew where his father was and how to get there. Then again, maybe Spider was just another harmless lunatic.

"Tell me what you know."

Spider nodded. "First thing you must understand, is that your father was not just some maniac with a craving for blood. There was a rhyme and reason for what he did. It took me some time to figure it out, but now I understand what he was doing."

"Which was?"

"He wanted to escape the stifling boredom of this reality. He wanted to be transported somewhere where there were no limits to anything."

"There is no such place."

"Isn't there? I thought so, too, at one time. But I was wrong. You see these books around us? None of it is light reading, my boy, it is study. All of these books and a hundred others gave me clues to the answer. They all mentioned a place beyond this reality, a plane of existence that was like nothing you could find here."

Eddy sat on the bed. "What are you talking about?"

"I'm telling you where your father went. Isn't that what you want to know?"

"Yes."

"Then listen." Spider lit another cigarette and dug a bottle of whiskey from a desk drawer and pulled off it. "Your father probably studied these same books and others as well. He heard mention of this place, maybe in the writings of de Sade or Crowley, it doesn't matter. He heard of this place and it was called by many names, but usually simply the Territories. A place where only few could ever go. A plane of beauty and horror. A special place."

Eddy had decided Spider was mad. But he listened. What did he have to lose? "Go on," he said.

"There was never any mention in any book of how to reach this place, only that you had to make your own way. Many have tried and most of their names would be familiar to you—Kiss, de Sade, Gilles de Rais . . . a hundred others. They said the Ripper went there . . ."

"Killers and Sadists," Eddy said.

"Yes, perhaps. That's how history looks upon them. But *maybe* they were something more. *Maybe* they were men who wanted to escape and saw that the only ticket to their heart's desire was through their own perverse creativity."

"You're saying that you have to murder, maim, and torture in just the proper way to get into this place?"

Spider clasped his hands together. "Yes! Yes, in a way. You have to impress certain individuals with your talents. They're lovers of *art,* you know, and the only canvas they respect is the human body. I've read bits and pieces about them. *The Sisters.* They'll let you in if you impress them with your skills, your imagination, your creativity."

It was madness, a perfect throbbing vein of madness and Eddy happily sipped from it, losing himself in it, intoxicated as Spider droned on and on and on. Murder was much like art, he said. Any fool could grab a brush and dip it in paint, splash a few meaningless strokes on a canvas just as any fool could grab a knife or a gun and commit murder. Both were forms of animal expression. But only a true craftsman, a skilled artisan, a creative *genius* could produce a canvas or a corpse that would take your breath away.

"It's more than mere hackwork with a knife, Eddy. It's artwork and only the most promising can even attempt it. Van Gogh used a brush, the Ripper used a knife."

Eddy listened, drawing slowly off a cigarette. "So this art . . . it is the key?"
"Yes!"

"And through it you can be invited into . . . *what?* Another dimension? An alternate universe?"

"Yes, something like that."

"And this is where my father is? This Territory?"

"Yes!"

Eddy chewed his lip. "And how do you know that?"

"It's a guess, really. But I've read a great deal about him. All there is, in fact. I know what he and his associates were doing. It points in only one direction to me."

"These Territories?"

"Exactly."

Eddy didn't know what to think. If nothing else, it was something. But could such a place possibly exist? It was the stuff of fringe science, very hard to wrap his brain around. "Do you know what has to be done to get there?" he asked. "Can you tell me?"

"I'll do better," Spider said. He took out a leather case and opened it. Inside were the tools of a surgeon, a butcher . . . or perhaps a somewhat eccentric artist. Everything from post mortem knives to bone snips and surgical saws. All gleaming. All meticulously polished and sharpened. "I'll show you."

It began.

MEMOIRS OF THE TEMPLAR SOCIETY (2)

"Here we are again," Grimes said smugly. "Brothers of sensation."

"As every week."

They were at Zero's house, drinking and discussing. They called the place the House of Mirrors because Zero had covered every conceivable space with mirrors for reasons he wouldn't comment upon. The house was bare save for these, a few sticks of furniture, beds upstairs, and hundreds of books describing every possible perversion. No one lived here, not even Zero. It was merely a meeting place. A club of sorts.

Zero refreshed their drinks.

"As I said," Grimes muttered, "here we are again."

Stadtler studied his drink. "And what's our pleasure tonight?"

"Yes, what exactly?" Zero said.

These two bothered Stadtler immensely sometimes. They seemed to communicate on a secret level that he was never able to broach. Theirs was a play of words, a subtle hint, a wink, a nod that spoke volumes to one another and left him completely in the dark. There was always a secret agenda between the two and Stadtler felt he would always remain a stranger to it.

Zero had something in mind tonight. That much was obvious, but direct questioning would only garner unpleasant looks from both he and Grimes. So Stadtler would have to wait until they were both ready to tell him what was on the agenda. He knew from experience it was the only way.

"I often wonder," Zero said, "what exactly it takes to unhinge the human mind. What factors have to be brought into play."

"Yes," Grimes agreed. "A fascinating concept."

Stadtler said nothing. He needed to hear where this was going before he commented on it. Unlike Grimes, he didn't worship everything Zero said. He was not a yes-man.

"Have you ever wondered about this?" Zero inquired.

"Sure, I wonder about a lot of shit," Stadtler told him point blank. "It all depends on the individual. Isn't that obvious? What drives you crazy may make me laugh and vise versa."

"Concise, as usual, my friend," Zero said. "I think you've hit on the crux of the entire dilemma. We all have fears, don't we? Hidden terrors of childhood that have become adult paranoias. It's only a matter of finding out what they are. Sometimes, I think, we're not even sure what they are ourselves. And, even if we knew, would we dare admit them? Think of the power it would give another over us."

"And what are you afraid of, Zero?" Stadtler asked.

"Of death, of course. Isn't that what we're all afraid of?"

"It's a universal fear," Grimes said as if he knew it all too well. "The end of physical existence. Nothingness. What can be more terrifying?"

Stadtler grinned. "You tell me."

Zero said, "What are your fears, Stadtler? Tell us."

"Boredom. It's the only thing that's really dogged me all my life. Sheer boredom. Nothing else even comes close."

"Really?" Zero obviously didn't believe him.

"Really. Don't try and dig in my head. There's nothing you'd like inside."

Zero smiled. "I think there are only two subjects worth our study, gentlemen: fear and death."

Grimes and he exchanged a secret look.

Stadtler lit a cigarette. "Explain that."

"What's to explain?" Zero asked in his typically evasive way.

"That pretty much says it all," Grimes chimed in.

"Then humor me. What are you two getting at? Scaring people? Killing them?"

"Would that bother you?"

"Yes," Grimes said, "would it?"

Stadtler took a slow, even drag from his smoke. "Not in the least."

Zero grinned like a cat. He had chosen his partners in crime well and it pleased him that they were willing to travel any road he selected. Stadtler saw the content, self-indulgent look on his face and wondered for a moment just how far this could possibly go.

"Are we going to take life?" Grimes asked.

"Yes," Zero assured him. "How else can we study death before and after?"

"And what about fear?" Stadtler said. "How are we going to go about studying that? If I might ask."

"There are ways. Let me tell you what I've been thinking," Zero said. "As I said, I've always been intrigued by what it would take to completely snap an individual's mind. And I don't mean just terrify them or give them a garden variety psychosis. I mean totally destroy their psyche, totally destroy what makes them a person. Wipe the slate clean, so to speak. Reduce this person to a basal level where he or she knows and remembers nothing but terror. *Then,*" he said in almost a whisper, "we could re-learn this person to our own fancy. Re-engineer their psyche."

"I'm not following you," Stadtler admitted.

"It's simple. Reduce this person through fear, strip their mind away, propel them backwards into a state of psychological infancy."

"Exactly," Grimes said.

"To what end?"

"Enlightenment and pleasure, if you will. Pleasure in the satisfaction we'll derive from destroying their will and life programming; enlightenment in that we'll ultimately understand the nature of horror itself."

"How do we go about it?"

"First we need a volunteer," Zero said.

"Who?"

"The streets are full of them," Grimes said.

"Then let's go find one."

It was the beginning of the end.

THE ZERO FACTOR

"I'm afraid you'll think I'm crazy, Mr. Fenn."

Fenn attempted a smile, but it was a bad one. Dr. Lochmere hadn't meant it as a joke, he supposed, but as far as he was concerned, all psychiatrists were crazy. They were no better than the loons they kept like pets. Maybe he was cynical, but he preferred to call himself a realist. And if ten years of homicide could do nothing else, it could certainly mold a man into a student of realism.

"You're a professional, Dr. Lochmere. I'm always happy to listen to a fellow professional. In my line of work, I rub noses with head doctors all the time. We can be of valuable assistance to one another."

Lisa nodded, sensing his dislike of her profession. "It just seems odd for me to ask your help in finding a man who *may* commit a crime. This is all very . . . vague, you understand. The man I'm searching for might not even be here at all."

"Maybe you'd better just tell me and let me decide."

"Fenn," she said. "Is that Irish?"

"Yeah, I'm afraid so." He laughed, but there was little humor behind it.

She looked amused. "An Irish cop."

He found himself grinning and it looked positively out of place on his hardened features, yet his blue eyes sparkled with mirth. "It runs in the family."

"I bet it does. My dad was a cop as was his," she chanced.

"And you broke the chain?"

"My brother Jeff works bunko in Vallejo. Same precinct as dad. He's terribly proud of him. He wanted me to go to school."

"Sounds like a good man."

A darkness crossed her face. "He is. You'd like him."

Fenn bet he would. This had all started as somewhat of a bothersome, uncomfortable meeting in a coffee shop with some female headshrinker . . . and what was happening now? Was he actually enjoying her company?

He was. And the fact that she was pretty in his eyes didn't hurt either.

"I need your help with a man called Eddy Zero," she said. "He was under my care at Coalinga."

"The state mental hospital?"

"Yes."

"That's where they keep some of the very worst. Serial killers, thrill killers, sexual predators." He shook his head. "Good God, why would a woman want to work in a zoo like that?"

"Why would a man want to work homicide?"

They shared a laugh.

"I never thought it would come to this," she admitted. "I never thought I would actually take it upon myself to track him down."

"And why are you?"

"Guilt, I guess. It wasn't my decision to release him. I was just a junior member of staff there. I had very little say. But I got to know him and what I knew I didn't like. He's a time bomb waiting to go off. I only hope it's not too late." She sipped her coffee. "You see, Eddy fooled the other doctors. Literally. He was a clever liar. They thought he was safe, so they let him go."

"But you never agreed?"

"Not at all. I spent three years at Coalinga and the entire time, my opinions were overlooked. Maybe because I was fresh out of school, maybe because I was a woman. Maybe both. I don't know. But the thing with Eddy was the worst. I never could stop thinking about him. Finally, I quit and took a job as a prison psychiatrist."

"Which joint?"

"Chowchilla. Central California Women's Facility."

Fenn wrinkled his nose. "Hell of a job, if you ask me."

"But I was needed there. My advice was respected."

He shrugged as if he found that hard to believe. "Are you still working there?"

"No, I quit over a year ago now. Other things to do."

A waitress sauntered over and refilled their cups. Fenn ordered a donut.

"So you think Eddy's here in my town?"

"He was. I hired a private investigator to find him. It wasn't that difficult. He was living here off and on for the past two years."

"And you know where?"

"No, not now. I stopped the investigation six months ago. It was costly."

"What did this guy do to be put into a mental hospital in the first place?"

"I'll get to that. Look at these first."

She handed him an envelope. One of several on the table before her. Her hand shook. "These are the most recent photographs I have of him. They were taken two years ago. His mother gave them to me. She's since passed on."

Fenn looked them over. They appeared to be Christmas photos. Eddy Zero was a gaunt man with a skeletal face and haunted, dark eyes. It wasn't the sort of face you'd forget after having seen it. Not particularly handsome, but attractive as all men who harbor tortured souls. The face of someone who had realized that his body was not a host but a prison, a machine that kept him in bondage.

Fenn almost felt as if he'd seen it before somewhere.

"Where was he living?"

She handed him a slip of paper. He looked over the addresses. They were all bad locations in a city full of them.

"You want me to check these out?"

"No, I already have. He hasn't been to any of them in some time," she explained. "As I said, I stopped the investigation six months ago, but I think he's still around."

"Why?"

"I'll get to that."

Fenn's donut came, but he didn't eat it. "I don't want to sound rude, Doc. But just what is it you want from me?"

"I want you to look at these," she told him, handing over a larger envelope. "Just look at them. I'm afraid they're rather unpleasant."

Fenn did as she asked. They were murder scene photographs. Not very pretty indeed. Taken by the police, no doubt. The lack of artistry and poor focus usually gave such things away.

"Look at them. Look at all of them."

"Murders."

"Yes," she said grimly. "But not just any."

And it was true. These were no ordinary crimes of slashing mania, the butchery here was precise, methodical. The work of a very demented, yet precise mind. The clothing and personal effects were arranged just so next to the bodies. The photos were all the same, the corpses different, but the methodology exact down to the smallest detail. The bodies had been eviscerated, the internals removed and cleansed of blood and then set alongside the cadavers in proper anatomical order and relation. The lips had been slit off, the eyes plucked free, the tongues severed. And again, whatever was removed was arranged in its proper sequence next to the body. The skin of each victim had been peeled free in a single sheet and secured to the wall with heavy pins. All the photos were duplicates of one another. It was incredible, if not somewhat ghoulish. The victims appeared to have been not so much murdered as dissected.

"Interesting," was all Fenn would say. He was starting to get one of his headaches. "Where did you get these?"

"My P.I. got them for me. He said he had contacts in your own department."

"My department? Are you saying these murders happened in San Francisco?"

"Yes. Some twenty years ago."

He slid them back into the envelope. "Did our boy have anything to do with this?"

"His father."

Fenn looked confused.

She looked in his eyes. "Did you ever hear of William Zero?"

"It's vaguely familiar." And it was. His temples were throbbing now.

"Are you all right?" Lisa asked.

He looked pale. "Yeah, go on."

"He disappeared twenty years ago, but not before he butchered those people."

Fenn looked pained. "Dr. Blood-and-Bones."

"Then you remember him?"

Fenn did. "The veterans in homicide are still talking about him. He's like their own personal bogeyman. I should've recognized that name. Zero. Christ."

Dr. Blood-and-Bones. The name had made national headlines years back. He'd slaughtered a dozen and vanished. Books were still written about him. He carried the same sort of grisly mystique and dark legendry about him as Jack the Ripper. William Zero. Dr. Blood-and-Bones. Ah yes, he remembered him all right. But unlike the Ripper, people knew *who* the good doctor was, they just didn't know where he was. In San Francisco, he was infamous. He'd never be forgotten. The old vets of homicide still grew pale when they spoke of him. They'd never gotten him and they'd never gotten over the fact. Fenn wasn't acquainted with the particulars of the case, but he seemed to recall that Zero hadn't worked alone.

"They never caught him," she said, as if saddened. "The police moved in on him mere hours after he'd disappeared."

"Tipped off?"

"We'll never know. He had two accomplices, it was discovered. One was named Grimes. He killed himself. The other—Stadtler—alluded capture. He was never caught. Yet, it's Zero everyone remembers, not these other two. And it's Zero I'm concerned with."

Fenn dug aspirins out of his coat and chewed them with a ferocity. The pain in his head was almost unendurable today. It got that way some days.

"I interviewed Zero's wife several times before her death," Lisa went on. "She knew nothing of what he was doing. His own father left them well provided for and William Zero never had to work as such. She knew he was an artist, even though he had graduate degrees in philosophy and medicine, a doctorate in medical anatomy. He had a studio at their old house in Pacific

Heights, she said, and he'd lock himself in there with his books and paints all day long. At night, he'd go out and walk . . . or so he said." There was something like fear in her eyes. "She figured his nightly jaunts were just part of the artistic temperament. Even when they became nightly, rather than weekly, she never suspected. She knew nothing of Grimes and Stadtler. He was no husband to her, she told me. And had very little to do with Eddy. He was a loner, but she never suspected she was sharing the same house with a monster. I knew her, Mr. Fenn. Just for a short time and she looked . . . haunted."

"I can believe that. But what does this have to do with Eddy?"

"Apparently, Eddy was fascinated with him. She hated it. She kept a collection of newspapers articles in a scrapbook. Articles about his father and his crimes. She would show them to Eddy, hoping he'd develop a hatred and fear of his father. But the opposite occurred. He worshipped the man."

Fenn nodded. It made sense. "And you think Eddy may attempt to recreate his father's horrors?"

"I'm sure of it. He's had a history of mental disturbance since his teenage years. Random acts of violence and cruelty. Assault, rape, attempted murder. He spent five years at Coalinga for blinding a man with a knife and stabbing his wife repeatedly. Luckily, both survived."

"He's dangerous," Fenn said.

"Exactly. Yet, my superiors released him. He pretended to be cured of his excesses. He's a talented liar as all psychopaths are. But he told me things he never told them, wouldn't tell them. He admires his father, Mr. Fenn. He wants to be like him, out-do him if he can."

Fenn butted his cigarette and shook his head. "This is mind boggling. And you believe it?"

"Yes. Absolutely. His mother believed it, too. Her greatest fear was that he'd return home and kill her."

"Jesus."

Lisa sighed. "I know how strange this must be, me coming to you with this. But I didn't know what else to do. If he plans to recreate his father's crimes, then I think it will be here, in the very city where his father did them."

"Well, you've convinced me. I look into it. I'll see if we can find him, nail him on something."

"I know it must seem like I'm trying to be some holy crusader, taking it upon myself to stop him. But my reasons aren't quite saintly, Mr. Fenn. Yes, I want him stopped, but I'd also love to do a book on him. He's a pure psychopath and from a medical point of view, that's fascinating to me."

Fenn smiled. "If all you wanted was a book out of this, Doc, you'd have gone at it alone with your P.I."

"Maybe."

He sighed, his teeth locked together from the pain in his head. "I'm going to do some checking. We have a few unsolved murders on the books. I'll do some cross-referencing and let you know what I find out."

"Thanks for listening."

He nodded. "I'd better be on my way."

He made a hasty exit and bolted out to his car. The throbbing in his head was lessening, but not by much. He had to get home and under the covers. Only complete darkness and silence seemed to help.

*   *   *

Of course, Fenn was no fool.

He didn't entirely believe all that Dr. Lisa Lochmere told him.

After his headache had fled and he was able to think again, he decided to do some checking. The best person to talk with was her private investigator. His name was Soames and he was no easy man to find. His offices were closed and his apartment locked. Fenn asked questions, but he got no good answers. People were paranoid of cops and Soames' whereabouts, they decided, were none of his damn business. The most he got was an admission from a neighbor that he "was ill". It wasn't much to go on, but after carefully checking the city hospitals, he found Soames, all right.

He was confined in the psychiatric wing of San Francisco General.

"I'm afraid he won't be much use to you, Lieutenant," Dr. Luce, the attending physician told Fenn. "Mr. Soames has pretty much been a regular here for the past four or five months."

"Why? If I might ask."

"He's suicidal. He entertains what might be called "black periods" from time to time. He's interested only in destroying himself when they come about."

"Will he be released anytime soon?"

"No, he needs intensive therapy," Luce said. "He's tried to kill himself some five times in the past months and he'll have to be committed for his own protection. At least for the time being. It's tragic. He has no history of disturbance that we know of. Tragic."

It was, Fenn thought, the idea that insanity can take one so suddenly, without warning.

"Can I see him? I won't upset him. Just a few simple questions."

"Well . . ."

"I just have to verify that he was working for a certain somebody."

Luce shrugged. "I'm afraid he's under sedation. He's conscious, but as to the validity of his answers . . ."

"Please. Just five minutes."

"All right. No more, though."

Luce led him through the wing and into a ward that was kept locked. The nurse on duty looked to be no more than thirty, but her eyes were those of someone twice that age. Soames was lying on a bed, restrained, his wrists bandaged from his latest suicide attempt. Luce left them alone.

"How are you?" Fenn asked. It was hard to screw up compassion for the man in this dreary and bleak place, but he was trying.

"Did you bring my cigarettes?" Soames asked as if Fenn were an old and trusted provider.

"No. I forgot them."

"Damn."

There were maybe twenty beds in the ward. Half of them were occupied. Most of the patients were sleeping off medications and reality. A few were awake. An elderly man without teeth was whistling nursery rhymes and winding invisible string around his index finger. When he was finished, he'd pull it free and start winding anew. Another was looking around the ward with blank eyes and spelling everything he saw. "Wall," he said. "W-a-l-l. Floor. F-l-o-o-r. Window. W-i-n-d-o-w." It went on and on seemingly without end.

"I wanted to ask you a couple of questions," Fenn said. "If you feel up to it."

"Questions?" he repeated. He looked confused and wizened, well beyond his true age of 55.

"Yes. If that's okay."

Soames shrugged, not caring one way or the other. "I'm a dead man," he said. "Why won't they let me die?"

"You'll be okay," Fenn reassured him. "You just need a good rest."

"Rest?"

"Sure, that's all. You'll be right as rain in no time."

"The doctor will kill me if she doesn't do it first."

"Oh . . . which doctor?"

"*The* doctor. He knows I've been poking around."

This seemed pointless, but Fenn kept on. "The doctors only have your health in mind. They want you to be well."

"You're wrong," said Soames.

"I'd like to ask you about Dr. Lochmere. Do you remember her?"

Soames began to laugh. It was a broken and pitiful sound. "Of course. She started this mess, didn't she? Or did I?" He laughed again.

"What can you tell me of her?"

Soames looked to be in pain. His lips twisted in a grimace, his eyes rolled wildly in their sockets. A tear stained his cheek. He fought at his bonds to no avail, then he settled down. "Do you have a knife?" he asked.

"No."

"A gun?"

"No."

"You're lying!" he snapped. "You're a cop. I know you have a gun. I can smell a cop a mile away."

"I checked it at the desk."

"Too bad." He fell silent for a moment. "There's no hope for me, then."

"Did you ever meet Dr. Lochmere?" Fenn pressed on.

"Oh yes. I met her. And she met me."

Fenn let that one go. "What did she want you to do?"

"Look for Eddy Zero." He began to laugh at that.

"And you found him?"

"Yeah, nothing to it. It took time, but I found him." He was sobbing now.

"I don't understand."

"No, and I won't let you," Soames said. "It's too dangerous. It's better to be ignorant."

"Just tell me about Lochmere."

"What's to tell? She hired me to find Zero and I did. I kept track of his movements best I could. He's a slippery one, that Eddy. Just like his dad." He looked around with bloodshot eyes. "Is that what you want to know? It's almost the truth."

"Tell me the rest."

"Never."

"Why?"

He ignored this. "Did I tell you I helped nail his old man? Dr. Blood-and-Bones? I did. If it wasn't for me, they would never have stopped him."

"He was never caught."

"No, but we drove him into hiding. It was something. I knew Zero. When I suspected what he was up to, I did a little digging. I had photos of Grimes doing things his wife wouldn't care for too much. I threatened to show them to her and, boy, did that old boy start talking then. He spilled it all about their little society and what they'd been up to." Soames looked weary. "I didn't believe it at first, so I checked. I went over there. To that house Zero kept."

"And?"

His eyes filled with tears. "It was a nightmare. I should've told the cops then, but I didn't. I waited. God knows why. Finally, I did, though. You know the rest, I'm sure. Zero got away. So did that other one. If only I'd told the cops sooner . . ."

"Why didn't you?"

"I guess I was afraid." He swallowed. "I'm afraid now."

"You think Zero's coming back?"

Soames ignored him again. "Get me a knife or razor, will ya? Anything'll do."

It was ridiculous. Soames was obsessed with taking his own life. He saw nothing else, save that William Zero apparently was coming to kill him. The rest of it . . . who could say if there was any truth to it?

"Well, rest up, my friend. You'll be okay," Fenn told him and made a hasty retreat.

He'd gone there with questions and come out with more. Dr. Lochmere *had* apparently hired him to track Eddy Zero. That much checked out. But how could any of that be related to his attempts at self-destruction? And what of this business about Dr. Blood-and-Bones? Was there a common thread here or just a lot of nonsense spewed by a crazy man? What secrets was he keeping?

It would take time to sort out. And Fenn decided he had all the time in the world to get to the bottom of it.

Thinking about it all gave him another headache.

LETTERS FROM HELL (1)

Dear Eddy,

This is a letter you'll never read. This is a letter that not you or anyone else will ever see, because I'm going to burn it to ash as soon as I'm done committing my thoughts to it.

If I don't, God help me.

I know you're out there somewhere, waiting for me. Just as I wait for you. We didn't know each other long. You maybe glimpsed me once or twice at that awful place, I can't say for sure. But I saw you. When they used to let you walk in the courtyard, I watched you. I began to time my life by your appearance below in the yard. I watched you through the steel mesh of my window. I envied you. Ultimately, I loved you. I wished I could walk with you. But they never let me out. No one from D-ward ever gets out.

Long after you were gone, I thought of you. I never stopped. I wanted nothing more than to be with you, to help you through the confusion of your life.

How can I do this, my love?

How can I hope to bring order to your life when I can't do the same to my own? I have no answer for that, I only have hope. I've made mistakes with my own affairs. I always choose the wrong men and this is something beyond my power to change (maybe I'll tell you why some day; it's a dark and twisted tale). I enter into relationships without much thought. I tell myself it's for love when in reality it's probably infatuation. I give myself totally to my men. Give them anything they ask and usually a lot more. They worship my face and my body and never, somehow, get any further than that. It's something I've accepted and decided I can't change. My mother was a beautiful woman and I inherited her looks, God help me.

One of my first lovers was a man named Rick and (as I learned later) he had been raised in a strict fundamentalist religious household. You wouldn't have known it at first. He was intense and seductive and given to violent outbursts that usually ended in passion for us. Those three things seemed to go hand in hand for me: intensity, seduction, and violence. And not necessarily in that order. If I was to tell you why, I'd have to tell you of my first lover and I don't think I'm ready to do that.

Let's just talk about Rick for a moment.

We had, in the three or four months of our relationship, explored nearly all forms of sexual pleasure. In fact, we'd exhausted most of the ordinary ones and it was at this time that I suggested we begin experimenting. I told Rick a few things I'd like to try.

"You can't be serious." He said this to me, storm clouds darkening in his eyes. Seeing that I was, he rushed about the room, destroying everything in his path. I found it all terribly exciting as I always did. I expected his tantrum to end in the usual manner, with him making violent love to me. It didn't. "What you're suggesting is perverted, it's disgusting. I won't be part of it." He said other things, none of which are important. I'd struck some puritanical nerve in him and there was no going back.

He walked out of my life.

And what did I ask him to do? You can use your imagination. Once accepted routes of sexual creativity have been exhausted, it requires one to walk darker, forbidden paths. Paths I've been down countless times.

I tell you of Rick as an example and nothing more. It will give you an idea of the course my loves generally take. They are disasters from the beginning and, as I have said, this is beyond my power to change.

But I can help you, Eddy. Believe me, I can. Because you're not going anywhere I haven't been. I know about lunacy. It rules my life.

And I love you. God, yes, I do.

When I find you, we'll help each other.

Yours,

Cherry

HOUSE OF MIRRORS

"I don't know what I expect to find," Lisa said. "Probably nothing. But it seems like a good place to start. If Eddy's in this town at all, then I'm sure he'll go there."

Fenn nodded. "I'm taking a lot of chances with you," he said. "I'll be damned if I know why."

"Because you want to stop him as I do."

Fenn looked thoughtful as he drove. "Yes, I suppose I do." But even with all that she told him, he still wasn't sure. He had other work to do, yet he was willing to help her track down some guy who might have been a thousand miles away. He was surprised at himself. He'd always been one who went with a sure thing and here he was tracking down a *maybe*. He supposed, realistically, homicide work was really just a loose collection of maybes that you fit together into a pattern. Yet, there was more involved here than just that. *Yes,* he wanted to stop Eddy Zero if he was indeed in the city; that was his job. But ever since he'd talked with Soames, there were suddenly too many questions in his mind. And, madman or not, Soames had seemed quite lucid on certain points. There was a hidden agenda here somewhere and Fenn wanted to know what it was.

Lisa said, "If you didn't want to be here, Mr. Fenn, you wouldn't be. I imagine you're a careful man. I'm sure that you weren't as sold on me and what I said the other day as you acted. But you've done some checking since then, and you know I'm not some crusading nut."

Fenn laughed. "You're a smart cookie, Doc. I did check you and our boy out."

"And?"

"And I trust my instincts. You're okay."

"Good."

"One thing, though. Probably none of my business, but why did you leave the prison? I got the impression you liked it there. I talked with your superiors there. Hope you don't mind. They were impressed with you. Couldn't say enough good things about you."

"I needed time for other things. Research, mainly, for a book I was working on."

"Where are you working now?"

"I'm not. I'm doing research."

"Listen, I was just curious."

"So now you know everything."

She was lying and he knew it, but he wasn't going to press it. There was a lot more to know about her. Maybe in time she'd be truthful with him. She was just another part of this mysterious puzzle.

"I'm sure it'll be a good book," he said.

She smiled and looked out the window.

"This house we're going to, I take it you've been by there already?"

"Yeah. I've driven by it, but I didn't bother going in. It looks like a bad neighborhood. I didn't want to get out alone."

Fenn chuckled. "Not too bad by day, but definitely sketchy by night."

"About what I thought."

He was watching her out of the corner of his eye as he spoke. Her hair was pulled back tight in a blonde braid and she wore glasses. Her face looked experienced, tough even. In her business suit and skirt, she looked like a lawyer. Emotionless, dedicated, and breastless. But her legs were nice: soft, tapered, sexy. He wondered what she'd look like without the glasses and her hair down. He found the idea exciting.

She looked at him. "Has anyone lived there since Zero occupied it?"

"No, not a person. It's been more or less up for sale for twenty years. Although, I imagine it's had its share of transients."

The streets and buildings became shabbier as Fenn drove. There was litter on the walks. Rusting, stripped cars at the curbs. Everything, both house and building and avenue alike, seemed to be painted a weathered gray. The people who watched them drive by all had the same hungry desperation in their yearning eyes.

And finally, the house.

The scene of the crimes of Dr. Blood-and-Bones.

"I almost hate leaving the car out here," Fenn told her.

"It's a police car."

"Doesn't matter in this neighborhood."

They got out and went up the walk. The street was deserted in either direction. Leaves and litter blew up the pavement.

*   *   *

The house was big and ugly and ominous. Like something lifted out of Poe or Lovecraft and dumped in this filthy back street. It was set up on a hill and they had to follow a set of crumbling, frost-heaved stone steps up to its door. The other houses were packed up against it, but beneath its towers and leaning turrets, they were unnoticeable.

"What a place," Fenn said, studying the sloping yard and its dead trees and arid grasses.

"It's very atmospheric," Lisa agreed.

"Most of the houses around here were like this at one time," Fenn told her. "But most were razed for housing and building space. But not this one."

Lisa tried the peeling, faded door. It was open. "Who owns it now?"

"Didn't I tell you?" he asked. "I spoke with the family lawyer. Eddy owns it now that his old lady bought it."

They went in and were struck by a feeling of desolation, of emptiness. It was impossible to imagine anyone actually living here. Laughter, joy, love, life—those things didn't belong. The place seemed haunted by itself, by its own flat neutrality. Dust twisted in the air and a cool breeze played in the halls. There was an entrenched feeling of insanity as if the house itself had lost its mind.

The grime and dust were disturbed at the bottom of the steps. There were dozens of footprints in this area.

Fenn's temples were beginning to throb.

"That's where they found the girl," he said. "Right at the foot of the steps. She was probably stabbed up there and fell."

"No idea who she was?"

"Nothing. No identification. Nothing on her prints. Her face was butchered so badly I don't think her own mother would have recognized her."

Lisa walked around, looking down corridors and into rooms. "I wonder if he came here, knowing what his father had done."

"You think Eddy killed her?"

She shrugged. "Who can say? The M.O. wasn't the same as his father's, certainly, but that doesn't mean anything. Maybe he's just getting going."

"Wouldn't that be something." Fenn shook his head.

"I know I'm grasping at straws here, Mr. Fenn, but I wouldn't be surprised. Somebody killed her."

"But in the same place as his father?" he said. "It's incredible. I've got an A.P.B. out on our boy. Maybe it'll turn up something."

They checked the house room by room. As they did, Fenn described to her where the girl had died and how. Lisa told him of the elder Zero and where in the house he had committed his own atrocities. It wasn't very appetizing conversation, but in this place, such talk seemed fitting. Its atmosphere demanded talk of dread and dismemberment; it had no use for anything but the darker prospects of human endeavor.

After a time, he chuckled and said, "You're not much of a first date."

"I've never been known to be."

Fenn was intrigued by her encyclopedic knowledge of crime and insanity, but mostly by the woman herself. He liked the way she looked at him, the way she called him *Mr.* Fenn rather than Lt. Fenn—there was something almost endearing about that, like a pet name—although he would've preferred just Jim. He liked her husky, sexy voice. And despite her catalog of grue and grim, she had a soft, winning quality about her that could reach right into your heart, he thought. The sort of woman who was a wonderful combination of beauty, brains, and confidence. She gave her best at all times and it made Fenn want to do the same. He felt he would follow her anywhere. He almost hoped that they never would find Eddy Zero, so their time together would never end.

But it would.

It had to and he knew it.

But there was always the present and it would have to enough. He could be with her now, listen to her voice, pretend that there was more here than there actually was. He told himself that he could merely ask her out to dinner, but he was afraid of the consequences. Her possible refusal was something he didn't think he could bear. That it would end before it really began.

He almost wished he were still married so there would be a reason he couldn't pursue her. If it hadn't been for the mystery surrounding her, surrounding Soames, surrounding *all* of this, he would've fallen completely.

"What do you make of all the mirrors?" he asked. There were dozens upon dozens.

"I'm not sure," she said. "Zero had them installed here. We know that much. But not why."

"Crazy fuck."

"I don't think we're going to find anything here," she said.

"No, I guess not. But we had to try." He popped a couple of aspirins and chewed them vigorously, willing the headache not to start.

"You should do something about those headaches," she said.

"I've tried. The doctors said there was nothing they could do."

"How often do you get them?"

"Irregularly," he lied. The truth being that they were starting to be very regular. "I've tried to figure out when they happen, like the doc said, so I could figure out if they were caused by some kind of stress. But there doesn't seem to be any reason. They just happen."

She touched his hand and it was nearly too much. "I want to thank you for being so helpful, Mr. Fenn," she said. "This is probably all a wild goose chase. You've been very understanding, very cooperative."

"Just doing my job," he said and they both knew it was a lie.

They walked back to the car, each secretly relieved to be out of the house.

"What now?" he asked.

"I don't know. I'll spend a few more weeks at this. I'm not beaten yet. I know he's here somewhere."

Fenn started the car. "If there's anything I can do . . ."

"I could go for a cup of coffee."

"You had only to ask."

He drove them quickly away from that malignant house and its decaying neighborhood. He chose a small diner that wasn't far from his own apartment. They sat and drank their coffee and he asked her about herself and all the while he thought about other things. How her lips might feel against his. How she might smell if he held her close. How she might look in the morning.

He was more than a little surprised at himself. Although he'd been divorced some six years, he'd had few dates . . . outside of a few sleazy one-nighters. Relationships could be ugly things, he knew, and he had no interest going back into that arena of psychological and emotional barbarity. And now this. He was quite happily falling in love like some giddy teenager. It was totally out of character for him. Yet, he was enjoying it. Enjoying the fact that love had put a new glow in his cheeks, new wind in his lungs, and a new and necessary need to keep living.

Last year, his fortieth birthday had come and gone and he'd consoled himself to the fact that this would never happen again. He was glad to be proven wrong.

His headache vanished as soon as they were free of the house.

*   *   *

When Lisa got back to her hotel room, she ordered some lunch and sat before the TV staring blindly at it. Things weren't going well and even she saw this. San Francisco was a huge city and there were hundreds of places someone like Eddy Zero could hide.

She had only enough money to last a month, no more.

Maybe she'd been deluding herself into thinking that four weeks would be enough time to find and contain him. It took Soames three times as long just to locate him in the first place. Eddy could've been in another city entirely or out of the country for that matter. But she couldn't bring herself to believe that. He was here, somewhere. And the murder of that girl in the old house only made her more sure of it.

It was over two years since the last time she'd seen Eddy. And in that time, her desire to work with him again had never dimmed. She supposed she was infatuated with him. Not physically, not emotionally, but professionally. A psychiatrist could spend a lifetime and never hope to meet a patient as interesting or challenging as Eddy Zero. He was the ultimate study. A pure psychopath who broke all of the rules and set new ones.

She pushed away from her lunch and went down to her rented car. She knew where she was going, even if she refused to even think about it. It took her about thirty minutes to reach Zero's house.

The House of Mirrors.

The atmosphere of gloom and depravity was the same as she pushed through the door. But it meant nothing, she told herself, merely an association the mind made with an old, empty house that had been the scene of several grisly crimes. She went up the stairs and stood for a time in the hallway where the girl had been first stabbed. There was some dried blood spattering the walls. Just a few drops, but enough to kick her heart into her throat.

She went from room to room looking for she knew not what. She was here purely on impulse and nothing more. She felt like a fool for even coming. In such a neighborhood, she'd be lucky if her car was still there when she returned to it. And there were worse possibilities. She was a woman alone in an empty house in a bad neighborhood. If someone had been watching her, they might've followed her in. Things like that happened. And if she was raped or murdered, who would hear her screams in this huge, enclosing tomb? And if they did, would they even care? Unlikely. People in this quarter were desensitized to such things long ago. Just another screaming woman.

The police had been all over this place, she knew, as had Fenn and she. Nothing of any possible bearing had been left behind. She passed the door which led to the attic and stopped. Did she really want to go up there? Alone? The attic was where Dr. Blood-and-Bones and his associates had done their bits of work. But that was twenty years past and she didn't believe in ghosts.

It was a nasty place, brimming with hate and pain. She told herself it was simple association once again, but she couldn't believe it this time. The beams overhead were festooned with cobwebs, the warped flooring layered in dust and grime. It took great personal strength for her to proceed. In her mind, she saw the crime photos of this place that she knew so well. The blood, the carnage, the skins tacked to the walls. It seemed she could smell them, ripe and sour like hides stacked outside a skinning shack.

"It's nothing," she said aloud and continued on. The sound of her voice echoing and dying, being sucked into these rotting timbers that had known so much horror, was disturbing somehow. She rounded a bend and a damp, dirty smell touched her nostrils. The floor here had been vacuumed of dust, even the paint seemed to have been leeched free. There was a dead thing resting in a circle of clean: a twisted clot of bone and fur boiled into a central mass. A cat, maybe. Its blood and meat was gone, blasted from the bone by some impossible, hungry wind. She'd never seen anything like it. Even the bones themselves looked pitted, abraded somehow. There were bits of flesh clinging to the nearest wall like blown insulation. A full-length mirror hung there, its pane caked with twenty years of filth.

What could've happened to the poor creature?

None of this had been in evidence before. It had happened since she and Fenn had been here earlier. In those few short hours.

She found her feet and ran downstairs and out to her car. Her breath was coming in raw gasps and her heart thudded like a drum. And it had little to do with exertion.

She drove away, her mind filled with hideous thoughts.

*   *   *

When Lisa got back to her rooms, the phone rang. It was Fenn.

"There's been another murder," he said.

"Where?"

"Near the shore. We think the body was dumped there. It was hacked up pretty good. Not like the girl in the house. More methodical."

"It's him," she said breathlessly.

"Maybe."

"It *is*."

"You can't know that, Doc."

"It's him. I know it now," was all she would say.

"Something else, too," he said with a sigh. "It's probably unrelated, but it concerns our Jane Doe. She was going to be buried tomorrow, but there was a fire at the mortuary. They're still sifting through the ashes. So far, they haven't found her remains."

Lisa felt something twist in her chest. Somehow, this wasn't unexpected.

THE NIGHTMARE FACTORY

In Fenn's dream, he was alone.

It was the single constant in these nightmares. Loneliness, solitude, madness. He was cold, freezing. He was naked and his skin was covered with gooseflesh that felt oddly like tiny bubbles ready to pop.

He was in a tiny room by himself, trapped in a square of blackness. He felt someone near . . . but where? Neither here nor there, but near and far, within and without.

He swept his eyes around in the mulling blackness, but could see no one or nothing. His fingers pulled at the length of rope and the coil of leather that held it to his ankle. As usual, they were immovable. Yet, he pulled, he worked, he strained against his bonds until his fingers ached and his heart pounded with ever-weakening, ever-irregular rhythms.

Beads of sweat stood out on his face and they felt huge and oily rolling down his cheeks. Maybe not sweat but blood. Coagulated blood. He could taste it on his lips—coppery and foul.

I'm bleeding to death, he thought, and there was no fear, only acceptance.

He reached out and the walls were made of glass. Moisture was beaded on them . . . or was it blood? His blood? That of someone else?

He looked up and there was a tiny slit of light. There were eyes in the slit, flat, emotionless, evil eyes. The eyes of a tormentor. A reptile.

He heard a voice: distant, cool, clinical. Was it asking him questions? The language was garbled like some guttural foreign tongue.

The eyes kept watching, detached, amused.

"Mama, mama, mama," he heard a voice say and it was his own. "Don't leave me here . . . the bad man's back again . . . mama? Please . . . mama . . ."

The eyes were staring, blatantly amused.

In the distance, a voice began to drone.

A drop of wetness struck his head.

Then another. And another.

A trickle of wetness now.

The eyes were watching.

The wetness was running down his face in warm streams. Water? Blood? Both and neither? The voice droned on. The eyes blinked and kept watching. He heard a broken sobbing coming from his throat and he was not frightened.

He was not afraid.

He was not afraid.

He began to scream.

The voice, the voice . . .

And then Fenn was awake, pushed up against the wall, his fingers pressed into the cracks of the cool plaster. With a tiny cry he pulled himself away and mopped sweat from his brow and under his eyes.

I'm going crazy, he thought, and the idea was terrifying.

I'm going crazy because only crazy people dream the same thing night after night after night. I'm losing my mind just like Soames.

Yet he knew it wasn't true. He wasn't going mad and the dream didn't happen every night. Maybe once or twice a week. But that was up from one or twice a month as it had been in the past. When had he last had it? Two nights ago. It was happening with greater frequency now. There was no denying it. And when things happen with frequency you can believe there is a reason for it.

Take it easy, he told himself. You're under a lot of stress right now what with Eddy fucking Zero and Lisa Lochmere. You're okay. Just keep a lid on it.

Keep a lid on it?

Sure, sure. Keep that lid screwed down tight until the pressure gets to be too much and it pops open. That's why they call it flipping your lid.

He reached over for the glass of water he'd left on the nightstand. He drank down what was left of it. Then he lit a cigarette.

The eyes, he thought, those goddamned eyes. And that voice. What the hell did it all mean?

Dreams were symbolic weren't they? Some said that. Others said they were just the mind's way of cleaning out the trash, sweeping the cellar of the subconscious clean for the day. If that was true, then he needed a bigger broom, because something in there wasn't moving. It was snagged like a nail in a wall.

He thought, for not the first time, of talking to Lisa about it. But he couldn't and he wouldn't. He didn't want her thinking he was some nut.

She wouldn't think that.

But maybe his greatest fear was that if he talked about it, he'd lose it completely and end up spending his days strapped to a cot like Soames.

He butted his smoke and closed his eyes.

There were no dreams.

LAIR OF THE SPIDER

It was late and Spider was still in bed.

Like a mountain moonflower, he rarely bloomed before darkness. There was nothing supernatural about this, he simply hated daylight. He hated the noise and the confusion and the crowds and most particularly, the people themselves. Staring at him. Always staring at him.

It was like he was freak or something.

The night was better. There were plenty of shadows to hide in, plenty of dark cubbyholes to lose yourself in. His particular eccentricities were well masked by the gloom. And in the seamy night world of San Francisco, he fit right in.

He pulled himself out of bed and went to the window. The moon was rising in the sky.

Out there, somewhere, he knew, the police were probably scurrying about like worrisome ants, trying to restore law and order. There was a killer in their midst, they probably thought. And they were right, or nearly so. But they didn't understand anything but the feeble evidence their near-sighted eyes gave them. And it was precious little of the big picture. They knew a murder had been committed, a young woman had been butchered, her life taken. But they didn't know *why*. They and their attendant psychiatrists probably thought the motive was lust or dementia. But it was neither. The reasons were far beyond what their limited mentalities could grasp.

It brought Spider no end of amusement to think of them and the reasons they pinned on the crime. They were idiots as all lawmakers and freedom takers were. They saw nothing but the most obvious.

Spider checked the time. Before long he had to meet Eddy and begin the night's work. It was time to get ready. He pulled out his battered leather case of knives and examined them one by one. He sharpened their blades and polished them with oil and a soft cloth. You could always tell the level of a craftsman by how he cared for his tools. And Spider's were gleaming.

He dressed before a full-length mirror, choosing the proper leathers and denims. It was important to look your best. When he took another life this night, he wanted said victim to realize that he or she wasn't merely dealing with some drug-crazed maniac. He wanted them to know they were being killed by a professional, a specialist. He wanted them to die knowing their great sacrifice was appreciated. That they were not some mere victim of blood-lust, but part of a greater good, a key to a door. It was the least he could do.

It meant a lot to him that they died knowing these things.

For he was a specialist, as was Eddy. Two experts plying a trade in the grand tradition of their criminal forbears.

He brushed his long hair and greased it just so, knotting it into seven braids. Seven, because he thought even numbers brought bad luck. He intertwined beads into the braids, using a system of color separation he'd read of in a book on necromancy.

When he was done, he was quite pleased. He was dressed to kill and wasn't that somehow fitting?

He went into his little kitchen and opened the refrigerator. There were few things inside. A couple bottles of imported German beer. Some celery and other assorted vegetables, tainted brown and rotting for the most part. Some herbs and flowers carefully wrapped in cellophane and a few bottles of murky liquid, all of which, he discovered in his studies, were useful in resurrecting the dead. He hadn't gotten around to trying them out yet. Next to a jar of graveyard dirt, there was something wrapped in bloodied tissues. He took this out and examined it. It was the left kidney of the woman they'd dispatched the night before.

He dropped it in a pan along with some lemon butter and pearl onions and fried it up. It wasn't bad, mind you, a tad bitter, but not terrible by any means. Not quite as sweet or succulent as he'd hoped for. But taste wasn't the thing here. Jack the Ripper had claimed in a note he'd done the same thing and it was Spider's belief that the Ripper had gotten into the Territories, so it was worth a shot.

When he was through eating, he washed up his dishes and drank one of the beers. Then he started putting on his make-up. Nothing extravagant, of course, no reason to stand out when you were a night-stalker. Just an even base of clown white and some dark grease on the lips and around the eyes. It gave him the unpleasant look of a wraith.

He liked it.

He gathered up his bag of instruments and some black raincoats for Eddy and he to wear during the messy parts. He left his flat and started down the street, whistling a tune. It was good for a man to have work, he thought, a purpose in life. His father had said that to him once and, dammit, if the old pedophilic cross-dresser wasn't right after all.

Spider wasn't without his worries. He was concerned about the police. If they were to catch on to who was offing the citizens of their fair city, all hell would break lose. They'd lock Eddy and he away for eternity, as they had with other visionaries. And the thought of that made him feel ill. He couldn't let it happen. They had to unlock the seal of the Territories long before then and slip into that more insightful realm.

He didn't care to dwell on such things.

For tonight, the city belonged to the night-stalkers. Tonight they would strip, cut, and bleed another and somewhere, he hoped, the Madonnas were watching over them, readying them for membership in the most exclusive club in all of reality . . . or out of it.

He walked on, whistling a merry tune.

EDDY

He, too, was readying himself.

Unlike Spider, he hadn't been sleeping all day. Sleep was something that was evading him a little more each passing day. He couldn't rest. The Shadows wouldn't let him. They kept after him hour after hour, pouring out their excesses to him. Weeping of their damned souls and failed existences. They were becoming more and more bothersome by the hour.

Each time he closed his eyes, they started screaming or laughing or crying, telling him of their needs, their wants, their anxieties. He almost cursed the day he'd taken Cassandra into that damn house. The only way he could keep them at bay was to open all the drapes in his little apartment and let the light chase them into the corners. And even there, they wept like mourning widows.

He knew who they were now, at any rate. Just nasty bits of earthbound souls. What was left after the good and righteous parts of them fled to Heaven or wherever it is they went. Left behind was the greed and vice and lust and hatred. All the bad things. He supposed the Shadows were his inheritance . . . being that his father had killed their physical bodies and left them to rot in that decaying house.

And as such, he figured he should care for them as best he could.

It gave him someone to talk with when he was alone. And he liked to watch them clinging to the walls or pooling on the floor like oil. If it wasn't for the bickering amongst them or the constant whining, he might've actually liked them.

"I have work to do tonight," he told them. "Please don't be a nuisance."

They slithered over the floor and wound around his legs like bothersome cats.

He stepped free and put on his black overcoat. He wore dark jeans and a simple brown long-sleeved shirt beneath. He combed his long dark hair and slipped on his sunglasses. He was ready. Unlike Spider, he dressed simply. He wanted only to be unremarkable in every way. It was important considering the nature of the work to be done.

He left his apartment and went out onto the street. He walked and no one paid him any mind, just another lost soul in the city. He avoided streetlights. He didn't want his shadow cast against the facade of a building, in case someone were to see. It would draw undue attention being that he cast not only his own shadow, but a vast, tumbling heap of others hissing at his side.

LETTERS FROM HELL (2)

Dear Eddy,

I'm still after you, so don't get any ideas you're off the hook.

True love never dies, my darling. Mine burns ever stronger.

There are things I have to say and I'm afraid I'll have to tell them to you of all people.

Ready?

I want to tell you about my father. Not my real father who died of pneumonia when I was an infant, but the man my mother married when I was six or seven years old. The man I thought was an angel sent from heaven to guide us and protect us, but was in reality a beast merely biding its time, just waiting to show its teeth and fangs. I want to tell you the truth, not the lies I manufactured for pure hearts. Only the truth.

I loved my stepfather. Please never doubt that. When I was a little girl I loved everything about him. A girl's father (surrogate father in my lamentable case) is her first love and she compares every other man she meets against him. He was a cop. When I was ten or eleven, he was terminated by the department. I didn't know why at the time. But I found out later by eavesdropping on conversations between my mother and aunts. He was terminated for his part in a pornography ring. I never learned the particulars. I didn't want to know them.

That was when my dream of him was shattered as the ideal parent. It only fell apart further, of course, as the years passed. He'd seemed like a good man before then. He was always kind to mother and my younger brother. He always came home bearing gifts and smiles and laughter. We adored him. None of us—not even mother, I think—really knew the beast he truly was deep down.

By the time I was thirteen, my image of him had fallen to memory. Yet, even though I knew he was little better than a common criminal, I still maintained a somewhat idealized view of him. Old habits are hard to break. Why mother stayed with him after that awful pornography business, I'll never know. Especially since she knew much of it concerned children. Love is blind, I guess.

I had never gotten over the shock of that affair. Much as I wanted to believe he was reformed, I had my doubts. I took to following him as he left for work each evening. He must've known, because he usually managed to lose me more than once, abandoning me in one bad neighborhood after the other—which in itself should give you an idea of the sort of man he REALLY was. Mother said he worked for a newspaper, but she never named which one. Maybe she even believed this. I don't know.

On the eve of my fourteenth birthday, the revelation occurred.

He thought I was sleeping at a friend's, while in reality I was hiding out waiting for him. I followed him to his place of work. It turned out to be an old, decaying warehouse off of Market. At least that's what it looked like from the outside. I slipped in there and discovered a very complex business taking place. It had nothing to do with newspapers. Oh, there were makeshift offices set up and people manning phones and desks. It was the scantily clad men and women moving about that raised my suspicions. Most of the men were in their twenties, I thought. The oldest of the women were about the same ages, the youngest no older than I.

I was looking around, being careless, I suppose, when I was caught.

"Hey, kid," a man said. He was obscenely fat and lecherous-looking.

I was terrified, but I did my best not to show it. "Yeah?" I said.

"You lookin' for Donny?" he asked, his eyes drinking me in.

I told him I was.

He put his hand on my ass and directed me up a set of stairs. I pretended to like him pawing me, but in reality I wanted to vomit. He left me at the stairs and went about his business.

I was curious by this time, so I went up.

Have you ever been in a movie studio? Well, neither have I. The place I found myself in was a sex factory. Oh, there were sets—torture chambers and dungeons—and cameras and recording equipment, but it was no studio as such. I was looking at things someone my age should never have been exposed to. Yes, I saw it all. And I think this was what destroyed my young mind. This is what pulled the carpet of innocence from beneath me. Not what followed, but this.

I was so shocked by it all. I felt guilty and dirty and damaged beyond repair. I remember backing away, not looking where I was going and not even knowing until I was already there. It was the voices of rage from the film crew that slapped me back into reality . . . and what reality? I had stumbled onto a live set where they were shooting a B & D film. The eyes of the director and actors were upon me. But they kept filming as someone shoved me out of the way before I stepped into the shot. A girl of my own age was lying on a bed. Her hands were bound, her legs spread wide. A woman in a leather mask was simultaneously whipping her with a leather thong and sliding a strap-on dildo in and out of her ass.

I ran out of there, half out of my mind.

That night, I heard my "father" come home. I expected the worst and I wasn't disappointed. He slipped into my room. He looked like a stranger.

"Don't pretend you're sleeping," he said.

I opened my eyes.

"Have you told anyone what you saw?"

I shook my head. Words were beyond me.

"They like you down there," he said. "They want to see more of you."

"I won't tell."

"Business is business."

To prove this pearl of wisdom, he raped me, then and there, with my mother sleeping only a few doors away. I had been a virgin up until that point. He raped me nightly for weeks. But that was nothing compared to what came next.

I became a star.

Yours,

Cherry

FLY AND SPIDER

"Spider? You around? I want to talk to you."

Gulliver listened. Beyond the door there was silence, an awful, heavy silence that got under his skin.

"Spider?"

With a badly shaking hand, Gulliver let himself in. Despite that seedy neighborhood of violent homeless people and drug addicts, Spider never locked the door. He was always open to visitors, regardless of their reasons and inclinations. Gulliver had once asked him if he wasn't worried about being robbed or killed, and Spider said, quite matter-of-factly, "Let them come; getting out won't be as easy as getting in."

He went in and was immediately struck by the stench. It was horrid. He had never smelled anything quite like it before, it was positively vile. Something had been cooked, but what? In his mind he pictured soufflés of blood and human hair, meat pies bubbling with gut cheese and creamy marrow.

He searched about and found no one. This was the point in a movie, he supposed, where a character would begin looting through the occupant's personal effects. And as he did so, the occupant would return. But Gulliver would have none of that. He was leaving now.

He had come to seek out Eddy, to keep Spider's filthy fingers off of him . . . but he knew in his heart and the deep recesses of his poetic soul that he was too late. Much, much too late.

He went back outside and the alley was still deserted. He breathed a welcome sigh of relief, brushing a dew of sweat from his brow. He started walking home, but just a few blocks away he caught sight of a slouched, almost bestial-looking figure. It was Spider. There could be no doubt. Even in that part of the city with its ready compliment of the eccentric, the disenfranchised, and the demented, Spider stuck out like a severed thumb. He was decked out in his leathers—comic book Goth chic—his hair braided and beaded, a leather case in one fist, something like a sheet of folded black vinyl in the other. If ever there had been a man . . . or something manlike . . . on a mission, it was certainly Spider.

Gulliver trotted along behind, keeping pace but not getting too close. He caught sight of his face once and was glad of it. Spider was made up like a ghoul. His face was painted bone-white, his eyelids and lips black. There was a reason to this madness and Gulliver planned to find out what.

So he tailed him.

"What the fuck are you up to now, Spider?" he said under his breath.

He kept a good half a block or more between himself and his quarry. If Spider found him following along, who could say what would happen? He was made up for something and Gulliver had a good idea whatever it was wasn't pleasant.

It took Spider nearly thirty minutes to reach the warehouse district. He was moving slow, his stride confident and sure. He never turned. The idea of being trailed probably never even occurred to him.

He went to the water's edge and stopped. He checked his watch in the glare of the rising moon. He nodded and looked about. His leather gloves shined like neoprene in the moonlight.

Gulliver hid in the shadows nearby, behind a row of shrubs. In the distance he could hear the throb and bustle of the city proper. Down here, it was quiet. There were warehouses and industrial sites dotting the waterfront, mainly failed and closed-up. It was a bleak and desolate place that would soon be bulldozed for urban renewal.

He heard voices and saw three figures approaching. There was female laughter and a low, even male voice. It was Eddy. He knew that much. He felt a tightness in his stomach, an expectancy.

There was talk and laughter as Eddy and Spider and the two women Eddy'd brought with him got acquainted. They were prostitutes by the looks of them. Was that what this was? Gulliver wondered. Just a little party and nothing more?

They walked off, chatting and giggling, the girls fascinated by Spider's get up. It was high carnival to them, but that was only because they didn't know Spider and the deadly machinations of his twisted mind.

Gulliver followed behind, keeping a safe distance.

Why am I even bothering?

He wasn't sure, but he'd come this far and he wasn't about to turn back now. If all they were going to do was a little fucking and sucking in the dark, at least he'd get some entertainment for his time.

They slipped through a gap in the gate of a chain-link fence that surrounded a former brewery. The place was empty and had been for . . . what? Twenty years? At least. Gulliver waited in the shadows until they were around the side of one of the buildings, then followed.

A loading dock had been forced open by vandals and he slipped in, hoping it was the way they'd come. It was huge inside, like being in some vast arena. Moonlight spilled in through the barred windows and he saw nothing but wood and rubble everywhere, the skittering of night creatures.

Then he heard a sound, a wet muffled noise.

He moved in its direction and stopped before a door. He heard voices: Spider, Eddy, but not the whores. Then another noise, like something heavy being dragged off. The voices faded in the distance. Gulliver stepped into the room. It was actually a corridor, he saw. There was no one in it, but he could hear them in the distance, laughing.

The floor was wet.

Moonlight glimmered off a smeared pool of something. A heavy, sharp odor hung in the air. Bile crept up his throat. Blood. A chill passed through him. He steadied himself against the wall. After a moment or two, he stopped shaking. Violent death was nothing new in this city, but he had never been this close to it before. It was garish and ugly and so very, very real. The stink of blood filled his nostrils, his lungs, his reeling head. He did all he could do to keep his stomach down.

He had to get away, to run, to hide. If they were to catch him so close to their crimes, it wouldn't be a good thing. Yet, like staring at the aftermath of a car accident, he couldn't leave. He couldn't pull himself away. He had to see, some graveyard curiosity had taken control and it demanded to be fed. Even at the cost of his own life, his sanity.

He started after them, freeing his shoes from the blood with a sticky sound. His stomach rolled with dry heaves.

Their trail was easy enough to follow, a smear of blood in their wake. He followed along, careful not to tread in it.

The corridor ended at an open door leading outside.

He could smell the fresh November breeze and something else quite horrible. He could hear them out there, talking amongst themselves. He peered out the door. There was a courtyard hemmed in by the buildings. Something was unzipped and there was a rattle of metal instruments. Eddy and Spider were putting on black vinyl raincoats, buttoning them up. A lantern was lit.

Gulliver watched them, stooping down, selecting knives in the brilliant, dirty light, discussing the bodies at their feet. They motioned in the air with the knives, comparing cuts like two butchers and he supposed that's what they were. What they did next was the thing that made him fall to his knees, the blood abandoning his buzzing head. They worked carefully. First stripping one body, then another, examining their prizes.

Gulliver crawled away down the corridor and threw up, collapsing face first in his own waste. He lay there like that for some time as reality spun out of control around him. In the courtyard, he could hear rippings and wet slashings as the knives did their gruesome work.

When he could finally think straight, he pulled himself up uneasily on all fours and wiped the vomit from his face with his sleeve. His brain was telling him run, but his body admitted it had no strength left.

He listened and it was quiet out in the courtyard.

Had they gone? Had they taken their victims somewhere else to work on?

There was hope. He had that much. If they'd left, then he could count himself lucky that they hadn't gone back the way they'd come. But if they were still around, this ordeal was far from finished.

He stood and went back to the end of the corridor.

And heard something in the courtyard.

He pressed himself into a corner and the nausea took him again. This time it wasn't a physical reaction, but one caused from cold, biting fear that swam through him. He covered his mouth with his hands so he wouldn't make a sound and shook, tears pressing from his bloodshot eyes.

They were still out there, all right. He could hear the sliding sound of vinyl and rip of knives over flesh.

Though he knew it would forever damage him and suck the soul right out of him, he had to see. He had to go look to prove to himself that it was indeed happening. He moved over to the doorway again, the breath in his lungs making a rushing sound in his ears.

They were kneeling next to one of the bodies. The light gleamed off their wet raincoats, the blades in their hands. It looked like they were carefully slitting the corpse's clothing free, but he could see that she was already naked, her legs long and bare, her breasts heavy, nipples standing stiffly like thimbles. Eddy and Spider whispered as they worked. Whatever it was they were doing, it was meticulous, painstaking work. As Spider carefully slit with what might have been a scalpel, Eddy began pulling a sheet of something free. It looked like a skirt with scarves dangling from it.

Jesus, they're skinning her.

Yes, very carefully and very slowly, the whore's hide came off in a gauzy membrane that the moonlight shined through. From what he could see—and surmise—they had slit open the woman's scalp, slicing down her neck and between her shoulder blades and ass, cutting vertically down each leg and around the bottom of her feet. As Spider surgically slit connective tissue, Eddy peeled her like an orange. It was exacting work, very time-consuming. But they went at it with a sickening finesse, cutting and peeling, the skin coming free in a single silken veil with a sound like stripped packing tape. It took them an hour or more and Gulliver watched them, disgusted, yes, horrified, yes, but oddly fascinated by the process . . . and too terrified to move. The most delicate work, of course, was at the breasts, fingers and toes. They didn't bother trying to peel the vulva and anus, they simply cut around them. Finally, they peeled the scalp and had their skin intact. At their feet was a raw, red husk.

As Eddy held the whore's hide up proudly, Spider examined it closely by the light of the lantern. Gulliver could see the woman's face, the ovals of her mouth and eyes, the flopping dark hair . . . like some ghostly hollow-eyed wraith from a horror film.

"Yes, yes," Spider said. "Not bad, not bad . . . a bit crude and workman-like in spots, but not bad at all."

"It's right then?" Eddy asked.

"Oh yes."

Trembling, Gulliver tried to climb to his feet, but the blood drained from his head and his knees went to rubber. He slid down the wall and went out cold.

*   *   *

He woke to the sound of footsteps coming towards the door. His heart thudded weakly in his chest, ready to burst like an over-inflated balloon. His teeth sank into his tongue and drew blood. A whimper clawed up his throat. Again, he tried to get to his feet, but his knees went to butter and deposited him softly onto the floor.

The footsteps stopped and he heard someone sit on the stoop mere feet away from him. A match was struck and he could smell cigarette smoke.

"Messy work," he heard Eddy say.

"But necessary," Spider said. "It has to be done in just the proper way."

Gulliver wanted to scream.

My God, he thought, *they're so damn nonchalant about it all. Like they're cutting meat for a cookout.*

He could hear Eddy drawing off his smoke and exhaling with a satisfied sigh, a laborer on coffee break.

"Why are you opening up her back like that?" Eddy inquired.

Spider was cutting with great effort, grunting and cursing beneath his breath. The wet sawing noise, like someone slicing frozen meat, was almost too much for Gulliver to bear.

"I'm exposing," Spider panted, "her vertebrae."

"Why?"

"Trust me," he said, hacking and cleaving, "there's method to my madness."

He heard Eddy crush his smoke out and join Spider with a swish of vinyl. There was a rattle of instruments.

"This membrane's hellish," Eddy grunted.

"Try the post mortem knife," Spider suggested, pulling something free with a wet snap. "There. Got it. Hand me the snips, will you?"

"I think you'll have to sharpen these knives again for next time."

And it kept on, this rather bored exchange as they cut and sawed and chopped and swore with exertion. After a time, Gulliver was desensitized to it all and he found his mind wandering. The most horrible part was the allusion to the next time. What sort of psychotic game were they playing here? And did they honestly plan to keep it up night after night?

I better get the police, Gulliver thought.

The butchering stopped and he heard the men wiping their hands and putting their knives away, stepping from raincoats.

"Help me with this," Spider said.

"Around their feet?"

"Yeah, they'll be easier to drag around like this."

Gulliver couldn't help himself. He peered out the door. They were tying lengths of rope around the cadaver's respective feet. The lantern was doused now, but the moon was bright. It was terrible. The women were little more than ripped open sacks of meat, internals and musculature trailing wetly.

Ropes were knotted and fastened, instruments gathered up. Spider's bag zipped shut.

"What are you doing with those?" Eddy asked.

"Just a couple of treats for later."

"Any good?"

"If they're seasoned properly."

"You should try marinating them," Eddy suggested. "It works wonders."

Gulliver wanted to vomit again. Murder. Mutilation. Cannibalism. What sort of dark cycle had he put into motion when he'd introduced these two?

Spider and Eddy were talking in low tones, laughing amongst themselves.

They were fiends, ghouls. Deranged beyond imagining. They killed and slaughtered with no remorse. Men like that wouldn't care to be interfered with. And if they were, murder wouldn't be beyond them. If Gulliver wanted to get out and alive, now was the time.

More sounds now. They were dragging the bodies to the door.

Run! Gulliver willed his legs, but they wouldn't move. The best he could do was a slow crawl away from the door. He curled into a ball in a dark corner, prayers falling from his lips. First Eddy emerged, then Spider, stinking of sweat and blood and primal things. They passed right by Gulliver without noticing him, hauling their respective bodies down the corridor and away, blood and bits of flesh raining from them.

When they were out of earshot, Gulliver scrambled to his feet and dashed out into the courtyard. He searched the exteriors of the buildings and found no way out. This theater of suffering had no exits save the one he'd come through.

He had no choice then.

He'd have to follow them back out or hide somewhere until they were gone. It wasn't much of a choice.

It took him some time to creep back up the corridor into the main chamber of the building. He had to move slowly, quietly, so he wouldn't be heard. The consequences at hand were great and he'd never been a brave man. But he was cautious and if luck would just hold out . . .

He made it to the end of the corridor and opened the door. Blinding light exploded in his face.

But that wasn't all.

The women were hung up before him, one by the feet, the other by the throat, back to back. Gulliver stood there, facing death, filled with it, his head reeling. A stink of blood and raw meat washed over him. The women had been gutted quite thoroughly, opened from crotch to breast. Most of the organs were gone, bone and bleeding muscle protruding at gashed angles. Their genitals had been severed free, replaced by gored holes. Their faces were grinning tissue and ligament.

The lantern was lit nearby, hissing with life, providing unwanted illumination. Their skins were tacked to the wall.

It was madness, yet there was a perfection about it all. These were not maniacal slashings, done out of lust or anger, but carefully plucked and dissected corpses. There was a method here, an insane one, but a method all the same. Both women had been mutilated in the exact, precise way.

Gulliver fell to his knees before their swinging masses, a pagan at the feet of his bleeding, slit gods.

"And what do we have here?" Eddy said, not surprised somehow. "Gulliver of all things."

He couldn't look at them.

"The little fuck has been spying on us."

"Have you?" Eddy asked. "Have you been watching us, Gully?"

Spider unzipped his case of knives. "Shall I carve him?"

Gulliver glared up at them, his eyes swimming in their sockets. He was as near madness as anyone Eddy had ever seen.

"I think you've made a grave error here," Eddy told him. "This isn't something we want anyone to know about. Not just yet."

Gulliver stared at him, unblinking. "Butchers," he managed.

"Let's kill him," Spider said.

Eddy shook his head, a man with a problem on his hands. He didn't look dangerous really, just confused. "What to do," he mused.

"If we let the little faggot go," Spider said, "he'll run to the police like the fairy he is. You know that as well as I do. We have no choice."

"Would you do that to us?" Eddy asked of him. "Would you betray us like that, Gully?"

"Course he would. Dirty queen would love to ruin everything," said Spider. "Let's quarter him."

Gulliver was waiting to die and under the circumstances, it seemed the best he could aspire to. There was a black voice of madness in his head, buzzing like insects, offering him a solemn and eternal peace. It didn't seem so bad. If he was crazy, maybe he wouldn't feel the blades when they spilled his life and peeled back his skin.

And then he heard something. A wet sound like dogs lapping at water bowls, like bones pulled through a meaty matrix of flesh. It had to be in his head . . . yet, Spider and Eddy seemed distracted, nervous even. They'd heard it, too. Was it the police? A last minute reprieve? Such things only happened in the movies. He was going to die and that was fact. His death would be bloody and painful. He could only hope that Eddy would take his life quickly so Spider wouldn't prolong the suffering.

But, for now, they weren't paying any attention to him. They stood fixed, rigid, confused even as he was. The air suddenly seemed different, heavier, busier, thrumming with impurity. It crackled with static electricity. It was cool and thick in his lungs, the air of a meat locker. And still that awful lapping sound, louder, louder, a huge and determined sound, that grisly moist ripping. The building seemed to tremble around them, dust pounding from the beams overhead, the floor uneasy with sluggish waves.

What in the hell is this?

And then he saw, just as Eddy and Spider saw.

She was causing the noises, the disturbances, the woman who wandered out of the darkness, out of a gossamer film of dirty light like some imperfection on the face of a mirror.

Something like a prayer of thanks fell from Gulliver's trembling lips. Here was help . . . or maybe something far worse.

The woman stopped just at the perimeter of the light. And what a woman. She was bloated without being actually fat. Her female proportions—hips, legs, breasts, cunt, belly—distended and heaving. She was totally naked and totally beyond shame. She reminded him of a women from museum paintings: heavy, bovine, flesh piled on in abundance. A renaissance women, out of place and time, from a period when large, voluptuous women were highly sought. She licked her lips with an obscene tongue, moonlight shining in her blood-greased tresses.

Gulliver screamed. There was no drama or forethought: the scream came ripping out of his guts and up his throat with a shrilling, broken sound.

It got the attention of the woman immediately. She came in his direction, something like white steam blowing out of the immense, sucking pores set into her pallid, metallic gray flesh. She left a snotty trail of something like afterbirth behind her that crept and rustled like the train of a bridal gown. She expanded like a puffer fish . . . face, lips, limbs, genitalia swelling grotesquely like someone undergoing anaphylactic shock . . . then deflated into some gaunt, mechanistic bone sculpture with glittering cherry pits for eyes. Her skin was like an elastic membrane through which dozens of plum-sized doll faces were trying to push.

"Pretty," she said. "How very, very pretty."

Gulliver pissed himself, thinking she was talking about him.

But she wasn't talking about him, but the sacrifices hanging there, the skins affixed to the wall.

"They've come," Spider said in a voice of reverence. He looked to be quite near religious ecstasy. He fell to his knees. *"Oh, dear Christ, they've come . . ."*

"Jesus," Eddy said. "The Sisters of Filth."

They? Gulliver thought. *They?*

Oh yes, *they.* He saw it now. She had not come alone but with some freakish thing that was attached to her by a snaking, fleshy umbilical . . . like some conjoined twin that had never truly separated. A boneless horror steaming with gray gas, swelling and fluttering, pulsing and throbbing.

Gulliver couldn't help himself: he screamed.

The other was a gas-inflated bladder that drifted three feet off the ground, a raggedy collection of leathery crow skirts formed of multiple blackened hides stitched together, the sutures of which randomly split as it expanded and deflated with its own clotted, phlegmy breathing . . . if breathing it was. Beneath them, he caught glimpses of a writhing mass of red meat. Tendrils of pulsating, bloody tissue kept trying to escape the confining stitchwork only to be sucked back in like ribbons of snot. It had no legs, only one yellow and scabrous arm dangling from the pelts and a skullish head with a white, seamed face like a puckered, waterlogged corpse. Each time it breathed, the mouth suctioned open and threads of pus trembled in the air with a sewer stink that made him want to throw up. Maybe it knew this, for it fixed him with its one remaining eye . . . a serous-yellow orb that looked much like a veined, fertilized ovum.

Gulliver felt his mind drawing into some black chasm within his skull. This was a fucking nightmare. He was hallucinating, he was tripping out of his mind. He had to be. And yet, he felt the minds of those things touch him and he knew they had names—the swollen one was *Haggis Sardonicus* and the conjoined one was *Haggis Umbilicus.* They were sisters.

"You've pleased us," said Haggis Sardonicus, her voice like the coo of a dove. "You've honored us."

She spoke for both of them, for her sister was incapable of speech as such.

Spider looked helpless, impotent next to them. He asked: "You are the Sisters?" His voice was eager.

"You flatter us, sir."

"And you've come to let us into the Territories?"

Sardonicus giggled like a little girl. "He is wise, sister. He knows."

Umbilicus rustled her agreement.

Gulliver was shaking so badly he could not string any words together.

"We want to go," Eddy said. "Into the Territories."

"In time, little one" Sardonicus said. "In time. We have to be sure. You can understand that, can't you? Only so many are allowed in every generation. We have to select initiates very carefully."

Gulliver swallowed down bile. She smelled like rotting orchids and black earth. Which was almost pleasant in comparison to the raw, hot stench of rotting fish that blew off her sister.

Eddy looked uneasy. He took a step back.

"And your names?" the woman asked.

"I'm Spider and this is Eddy Zero."

"Zero?" she said. "Zero?"

"The Doctor's son."

Haggis Sardonicus nodded and seemed pleased by this. She grinned like a wolf with a fresh kill, a foul sweat exuding from her pores. Her sister expanded and deflated rapidly. "Just as lovely as your father, too. What a rare treat."

"And when can we go? How—"

"In time. When we see more of your artistry. Only then. Our club is quite exclusive."

Spider seemed happy.

"For now, maybe you'll leave that one in our care," she said, licking her stout, swollen lips. "My sister fancies him."

Gulliver felt a wild, irrational fear slam into him. He'd take the knives first, he'd use them on himself before he let that horror touch him. He began to crawl away even as Eddy and Spider blocked his path. That would have been it and he knew it. It would have ended right there . . . but there came an interruption.

"Hey!" a voice called out as a flashlight beam panned the room. "What's going on here? What are you people . . . *oh dear God . . .*"

He was a night watchman of some sort or maybe a member of a neighborhood vigilance committee. No matter, because Sister Haggis Umbilicus went right at him. Her stink washed over Gulliver and it was the reek of split carcasses boiling with fly larva upon a battlefield. The old man screamed once and she had him. Her hair writhed like hookworms, her puckered mouth howled, and she unzipped herself, opening like some monstrous black hood, sucking him into the whirlwind meatstorm of her anatomy where he screamed but once before his brain pulped like a soft pear in his skull and his eyes were plucked from their sockets by slimy optic stems and his bones were literally sucked from his skin. He was pulled apart, slit and smashed and turned inside out. He became part of Haggis Umbilicus. She closed back up like a clamshell and he was gone.

Gulliver seized the only chance given him.

He was on his feet and running before Eddy and Spider could hope to stop him. He was out the door and in the night air, the stench, the sickness behind him. If anyone followed, he never turned to see, he knew only escape and that's all he needed to know.

He slipped through the gate and pounded up the street, heading away from the brewery and those gruesome hell-witches and their pawns. He was alive, but his mind, he feared, would never be the same again.

MEMOIRS OF THE TEMPLAR SOCIETY (3)

The Society had their guinea pig now.

She was a teen-age prostitute named Gina. She came to the house and they all had drinks. Hers was drugged. She fell into a deep sleep and woke naked and chained in an upstairs room. There were no windows, only a single light bulb of low illumination for amusement. It was turned on and off at irregular intervals. The walls of her little prison were adorned with mirrors in which she could study her own descent into darkness. One mirror—a small, unimpressive oval—was a two-way glass through which her destruction could be observed by members of the Society.

It was perfect.

Zero decided it would take some time to break her sufficiently. Months, perhaps. And in that time, she would be alone, completely alone in those intervals of irregular dark.

They had their fear victim now and it was time to move onto new things as solitude softened her a bit. Stadtler wasn't entirely happy with any of it, but he went along with it. Like a good SS trooper, he told himself he was only following orders, those of the Society . . . or Zero, because they were basically the same thing.

Although Grimes and Stadtler only came to the House of Mirrors for their weekly meetings, Zero was there much more often. To study his books, he said, or to throw a bit of meat to their captive.

One meeting night, Grimes was late.

"I have an interesting theory I'm playing about with," Zero told Stadtler. "Want to hear it?"

Stadtler gulped his drink. "Why not?"

Zero began, "Say you take two individuals of the same physical type. Twins of a sort, identical, but not related in blood. You place each in a room like the one our Gina occupies. You break each down. You ask the first to tell his life story in minute detail, leaving nothing out—his life, his loves, his history, his occupation in great detail. At first he refuses, of course. But when you starve him long enough, he'll comply. Oh yes, he'll talk, he'll tell all. And by this time, of course, he's nearly mad, so he'll do anything. He spends days telling you his life. And you record it." Zero paused, lighting a cigarette. His eyes were blazing. "Now, you break down the second man far beyond what the first man endured. You destroy him as we plan with our little Gina. You drag him down to a point where he remembers not who he is or was. You transform him into a psychological infant. Then, over a series of weeks and months, you leave him in complete darkness with nothing to amuse his vacant mind save for the recording of the other man's life which you play over and over again. Night and day. While he's awake, while he's asleep. It's the only information he receives, the only external stimulus. After months of this, what do you have?"

Stadtler shrugged. "A crazy man with no memories tortured by the recording."

"Maybe. But maybe you have a duplicate of the first man."

"That's impossible."

"Is it? Remember, your second man has no memories, no knowledge of self, only a burning desire as we all have to be someone, to have an identity. His basal psyche adopts the first man's life in order to give itself a sense of worth, of identity."

"But his other life is still there. Regardless of how you fuck his head up, something might trigger him to remember."

"Possibly. But you forget that his subconscious remembers the terror associated with his former life, it buries it deep, it wants no part of it. It adopts the new life because there's freedom hanging in the balance and because it has nothing else."

"I suppose it's possible."

"It's certainly possible, particularly with the added leverage of certain psychotropic drugs."

"The idea is . . . well, horrible."

Zero ignored that, moral and ethical platitudes having no place in his research, as he called it. "And if you were to take it further," he said, "if you were to place this second man in a prolonged drug-induced hypnotic trance while the recording played and then take him out of it once there was no doubt he had become the first man, he again would remember nothing. But you could plant a suggestion in his mind, a word that would trigger his artificial memory. He would simply be a man coming out of amnesia, his true life buried forever."

Stadtler finished his drink. "That's all and fine, but who would you do it to? You'd have to have two men that were nearly twins."

"What if I knew two such men?"

"Who?"

"Grimes and another."

"You'd do that to him?" Stadtler asked.

"In a second. He's perfect. Overflowing with fears to be exploited. Think about it."

Stadtler did and he didn't like it one bit.

"It's mad," he said.

Zero smiled. Those were the exact words Grimes had said when Zero suggested they do the same thing to Stadtler. But unlike Grimes, Zero had already found Stadtler's body double.

There was no more talk of it that night. There were other things to be done. Zero suggested that tonight they explore the nature of death. They had a pimp supply them with the proper girl and in the attic, while the mirrors watched, they set to work on her.

It was the first of many nights they would do this.

Dr. Blood-and-Bones had been born.

SWEET MR. BILLY

Lisa Lochmere woke the next morning with Eddy Zero on her mind. It had been two years since she'd last talked to him and in all that time, he never strayed far from her thoughts. Eddy was a constant.

But there other things on her mind as well.

Not the least of which was what she'd seen in the House of Mirrors. That animal in the attic—be it rat or cat—had been stripped of its meat. This much was fact. Like some great and hungry wind had sucked away its flesh and had bleached the floorboards in the process. And what could do that? What could suck meat from bones? Dust and paint from boards? There seemed to be no logical answer. Her scientist's brain drew a complete blank. These things alone didn't bother her as much as the fact that everything seemed to have been drawn *towards* the mirror. That was the truly odd and disturbing thing.

She wasn't one who liked mysteries.

And this particular one was very unsettling.

Speaking of mysteries, her mind came back to Eddy again. She was certain now that he was in town, imitating his father's reign of terror. She had no hard evidence, she just *knew*. It was pure intuition. He was out there somewhere plotting the deaths of innocents. And all to feed the twisted ego-machine his mind had become. Fenn had faith in his methods to stop him, but Lisa did not. She better than anyone else in the world outside of Eddy himself knew what he was capable of. Knew just how clever he was.

It was strange how it was all working out. She'd arrived in town and just about the same time there was a murder in the house of William Zero. Eddy? She thought so. And the other one yesterday? She thought that it was his work, too. Just a feeling, really, a sixth sense. There was a certain logic to the fact that the first killing had started where Dr. Blood-and-Bones had more or less ended. At least in her mind. And it had all started with her arrival in San Francisco. If she didn't know better, she would've thought she was the catalyst somehow for the nightmare to begin again.

But that was crazy.

Eddy had told her many things during their sessions. Things he never dared repeat to the other doctors at Coalinga and only when she'd shut her recorder off. He wanted to be his father, recreate his crimes and perhaps outdo them. He had planned it all out, he informed her, how it was to be done. And soon as he had the other doctors fooled and was released, he'd put his master plan into motion. He was a clever one. In time, he did what he promised.

He effortlessly fooled Quillan, Reeves, and Staidmyer. Those idiots never even suspected they'd been manipulated by a master. If the idea of a sexual psychopath on the loose wasn't so frightening, Lisa might have laughed herself.

But Eddy was no garden-variety psychopath (if there was such a thing), which is why he was so fascinating from a professional standpoint. His delusions seemed less a sickness and more role-playing. He flaunted his insanity with all the self-indulgence of a hammy thespian at times; at others, he pretended sanity with a practiced finesse. He was a dilemma to say the least. So as far as the law was concerned, he was quite sane.

Which is just another reason Lisa thought the science of mental health had a long way to go. In her opinion, no two people suffered in exactly the same way from any particular dementia or psychosis. It was always a matter of the individual—his or her history, peculiarities, childhood, personal biases. There was no set pattern, no pat description of any illness, no parameters that could be perfectly defined. It always depended on the individual.

Sometimes, she wondered why hunting down Eddy was so damn important. She spent money and time searching for a man who, once captured, would no doubt be out of reach to her forever. His case would invariably be turned over to someone else. Yet, even with this in mind, she couldn't stop. She told herself she wanted to do a book on him. The son of a serial killer recreating dad's crimes. It was a fascinating concept.

Another book. Like the one she wanted to do on Cherry Hill.

But she didn't like thinking about how that one had ended.

Cherry manipulated you as easily as Eddy did his other doctors.

There was no point in going over that again. There was only Eddy now. He had to be stopped, one way or another. If she got a book out of it, fine. But her primary reason was stopping him. Nothing else. She was a criminal psychiatrist and her job was to identify dangerous individuals and get them off the streets.

But was that the only reason? Mere professional curiosity? Duty?

Of course, she told herself, what other reason could there be?

Passion, maybe? Was there more than a book in mind here, more than service to her fellow man? Something else entirely? Like maybe an emotional and sexual fixation? She refused to accept that. Her obsession was purely professional. There could be nothing else. The truth was Eddy had been in her thoughts since Coalinga. Even when she was picking Cherry Hill's brain for that damn book, Eddy had been the reason. Cherry was infatuated with Eddy. Lisa had to know why.

Because maybe you could understand yourself if you understood her.

Lisa grimaced at the idea.

But the plain facts were that she had a history of involvement with dangerous, desperate men. They excited a raw and primal urge within her. And Eddy was nothing if not those things.

Her fascination with desperate men had started early.

When she was fifteen, her parents divorced. It nearly destroyed her. Outwardly, they'd seemed to love each other, but inwardly, the love hadn't existed in some time, she learned later. Her sense of continuity, of family, was obliterated. Although it was easy enough now to understand how love dies, then it was unthinkable. She loved her father desperately. She and her brother went with her mother to Sausalito. It was the worst time of her young life.

Lisa spent the next few months alone. Oh, her brother and mother were around, but she avoided them like the plague. Her old friends were long gone and she only wanted to be alone. Nothing more. She began taking the bus into Frisco two or three times a week to go to the movies. Even now she had no idea what films she saw. She just went and stared blindly at the screen.

And then came Billy.

He sat down by her one day, a tall, handsome man with a beard and dark eyes. They started talking about this and that and soon she was spilling the sordid details of her life out to him. He listened patiently. He never judged. He spoke only when she wanted him to and the things he said were so . . . wonderful. Sometimes a stranger is the best person to unburden your problems on. They have no personal interest. No reason to keep you happy or down. They merely listen and offer calm advice. This is what Billy did. They met every afternoon for months. Sometimes they sat in the theater, sometimes they took walks in the park. He became a constant in her life. He was always there, come rain or shine and she needed that. He was always waiting for her.

It wasn't long before she fell in love with him.

Oh, he didn't know or pretended he didn't for some time. They'd just talk and walk and watch films. It went on like that for weeks. Lisa worshipping him, loving every word he spoke, and he being kind and understanding.

Then they made love.

The first time was in a copse of trees in the park. It was her first time. And it was beautiful. Billy was very sweet, very patient, very understanding. At that moment Lisa loved him more than life itself. After that, the sex got more frequent. They did it everywhere. In alleys, in cars, in deserted buildings, in public restrooms. Even at her house when her mother was out. The more dangerous the location, the more aroused she became. The thrill of discovery filled her with hot blood. And the thrill of screwing a teenager pushed Billy into new heights of perversion as the couplings became more and more crude. But Lisa never backed down, not even when he started hurting her. In fact, despite herself, she liked it. The more obscene, the more violent, the better.

Then . . . Billy was gone.

Where? She never learned. Not then.

She never saw him again. She kept hoping, though. She kept waiting for him in their secret places, putting ads in the lovelorn columns that she hoped he'd catch. All to no avail. Billy was gone. And there was a gaping hole in her young, somewhat distorted life.

In time, there were other partners, of course. A parade of them. But they weren't Billy. Lisa heard only him as they whispered obscenities in her ears, felt only him as they thrusted inside her. She began to think of him as a user. A monster who'd taken advantage of a teenage girl's vulnerability and then tossed her aside when he grew bored. After all, he was well into his forties, she assumed. But much as she wanted to believe that, that he was some despicable pedophilic monster, she couldn't. Her heart still pined for him. The fire in her veins never cooled.

As time passed, she put him out of her mind. There were always others willing to keep her bed warm. In high school, in college. But the gentle ones were only gentle, the abusive ones only abusive. They were never Billy.

Slowly he slipped from her mind.

Then in college she had her first semester of criminal psychology. The instructor had the students, as a final exam, form profiles of various criminal types. Her assignment, drawn quite at random, was William Zero. Dr. Blood-and-Bones. And it was in the pages of a text on abnormal psychology that Billy and Lisa re-met. She never forgot his face. She never forgot his eyes. When she saw them staring out at her from a grainy photograph, she nearly fainted.

Billy was William Zero, of course.

Her teen-age lover was a fiend of no little repute. He spent his afternoons with Lisa, his evenings with *others*. And he wasn't quite as kind with them. Why he never killed her, she never knew.

She never wanted to.

Time passed and she tried to forget. And then came Eddy Zero, his son. Lisa was assigned to his case. Things had come full circle. From one desperate man to the next. Why did it seem that her own destiny was intricately woven into that of the Zeros? What were the chances she'd end up with Eddy? A chance encounter with the elder Zero was one thing, but to end up as his demented son's psychiatrist almost tweaked the tit of chance a little too much.

Fate? Providence? Predestination? Plain old shitty bad luck?

Sometimes she really had to wonder. But as unscientific as it was giving such things credence, peoples' lives often seemed intertwined in the most unusual ways.

But Eddy . . .

Just as she was beginning to understand him, getting to know him, he was released. Not her doing, of course. Not her decision.

Shortly before that happened, she'd called him into her office for an evening session and all had been going well. Suddenly, without provocation, he'd stood and walked behind her. An orderly was out in the hall, dozing no doubt. Eddy began to massage her neck and, despite herself, it had felt good. His touch sent an electricity through her veins. She stood finally and told him to stop. *What're you afraid of, Doc? That you'll like it?* he'd asked. And that was closer to the truth than he'd ever know. He began to kiss her neck, then her lips, his hand going under her skirt. She told him to stop or she'd call the orderly. But there'd been little strength behind those words. He pushed her down onto the desk and yanked off her skirt. She should have called for help, but she didn't. That was the most disturbing part of it—she *didn't.* No, she laid there across the desk, panting and trembling as he'd slid himself out of his pants. She fought, but it was half-hearted at best, not enough to stop a child, let alone a man. Then his cock was pressed against her, beginning to penetrate. *Feel good, Doc?* he'd said with that piggish leer on his face and a look of utter amusement in his eyes. Then he'd stopped.

And it wasn't because she'd fought him off.

Her struggle hadn't been enough to dissuade anyone. He'd stopped because he'd wanted to. He'd never intended to carry it through. He merely wanted to see if he could push her buttons and he had. He wanted to show her that he could take her anytime he wanted and that she lacked the will-power and self-control to deny him.

And he was right.

Even now, the whole affair made her feel dirty inside because . . . well, *because* she'd wanted him to fuck her right there on the desk. There was something about him that was exactly like his father and it excited her in ways she hadn't felt since the last time "Billy" had laid his hands on her.

She liked to think Eddy tried to rape her—it was easier on her con-science—but it wasn't entirely true. She'd wanted him inside her and there was no getting around that unpleasant fact.

Thinking these things gave her a headache as they always did. It made her wonder who needed the therapy here. Professional interest? Sure, but not just. Some part of her wanted to finish what Eddy had started.

That's bullshit.

But was it? Was her only reason for hunting him down some dull book that would only be read by equally dull academics? Or was it that Eddy was the most desperate and dangerous man she'd ever encountered? And being so, the most exciting lover she could imagine. The image of his father.

She refused to accept that.

Her head was reeling with conflicting thoughts and emotions. Her temples throbbed and she felt nauseous. It had been so long ago, sometimes she wondered if it had even happened.

Did it? Did he really try to rape you or did you just fantasize it all?

Yes, yes, of course he did. The bastard.

You were asking for it. He excited you like his father did. You wanted him.

No! He tried to rape me!

It's only rape when you don't want it. And you wanted it to happen and he knew it.

That's not how it was.

Then how about now? What are you after this time?

I'm a psychiatrist. I have no feelings for him. It's my job, my duty to get him off the streets—*and into your bed?*—and into a hospital where he can't hurt himself or anyone else.

Filled with self-loathing, she dragged herself into the shower. She wasn't going to think about this crap anymore. She stepped beneath the spray and let the badness wash down the drain. The hot water was invigorating, somewhat arousing. She soaped her breasts and urged the nipples into erection. Her right hand strayed, tracing a line down her belly and between her legs. She inserted her middle finger into herself and began a slow and easy motion that urged a gasp from her throat. She saw Fenn in her mind pushing in and out of her. The image was mildly exciting. His face melted and her dream lover became Eddy Zero. Her fingers worked more feverishly now, sliding in with a frantic motion that made her knees weak, her heart pound. And then Eddy was gone, too, and she saw only herself. A woman masturbating in a shower. The picture of which was intensely exciting. It made her feel dirty and this teased her into new realms of pleasure. When the orgasm came, it was complete and draining. She shut off the shower and climbed back into bed, laying there, gasping for breath.

Feel good, Doc?

She closed her eyes and slept.

FENCING

That evening she met Fenn at a pizzeria in Russian Hill and they shared an arugula and prosciutto thin crust and a carafe of Chianti. It was exactly what Lisa needed to forget her worries. Good food, alcohol, and small talk. When not being a cop, Fenn was very funny. His stories of his previous marriages were hilarious and she found herself laughing like she hadn't in ages. The only thing she didn't like about it all was that the entire episode had the uncomfortable feeling of a date.

Eventually, more serious matters reared their ugly heads.

"Tell me what's going on," she said after a time.

"What makes you think anything is?"

"I get the feeling you're trying your best not to talk about something."

"All right, Doc. There's been two more killings."

"I thought so. Why didn't you tell me?"

"Because maybe I was enjoying myself for the first time in years."

He looked hurt. She'd hurt him by bringing this business up and in hurting him, she felt she had hurt herself. Which made her wonder what exactly were the depths of her feelings for him.

"Two more. Found them this morning in an old brewery."

"What was the method?"

"Nothing like our Jane Doe," he said. "More like the one yesterday. In fact, exactly like the one yesterday in some respects except that they were skinned and . . . nearly dissected."

He elaborated on what was found: the peeled skins, the almost ritualistic removal of organs.

"The left kidney was missing from that one yesterday. These two we found today were missing livers. What does that tell you?"

Lisa said nothing.

"What does it tell you?" he asked again. "Answer me."

"You tell me."

"All right, Doc. How about cannibalism?"

"You're guessing."

"Why else? Why would someone want those things?"

"You're asking me to speculate."

"Fine. I'll tell you then: These organs were taken for the sole purpose of eating them. I think our boy is much sicker than you could possibly imagine."

"That's pure conjecture."

"Is it? What else could the reason be?"

"That remains to be seen. It's not unusual for a serial murderer to take trophies from his victims. In fact, it's fairly common. They like to gloat over their deeds. In cases of sexual sadism—and my guess is that these are sexually-motivated crimes rather than instances of mass murder for profit or gain—the psychosis of the killer revolves around the fact that they've been wronged or mistreated in some way and this is their way of punishing society. That would be typical."

"Did Eddy Zero feel he was mistreated?"

She shrugged. "Eddy was a tough nut to crack . . . and you'll, of course, forgive my inappropriate choice of wording. His motivations were obscure other than he believed he would *find* his father by *becoming* his father. But at the seat of it, at the core, I think he blamed society for forcing his father into hiding or beyond the reach of the law."

"So you don't think Eddy is cannibalistic?"

"No, not offhand. But his psychosis was very complex. I can't say with any certainty that he couldn't have developed such tendencies."

"Wait until the newsies find out we have a cannibal on the prowl."

Lisa felt cold inside. If she'd ever felt any desire for Eddy Zero, that was gone now. She felt only contempt and pure disgust. Anyone who could resort to such a thing was a monster. Then again, there was no proof that that's what it was about. Either way, it was morally repugnant . . . though professionally interesting.

"Did Eddy have any anatomical training?"

Lisa shrugged. "Not that I know of. I don't even think he went to college."

"Well, whoever killed these three women sure as hell does. Roget, the medical examiner, says there's a method to these cuttings. Not one he's familiar with, but a method all the same. Almost professional. Like the purpose was not simple mutilation, but dissection."

"Just like William Zero."

"Exactly what Roget said. And he should know. He was involved in that mess twenty years ago."

Lisa lifted her wine glass, but it was empty. God, she needed a drink. "Any relation between these and our Jane Doe?"

"Roget can't be sure. The first was a crime of passion, he said. Slashing mania. Blood lust. These others are far more methodical. Whoever did them, took their own sweet time. Roget thinks surgical instruments were used." Fenn let that sit a moment. "He's pretty sure our boy has fairly extensive anatomy training. The livers were severed expertly. And the kidney isn't something just anyone could find. It's not very obvious. It would take a pro to locate it and remove it so skillfully."

That said, the meal was certainly over. Fenn paid despite Lisa's insistence on paying for herself. Outside, they found a bench up the sidewalk and sat on it, enjoying the night. Fenn lit a cigarette and drew deeply off it.

"Can I have one of those?" Lisa said.

"I didn't know you smoked."

"Only in times of stress."

"There's more," he said. "The remains of a third body was found at the crime scene this morning . . . but only fragments. Bones mostly. They appear to be badly weathered, Roget said, but the blood stains are recent. There's some speculation as to who they might belong to, but there's an old guy missing, a member of a neighborhood watch."

Lisa was thinking about the bones and connecting them to the animal remains in the attic of Zero's house. Logically, there could be no connection . . . but the deeper she got into this the more logic became suspect.

Fenn smoked and stared at her without really meaning to do so. "I didn't have time to tell you something on the phone last night, but our Jane Doe's not the only one missing in that blaze. There was an undertaker name of Fish who was supposedly working on her. His remains haven't been located either. And his car's missing."

"Find this Fish and you find your body. He must have torched the place to cover his body-snatching."

"It still doesn't make much sense. This guy Fish has been with the mortuary for over fifteen years . . . why snap now? Why throw it all away to snatch one corpse? Not to be crude, Doc, but if he's into the dead he must have more than ample opportunity to satisfy his cravings. Why end the gravy train?"

"Well, if he was a true necrophile—and I'm speculating wildly here— then he may have been overcome by his own desires. Most necrophiles are compulsive. Some just collect things taken from the dead, everything from jewelry to locks of hair. Some only kiss and pet corpses, others need to violate them and sometimes tear them apart. Fish's compulsion may have been growing steadily for years until he had to have a female corpse he could completely possess. Again, pure speculation."

Fenn shrugged. "Well, there's nothing in his apartment and he hasn't been seen at any of his hang-outs."

"He'll turn up, I would think . . . once his desires are sated."

Fenn grimaced, then said, "You don't think Eddy took it?"

"I have no reason to. During our sessions, he never spoke of any leanings towards necrophilia."

Fenn laughed without humor. "But, then again, did he ever mention any leanings towards cannibalism?"

"Touche."

Fenn touched her hand. "Listen, Doc. I'm not trying to be a smartass. Believe me. You know more about Eddy than anyone. But I think if this is his handiwork, then he's only gotten a lot worse since you last saw him."

Lisa nodded. "I just wonder where this is all going to end."

There was nothing further to say after that. Fenn drove her back to her hotel and they said their good-byes. If it was a date Fenn had in mind, it hadn't worked out that way.

The desk clerk stopped Lisa on her way up.

"There was a man here asking after you."

Lisa's flesh went cold. "Did he leave a name?"

"No. Refused to. He was waiting in the lobby, but he's gone now."

"Could you describe him?"

The clerk looked skyward. "Oh, short, stocky. Early forties. Clean shaven. Brown hair, thinning. He had a blue leather jacket on. Rather stylish and well-groomed. You might want to try the lounge."

Lisa did, but there was no one in there that matched the clerk's description. A few businessmen ogled her, but that was about it. She went back up to her room and stretched out on the bed, wondering who her visitor could have been and, worse, what he might have wanted. It seemed, in her mind, that everything these days was connected to Eddy Zero and her instinct told her that this was, too. The description the clerk gave her did not match Eddy, yet she knew there was an association there. One that she'd soon find out about.

She must have dozed, because when she opened her eyes it was after two and the phone was ringing.

"Dr. Lochmere?"

"Yes?"

"I hear you're looking for Eddy Zero . . ."

BUTCHER SHOP

Lisa had known Gulliver little over an hour and she was doing everything she could to present herself as a tough, non-nonsense psychiatrist: cool, clinical, emotionless. She wanted him to sense no weakness. After all, he could've been some nut, maybe even an accomplice of Eddy's leading her to God knew what fate. He had insisted that it be just the two of them. No police, no third parties. She either trusted him or he walked away . . . and if he walked away, she lost her connection—however tenuous—to Eddy.

She was hardly naïve, of course. She better than just about anyone understood all too well the depravity of the human mind and the violent demons hiding therein. Yet . . . something in her wanted to trust Gulliver. It wasn't just the connection to Eddy either. Gulliver seemed like a gentle soul, one who was as frightened of what Eddy had become as she herself was fascinated.

So, going on intuition and nothing more, she allowed this strange man to lead her into an abandoned brewery. She was either tough and fearless or very fucking stupid.

She didn't want to think about which one it was.

She picked Gulliver up over in Haight-Ashbury and he spilled his story soon enough . . . or, perhaps, a very bare bones version of it. Lisa had the oddest feeling that he was leaving most of it out. She didn't tip him off to the fact that she knew about the brewery murders; the ball was in his court and she wanted to give him the space to bounce it in any direction he chose.

"Damn," Gulliver said when they pulled up to the curb. "Look."

The building was a crime scene: it was taped off and sealed. There were no police around. It was late in the day and they had been combing the scene since yesterday morning and must have called it quits. At least, for the time being.

"The cops know. They must have found the bodies."

"Let's go in anyway," Lisa suggested, wanting to see. Whether that was professional interest, morbid curiosity, or something much darker hiding in the basement of her psyche, she did not know.

"They throw you in jail for things like that."

"Let's do it anyway."

Good Christ, listen to yourself. You're practically panting with eagerness.

Gulliver seemed to sense that and moved a little farther away from her on the seat.

"Well?"

He sighed. "All right."

It was simple enough to get in. The doors were taped, but the windows no longer had any glass in them.

If the exterior of the brewery was unimpressive—a bleak stone monolith ravaged by time and weather—then the interior was another matter entirely. The floors were warped and cracked, the walls peeling, the ceiling punched with holes. It was like being inside a corpse. There was a singular air of bleeding decay and corruption, a creeping morbidity that seemed more appropriate to a mausoleum than a place where beer was once bottled.

"What an atmosphere," Gulliver remarked. "They ought to film horror movies here. It's even worse by daylight."

"Like a morgue," Lisa said.

"That's appropriate because this is where it happened," he said. "I wish I'd never followed them."

"Do you know anything about this building?" Lisa asked.

"What's to know?"

"This is where Eddy's father and his little society butchered a few of their victims in the early days."

"You're just a wealth of knowledge, Doctor. You might have mentioned that before when I told you about this place."

"Yes, I should have. I'm sorry."

He ignored that, looking around. He was clearly disturbed by this place. "All this ambience at so cheap a price. I'm tempted to buy."

Lisa grunted. She didn't pretend to understand his sense of humor.

"It's for sale, you know. Has been for years."

Like most failed industrial sites in America, the brewery was an eyesore and as such, available for a song. The realtors were desperate to be rid of it. And especially so considering its ghoulish history. Atmosphere, it seemed, was cheap these days.

"This is where they were hanging," Gulliver said with dread in his voice. They were stopped before a doorway. Hooks were suspended above. The floor was dark with what might have been dried blood. And a lot of it. "Right there. They were tied by the ankles with ropes . . . and strung up." He was sweating.

Lisa said nothing. Dust twisted in the air and she could feel sawdust on her tongue with each breath. There was a stench of stale beer and pungent yeast in the air and something worse beneath it. The room they were in was huge and had probably housed vats at one time.

"Okay," she said. "I believe you."

"Quiet," he said.

"What?"

"Ssh. I heard something."

Lisa humored him and listened. Pale afternoon sunlight filtered in through grimy, broken windows. Motes of dirt and dust danced in the beams like flakes of snow.

"Nothing," she said.

"Shut up," Guliver snapped. His eyes were wide and fearful like those of a rabbit listening for a fox. He was shivering.

Lisa shrugged. "Just your imagination. This place could do it to anyone."

He didn't look convinced. "I heard something, I know that much."

"Let's get out of here then."

"No. Not until I show you everything."

Lisa shook her head and followed along. What the hell am I doing? she asked herself. This guy might be crazy. But she didn't think so. He was frightened. Scared shitless, even, but not dangerous. The smart thing would have been to ask Fenn to meet them here in this charnel house. But she hadn't done that and part of her was glad she hadn't broken her promise to Gulliver of no cops. Another part, however, thought she was a damn fool.

What if Eddy and this Spider were still around?

Gulliver led on, through the door and down a hallway littered with debris, past a block of offices with grimy windows. "You notice anything strange?" he asked.

"This whole business is strange."

"No, really. Old, abandoned places like this are always magnets for teenagers. Places to get drunk, high, cop a feel, get laid—whatever." He looked around. "But not this one. No beer cans or wine bottles, no graffiti. Nothing. What does that tell you?"

"Only that most teenagers have more sense than we do."

He faked a laugh. "I wonder what the reason is."

Lisa didn't want to think about it because there was something utterly wrong about it.

The hallway floor was streaked with blood.

"They dragged the bodies from out there," Gulliver said, indicating a doorway in the distance.

There was a quick shuffling sound from the floor above. They both stopped this time. Gulliver looked pained. "I didn't imagine that one."

"No, I heard it, all right. Mice, probably."

"Or rats."

"Great," Lisa said, hugging herself, her tough act long forgotten. "Rats in the walls."

"What a dump."

When Lisa thought of the atrocities committed here, it was almost possible to believe that the place could be haunted.

They moved on, the shadows deepening. Gulliver carried a small aluminum flashlight. He turned it on now. The light flickered and died. "Shit," he said, banging it against his knee. "Pissing thing."

"We don't need to go any farther," Lisa said.

"Yeah, let's get the hell out of here."

And they did, practically running from the place.

Fenn was outside.

He didn't look happy. "What the hell is this?" he asked.

It took Lisa about five minutes to outline the whole thing to him. When she was done, he looked suspicious. He told her that one of the neighbors had called her plate in. When it was referred to him, he explained that she was working with him. He had covered for her, but from the look on his face it was obvious he was questioning that decision.

"So, you came out here with some guy you don't even know?"

"I'm not a child," Lisa snapped. "I don't need your protection."

Gulliver looked uneasy. "Listen, I'm not some freak—"

"That remains to be seen."

"I don't need this shit," Gulliver said.

"But you'll take it anyway. You're a material witness to a double homicide."

Fenn made Gulliver go through it all again.

"There's something I just don't understand," he finally said. "Why on earth were you following them? What was your reason?"

"I just wanted to see what they were doing. I was worried about Eddy, I guess. Spider's one crazy dude. Take my word for it."

"I guess I'll have to."

Lisa didn't like this at all. Fenn had changed from the warm, friendly man she knew into a cold, cynical cop. He was treating Gulliver like he was guilty.

"You were worried about Eddy, you say?"

"Yeah."

"Were you lovers?"

"No!"

"But you're gay, aren't you?"

"Yes . . . no . . ."

"I thought as much. In my job it gets to where you can smell guys like you."

Lisa was getting pissed. "Goddammit, Fenn. What the hell are you doing? He came to me of his own free will. He's putting his life in danger by fingering Eddy. What in God's name does his sexual preference have to do with anything?"

Fenn smiled cooly. "You're too trusting, Doc."

Christ, he's a homophobe, she thought. Just great.

"You're going to have to come to the precinct with me, Gulliver."

He looked shocked. "Why? I haven't done anything."

"Routine questions, that's all. As I said, you're a material witness."

"Shit," he said.

"Listen, I'm not flying solo on this case, Gulliver. There are other people who'll want to talk with you. It's merely procedure."

Lisa gave Fenn a dirty look. "I'm sure he won't keep you long."

"I'll just bet," Gulliver said under his breath.

MIDNIGHT MANIAC

At San Francisco General, Soames was dreaming.

He was at the House of Mirrors again and it was twenty years ago. There were mirrors everywhere. He was staring at several dozen reflections of himself. There was a stairway ahead, leading into the murk. He caught sight of a figure—a girl, he was sure it had been a girl—racing up the stairs on all fours. His heart hitched in his chest, sweat trickled down his back. He turned, feeling someone behind him.

There was no one.

The girl had looked like Gina. He'd gotten her for Zero. Was she the one Grimes said they were keeping in a cage? He couldn't remember. Maybe it was just some kid . . . some other victim. He swallowed down his unease and followed, knowing, ultimately, that he was part of this. He could try to disassociate himself from the crimes of Zero and his little society all he wanted, but he was still part of it.

He saw the girl again.

She was paused at the top of the steps. She was panting like a dog.

Dear God, what have they done to her?

"Hey!" he said, climbing after her. "Come back here!"

He could see her waiting for him, veiled in murk. She was young, sixteen, seventeen, if that. And if his eyes didn't deceive him—quite naked as well. Was it Gina? He couldn't say. This poor thing looked mad, starved. What did that say? Was Grimes telling the truth?

"Listen, I won't hurt you," he said. "Come down."

Silence.

She giggled softly and disappeared.

"Damn kids," he said.

He continued up the steps. It seemed hotter on the second story, humid even, and a damp jungle heat seemed to drip from the walls. He took off his coat and slung it over his shoulder. Within a few minutes, he was sweating profusely. He was thinking of the girl as he began his explorations. Could it be Gina? He saw her eyes only once and he supposed, more than anything, that was what had brought him up here. There'd been something in them, a wet glimmer but nothing more. The eyes of a dog.

It was quiet upstairs, deathly so. Nothing stirred nor breathed. The floor, he saw, was jutting up in places, the tiles ruptured. There was an even, undisturbed layer of dust over them. Surely, the girl had come this way, but if she had, where were her footprints? Soames looked behind him, scanning the floor with his light. His own were in evidence. Where had she gone? It was vexing. She had to be here. He moved on, the air thick with dust, heavy and hot, hard to breathe. The mirrors were everywhere.

The corridor stopped and ran in both directions. He chose the left passage. It was as good as anything. There was a room ahead, without a door. It looked large. He heard a brief whisper of footfall.

"Girl?" he asked. "Are you here?"

Nothing. She had to be there, though.

"Girl? C'mon out, I won't hurt you."

He found himself unwilling to go farther. He couldn't bring himself to cross the threshold into the room, yet he couldn't go back. There was a mystery here that called to him and what it might say when he got face to face with it terrified him.

The room was huge, cluttered with shattered packing crates and lumber. The air was clotted with dust, the light barely able to penetrate it. She was here, somewhere. He knew it now. Some inner network told him so. It was unbearably hot now, his shirt plastered with dampness to his back. He tasted salt on his lips, sweat ran in his eyes. It was like a maze in there. He threaded his way around shadowy hulks. Furniture? Something was dripping nearby. He played the light around. He could hear a lapping sound like a hound slurping from a bowl of water. He smelled the girl before the light found her: a stink of yellow disease, suffering, and human waste.

She was squatted in a corner on a filthy rug, her back to him. Her nakedness was streaked with dirt, her hair full of dust and broken cobwebs. There were feces on the floor. Much of it dried and breaking apart, but some of it quite fresh and fly-specked. Some of it was smeared on the wall. It looked as if she had been painting with it, forming crude designs and barely recognizable letters.

An animal. Zero's broken her down and is keeping her like a pet.

The horrendous stench and shit on the floor was evidence of that, as was the water bowl and a few well-gnawed bones and rotting scraps.

"Hey," he said. "I won't hurt you."

She ignored him.

"C'mon, it's okay . . . really."

He went to her, reaching out and touching her shoulder. Her skin was clammy, more so like meat from a cooler. She looked up at him through greasy strands of hair, grinning with dirty teeth.

"Jesus Christ," he muttered.

It *was* Gina.

"Gina?" he whispered. "It's me . . . Soames."

She was humming a tune beneath her breath. Her eyes were empty, blank, and insane. Drool ran down her chin. When she tried to speak, all that came out was a guttural, grating noise almost like a dry barking. And the reason for that was quite obvious: they had cut her tongue out.

"My God," Soames said under his breath. "My . . . *God.*"

She cocked her head to the side whenever he spoke her name. There was an association there, but she couldn't quite grasp it. Like a confused puppy, she could only cock her head in confusion. Soames reached out to touch her and she started, baring her teeth. Her eyes were black and glassy.

"It's okay, Gina. Really, it's okay."

She seemed to relax by degrees. Softening . . . but wary, still very wary.

"I'm your friend."

Yes, I'm your friend that handed you over to these monsters. Such a good friend I am.

She nearly smiled as if the word "friend" was another good association, one that made her feel relaxed. She uttered a strange sort of cooing sound, reaching out towards Soames' outstretched hand . . . then she shifted her gaze over his shoulder and her eyes went wide. She jerked away from him, whimpering and curling up in a ball like a whipped dog.

Soames turned and saw someone in the doorway. A tall, cruel-looking man in a dark suit.

Zero.

"What the fuck are you doing here?" he asked. "I didn't send for you."

"I thought maybe . . ."

"You thought wrong. You trespassed and now you know about one of my little secrets." His jaw was making a side to side motion as if he was chewing on something. "I've been looking for a new subject to put in the cage. You might do quite nicely."

"Like hell I will."

"Then you better leave . . . and Soames?" Zero said, fixing him with his dark simmering eyes. "Don't get any misplaced heroic ideas about bringing the police into this. I've got enough on you to put you away for thirty years."

Soames was angry and disgusted. He wanted to beat Zero down, kick him until he was bloody and begging for pity. He wanted to shout in his face, *I might get thirty years, but you'll fry in the chair at San Quentin!* But he didn't. And it wasn't just what Zero held over his head, which was considerable, but the fact that he feared the man. There was an unmistakable sense of power and mastery to him, sadism and brutality. Yes, he might have been able to beat him down, but Zero would do something far worse to him and he knew it.

"You can leave now," Zero said and it was not a polite suggestion.

Soames stumbled blindly for the door, his breath barely coming, his heart banging against the bars of his ribs.

Zero snapped his fingers. "Gina. Come to me. No . . . *crawl* to me. That's a good girl."

Gina slinked across the floor like some human worm, inching slowly forward, whimpering in her throat. Soames smelled a hot stink of fresh urine and knew she had pissed herself out of pure terror for her master.

Then Soames was out in the corridor, shaking and nearly delirious. There was the sound of Zero patting her head and what sounded like him scratching her. "There's my girl. Now you need to learn to obey. You know I don't like you showing yourself to strangers. You'll have to be punished. You know that, don't you?"

Soames made it to the stairs. Zero was going to kill her now and he knew it. He could hear a muted whimpering, but it wasn't from Gina. It was coming from a door opposite him. The terrible sound of a man crying . . .

Soames woke up.

Just the same dream he had off and on for two decades now. A replay of that fateful night.

Tormented and beyond hope, he pressed his face into his pillow and wept.

MATERIAL WITNESS

Gulliver also felt like weeping.

He was sitting in an interrogation room at Southern Station. Fenn had brought him in here and left. That was twenty minutes ago. What was the bastard up to? Maybe he didn't want to know. If he'd just minded his own goddamn business, none of this would've happened. Why the hell had he bothered following Spider anyway? What had he hoped to prove? And why did he bother tracking down Lochmere? All mistakes. All terrible mistakes.

The door opened and Fenn came back in. He had a yellow legal pad and a pen. Gulliver hated the sight of him. Thin, muscular, with cold gray eyes and a hardened, emotionless face. He'd known too many like him before.

"Okay, Gulliver. Let's talk turkey. Shall we?"

Gulliver nodded.

"First off, I'm still not convinced with what you've told me. Why did you follow them?"

"Curiosity."

"That doesn't bite with me. Just curiosity? Did you wanna watch? Maybe see what real men do with women?"

Gulliver had been waiting for that. His reply was all set. "Yes, that's it exactly. And now I know. Real men butcher women."

"I don't need your mouth."

"Then don't give me any."

"All right. How did you learn about Dr. Lochmere?"

"Simple. She's been at every club in town asking questions. Just about everyone knows about her."

Fenn wrinkled his brow. "That's bad. If you can hear about her, so can Eddy."

"Most likely."

"Now, how about your full name?" Fenn said.

"Gulliver."

"Real name."

"Francais Simmons."

"Good. Now address, social security number. Anything pertinent."

Gulliver gave him what he wanted.

"Great," Fenn said. He drew some photos out of an envelope and slid them over to Gulliver. "Is that the man you know as Eddy Zero?"

Gulliver studied them for a time. "Yeah, I think so."

"Is it or isn't it?"

"Yes . . . I think so. His hair's longer now."

"I'll be back," Fenn said, going to the door. He paused before it and turned. "Why Gulliver?"

Gulliver shrugged. "I liked that book when I was a kid. *Gulliver's Travels.* I've been on some travels of my own since then."

Fenn laughed. "I'll just bet you have."

Asshole. Now Fenn was going to leave and check him out on his laptop and when he returned, then the fun would start. Fenn would have a good time then. Gulliver cursed under his breath. How the hell had he gotten himself mixed up in this? It was crazy. Fenn would return in a few minutes with Gulliver's police record. There'd be no stopping him then. Just another bigoted, right wing homophobic asshole whose old school world was falling apart around him. They were all alike, these cops. Their innate ignorance and intolerance was a symbol of office.

Fenn came back with a stack of computer printouts. He sat down. There was no avoiding the shit-eating grin on his face.

"All right, Francais . . . or should I say pastor?"

"Fuck you."

Fenn laughed. "It looks like you've been a naughty boy in the past. Shoplifting. Check kiting. Male prostitution. And here's a good one. Soliciting minors for sexual—"

"That one wasn't proved. It was sheer bullshit. A couple of dumbass cops tried to pin that one on me because I was convenient. You know how cops are. They don't breed 'em for smarts."

"So you say. It doesn't matter. The whole purpose of pulling your file was just to find out what sort of man I'm dealing with."

"And are you satisfied?"

"Very. I take it you don't like cops?"

Gulliver grunted. "What's to like?"

"We protect you, mister."

"Is that what you do? I've never heard it put that way before."

"What the hell do you mean by that?"

"I mean I'm trying to cooperate and you're treating me like the criminal."

"No, I'm just trying to get the facts straight."

"I've told you everything six times now. If you don't have it straight by now, you have a serious learning disability."

"You need to watch that mouth, princess."

Gulliver shook his head. "Why are you cops all the same? Why are you all such homophobic bigots? Is it the training? Surely, the department couldn't possibly put together such a collection of inbred assholes merely just by chance. You're so damn predictable. All of you."

"Aren't we both," Fenn said. "I tell you what, Gulliver. I won't be an asshole if you won't be. We'll treat each other with mutual respect. Trading insults is only gonna slow things down. No more name calling. Your sexual preference is your own business."

"Fine with me. Only, get it straight: I'm not a homosexual, I'm bisexual. There's a difference."

Fenn wrote those items down. "Okay. Now you met Eddy and he asked about his father? If you knew him?"

"Right. I said I didn't. I said I knew a guy who might . . ."

Gulliver went through it all again. Two, three more times.

"I guess that's it then, Gulliver. There's only one more thing I want to ask you."

"Shoot."

"What's your opinion of Lisa Lochmere?"

"My opinion? I don't know. She seems okay. A little tense, wound a little tight. Why?"

"I'm curious."

Gulliver thought it over. "You're in love with her, aren't you?"

"Is it obvious?"

"Yes."

"Keep it to yourself, if you would. Now what's your opinion."

"I haven't known her long, but I'd say she's mysterious. That neither of us really know what she's about," he said. "She has a secretive side. A secret agenda, I'd guess. She's someone with skeletons in her closet."

Fenn nodded. He'd pretty much had his own thoughts just put into words, Gulliver figured.

"All right. A couple of my colleagues want to question you now."

Fenn left and two other cops came in. One black and heavy, the other thin and white.

"I'm Detective Moore," the black said. "And this is Gaines. This won't take long."

"Now," Gaines said, "tell us everything and don't leave nothing out, *princess* . . ."

LETTERS FROM HELL (3)

Dear Eddy,

Sometimes I dream about you.

Don't ask me why, because I know you would if you were here. Let's just accept the fact that I do. I dream of many things, but I tend to think even the dreams that aren't about you, are about you. In a symbolic sense, if nothing else.

There's one dream I have all the time.

It began during those long days and nights in D-ward, when I had nothing but dreams to sustain me, to break up the monotony of months and years.

In the dream we're at Coalinga. Together we walk hand in hand through the courtyard. You're so handsome, my breath dies in my lungs and my heart refuses to beat. Barbara Cartland aside, I feel like a nubile little girl on her first date. We walk the denuded lawn and the wind smells of dead flowers and rain. Your lips touch mine and I hear thunder . . . somewhere. Maybe in my own head.

I feel two things then: enlightenment and misery. Enlightenment because I realize I love you and I always have, and that you love me. Together our hearts beat in a single rhythm, our feet travel the same darkened paths. Yes, enlightenment in the purest sense. And misery . . . dread, gnawing misery because I know there are those who would separate us, would take you from me and lock me away forever in that cold dungeon they call D-ward. A place of nightmares. A pit of loneliness and gloom where all the weeks pass in a mindbending blur of sedatives and starched straightcoats and darkness. Misery like nothing else.

You tell me not to worry and we walk on through the gates and into the world. We pass through a field of yellowed grasses and we come to another gate. A cemetery lies beyond. Crumbling headstones jut from the uneven ground, their epitaphs rendered gray and meaningless from time and weather. This is our place. I know it. Where it begins and ends.

You choose a crypt covered in dead creepers and wilted wreaths. There's a smell of October wind in the air: death, certainly, but the spice of resurrection, too. We go in. Together, hand in trembling hand, we read the names of the dead from their tarnished markers set into the damp, breathing walls.

You lay me down on a marble slab and cover me in dead roses.

We make love then.

In that place of cold and insects and tunneling vermin.

As you love me your face changes. It becomes that of my father and a hundred abusive lovers in-between. Then it wilts and runs like wax and it's only you.

Your tongue tastes of dirt and death.

"You belong to me," I say. "Only me."

And I hear a great bell tolling and peals of laughter. Rats scratch in the walls of our honeymoon nest, spiders spin webs and court eternity.

Then I hear the sound of running feet. They are loud footfalls, deafening. Hundreds of marching feet clad in Nazi jackboots. The iron gate to our little cottage is thrown open and men in white uniforms pull you from me.

And you are gone.

I cry and scream. My nails rake their faces, my teeth tear at their throats. All to no avail.

And then I'm back in my cold, bleak room with the rusting bars and iron mesh over the windows. I see a bloated orange moon in the sky and black, scudding clouds. The wind calls my name and tree boughs creak.

And I start to scream, knowing I love you.

Knowing true love never dies.

It only waits in dark places.

As I do.

Yours,

Cherry

THE GRIM RESURRECTION OF CASSANDRA LOOMIS

The night Cassandra came back from the dead was unexceptional in every way: no moaning wind or blowing leaves, not so much as a stray raindrop or a distant clap of thunder. It was a warm and dry night, moonless, the stars bright, the breeze negligible. It was the sort of night lovers walk hand in hand down shadowy lanes and make love in vacant, grassy lots or beside country streams. The atmosphere was light and in no way ominous or remotely threatening.

This was the night she chose, or was chosen for her.

Her body was found in what was known by some as the House of Mirrors. A derelict looking for a place to sleep had wandered in as they did from time to time. He'd called the police, of course, but not before he'd looted through her pockets and taken everything of any possible value, including her ID.

Then she became Jane Doe. Dead, lost, but not unaware.

The following days were abysmal. The medical examiner and his attendant flunkies were the first to extricate her from the locker she was kept in. Before them, only cops came to visit and a few despondent souls looking for missing loved ones. The former group was insufferable. They'd stand about, gazing down with barren eyes, telling dirty jokes or studying her wounds and usually at the same time. One or two of them made comments about her breasts and legs. The latter group always looked shell-shocked. Their eyes were hollow, their hearts heavy, their voices weak. If they were grateful that the wrecked and flayed face they looked down upon didn't belong to their lost sheep, you could never tell. They came in numb and were led away in the same state.

Cassandra watched them come, watched them go, her mind racing around in the bleak corridors of her decaying brain. She wasn't sure why the lights never went out completely, but they didn't. Awareness still flickered in that skull of hers, relentless and undying, a dim but steadily burning light.

The medical examiner's name was Dr. Roget. The name reminded her of cheap champagne. So did he: a raw stink of liquor came off his sour breath. He and his flunkies took their time cutting and probing her secrets. Biopsies were taken, fluid samples sucked free, wounds measured for depth and angle of infliction. Her scalp was peeled and her skull was opened like a can of peas, its bounty dropped into a dish and weighed, sliced, and picked at. Her organs and tissues were likewise examined with total indifference. She was no longer a human being in their eyes, just a cadaver, a carcass to be folded, spindled, and mutilated. They did a good job of it. She was disgusted by the process at first, then amused, and finally bored. It only proved that one could get used to just about anything in due time.

When Dr. Roget had finished his little report on the deceased, he sewed her back up again. It was anything but a neat job. Cassandra had known little about autopsies before her own, but she came away with an extensive knowledge. A tailor or a butcher could've zipped her back up; it took no anatomical knowledge or specialized skill. Roget hummed a showtune beneath his breath—*Hello, Dolly? Oklahoma?*—and stuffed her organs back in their slots and if they didn't fit, he shrugged and packed them in any available recess that would accommodate them. He didn't even bother trying to fit the brain back in its housing. He dropped it in her body cavity and started stitching, a cigarette dangling from his lips. A bit of ash fell in, but who was complaining? When he was done, she was sewn from crotch to throat in a great Y-pattern, closing out the post.

Roget dropped his rubber gloves in a medical waste vat and said, "Another day, another dollar."

The flunkies covered her back up and rolled her gurney back into the meat locker. She was slid into her own cubicle.

"Next stop, worm city, baby," one of them said and closed the hatch.

Cassandra was alone for some time after that. Days? Weeks? Months? It was hard to say. The dead lack any definite sense of time. The next thing she knew, she was sprawled on a slab in a funeral home. Two morticians, both men in their twenties, attended to her final needs. She was embalmed and then meticulously washed before a cheap casket was selected. She was a charity case, so the state wasn't about to pay for anything regal.

"She looks pretty good," Fish said. "Considering."

Mick nodded. "You're an artist. That's what you are."

"I wish I knew her in life. Look at those tits . . . yummy."

"You're sick."

"Don't I know it."

Mick shook his head and went about cleaning the instruments.

Cassandra was appalled by the exchange, but not truly offended. The dead did not offend easily. She was almost flattered by Fish's comments. If he hadn't have been such a drooling pervert, she might have loved him. Though her mind was quite active, her body remained numb and frigid like frozen meat. She could feel nothing, only sorrow and despair, the fear of eternity. But she never gave up. She worked at her nerves and stiff muscles, massaging them into compliance. Oh, they'd do her bidding yet, one way or another.

"Any plans tonight?" Fish said.

Cassandra felt herself brighten, thinking she was being addressed . . . but no, Fish was talking to Mick.

"Not much. Early night. I've got class in the a.m."

"You need to live a little, my friend. I've got a couple of Puerto Rican cuties lined-up. Why don't you come along? They speekee very little English and they're barely legal, you know what I mean, but they love to fuck."

Mick sighed. "You're gonna get your ass in trouble, my friend. Mark my words. You can't run around poking teenagers without paying the piper sooner or later."

"Ah, I'm fixed, shooting blanks. I leave no calling cards."

"You're still having sex with minors. It's gonna catch up to you."

"My ass it will."

"One of these times, one of your girlies is going to tell her hot-blooded Puerto Rican daddy and your ass'll be lying on this slab."

"Shit."

"Statutory rape, Fish. Courts don't look kindly on it. You'll do time."

Fish laughed. "Not me."

But Mick was wrong, Cassandra knew. Evil parasites like Fish rarely were punished and they always seemed to get away.

"I wonder who offed this babe," Fish wondered aloud.

"They don't know. They don't even know *who* she is."

Fish laughed. "And what the fuck do we care, eh, Mick? We tag 'em and bag 'em and dump 'em in a cheap box and we get paid."

"Yeah, I guess."

"Look at that face," Fish said. "A butcher couldn't even love that."

Cassandra's face, of course, had been gashed repeatedly by Eddy's knife. There were cuts and gashes everywhere, but her face was still the worst: it had been carved down to meat, nearly down to the skull. The wounds had been cleaned and somehow they looked more ghoulish without blood to lend them color or character.

"I can't imagine what kind of sick sonofabitch could do something like that," Mick said.

"Yeah," Fish agreed. "A freaking waste. Bet she was a good lay in her time. Nice tits."

"You sick fuck."

"Well, shit, look at her. I mean, bag that face, but that body . . . not bad at all." Fish stroked the cold mounds of her breasts. "Too bad, sweetheart. You died too soon. We could've had fun."

"That's enough," Mick said, getting angry. He was larger than Fish, more muscular. Cassandra was practically in love with him. Here was a man who'd fight for her virtue, dead or alive.

"Lighten up, man."

"C'mon, let's get her in the box," Mick told him. "Time to get home."

"What's your hurry?"

"I got things to do."

"So, get out of here. I'll take care of her myself. I need the overtime."

"You sure?"

"Yeah, beat it."

Mick left and Cassandra felt herself cringe. He wasn't going to leave her alone with this degenerate, was he? Yes, it seemed so. Of all the indignities. After Mick was gone for ten minutes or so, Fish stood there, staring at her for the longest time. He left the room and came back. Cassandra didn't like the look in his eyes. Nor did she like anything that came next. But she expected it. Even in death, there was no peace for her. Fish climbed up on the slab and unzipped himself. His member was huge and throbbing. This wasn't the first time for him. That was easy enough to see. He greased himself with petroleum jelly and forced her legs apart. It didn't take very long. Cassandra couldn't feel any of it. She was only aware of the motion of her body as he thrust into her. She felt repulsion and hatred, but nothing more. His semen was hot inside her. She could feel it working at her loins, unlocking the ice prison of her dead cells. The warmth spread and her nerve endings began to tingle, her muscles began to ache. He had given her life. Life could only come from life and so it had. Her entire body was pulsing with heat.

Fish hopped off the slab and washed himself thoroughly. He had considered giving her a long and thorough fucking, but he had to think about his dates later that night. He had to have some spunk left for the Rican girls. Besides, it always had to be fast when you knocked off a quickie with a corpse. The thrill of discovery was part of the allure, but you couldn't push it. He had long experience at deflowering the dead and he wasn't about to risk any of it coming to an end.

He sat down at the desk and scribbled a few pertinents for his boss, thinking about those Puerto Rican girls and what he was going to make them do. The paperwork took well over thirty minutes to complete. The entire time, Cassandra was knitting up inside, the life given her spreading out, cells renewing and dividing as kinetic organic energy flooded her system, and she was reborn . . . not the same, she would never be the same . . . but revitalized and rekindled and remade if only temporarily.

Without further ado, she rose.

Fish's reaction was kind of a disappointment because he didn't scream as she'd hoped. He just looked at her with surprise, with awe, with a sort of *what-the-fuck?* look on his face as if it was a practical joke. And when he saw that it wasn't, a guilty fear stole over his features that she could now tell the world what sort of monster he indeed was. He sat there like that for a few drawn-out moments, his eyes wide, his lips trembling with questions. Then the color abandoned his face and his composure seemed to go with an almost audible snap.

"MICK! MICK! MICK! HELP ME FOR THE LOVE OF CHRIST—"

Mick was long gone, of course.

Fish screamed and babbled out incoherent sentences as cool sweat boiled from his pores and washed down his face. It was the sort of sweat that always beaded the faces of people in situations like this in old horror comics, Cassandra recalled. Paralyzed with fear, the scream winding down into a gobbling/whimpering sort of noise, Fish slid from the chair and fell to his knees. This was his next primitive reaction. Since he couldn't run and screaming brought no help, he kneeled at the feet of his risen goddess, sobbing and squealing, hoping for mercy.

Cassandra felt only pity for this wreck of humanity before her. She took him in her arms. His eyes bulged in their sockets, his mouth formed airless words. He was trembling like a babe.

"You'll . . . be my victim," she whispered in a dry and gritty voice, a hiss, really.

"Please," Fish muttered.

She pressed her forearm against his throat and placed her other arm behind his neck. She applied what she thought would be subtle pressure, but it was great and irresistible. Fish's eyes rolled like marbles, like white yolks, spit foamed from his mouth and his neck went with a sharp, wet snap. He slumped in her arms, the air thick with the reek of his voided bowels. She let him fall.

She found a laundry bag out in the garage. She figured the clothes in it must have belonged to the dead. She dumped them out, selecting a foul-smelling business suit for herself, and brought the sack back into the mortuary. She stuffed Fish into it. Though she was starving, he was far too warm to be palatable. A little ageing would tenderize him.

But there was no need to go hungry because she was standing in the middle of a well-stocked larder.

A prisoner to her own ravenous hunger, Cassandra located the corpse of a woman who had yet to be embalmed. She slid the drawer out, looking down at her and told herself she must be sickened by what she was contemplating. But there was no nausea and precious few pangs of moral guilt. Some things simply did not survive the resurrection process. What societal taboos remained in her brain were like distant memories, dream imagery glimpsed halfway through the day that made precious little sense.

"No," she said under her breath, sliding the drawer shut. "This is wrong and I know it's wrong."

But her hunger remained and it growled and tore at her belly. It had claws and teeth and unless it was satisfied, it would only get worse and somehow she knew this. It was not the appetite of the living, but something far darker, a gnawing agony like needles inserted into her stomach. A hunger born in dark graves and narrow boxes. The starvation of entombment.

She slid the drawer open again . . . but slowly, very slowly, teasingly and seductively like a man slowly pulling the sheet away from the voluptuous body of his lover. She revealed her food in this way and the hunger inside grew wild, almost violent in its demands.

Letting out a cry, Cassandra seized the woman's corpse and tore into it with her teeth, shattering the skull against the floor and tearing her scalp free. She snapped away plates of skull until the buttery-soft folds of the brain were exposed. At first, she tore at the gray matter with wolflike bites, then she began to nibble at them, scooping them out with her fingers and savoring each delicate bite. She gnawed the flesh from the left leg and right arm, stripped the throat, and dug deep into the sweetmeats of the cadaver's distended belly.

When she was finished, she was laying next to the corpse's grisly remains, her naked body painted with gore. She hummed a song as she licked her fingers. She knew that she could have easily laid there, picking away at it for hours until there was nothing but bones, but that wouldn't do. Someone might come at any moment and she needed to be practical.

She washed herself up a bit and donned the smelly business suit.

Once she had Fish's remains safely in the trunk of his car along with a variety of cosmetics to reconstruct her face, she returned to the mortuary. She had definitely made a mess of things. Questions would be asked. She needed to tidy things up. Out in the garage she found a can of gasoline and doused the mortuary. When she left it was blazing.

There was work to do. She would need a place to stay and clothes to wear. She wasted no time; she got busy.

Then she'd seek out Eddy. Who could say what sort of trouble he'd gotten himself into during her absence?

God only knew.

With that in mind, Cassandra drove off into the night. And while the police searched for an embalmer named Fish, the true malefactor went about her business at leisure.

A BOY AND HIS SPIDER

Eddy sensed something in the air of the city and it wasn't a good thing. There was danger near and he had no idea how he knew this but he did. He felt it in every fiber of his body. Something had either gone terribly wrong or was about to. The feeling was needling every cell in his body, tearing him from the inside like tiny claws. Any number of things could have happened. Spider could have been picked up (not that he'd talk or anyone would understand him if he did). They could have been identified. The police could've been on their way to his door right now. There was any number of things that could have gone south here. He couldn't say what, but he knew that it had.

Night had fallen when he left his flat. The Shadows came with him, much as he tried to leave them behind. Perhaps they were warning him in their usual inexplicable ways. Maybe they'd keep this danger away from him or at least warn him of it when it got close. It took him about thirty minutes to make it on foot to Spider's lair. When he got there, he waited across the street, studying the alleyway and Spider's door, seeing if anything was amiss.

All looked well. The Shadows congregated around him. He found himself growing hot with anticipation of what he and Spider might do this evening.

He went to the door and slipped in without knocking.

Spider was crouched on the kitchen floor, paging through a weighty book.

"Is everything well?" Eddy asked.

"Yes. I've sharpened our knives up. We're all set."

"Good. Whores, then?"

"Why not? It's so much easier that way."

Eddy sat down and lit a cigarette. He could hear the Shadows scratching to get in against the outside door where he'd left them. Now that he had completely accepted their near-constant presence, they obeyed him. In many ways, they were much like pets. A bit of attention now and again and they were most faithful.

"Did you hear something?" Spider said, flipping pages.

"No, nothing."

(let us in we don't like it out here)

Eddy ignored them. "Have you eaten your treats yet?"

"Oh, yes. They were quite good. I marinaded them in lemon and Worcestershire sauce. Yummy. I should've saved you some."

(he's insane this one he's completely mad he's not in command of his faculties like you if they catch him he'll talk. Be careful)

"I will," Eddy said.

"What?"

"Oh, nothing."

Spider set the book aside. "I think a few more and we'll be all set. They're ready to let us in. I feel it."

"What about Gulliver? Do you think he'll talk?"

"To the police? No, his kind are scared of cops. He'll keep quiet. And if he doesn't, we'll have to pay a call on him."

"I have to go," Eddy said. "The warehouse at eight?"

"Of course."

"See you then."

Eddy went back outside and the Shadows smothered him in a cloud.

(you should kill him eddy he's dangerous you don't need him now you can get into the territories all on your own)

"No. Not yet."

(you owe us your family owes us we're hungry . . . give him to us we want him now)

"When I'm ready and not before. You'll have to be patient just as I've had to be patient."

Eddy walked back to his place and got ready for the night. Before he went to the warehouse, he planned to pay a call on Gulliver. It might be a good idea to straighten things out before he got them into trouble. He would let the Shadows have him and then they'd quit their constant griping. All they ever thought about were their own bellies.

Moments after he'd left Spider, the police moved in.

BONES

They were driving back to the House of Mirrors.

Fenn had suggested a drink, but Lisa had other things in mind. She was obsessed with the idea of finding Eddy Zero, he was beginning to think. But he supposed that anyone that was any good at what they did were slightly obsessed. It only stood to reason. There'd been more than one instance in his many years as a cop that he'd displayed similar compulsive behavior. Sometimes that's what it took to get the job done.

"I know you don't want to do this," Lisa said. "But just humor me, okay? One of these times, we're going to get lucky."

"Or unlucky. It depends on how you look at it," he said.

"I don't understand."

And she didn't, poor driven thing. "What I mean is, I really don't relish the idea of running into Eddy and Spider in a deserted house at night. Don't get me wrong, I've dealt with plenty of bad boys in my time. I know how to take care of myself. But we're dealing with two psychopaths here. Your basic criminal—thief, purse snatcher, mugger—are cowardly by nature. They'll run at the first sign of trouble to save themselves . . . but a psychopath, they're unpredictable."

"Maybe we should get help," Lisa suggested.

Of course, that's what they should have done. But Fenn was just crazy enough to want to go it alone. He hated the idea of sharing Lisa with anyone else, even if that meant the safety of a couple of cops for back-up.

"There's something I should tell you, Mr. Fenn," she said and he could sense a certain menace in her tone. "I came back here by myself the other day after we were here. I don't know why, but I felt I had to."

"And?"

"And I saw something very strange."

"Tell me."

She did. It didn't take long. It was just something about a dead cat that had been stripped of its meat. He didn't see the connection.

"Don't ask me to explain any of it. All I know is that it scared the hell out of me and I don't know why," she said.

"Who could blame you? Alone in this damn place." Fenn was sincere. "My imagination was doing a little number on me when we were here the last time."

She nodded. "Except I don't think it was my imagination."

"We'll see."

He knew Lisa well enough by now to know that she wasn't the imaginative type. If she saw something that didn't properly fit into her scientist's view of the world, then chances were, it was something strange. But what it could possibly have to do with the matter at hand, he couldn't say. It was enough for him that they'd be alone together—he hoped, at any rate—and that was enough for now.

He loved her, he knew. There was no getting around that. It was unconditional love for he still knew very little about her. Gulliver seemed to think she had a hidden agenda and Fenn agreed. But it was reaching the point where he really didn't care anymore. When the time came, she'd show her secret face to him.

And would that be a good thing or bad?

Finally, they arrived at the house.

They took flashlights and went in. It was like a crypt in there at night: dusty, silent, a smell in the air of plaster rot and subterranean drainage. But, as before, there was something more, a palpable miasma of decay in the air that was not so much physical as spiritual.

"Christ," Fenn said. "What a place."

"You feel something?"

"Yes."

"Me too," she admitted, knowing for sure it wasn't just her imagination.

They didn't waste any time trying to figure out what it was. They went directly up to the attic. The dead animal had no real smell, just a yellow ghosting odor of old death. They played their lights over the bones and Fenn studied it minutely for some minutes.

"What do you make of it?" Lisa asked after a moment.

He shook his head. "The same thing you did. It looks vacuumed clean. Like its matter exploded and was drawn towards this wall. Right at that fucking mirror. Crazy."

"What could do something like that?"

"Maybe we'd better ask Eddy about that."

Fenn examined the mirror itself. He ran his fingers over it. The glass felt warm. "I'd love to know about the mirrors. Zero filled the house with them. Nobody ever really knew why."

"There was a reason, I'm sure, but the man who knew is long gone."

Fenn lit a cigarette, wiping the mirror's grime from his fingers. "That's something else that's bothering me," he said between drags. "Old Doc Blood-and-Bones disappeared twenty years ago. And since, no sign of him. What gives? Is he still hiding out? Is that even possible?"

"Possible, but not probable. You have to keep in mind the kind of guilt one suffers in association with crimes of this nature. Many murderers aren't caught simply because they kill themselves before the law gets to them. The guilt proves to be too much."

Fenn was massaging his temples. "So you think he committed suicide?"

"Probably. Otherwise, we would have heard of him. An obsessed individual like Zero could only hold back so long before killing again. And he would do it in his trademark style of dissection. He couldn't change his M.O. anymore than the color of his skin. If he was active, there'd be no hiding the fact."

Fenn nodded. "You're probably right. Let's get the hell out of here."

They went back out to Fenn's car in silence. His headache was back in full force. It had drained the color from his face, set his lips to trembling.

"With any luck," he said, chewing aspirins, "we should have Spider pretty soon. I have a couple of boys watching his place. They'll get him if he shows his mug."

"Then we're almost there," Lisa said, relieved. "We should wrap up this mess before long."

But she was wrong.

NIGHT TERRORS

He wasn't out long. But as soon as he got back to his apartment, Gulliver knew something was wrong. He'd gone out for a bottle of scotch and a newspaper, deciding it would be in his best interest to stay home tonight. The door, which he was certain he'd locked, was ajar.

Get a cop, he thought, then dismissed the idea. *A cop.* Yeah, that was the last thing he wanted after the shit they'd put him through. If he was being gang-raped by the KKK, they would have been the last ones he would have called.

He pushed through the door, moving carefully, trying to be silent, but seeming to make all manner of noise. He set his bag down and stood in the entry. Nothing seemed to be out of order. He hadn't been robbed, unless he'd surprised the thief and said thief was now hiding somewhere on the premises.

A certain anxiety ate at him. Although he was sure he had locked the door, there was always the possibility he was wrong. He'd forgotten before. He toyed with the idea of turning around and leaving, marching straight down to the phone on the corner and calling Fenn. With what was going on, Fenn would probably come right over. But if he did and there was no one around, that would only reaffirm Fenn's belief that Gulliver was nothing but a sissy, a girly pretending to be a man.

And Gulliver had already decided he'd have nothing more to do with that bigoted sonofabitch. He had no patience with rednecks.

Forget cops. You're on your own.

He moved slowly into the living room, found it empty, and went into his bedroom. It was also unoccupied. Feeling relieved, he went into the kitchen. And felt hands come up behind him and shove him against the refrigerator.

I'm fucked, he thought dismally and turned.

A man was standing before him dressed in a long black coat. He had a knife in his hand, a huge, nasty thing that looked like some wicked surgical instrument. Its razored edge reflected impure light into Gulliver's eyes.

It was Eddy; there was no doubt of this.

"Jesus," Gulliver gasped.

"Afraid not." Eddy described arcs in the air with his blade, the swooshing sounds were unnerving. "I think we should talk," he said calmly.

"Get away from me."

"You ran off on us the other night, Gully. You never let me explain. I was afraid you misunderstood the entire situation."

Gulliver nearly laughed. "There was nothing to misinterpret, Eddy. I saw what you were doing. I saw those women, those things you called up."

"Maybe you imagined it all."

"Maybe I did. I'm trying to forget."

Gulliver tried to play it cool. Only a calm head would get him out of this mess. Rushing Eddy would bring an ugly death that much faster. He had to reason this out, sympathize with Eddy, let him know he was his friend.

"You don't need that knife, Eddy," he said, fighting against the urge to gasp for breath. "I'm your friend. If you want to talk, let's sit and talk. I won't run."

"I'll keep it, I think. I'm growing rather fond of it. You'd be surprised what this can do to a person."

"What do you want?"

"A little information is all," Eddy said. "If I get it, you'll live. If I don't . . ."

"Anything." How could he have ever found this maniac attractive? He was a drooling, delusional psychotic. He needed to be locked up. He needed to spend his days in a cage with the rest of the animals.

"Have you talked? Maybe to the police?" Eddy inquired.

Gulliver's head was shaking and he wasn't sure whether he'd done it or fear had. He suddenly had to piss very badly. "No, of course not. I hate cops. Ask anyone. They've been nothing but a nuisance to me since . . . since I came to this goddamn town. I wouldn't turn you in, Eddy. Christ, no," he said, trying to sound believable. "Besides, if I did, you and Spider would kill me. Don't you think I know that?"

"You're lying. I can see it in your eyes."

"No, Eddy. Really, it's the truth."

Eddy came forward like an automaton, teeth barred, saliva running from his mouth. The blade was in motion again. It came at his throat in a swift, gleaming arc and stopped inches from its target. "The truth," Eddy said flatly. "Or I'll cut it out of you, Gully."

"I didn't want to tell," Gulliver whimpered. *"She* made me."

"She?"

"I heard she was asking around about you. In every club I went to, I heard about her and her questions about you."

"Who the fuck are you talking about?"

Gulliver's face was drained of color. If Eddy wanted blood, he'd have to cut somewhere else. "The psychiatrist. Dr. Lochmere. Lisa Lochmere."

Eddy took a step back, his eyes darting in confusion. His lips trembled, his head was shaking. Then a dark and rapacious grin twisted at his lips. "Lochmere? The bitch from the asylum?"

"She said you'd been her patient."

"So I was. You contacted her and she brought you to the police? Made you tell?"

"Yes. But they already suspected it was you. She'd been hunting you, waiting for you to show up here. She even had a P.I. on your trail for a time."

"Clever thing, isn't she?"

Gulliver was glad for the distraction. His breathing slowed, but only slightly. "You'd better get out of town, Eddy. You shouldn't even be here. They might be watching." It was a bad lie, but worth a shot.

"They're not."

"You can't be sure. This cop that's working with Lochmere—Fenn's his name, Jim Fenn—he's a smart one. A real prick in every way. You better watch your tail. He's coming for you."

"I'd better deal with you first."

Gulliver looked shocked. "Why?"

"Why? Why should I kill you or why did I kill the others?"

Anything to slow him down. "The others."

Eddy shrugged. He lowered the knife and slid a cigarette out of the pocket of his coat. He lit it with a stick match. "It's all very complicated, Gully. We didn't kill them just to *kill*. It wasn't that simple. Spider and I talked about that a lot. Debated whether we really enjoy it or are just doing our duty. I think it's both for me."

"Duty?"

"Yes. Have you ever heard of the Territories? No, I don't expect so. It's something only the very desperate speak of. Men like Spider, like my father. It's an escape of sorts. A place where there are no limits to a man's creativity, shall we say."

"Where is it?"

"The Territories? Not on any map. You can only get there by impressing certain individuals with your talents, your art. You saw the woman and her sister. She's the one. She took my father. She wants to take me. But first I have to impress her."

"You're insane," Gulliver said and instantly regretted it.

"Well, yes, just ask Dr. Lochmere. That silly cunt wants me in a cage so she can pick at my mind. I'll make a nice study for her. And when she's done, she'll drop my brain into a jar of alcohol."

The cigarette was dropped to the floor, crushed out under a boot. The knife came up again.

"She wants to help you, Eddy."

"My ass."

Gulliver just stared. His mind was drawing a blank, but he had to say something, had to stall for time.

"Spider and I are going out again tonight," Eddy said. He checked his watch. "But I think I have enough time to play with you."

Gulliver saw something out of the corner of his staring eyes. It was a cast iron frying pan he'd fried eggs in that morning. He was thankful for the first time in his life that he hated putting away the dishes. His hand was on it at the same time Eddy made his move. He rolled to the floor with the pan in his grip. Eddy's knife sank into the table.

"Why don't you just accept it?" Eddy asked. "It'll be so much easier that way. You may hit me with that, but I'll surely gut you."

"Then they'll find my body and you unconscious next to it."

Eddy shrugged and came forward slashing. Gulliver deflected the first few blows, but eventually Eddy out-guessed him and sank the blade just above his knee. The pain was instant and overwhelming, but it gave him the time to bring the pan around with full strength. It landed with a hollow thud and Eddy went down with all the grace of a bowling pin, the knife spinning from his fingers, blood trickling from his mouth. Gulliver made his move, limping from the apartment and moving uneasily down the stairs.

"This isn't done, you little queen," Eddy called after him. "Not by a long shot."

Gulliver made it out to the sidewalk and dialed 911 on his cell before he collapsed in a heap. By the time Eddy came, there was already a knot of gathering street people. He vanished into the shadows.

LETTERS FROM HELL (4)

Dear Eddy,

I remember it was storming the night it began.

I'd been free for about a week, I think, and it seemed to rain every day. I took my time getting to San Francisco. I knew you'd still be there. That's where they sent you, wasn't it? After they'd let you out. It wasn't easy finding that out. It would have been impossible had I still been at the asylum. But a year or so after you left, I was sent to the prison. I had limited freedom there. My family started getting money to me. I used it to bribe guards. It was a simple matter for them to track you down via the prison's computer system. It links up with the state's penal files where they keep track of people like you and I.

I went to your little apartment first. You weren't there, but your landlady told me where to find you.

If she'd known who I was, she would've locked the door.

I hadn't been in a bar in years. How many, I couldn't remember. They hadn't changed any. Why you'd chose such a redneck establishment was beyond me. I went in and saw you soon enough. You looked at me once, but you didn't recognize me. It had been some time, I suppose. All those other men were looking at me and thinking their thoughts. It gave me a charge. They probably wanted to get me out in their cars. They had no idea.

I sat down by you, remember? I ordered a glass of wine and you drank beer. You didn't even look at me. You'd sunk pretty deep.

"It's been a long time, Eddy," I said.

You looked shocked that I knew your name. "Has it?" you said.

"Oh, yes. You don't remember me?"

"No."

It hurt when you said that. But I'd expected it. "I used to watch you walking in the yard at Coalinga."

"You were there?"

"D-Ward," I said. It was enough. "They never let us mingle."

"So I heard. You got out finally?"

"I'm here, aren't I?"

You laughed at that. The sound of your laughter was beautiful to me. It drew strange looks from others, though. But that was just because they'd never been there, they couldn't know our secret joke.

"Where are you heading now?" you asked. "What are you gonna do?"

"That all depends on you."

Our eyes met and I think we both knew what was coming next.

"Who's she?" a voice said.

I turned and there was a girl standing there giving me dirty looks. She looked like some kind of heavy metal whore in her leather and studs. Her face had a weary, worn look to it. I thought she was kind of attractive in a depraved sort of way. She had nice legs and a very elegant neck. I wanted to sink my teeth into it.

"She's our guest, Christy," you said.

"I thought we were leaving," she said.

"We are. All three of us."

Christy didn't like the idea. But she didn't argue.

You had a van outside and we climbed in. There was a Thermos of whiskey and some coke in the back. We sat in a circle and drank. After Christy did a few lines, she didn't care who I was. The three of us got down then. She had her hands all over you. She didn't give a damn that I was there. She wanted it and in a bad way. You obliged. She had her clothes off by then and so did you. It wasn't long before mine were off, too. I held her head between my knees and squeezed her breasts while you rammed into her. She was really into it. I don't think she'd ever done anything like that before, but she was hot for it. While you fucked her, I pressed myself against her wet mouth and she ate me. It had been so long since anyone had done that. God, how I came.

That's when I took out the straight razor.

You just smiled.

Christy never saw it, never knew it was there until I drew it across her throat. Her tongue was still inside me. It was the best orgasm I ever had. She was bleeding and scratching me, but I held her there until I was done and her moaning was just a wet gurgling. You kept thrusting in her. I could barely stand it. That's when you took the razor and cut her eyes out. I think she was unconscious by the time you finished. Maybe dead. It didn't matter. By the time you got it out of your system, she looked like raw meat.

Then you took me.

I had wrapped my legs around you and you fucked me so hard I thought I was going to die. Maybe I did just a little toward the end. When we were done, my ass was red with Christy's blood.

"She's dead," you said dully when you pulled out. "What do we do now?"

I remember smiling, her blood hot all over me.

The van was Christy's and we left it in the lot. And her in it. We cleaned up ourselves the best we could with her clothes and then we got in my car and went to your place. A hot shower felt good.

And then we were cruising again.

I was driving and you didn't ask where we were going. I think you knew.

There was nowhere else to go.

"What's your name?" you finally asked.

"Cherry," I told you. "Call me Cherry."

"Cherry," you said, rolling it off your tongue. It tasted sweet, didn't it? "I like that."

We had to get another car. That much was apparent. I didn't like the idea of driving the one I had. It made me nervous. We drove for a long time. I kept expecting to hear sirens. But it would be hours if not days before someone decided to look in that van. There was nothing to worry about. I got us across the bridge to Marin and we kept driving.

I don't remember the name of the first town. It wasn't much of a place, was it? Just a little town with a motel and a couple of gas stations, the first place we came to after leaving the off ramp. The rain had stopped and the wind was blowing. I remember the moon coming out, huge, swollen, watching over us. We pulled into the parking lot of that little bar and waited. You put the hood of the car up and stood in the shadows.

It wasn't long before that man came by.

"Problems?" he asked, more than happy to help out a woman in distress.

"Yeah. My car won't start," I said. "I don't know what to do."

"Well, you just let me have a look," he said and dropped me a wink. Oh, men are so predictable. He'd get my car going again, but for a price. He had no idea how expensive it would be.

He bent over and looked at the engine. I was right behind him, pressing up against him. He liked that.

Until I jerked his head back and cut his throat.

Yours,

Cherry

NIGHT CALL

Lisa was taking a bath when the phone rang.

Its shrill cry jarred her nerves. She didn't want answer it, but she knew she had to with everything going on. She wanted nothing better than to lay back in the hot water and work the knots from her muscles and the aches from her head, but she had no choice.

She wrapped herself in a towel and ran into the bedroom, grabbing the portable.

"Hello?"

"Good evening, Doctor."

She felt a chill sweep through her. Her blood was ice. "Who is this?"

"You don't recognize my voice?"

"No and I don't have time for games."

"Cherry Hill," the voice giggled. "You might remember me from Coalinga, from Chowchilla. Don't pretend you don't remember me."

"I remember you." And Lisa did. The bells were ringing, each one of them a warning bell that felt like it was going to split her head open.

"I'm glad you remember," Cherry said. "If it hadn't have been for you, I might still be at that place. I'll never forget you for getting me out there and I'll never forget what you did to me there."

Lisa's throat was dry with panic. "What do you want?"

"I want you to stop looking for Eddy Zero."

"Why?"

"Because it's what I want. You always liked to please me, remember?"

"Cherry, listen to me. Why don't I meet you and—"

"And you'll see I get the help I need?"

Lisa felt weak inside. "It's for your own good, Cherry."

"Stop looking for him," the voice said. "If you find him, you're going to find me . . . and you don't really want that, do you?"

The line went dead.

Lisa climbed back in the tub, her lips forming words that she was unaware of. Even the hot water couldn't stop her from shaking. There are always worse-case scenarios in life and she had just encountered one of them.

Cherry Hill.

Cherry Hill.

My past is coming back to haunt me, she thought and it was the truth. Knowing it, it was all she could do not to slit her own wrists.

MEMOIRS OF THE TEMPLAR SOCIETY (4)

Stadtler, Grimes, and Zero were busy men. They pretended to be certain people during the day but at night they were something else entirely. In the passage of weeks since they'd drugged the girl and began their explorations of death, they had the blood of five women on their hands. The guilt was taking its toll on Grimes and Stadtler. Both were mere shadows of the men they'd been before striking this peculiar partnership with Zero. They rarely ate now. Even pot-bellied Grimes was beginning to look thin and Stadtler was a skeleton. They jumped at any sudden noise and saw the police everywhere. The study of death was destroying them both physically and psychologically.

Only Zero seemed to be enjoying himself by that point.

He hadn't changed. Every fresh killing left him in a sort of euphoria that frightened the other men. He seemed to draw his strength from killing, taking life from death. He had become sort of a parasite who ran down like a clock in-between murders. The other two never saw him between meetings, they couldn't know the listless, drained creature he became until he got his fix.

They met on their usual night and plotted.

"Back to work," Zero said, sipping brandy.

Grimes said nothing.

"How many do you plan on killing?" Stadtler asked.

"You mean, of course, how many do *we* plan on killing?"

"Yeah, whatever." Stadtler didn't argue. Zero knew as well as he did that they were just dupes, that it was Zero who called the shots. He selected the victims, he oversaw their murders, and he did the actual cutting on their corpses. They were merely followers, little more than indentured servants who were in so deep by that point that they didn't know how to get out and were terrified of what Zero would do to them if they tried.

Zero smiled. "We'll dispose of as many as need be. Our study is just beginning. The science is the thing. The murders are a means to an end, nothing more. When we've learned all we can, we'll be done with the dirty work."

"We can't hope to go on like this," Grimes said.

"And why not? What will stop us?"

"The police for chrissake, Zero. Do you think they're just ignoring the bodies they find?" Stadtler said, his voice nearly neurotic in tone. "There's a hundred men if there's one out there right now hunting us down."

"They'll never find us. Not if we use our brains."

"I don't know if I can do it again," Grimes admitted.

Zero looked amused. "You two aren't coming apart on me, are you? We struck a bargain."

Neither spoke a word.

"What you need is diversion," Zero advised in a genial tone. "Our subject upstairs is softening up nicely. She's beginning to call out for her mother. It's delicious."

Grimes seemed to come to life. "Why don't we toy with her a bit?"

"Not just yet. She's not ready yet."

"Soon?"

"Very. But tonight . . ."

"The streets?"

Zero grinned. "Yes, our study continues."

SPIDER'S WEB

Fenn dropped Lisa off at her hotel earlier and wasn't invited up as he'd hoped. He supposed his love of her was wishful thinking at best. In a way, he thought he should just lay it on the line and tell her how he felt. But at the same time, he feared it would damage their working relationship and what friendship they'd managed to accrue. It was all so terribly strange. He hadn't felt so nervous about pressing his attentions on a woman since he was fifteen. And, if nothing else came of this, it was good to feel that way again.

He drove around for some time, thinking of these things.

When he got back to Southern Station, there was a good deal of activity as there always was that time of night. Hookers, pushers, pick pockets, and all manner of street garbage were being dragged in and processed. Some were quiet, others screamed and fought. Such was the atmosphere of a city precinct at night. Fenn worked days now, but he still did night duty. There seemed to be no set hours for a homicide detective.

"We've got him," a voice behind him said.

It was Gaines. "We got your boy, Jim. He's in holding."

Fenn smiled. "Spider?"

"Yeah. He's one weird bastard, too."

"Bring him on up then."

Gaines left and Fenn went to his desk, getting a pad of paper and a folder of crime photos. He went into an unoccupied interrogation room and waited. He felt nervous and he wasn't sure why.

It took three uniforms and Gaines to bring Spider in. He was in cuffs and leg irons. Fenn had never seen anything like him. He was dressed in a knee-length black leather coat, his hair knotted in braids and set with gleaming beads. His face was painted white, black grease around his eyes and on his lips.

"Motherfuckers! Get your fucking hands off me!" He was squirming in their grips like a snake. Fenn half expected him to slip right out of the cuffs.

"Take it easy," Gaines said. "Take it easy!"

"You don't know what you're doing! You don't know what you're involved in!"

"Sit him down," Fenn said. God, he got so sick of these fucking deviants. He longed for the old days when he could have beaten them into submission.

They did, but not without great effort. Spider apparently had the strength of the insane. If it wasn't for the bonds that held his arms and legs together, he would've surely overpowered all three men with ease. Fenn had never seen such raw hatred in a man's eyes.

"He ain't going anywhere," one of the uniforms said proudly. They were on either side of him, holding him down. Gaines was behind him, twisting his cuffed wrists up. If Spider fought too much, his arms would break.

His lips curled in anger, drool ran down his chin. His eyes were nearly as black as the make-up highlighting them.

The door opened and Moore came in, his black face sweaty. He was carrying a leather case that had been tagged as evidence. He set it down before Fenn.

"He was carrying this. Take a look."

Fenn did so. It was loaded with knives of every conceivable sort. "Jesus. You gotta love a perp that comes with his own evidence."

So many knives. So goddamn many knives. Fenn felt a dull throb at his temples. He could just imagine all the cutting and pain. It made him want to use his fists. He made himself relax. "Why, Spider?" he asked. "Why did you do it?"

It was a simple question, a pretty shop-worn one for cops, but he knew that the answer—if he got one—was going to be interesting.

"Answer the man," Moore prompted.

Spider grinned and chortled deep in his throat. There was a certain sarcasm in his laugh as if he were asked something far too obvious to answer.

"Because I'm a lunatic," he said.

"And that's the only reason?"

Spider laughed loudly this time. "It's too late to stop any of it now."

"Any of what?"

Spider shook his head. "You're too bloody stupid to even understand."

"Better cooperate," Gaines told him, twisting his arm a bit, "you're in deep enough shit."

"Humor me, then," Fenn said.

"You couldn't grasp what I'd say," Spider told him. And it was obvious to all that he wasn't being merely derisive; he actually believed what he said.

"C'mon, Spider, for chrissake," Moore said.

"What's your real name?" Fenn asked. "The one you were born with."

"I'm crazy, I tell you," Spider maintained. "I can't even remember what I am, let alone *who* I am. This body is a shell, this life is synthetic. Soon I'll abandon both to make the trip."

"You ain't taking a trip anywhere," Gaines said. "They like to keep the animals in their cages at San Quentin and that's where you're fucking going."

"You don't know anything."

Moore shook his head. "Crazy like a fox."

"Your prints are already being processed," Fenn said, trying to remain calm. He'd never dealt with a true serial murderer before, but he supposed it was important not to upset them.

"Then when you find out who I am, tell me."

"Do you know where Eddy Zero is?"

"Eddy Zero?"

"You know who I'm talking about. Where the hell is he?"

For the first time, Spider looked less than confident. He seemed somewhat puzzled, frightened even, though it was hard to tell under all the make-up.

"If you help us get Eddy, maybe we can help you."

Spider spat a stream of mucus at him. "You'll never find him. Never."

Gaines gave his arms a nasty pull. "Be civil, freak."

"Where is he?"

"I don't even know. I'm a lunatic, can't you see that? How do you expect me to recall all these details when I don't even know the difference between right and wrong?"

"Make it easy on yourself, Spider," Moore said.

Fenn lit a cigarette. He wondered if he should call Lisa in and let her have a go at this nut. He had no idea even how to proceed with something like this.

"Eddy's much smarter than you, boss," said Spider. "You can lock me up all you want, but he'll carry on with our work until the time comes."

"The time of what?"

"Oh, you silly bastard, wouldn't you like to know?"

"Yes, I would."

"The time of departure," Spider laughed. "The time we leave the here and now for the Territories. When they come for us." Spider looked from Moore to Fenn. "See, I told you you couldn't understand."

"Help me," Fenn urged him.

"If I could I would, boss," Spider admitted. "The road to true knowledge is a long and grim journey. It's not for everyone."

Fenn tried a different angle. "Who are they? The ones that come for you?"

"The Sisters, of course."

"And who the hell are the sisters?" Moore asked. "Do they have names?"

"You cannot know their names."

"This is bullshit," Moore snapped.

But Fenn was beginning to wonder. Yes, it was bullshit to them, but to Spider and Eddy, it meant something. But what? What sort of insane relevance did it have? "You seem to be a bright boy, Spider. I want to help you. So, why don't you help me? Tell me about these sisters and Eddy. Tell me what it all means. We're going to find out from Eddy when we pick him up, anyway. And I'll just bet he'll do anything he can to save his own ass and sink yours."

Spider laughed. "You don't know Eddy. You don't know who he is."

"He's the son of a psycho. We know that."

"Like I said, you know nothing."

"Put him back for now," Fenn said.

They hauled him away and he went quietly this time, giggling at some joke no one could pretend to ever know. Fenn didn't like this at all. He'd thought it would be much easier, somehow. Maybe it was time to bring Lisa in. If there was logic here, maybe she'd see it.

After all, nutjobs were her specialty.

TERRITORIAL

Fenn let Spider spend the night at the hands of the other detectives. They would pull him from his cell every two or three hours and give him a good going over. It was standard procedure, sleep deprivation. Tried and true. He was being held on charges of multiple homicide and murder conspiracy. He was looking at life if he was lucky and lethal injection if he wasn't. Still . . . Spider looked upon it all as some kind of cheap amusement. He refused a lawyer because he said he did not recognize the law of the State of California.

If he was shooting for an insanity defense, he was making a good job of it.

Fenn met Lisa for breakfast the next morning, before he went to the precinct.

"I talked with Gaines an hour ago," Fenn told her. "They got nothing from Spider last night. Just the same shit he was telling me."

"The Territories," Lisa said.

"Ever come across that one before?"

Lisa shook her head. "Can't say that I have. But I'd like to talk with him."

"I'd appreciate it," Fenn said, dipping into his eggs. "We've gone easy on him so far, but that can't last. He's a strange one. Doesn't want a lawyer. Admitted to Gaines that he killed them, but won't implicate Eddy. Not directly."

"I'll interview him, see what I can get."

"Good. We have a psychiatrist, but he's a shit and he doesn't have the sort of experience you've had."

"This isn't going to be cut and dried," Lisa said. "I can feel it. Compulsive killers like Spider create very elaborate fantasy systems to justify their crimes. They create immense psychological barriers to hide behind. This is going to be a very complex situation, if these Territories are any indication."

"I suppose. I'd love to know what he means by these 'sisters'."

"It probably means nothing. In my experience, deluded individuals always have some guardian protector they cling to. That's all this is, I'm sure . . . but getting him to tell us about them will be problematical."

"Yeah, but you didn't see his eyes. He really believes in them."

"I'll just bet he does."

*　　*　　*

"Tell me about the Territories," Lisa said.

They were in an interrogation room. Spider was shackled to a chair. He smiled up at her and then closed his eyes.

"And why do you want to know that? Can't you see I'm a monster, a fiend?" He fought at his bonds, hissing, then collapsed, giggling. "I'm so terribly deluded, Doctor. I want only to kill people."

"I only want to help you. There's no need for sarcasm."

They were alone in the room, but Fenn and a few other detectives were watching through the glass, ready to burst in at a moment's notice. But it wouldn't be necessary, being that Spider's hands and feet were immobilized.

"Did I tell you I knew Eddy?" she said.

"No, but I'm sure you will."

"I'm not lying. I was his physician at Coalinga. He was under my care. We got to know each very well."

"He never mentioned you."

And was that good or bad? Lisa wasn't sure.

"I treated him for several years. We talked of his father a great deal. Eddy idolized him."

Spider was interested now. "The Doctor." He said it with awe in his voice. "Gone off to the Territories. We'll see him soon, I think."

"Where are the Territories?" she asked.

"I'm so bored with that one. But, very well, you seem educated." Spider yawned and closed his eyes again. "It's a place beyond here and now. So close you can almost touch it, but so far away you could never reach it in a thousand lifetimes. Not unless you know how, not unless you impress the Sisters. Eddy's father got in and many others through the centuries. Call it an alternate universe. That will tax your brain less."

Lisa considered it. "Interesting. I've always wondered what happened to William Zero, as, I imagine, many others have."

"Now who's being sarcastic."

She smiled thinly. Sarcasm had not been her intention. She was trying to get Spider to draw her into his fantasy world. Once she had a firm footing on his delusions, she could begin to pick them apart.

"How did he do it?" she asked. "How do you get into the Territories?"

"It's not easy. It takes work and devotion to your craft."

"But how?"

"By the very nature of what he did."

"By killing people?" she chanced.

"No, by the *way* he killed them. There's a ritual involved. That's the only way you can get through. Why do you think he was never caught? He slipped away where no one could follow."

"And you and Eddy are trying to do the same?"

"We're not trying, we've done it. We're close now. A few more and they'll take us away. They told us so. That's why it doesn't matter if you lock me up or not, one day—and soon—they'll find this cell empty."

"I see."

"No, you don't. Not yet. But if you keep poking around, you'll find out. And by then it'll be too late."

Lisa just nodded. She was thinking about Eddy and his connection to Cherry Hill.

Stop looking for him. If you find him, you're going to find me . . . and you don't really want that, do you?

She grimaced. As if she didn't have enough problems already. Was Cherry Hill mixed up in this too? And if so, how? Was her infatuation with Eddy still alive? Was she working with him? God, the idea of that was truly chilling. If it was true, then Lisa's past truly was coming back to haunt her. Eddy, Cherry . . . well, why not Dr. Blood-and-Bones too?

You unleashed a monster in Cherry, keep that in mind.

No, the monster was already there, Lisa thought.

You threw open its cage and set it free.

Lisa had had enough. She had a few answers now, but none that made any sense. Fenn was right: Spider's belief in all of this was somewhat un-nerving. But it meant nothing, of course. If they could just get Eddy in here and see what he had to say. It could all prove most interesting if he, too, was compelled by similar delusions. A shared psychopathy was a rare thing.

"We have to go," Fenn said when she came out.

"Where?"

"The hospital. Eddy attacked Gulliver last night."

DOWN AND OUT

When they finally got to Gulliver's room, they found him staring off into space. There was a Bible resting on his lap. His right leg was exposed, swathed in bandages. He looked very old, very wasted. He saw them and simulated a smile.

"How are you feeling?" Fenn said, clasping his hand and shaking it.

The exchange of warmth between the two of them startled Lisa. Had she missed something? Some male bonding? It seemed out of character for both of them.

"Okay. Knee hurts, but not as bad as last night. Really wonderful stuff those nurses are giving me," he said. "You could cut your leg off and never so much as shrug."

"We're sorry to hear what happened," Lisa said.

"Not your fault."

Fenn couldn't help himself. "What happened?"

Gulliver sighed and shook his head. "I went out for a bottle of booze. Decided I'd best stay behind locked doors for the meanwhile. I wasn't gone more than fifteen minutes. When I got back, the door was ajar." He looked pale. "I thought it was funny, but like an ass, I went in. Eddy was there."

"My God," Lisa said in a whisper.

"What then?"

"I'm afraid I panicked. I couldn't help myself."

They both waited for him to go on.

"He had a knife. He had it against my throat and . . . I told him things. I was scared, I guess." He breathed deeply, steadying himself. "He knew I'd told somebody about seeing him and Spider. I tried to lie to him that I hadn't, but he knew. Somehow, he knew."

"You didn't have a choice. You had to save yourself," Fenn said.

But, much as Lisa respected his warmth and comforting words, she had to know. "Did you tell him about me?" Her voice was oddly airless.

"Yes. I told him everything. I opened my mouth and I couldn't stop. He knows about you. He knows you're after him."

"It doesn't matter," Fenn told him.

But Lisa thought it did. If Eddy got to Gulliver, he could just as easily get to her anytime he wished. But she was being selfish and cruel. This was no time to be worrying about herself. Besides, she'd come to find him and the chances of that were very good now.

"He would've figured it out eventually. He's clever," she said.

"What did he say?"

"He told me he and Spider had killed those women for a reason."

This is what Fenn had been fishing for. "And why was that?"

Gulliver looked uncomfortable. "So they could go to some place called the Territories. It's where his father went."

"Shit," Fenn snorted. "It's the same thing Spider's been saying."

"You have him?"

Fenn nodded. "He won't be hurting anyone for a long time. We'll get Eddy, too. Sooner or later."

"Did he say anything else?" Lisa inquired. "Anything about 'the sisters'?"

"The Sisters." Gulliver said it and from the pinched, compressed look on his face, he wished he hadn't. He pressed himself down into the bed as if hoping he'd lose himself in it.

"You know something about them?"

"I suppose," he said dryly, "that I should tell you that part . . ."

He did. The telling didn't take long. He closed his eyes as his lips did the work. He didn't want to see the looks on their faces.

"I ran then," he concluded. "That's the only part I left out the other day. It was too crazy to mention. I'm not even sure if it happened."

Lisa and Fenn looked at each other.

"And they just walked up?" Fenn asked. "Out of nowhere?"

Gulliver shrugged. "I guess. They weren't there one moment, the next they were. One was naked and fat, hideous . . . the other, it was a thing."

"You really believe you saw them?" Fenn said. "The truth now."

Gulliver looked in his eyes, unblinking. "Yes."

"It's not possible."

"Maybe not. But I saw it. Now you know why I left it out."

Fenn wasn't sure what he felt at that moment. Oh, he knew the man was telling the truth or what he believed to be the truth. But there couldn't have been anyone else there, unless it wasn't just Spider and Eddy involved in this. The entire scenario was getting crazier by the moment.

"I'm not saying I believe or disbelieve you, Gulliver. But I need time to think on something like this."

"I think we all do," Lisa said. "We'll stop back later."

"There'll be a cop at your door from now on," Fenn informed him. "Just to be on the safe side. Is there anything we can get you?"

"No, I'll be all right now."

They left and went out to Fenn's car in silence.

"He's telling the truth," Lisa finally said.

"I know and that's what bothers me."

And it did, just as it bothered her. This mystery of sorts was changing and mutating every time they thought they had it nailed down.

"Spider spoke of the Sisters like they were gods of some sort, not real people," Fenn recalled. "I had the impression he was referring to supernatural beings."

"Do you believe in ghosts, Mr. Fenn?"

"Hell of a question from a head doctor."

"Do you?"

"No, of course not. And neither do you."

"Who are they then? These Sisters?"

"I don't know," Fenn said. "But if they're not real flesh and blood, I'm handing in my fucking badge."

THE ENIGMA OF SPIDER

Like Fenn, Lisa wasn't sure what she made of this newest development. She spent a great deal of time thinking it over. Such a dilemma demanded to be approached from all possible sides.

If what Gulliver had told them was true, then something mad was going on here. It seemed to be his impression that these women weren't human, but then he was under a great deal of stress at the time. They may have been quite human, but if they were, then that created even more questions. Was it even remotely possible that Spider and Eddy had two female accomplices? It seemed unlikely. Demented as Spider was, there was a certain cold rationality to what he'd said.

Lisa believed that *he* believed the Sisters, as he called them, were not human but something else entirely.

Accomplices?

How about Cherry Hill?

No, no, not her.

And why not?

Yes, why not? Cherry was involved, Lisa was sure of that now, she just didn't know in what way. Could she be an accomplice? Was that possible?

It seemed unlikely. She remembered Cherry quite well and she hardly fit the description of the one—*fat, hideous*—or the other—*a thing*. No, Cherry had been a very attractive woman. She could hardly imagine a set of circumstances where Cherry would not be considered beautiful. If Gulliver had seen her, he would have been smitten. All men were . . . at least until her true nature was revealed.

And you sure helped that along, now didn't you?

She wasn't going to think about that. Spider had talked to her of many things. If he and Eddy indeed were working with another woman, he would have told her. He was nothing if not honest about it all. But he was deluded. There was no arguing that point. He was seriously, dangerously deluded. He believed Eddy's father had slipped off to some alternate world called the Territories. He believed the only way he and Eddy could follow was by committing a series of brutal, yet creative murders that would gain the attention of these Sisters, who in turn would show them the way. It was a very complex mania in its own way and Lisa wondered if it was of Eddy's creation or Spider's or a collaboration of the two. She knew little of Spider save what he chose to tell her and they had as yet to find out who he really was. But she knew Eddy. And he'd never spoke of these things to her in their sessions. Only of wanting to recreate his father's crimes. She wanted dearly to know where these mutual obsessions had come from. The very idea of two apparent psychopaths sharing a common psychosis was fantastic. Her book was looking better with each passing day.

Or worse.

It all depended on your point of view.

And Lisa wasn't even certain what hers was any longer. Professionally, she was fascinated like never before; personally, as a human being, she was terrified. First Dr. Blood-and-Bones himself (Mr. Billy, heh, heh). Bad enough. Then a son who worshipped him, a son with the proper psychological make-up to repeat his atrocities. Even worse. And finally, said son hooking up by sheer coincidence with another lunatic who shared his tastes and outlooks. It was scary. Add a pathological murderer like Cherry Hill in the mix and it became an absolute nightmare.

Christ, where would it end?

And what of Gulliver? Could he possibly have seen what he claimed to? Was it even remotely possible that there was more going on here than mere human dementia? A larger picture that paled everything that was set against it? The Territories? The Sisters? There could be no truth in it.

Do you believe in ghosts?

She'd said that to Fenn and had been completely serious.

Can you believe in something much worse?

A place where people like Eddy and Spider and Zero himself were honored guests?

Bullshit. Sheer dementia.

She had no idea what she believed anymore. She only knew that Spider had pretty much said the Sisters were discarnate entities of a sort and that Gulliver claimed to have seen them. And she knew she believed them both and in the process was beginning to disbelieve in herself and the constants of physical reality she'd always held so dear.

It was maddening.

Time to see Spider again.

*   *   *

It was an easy thing to arrange. Fenn was as confused as she was about all this and he was more than happy to let her have another go at his resident psychopath in hopes of unraveling this insanity.

Back into the interrogation room.

"Well? What now?" Spider inquired.

"I have more questions. I don't even know where to start."

Spider rolled his eyes. "Cheap drama," he muttered under his breath. He was dressed in a jail uniform now and his face was cleansed of make-up. His beads and jewelry were gone. He was just a wiry youth with a pale face, too much hair, and more tattoos than a sailor. His eyes were intense and shiny like those of a mad dog just before it bit.

"When Gulliver saw you and Eddy the other night," she began, "he said he saw someone else too."

"The Sisters?"

"Yes."

"What of it?" He seemed unconcerned.

She was taken aback by it all. Spider was freely acknowledging their existence, that they had indeed been in attendance that evening. It wasn't what she wanted to hear at all.

"I want to know about them."

"And I want a cigarette."

"This is a non-smoking facility," she reminded him.

"Then pedal your questions somewhere else. Either I get an ashtray and cigarettes or I'm done talking."

She again explained the no smoking policy, but Spider was buttoned-up tight. He would not even admit she existed. She tried again and again, but he just stared off into space.

She went to Fenn and he okayed it. His boss was going to be pissed, but if it meant getting closer to some answers, Fenn wanted him to smoke his lungs out. Whatever it took.

Once Spider had a few drags in him, he relaxed. Maybe he relaxed too much. "You worked with Eddy at Coalinga. Did he fuck you?"

Lisa reddened, but shook her head. "It wasn't that sort of relationship."

"I was just wondering. He has a way about him. He can make women do just about anything. They can't refuse him. I've watched him work. He flirts and teases, gets them hot and bothered and—"

"Spider, please, let's stay on topic."

"—then once he's got them worked up, he turns away from them. They practically crawl after him. I've seen them beg for him to use them."

Lisa squirmed in her chair, thinking of the night Eddy had nearly raped her. But it hadn't been rape. She didn't think she'd ever wanted anybody as much as she wanted him that night. She could practically still feel the engorged head of his penis begin to push into her . . . then he had withdrawn. Spider was right: he did have a gift. She knew it was true. She'd practically begged him to screw her that night. It took great strength to get free of the trap he'd laid.

"I'm waiting," Spider said.

God, she felt flushed hot from head to foot. She had to concentrate. She had to get goddamn Eddy Zero out of her mind. She was a professional and she had to act like one.

"The Sisters," she said. "Tell me about them."

"Ah, yes." He shrugged. "Their history is a bit hard to trace. It took me years of research to even find out they existed."

"Then you're saying they're not human?"

"Not in the usual sense. I thought I made that abundantly clear?"

Lisa was at a loss for words. Had she not been a psychiatrist, she supposed she would have left now. It was all madness. "Tell me about them."

"The Madonnas," he said. "They're called that sometimes, too. I think the Marquis de Sade preferred that title. I'm not sure of its meaning. Regardless, they're not sisters as such. Only insofar as common experience goes. One of them has a rather hacked-up appearance, you know. As if she was pulled apart and sewn back up in a hurry. I've read certain hints that she's Crippen's dead wife."

"Crippen?"

"Dr. Crippen. Don't you know your criminology at all?" He seemed impatient with it all.

"Yes, I know who Dr. Crippen was."

"I've read that might be her. Other sources disagree. I don't think it's important, do you?"

"Probably not."

"It's like Gulliver told you: one's heavy and big-titted like a wench from an old painting, you know? The other isn't even human exactly, just a hacked-up, shredded thing."

She found that interesting because she'd never told him exactly what Gulliver said, yet he was certain Gulliver had given her the specifics.

"And they're joined?" she asked.

"Yeah. There's like a birth cord connecting them . . . so maybe they *are* real sisters. Maybe they came from the same womb."

"So if you kill in a certain way . . .?"

"Yeah, they come. It's like bait to them. The Sisters open the gates to the Territories for certain aspiring, creative individuals. They're lovers of art, you see. And the only art form they recognize is that of atrocity. Hence, human flesh is the medium and the canvas. The knife being the instrument with which it is shaped, re-invented to one's own personal view of masterpiece. It's all quite simple, isn't it? Impress them with your talents, they let you in."

She felt empty inside. His madness was so lucid, so real, it was infectious. "And the Territories?"

"A sphere of existence, nothing more. Different from this. A place of experience and enlightenment that the human mind can scarcely conceive of." He paused, lost in thought. "I don't know much about science, except that which I find useful. I only know it's there. I've heard it described as a world between worlds, a neutral ground between this dimension and another. An extradimensional back alley of sorts, a cubbyhole of alternate reality."

"And the Sisters travel from there to here?"

"Why not?" Spider asked of her. He butted his cigarette and lit another. "But there's something else you wanted to ask me, isn't there? Something more pertinent to the matters at hand."

He was quite perceptive, she noted. "Gulliver said he saw them. If he hadn't told us that, I would say this is all a delusion of your own creation."

Spider giggled. "You can trust that old queen, can't you? They exist."

"The police want to know if these Sisters aren't flesh and blood. If perhaps you and Eddy have two female accomplices."

"That's crazy," Spider told her. "There's only the two of us."

"Then you insist the Sisters are of supernatural origin?"

"I don't know shit about the supernatural, Dr. Lochmere. They exist. They have flesh, but it's not like our flesh. They're not ghosts exactly and they're not residents of this boring world."

"I see."

He laughed in his throat. "No, you don't. You think I'm crazy and I probably am. But I'm *not* wrong," he assured her. "I have books at my flat. You can read of the Sisters, the Territories, other things your science doesn't recognize in them. Whether you believe them or not, that's up to you."

"Then others have known?"

"Countless."

For the first time in her career, she was actually frightened by what she was hearing. The delusions of others never held any weight for her before. But this was different. Spider believed this. As did Eddy, she was sure. It had been written in books by others. And Gulliver had seen it with his own eyes.

"Have they found another body yet?" Spider asked. "I'm sure Eddy's carrying out our plan without me. He's quite dedicated, you know."

"I haven't heard."

"No matter. Others will turn up and soon. Eddy's as industrious and compulsive as his father. I imagine he's keeping busy."

"I'm sure," Lisa said. "One more question, if I may."

"Of course."

"Do you know a woman who calls herself Cherry Hill?"

"No. Do you?"

"Is she working with you and Eddy?"

"I said I don't know any Cherry Hill. Who the hell is she?"

"It's not important."

"Goodbye then, Herr Doctor," Spider said. "We won't see each other again, I'm guessing." His grin deepened. "What's the old nursery rhyme? *Run to bed children, before it gets dark?* Yeah. Take my advice, Doc. Run away. Get the fuck out of here. This isn't for you, but if you keep nosing into things, you'll be taking a trip to the other side. You won't like it there."

She broke off the session and went to the door.

Behind her, Spider said, *"Before it gets dark."*

She stumbled out of there, visibly shaken, creeped out in ways that surprised even her. There was something happening here. Something unnatural and eerie and she was scared. The next thing she knew, she was falling and Fenn's arms caught her.

APPETITE

Later that night.

Fenn and Lisa were in her hotel suite, staring at plates of room service. The filet mignon was thick and simmering in pink juices, the baked potatoes steaming with butter and sour cream, the salads crisp, the bread fresh from the oven . . . yet, they did little but pick at their food. Fenn was distant, beyond words. Lisa was trembling, both inside and out.

"Spider's dead?" she said for the fourth or fifth time. "I just can't believe it. What he said to me was true then, wasn't it?"

Fenn nodded. "He must've been planning it."

"It was more that. That nursery rhyme he kept repeating. It had some relevance, I'm sure of it. My mother used to say that before we went up to our rooms for the night, 'Run to bed children, before it gets dark.' I know what she meant, but what did Spider mean?"

"You're probably reading too much into it," Fenn explained to her.

"Maybe."

There was no point in arguing, Lisa decided, because he was essentially right. Any sane person would have come to the same conclusion. But she was certain Spider's words were important somehow. They had to be. In some mad way she could never hope to divine, it was the summation of everything he'd told her. The final parting shot.

"A guy like Spider has a big ego, Doc. He can't just die gracefully, he has to make a dramatic exit complete with prophetic last words," Fenn said. "You know how guys like him are."

"Tell me what happened."

"I wish I could. You were the last one to talk with him. He was alone for less than an hour. Gaines went down to give him a going over and he was dead. Simple as that."

"There's nothing simple about it," she reminded him.

He nodded. "The question remains: How did he do it? How the fuck does a guy with one free hand cut his own throat and then hide the razor?"

"The razor's got to be somewhere."

"If it is, we have yet to find it."

"He seemed so certain the Sisters were coming for him," she said, almost as if she were surprised they hadn't.

"Well, they better pick his ass up at the morgue then."

"You think that's all bunk?"

"Don't you?" Fenn said. "You can't actually believe in any of that shit. You're a psychiatrist for chrissake, you've heard it all before. Just another nut with another nutty tale."

She nodded, as if in agreement. But she didn't agree. She was starting to wonder about the whole thing herself. Everything about this entire situation was just getting too damn weird. Eddy and Spider linking up. Gulliver's sighting of the Sisters. What she'd seen in the house. Spider's convenient suicide with a razor that couldn't be found. And Cherry Hill's sudden appearance. It was all circumstantial and terribly confusing . . . yet why did she feel certain there was a common thread that would link it all together?

"We have to concentrate on Eddy right now," Fenn said.

"I suppose."

"If what Spider said is true, then Eddy will keep killing until we stop him."

"I have no doubt. It's just that I'd like to know more about Spider. I mean, for God's sake, we don't even know who he was."

Fenn chewed his lip. "It is a little incredible, isn't it? In this day and age with all our technology and databases, we still can't identify one man."

"How about his things?" she asked. "Isn't there something at his apartment that could help us? A bill, a letter, anything?"

"No, not a goddamn thing. Spider appears to be a man without a past. He had plenty of junk, all right, but nothing we could use. Not even a fucking library card. And the books. Christ, there must be a couple hundred piled in that damn rathole."

"What sort of books are they?" She wanted to look at them, but she didn't want Fenn to know.

"Lot of stuff on witchcraft, the occult. Historical stuff. Criminology texts. Religion, mysticism. You name it. Quite a few written in foreign languages, some bound in leather. Moore knows something of books. He says some of them are worth a bundle." Fenn shook his head as if trying to make sense of it. "But most important to us are the anatomy texts. He had quite a few. Apparently, he'd been studying his craft for some time. We found other books on surgery, forensic pathology."

"Quite a student. I wonder what the occult and religious books have to do with this."

"Who can say? You'll have to figure that one out."

"I guess."

He pushed his plate away. "I can't eat. I'm too goddamn stressed out."

She agreed. She took the bottle of wine they'd ordered and sat on the sofa with it. They drank it in water glasses until there was none left. They spoke very little. There seemed to be little to say.

Fenn was sitting close to her and she knew what was coming. When he kissed her, she didn't object. When his hands sought her breasts, she didn't stop them. He did what he wanted and it was only his gentle ways that made her intervene.

"You don't have to be soft and tender with me," she instructed him, unzipping his pants and freeing his erection. She took it in her hands and then between her lips.

She peeled off her blouse, then dropped her skirt. "I like to be fucked good and proper," she told him. He came at her with the sort of hunger she liked to see in a man's eyes. He squeezed her nipples and licked them.

"Bite them," she panted. "Yes . . . oh yes . . ."

He grabbed her roughly by the thighs and thrust into her without warning and her eyes rolled back in her head. Their tongues found each other, but only for a moment. She wanted to see, she *needed* to see his cock ramming into her. When she did, she began to shake and moan.

"Fuck me," she cooed in his ear. "Fuck me like you hate me."

And he did, pounding into her until her body tensed and she came violently, her nails scratching down his back and her teeth biting into his shoulder. Then she pushed him on his back and finished him with her mouth. When it was done and his taste was in her mouth, she felt better.

She only wished he'd used his fists on her.

LETTERS FROM HELL (5)

Dear Eddy,

Wonder and enlightenment.

Two states of being.

I experienced both that night. I was constantly in awe and wonder of you. When that greasy bastard in the parking lot started to fight, you were there in an instant, hitting him over the head with that empty beer bottle. What a sound that made! Hardened glass impacting with flesh. He was a tough one, wasn't he? Throat slit, bleeding like a pig, and still strong enough to take eight or ten good shots from that bottle. The top of his head looked like hamburger by the time he went down. It was incredible. My, but they hang on to their miserable lives, don't they? It's practically a crime.

I suppose I was taking an awful chance by having you lay him across the seat while I worked on him. Ah, well.

I didn't mean to take his head off. Sometimes, in the heat of the moment, I become a slave to the violence and addict to the blood. I'd be lying if I didn't admit how death and blood get me off. I think when I pulled his head free, I came. It was just too much.

But where was I? Oh yes, wonder and enlightenment. The aforementioned things filled me with a sense of wonder. But enlightenment. That came when I realized what our purpose was. You and I. We had a purpose that we could only fulfill together. Alone, we were just two threads, but woven together we formed a rope. We became a noose that was hungry for necks to stretch. And we found them, didn't we? Oh yes, we certainly did.

Yours,

Cherry

MEMOIRS OF THE TEMPLAR SOCIETY (5)

"When was the last time she ate?" Stadtler inquired.

Zero grinned. "It's been some time, I think. It's part of her conditioning, you know. She's fed only when I fear lack of sustenance might cause her physical damage."

The three of them were watching Gina through the two-way mirror. She looked terrible: thin, wasted, eyes blank. She was curled in the fetal position on the floor amongst her own waste.

"It's disgusting."

"Perhaps," Zero said. "But we've broken her now, don't you see? Her mind belongs to us, ready to be molded to our own liking. Who she will become now is up to us."

Grimes said, "Now things get interesting."

"She was very strong," Zero said. "I never dreamed it would take this long to break her. But now I know that it can be done. That's the important thing: The knowledge that the human mind can be destroyed, wiped clean of memory. The next step is to replace what she lost."

"You still think you can do it?" Stadtler said.

"More than ever. I'm sure of it, in fact."

Stadtler shook his head and lit a cigarette. "Any sadist can break a mind given time. There's nothing unusual about that."

"But so completely?" Grimes wanted to know.

"Yes. It's just a matter of brutality."

Zero looked angry. "How about you, Stadtler? Can your mind be broken?"

"Of course. But it would take you years."

"Do you really think so?"

"I'm sure of it."

Stadtler never caught the look that passed between the two men. If he had, some of the trouble could have been averted.

AMONG THE MISSING

Fenn's first marriage lasted seven years; his second, less than three. Both had lacked something. Some indefinable thing he hadn't been able to put his finger on. Until now. Both relationships had lacked passion, had lacked desire. Through familiarity, he and his former wives had gotten bored. There was never any sexual experimentation. Lights off, missionary position. It became terribly boring after a time. He knew there was more to a relationship than sex, but it was an integral part of a union. And when it went, it led to the disintegration of the more important things until there was nothing left.

He could never imagine that being a problem with Lisa. Marriage wasn't something he was thinking of quite yet, but when the time came, he felt he could enter into it knowing she would never fail to excite or interest him. Such a creature of beauty, grace, and intelligence on the surface . . . but beneath, when the lights went down, an animal. And what man could ask for more?

Fenn was at his desk, musing over these things, a huge smile on his face. Even when Gaines walked up, looking very grim, he still smiled.

"Bad news," Gaines said.

"What now?"

"Spider's apartment. It's been robbed."

"What?"

Gaines shrugged. "Somebody broke the seal and went in. Robbed the joint."

Fenn felt his face falling. "What did they take?"

"Books. Not all of them, just a dozen or so. And everything in the refrigerator. All those jars of shit he had in there."

"That's all?"

Gaines nodded.

Fenn looked angry. "I thought all those jars were removed for analysis?"

"They were going to be this morning. The DA said they weren't relevant the other day, so we didn't bother."

"Jesus H. Christ. Why wasn't I told about any of this? That bastard's been sticking his nose in my investigation and you didn't bother telling me?"

"Shit, Jim," Gaines said apologetically, "I thought you knew. Besides, those jars were just full of dirt and powders and crap."

Fenn's smile was light years away now. "Fuck," he said. "Fuck."

"Sorry, Jim, I—"

Fenn couldn't believe it. Gaines knew anything and everything at a homicide scene was important. What the hell was he thinking? And what the fuck was the DA doing this time? But he knew, God yes, he knew. Seigersen, the DA, had the knives and he had Spider's confession. His case was wrapped up now. Another maniac off the streets. More political points scored. As soon as Eddy was brought in, it was all done from an investigatory standpoint as far as he was concerned.

Christ, the system sucked.

His cell jingled and he put it to his ear. "What?" he snapped into it.

"Fenn? This is Dr. Roget. We got big trouble here."

What the fuck now? "I'm listening."

"Spider's missing."

His face was falling again. This time it hit the floor. *"Missing?"*

"Gone. His body's gone."

"Christ in Heaven," Fenn said under his breath. "What the fuck do you mean it's gone?"

Roget proceeded cautiously. "It was put in a locker last night. This morning we went to get it for the post and it wasn't there."

Fenn felt like crying. "It was snatched for God's sake?"

"I'm only stating the facts. It's missing."

"How could that happen?"

"I don't know. It must've happened last night some time. That's my guess. There's only one or two technicians on duty Sunday night."

"So somebody slipped in and stole a fucking body under the noses of your boys?"

"I assume so, yes. It's rather doubtful it walked out under its own power."

"Well, Doc, we're really in the shit then. The newsies haven't found out about our missing Jane Doe yet, but when they do and hear about Spider . . . Seigersen will have all our asses. You better find that stiff, goddammit."

Roget grunted. "And where do you suggest I begin?"

"I don't really care, but you better find it."

Fenn hung up. First the Jane Doe, now Spider. Coincidence? Not fucking likely. Eddy Zero had to be behind this some how. He just had to be.

Fenn's headache was starting again.

And then Gaines came through the door. "We got another one," he said.

CONFESSIONS OF DR. BLOOD-AND-BONES (3)

It was a night of revelations.

I picked up a prostitute and her name was Rachael, I believe. Not that it mattered. I can't seem to recall if she was beautiful or not. I took her back to the house. Most of my work was done there now. I was tiring of the brewery. She asked me why I lived in such a barren and cold place. I don't remember my answer, only the question posed by those soft, unknowing lips. It seems to haunt me still.

I had few worries then. Even the fact that Soames knew everything didn't bother me. That worm didn't have the courage to go to the police.

I was one with myself, my universe.

I took her up to the attic, to my workshop of sorts. She didn't seem to notice the stains on the floor or the heavy, salty smell of death in the air. And I didn't let her go into the next room to see the tapestry of skins. She saw only the money I'd promised her. She saw nothing else, wanted nothing else. Even my instruments gleaming from their hooks on the wall didn't deter her. How sweet she was. She lay on the floor, on a blanket I had provided. She couldn't have known how I appreciated her sacrifice as she closed her eyes. She could never know of the pleasure she gave me selflessly, the pain she forced upon my dreaming brain. She could never know of the torment that twists in an artist's soul and that she was my only possible mode of release.

I slit her throat and she died quietly enough.

I got down to work with little hesitation, peeling her skin back in the accepted manner. It was very painstaking work to do alone, but Stadtler and Grimes had no stomach for it. I was close, I was very close and I knew it. It took me hours to peel her hide free. When I was done, I tacked it to the walls with the others.

There was no time to stop and smell the roses, such as they were. I started in with the knives, creativity flowing from my impassioned fingertips. As I exposed muscle, nerve ganglia, and internals, I was pushed to new and fevered heights. I plucked her eyes free, then her tongue. I worked diligently, possessed by my own irresistible need to destroy and then create.

It was more exciting working alone, I found, without Stadtler and Grimes around to complicate things. They were gone now, each to his own reward.

It was about this time, as I neared completion, that the revelation came unbidden. I didn't ask for it; it arrived and nothing could have been the same again.

The light bulb overhead dimmed and then exploded with blinding brilliance, casting a sickly glow over everything. And though fragments of the bulb rained over me, the filament continued to burn of its own volition.

I heard something like a great and awful sigh and there was a hot blast of stinking wind. For just a moment I heard the sound of crying, of mourning, of animals lapping at wounds. That and something like glass breaking underfoot. Then nothing but a heavy, unnatural stillness. I was stopped, scalpel in hand, waiting for something.

I had arranged dozens of mirrors on the walls. Not for any particular reason other than vanity. I liked to watch myself work, really. And it was in one of these mirrors that I now saw the face.

It was pressed to the glass like that of a child peering through a window. With a minimum of effort, she stepped free.

I didn't know who she was or what she wanted, not entirely. She was hideously fat, naked, her rolling skin slicked with oil or sweat that seemed to bubble from suckering pores like blowholes. Her breasts were huge and heaving, standing full and firm, desirous of lips to ply their swollen nipples. Droplets of gray sour milk dripped from them. The stench was appalling.

I believe I hit the floor. My legs went right out from beneath me. I tried to speak, but all that came out was gibberish, mindless gibberish.

"Pretty," she said, staring at the near-dissected woman on the floor. "How very, very pretty."

It struck me that she wasn't so much fat as exaggerated, everything enlarged and ripened and horribly distorted . . . like a reflection in a funhouse mirror. Even the chasm between her legs was an impossible, wet cavity that could have swallowed a man whole. She stood there, her entire body breathing, expanding and deflating like some grotesque, fleshy balloon.

When she was inflated, she was bulbous and swollen; when she deflated, she became a bag of membranous flesh with an exaggerated, profuse architecture of bone beneath—knobs and rungs, crevices and chasms, spirals and ribbed protrusions and what looked like the teeth of gears. All of it was in motion, some grim interface of tissue and machine. Grinding and whirring sounds came from her as did slopping and gushing noises. She was like some swollen, intricate biomechanical device. A machine devouring flesh or flesh devouring machine, or perhaps both dissolving into some nameless hybrid.

"You are an artist," she said, fixing me with a look of starvation I'd only seen in the eyes of hungry children in destitute countries. "You are a maker and unmaker, a creator and destroyer."

I nearly screamed with horror. Her voice had a moist, slopping sound that reminded me of fish being gutted.

She began to inflate again into a swollen, rubbery-lipped thing with a great slobbering mouth licked by a dozen red tongues like fattened, peristaltic blood worms. Her eyes—glossy pink scabs—sank away into the sea of flab. She held out one machined-looking hand, the digits plump and scalloped, the nails long and black-green like her lips, the color of insect blood.

"You do us honor. A great and timeless honor."

She took a heavy step forward and I saw that she had been pulled apart at some time in the past and hastily reassembled. The workmanship was crude, unskilled. She had the look of a puzzle fitted together by an impatient, angry child, pieces forced into place when they wouldn't fit smoothly. And when she moved, it was insanity.

It was then I noticed that she was not alone.

Oh no, there was another just behind her that floated just off the floor, rising and falling like a hot air balloon. How to describe what I saw? A great, heaving mass like a distended sack made of blackened, slime-greased hides stitched and sewn together into a common whole. At the top, there was a head . . . or something like a head. It was laying on the left shoulder as if the neck that held it was broken. It had a bleeding, puckered mouth like a sea lamprey and hair like rotting marshweed that was red and crawling like blood-fattened worms.

It had no legs that I saw, just a few strands of coiling tissue. Fingers of gray gas steamed from it. One long, rawboned yellow arm hung from a scarified socket, the fingers being the black talons of a beast. It breathed in the manner of the other, swelling and deflating. Each time it expanded, seams of crude catgut stitching popped open and I saw red meat pulsing forth and what I thought was a face . . . no, two faces, two bloated white conjoined faces budding from a single growth. They looked like they were splitting apart through some crazy binary fission. It was like the thing was giving birth to them.

"Who are you?" I asked when my voice finally came, though I knew who they were. They were the things I had read of in books: Haggis Sardonicus and Haggis Umbilicus.

It was then I noticed that an umbilical connected them as if the floating thing was the woman's sister, something that never quite came to term in the womb. They both had the look of carcasses that had been dissected and stitched back up.

"We are the Sisters," the first said. "We can take you away from all this."

"Where?"

"To a place far but near. A place where an artist such as yourself would be appreciated, revered."

I wanted to go. This was my goal from the very first. "Tell me of it."

She did, but she insisted I finish my work. She gasped and shuddered with orgasms as I cut and sorted through the whore, dissecting her with trembling fingers. Her sister pulsated with glee.

"Come," she said when I was finished.

"We leave now?"

"Yes, oh yes," she told me. "But you can't make the trip without preparation. You cannot go in your present state. You must be unmade."

As I had prepared corpses for them, they now prepared me. As I screamed, they peeled my hide free. But it was only the beginning.

BODY DUMP

"A fisherman found them," Detective Moore explained. "He was out for some kingfish and he hooked this instead. When the uniforms got down here, they found the second one."

They were standing on the banks near Candlestick Point Pier. A cool mist was drizzling from a sky the color of dirty cotton, a chill breeze coming in off the bay. Fenn could feel it deep in his bones and beyond. He shivered.

"Fuck of a day for this," Moore went on. "Looks like Eddy was a busy boy last night. There's no end to this shit."

Fenn nodded. He stooped down next to the first corpse and pulled back the plastic sheet that had been draped over it. It was a woman, they knew that much, and only because Eddy hadn't gashed up her sex. Beyond that, it was hard to tell. She had been peeled and ritually dissected as usual. Her skin was missing along with most major organs. Whether he had tossed her off the pier or not was anybody's guess. The coroner figured she'd been in the water since last night and the fish had wasted no time nibbling on her.

"How's a guy supposed to sleep at night after looking at this butchery?" Moore wanted to know. "How the hell can you ever let your kids leave the house without wondering if you'll see 'em again?" He shook his head and stalked off, chewing antacid tablets.

Fenn could say nothing. There was no longer anything left in him. He'd spent what cold comfort he'd had on himself, there was nothing to give. Nothing at all but a black knowledge that Eddy Zero was only just beginning.

"We've got to get a handle on this," he told Gaines. "The bodies are piling up like cordwood and we're sitting around with our thumbs up our asses."

"Everybody's doing their best, Jim. You know that."

"It's not enough."

And it wasn't. They had a name, a face, but they still couldn't find Eddy.

Fenn walked up the bank, a stink of dead fish and industrial waste in his nostrils. Roget was finishing his cursory examination of the second body. It had been skinned, too, opened from crotch to throat, a great deal of the anatomy cut free and placed in bleeding piles next to the body. Fenn looked away. The carved, skullish face was leering up at him with empty sockets.

"The same?" he asked.

Roget shook his head. "Not exactly. Your boy removed the entire reproductive system this time. Clean job. He'd have made quite a surgeon."

"It runs in the family."

A car pulled up in the distance and he saw Lisa step out. She was wearing a brown leather skirt and blazer, dark stockings embroidered with leaves. Her hair was pulled back in a braid, her glasses on. The other men watched her legs as she came forward and so did Fenn. In his mind, he pictured the two of them fucking like dogs in the backseat of his car.

He went to meet her.

"Don't bother," he said, going up to her and looking hopeless. "There's nothing to see."

She touched his hand. "Let me look anyway."

He wanted to say no, but he couldn't. Just gazing into her face took his breath away and he knew he'd give her his soul if she but asked. Sometimes, like now, her beauty frightened him. It was so cold, like river ice. Cold and emotionless.

"I'll be all right," she assured him.

They toured the bodies and she looked, unmoved, at them. Then she broke free of his hand and stalked away.

"Everybody done here?" Fenn called out.

No one said anything; a few CSI techs nodded, pale and beaten wrecks.

"Then let's clean this mess up."

He followed Lisa back to her car. She sat behind the wheel, her face colorless, her knuckles white as she gripped the steering wheel.

"You okay?"

"I think I'm going to be sick," she said honestly.

Her door opened and she did as she promised.

Fenn wished it were that easy for him. Murder scenes gave him a bad feeling inside, but he was never disturbed the way he figured he should have been. And sometimes that worried him. It was as if he'd waded through corpses in another life, become immune to the carnage, and was unable to feel anything.

*   *   *

They weren't hungry again that night.

They spent the evening in Lisa's hotel room, before the blaring TV set, making love and saying very little. When they got back from the shore, Lisa took a bath and Fenn drank three gin and tonics, courtesy of room service. Everything seemed to be out of the question but getting drunk. He'd never felt so hopeless in all his born days. He hadn't told Lisa about Spider's body being missing or the theft of the obscure objects from his flat. He would eventually, he knew, to get her opinion on it all. But later. The last thing he wanted was to talk about any of that. It only made him feel that much more helpless.

When Lisa finished her bath, she came out in a robe and gave him a massage. It felt good, releasing the day's tensions and igniting new ones. They made love orally and drank wine from room service. As they grew more intoxicated, they became more adventurous and began pouring the wine on each other and sucking it free. Fenn wasn't sure how it came about, but he ended up cuffing her to the bed and fucking her from behind. Afterwards, they slept.

Later, as they lay naked and sticky with wine, Lisa said, "You might as well tell me what's on your mind."

"You really want to know?"

"We're in this together," she told him. "Tell me."

He did. And felt somewhat relieved in the telling. He proceeded in an almost soothing tone about Spider's body and theft from his apartment. As he grew more calm, she seemed to slowly fill with anxiety and dread, almost as if she had drawn it from him.

"This is all so insane," she said. "I never thought—"

He held her. "None of us did."

"Who do you think robbed his flat?" she asked.

"I know what I think. But what do you?"

"Eddy." The word fell from her lips heavily.

"Yeah. Who else would?"

Lisa looked into his eyes, her face lacking expression. "He took the body, too. I'm sure of it. No one else would have a reason."

"And our Jane Doe?"

"Probably that one, too"

Fenn lit a cigarette. "I agree. But why? Why would he risk his own freedom by waltzing into a morgue and snatching a body?"

"He has his reasons." She looked scared suddenly. "I don't know what they are and in a way, I don't want to. But it's all tied up with this business of the Territories and the Sisters. It has to be."

"If that's the case, then he's crazier than anyone thought."

There seemed to be nothing further to say. They fell into their own respective silences and thought.

Fenn saw Eddy Zero as being more dangerous than ever. He didn't put too much stock in any of this business about the Territories. It was a delusion shared by a couple of psychopaths and as such, it wasn't something he planned to lose much sleep over. He didn't really care why Eddy was doing what he was doing; that was the provenance of head doctors like Lisa. He saw only the basic, immutable facts of the situation: Eddy Zero was a pathological murderer and the sooner they got him behind bars, the better.

And once that happened, Eddy could dream of his never-never lands until his dying day. And that's all that really mattered to Fenn and as a cop, he could let nothing else cloud his judgment. He didn't give a good goddamn what Eddy was doing with Spider's things or with the cadavers. It had little bearing in his mind. The only thing that threw a very large, untidy wrench into his thinking was Gulliver and his insistence that he'd seen these Sisters. That would work out in time, he decided.

Lisa, however, was very much concerned with the peculiarities of this case. Given what Gulliver had said and Spider's firm belief in the Sisters, she was slowly being pushed towards acceptance. She couldn't pretend to understand much more than the basics of it, but she had a nasty, undeniable feeling that there was a very real dark truth behind it all. And the fact that Eddy had chanced taking those things from Spider's flat and stealing his body only made her that much more certain that there was a bit more to Heaven and Earth than she'd ever dared guess. It all decayed her belief in reality and she didn't like it one bit. William Zero had known and now his son did, as Spider had. Not that any of this really changed anything. Even if the three of them thought in their own delusive ways that murder was only the means to an end, it was still murder. And the three of them were still quite insane, in her opinion, regardless of their motives.

And what about Cherry?

She refused to consider that just yet. She only knew without reservation now that she was not interested in Eddy in anything but a professional manner, that he was no better than his father. Just another deranged monster. If Eddy had set out to become William Zero, apparently he had finally succeeded. Like father, like son. Another butcher with a sense of self-importance bearing the family name. Zero. That pretty much said it all.

And what of Fenn?

Did she love him? She wasn't entirely sure one way or another. She only knew that for the time being he made her feel good, safe. And what else really mattered?

"Where do we go from here?" Lisa said. "As far as Eddy Zero goes."

"Good question."

"He has to be seen eventually."

"Yeah, but we can't wait that long. We have to bring him in. I don't know how, but we have to." He took even, slow drags from his smoke. "Out there, somewhere, he's probably at it again and we can't do a fucking thing to stop him."

"Have you given any thought to stationing a man in the old house?"

Fenn nodded. "Yeah, but I don't like the idea. I have uniforms patrolling by every few hours, but putting a man in there . . . I don't know. Too many risks." He sighed and butted his smoke. "Eventually, I might not have a choice, though. It might be our best bet but I hate to have to order anyone to do it."

"What if you had a volunteer, Mr. Fenn?"

"Who? Who would . . ."

But then he knew. He saw it in her eyes and he wished the subject had never come up. Because it was a good idea and he hated it.

And he felt frightened way down deep.

THE FRIGHTENED MAN

Early the next morning, Fenn was over at San Francisco General in the psychiatric wing. Dr. Luce told him that Soames was no better or worse than on his last visit. Again, after some finagling, Fenn was allowed to see him.

"I want to know about Eddy Zero," Fenn said.

"Then you want to know an awful lot, my friend."

"Tell me."

Soames' eyes pinched closed. The lids were red and swollen as if he'd done a lot of crying. "I can't."

"Why?"

"You don't understand. The Doctor—"

"Zero is long gone, Soames," Fenn said. "He can't harm you now."

"Maybe not. But there are others."

"Who?"

Soames said nothing. A tear was rolling down his cheek.

Fenn had to proceed cautiously. If he upset the man too much, Luce would send him away and never let him back in. And Soames was a wealth of information. Fenn didn't know this to be fact, it was just a feeling that Soames was somehow important in all this. The only man who held the key to the mystery of Eddy Zero and Lisa Lochmere and the rest of this God-awful mess. But how to get said key. That was the question.

"I need answers, Soames. I need to know what you know. You found out things during your investigation, didn't you? I need to know what."

"I lost my mind during that investigation. I don't know what held it together before, but that was the final straw."

"Tell me about Eddy Zero. What did you learn?"

"Nothing."

"Did you tell Dr. Lochmere everything you found out?"

Soames was silent for some time. Then: "I won't tell you. I can't tell you. I'm a coward. Can't you see that? You'll have to find out on your own."

Fenn sighed. "All right. Where do I start?"

Soames grinned madly, his eyes wide and shining. "You start with Cherry Hill," he said and began to laugh.

He never stopped.

THE NIGHTMARE FACTORY (2)

After Fenn left the hospital, he had a terrible headache. He went straight back to his apartment and collapsed on the bed. He had more questions now than before. It seemed that happened every time he spoke with Soames. Questions and more questions.

Cherry Hill?

Now who the fuck was she and how was she mixed up in this?

Fenn closed his eyes and sleep came fairly quickly. As always when his headaches struck, sleep was the only true cure.

Moments later, he began to dream.

Help me, a voice was saying in the dream.

He didn't know whose voice it was. It could've been his own. Everything was alien in this dark little place.

Another voice was talking.

Constant, endless.

Eyes were watching.

Who are you? Who are you? Who are you? Do you know who you are or where you are going? Answer me.

Fenn wanted to scream . . . but no, his mouth was open and he wasn't screaming. He was crying. He was curled up in the fetal position, sucking his thumb and not knowing why.

Mommy, that voice . . .

He heard a terrible wailing, a rushing sound. Was it the blood surging through his veins? It was so warm here now. Warm and wet and dark. He had everything he needed here. He was happy, content.

Sounds, voices.

Not the bad voice . . . or was it?

He felt himself being pushed down, down, being squeezed, manipulated by hot warmth.

Light, blinding light and fierce cold.

Metal instruments.

A cry of pain.

His own?

Drawn into the light, into the light . . .

So cold . . . mommy . . .

He woke up screaming.

FEMME FATALES

While Fenn was waking from his dream, Lisa was in the hotel lounge picking at a plate of pancakes. It was dim in there, not brightly washed by sunlight like the adjoining cafe. This was a place for drinking and brooding, but she was in no mood for bright lights.

There was only one other person in the lounge. A young, dark-complexioned woman dressed in a black business suit with matching skirt. Their eyes kept meeting from time to time and Lisa wondered if they'd known each other somewhere before. Finally, the woman came over.

"Would you mind if I sat down?" she asked. She had donned dark Wayfarer sunglasses now.

"Not at all. I could use the company."

She sat. She was a tall woman, svelte, long-legged, very attractive.

"I'm not bothering you, am I?" she asked.

"Of course not."

"This may sound terribly strange, but I have a feeling I know you from somewhere."

Lisa looked startled. "I was just thinking that very thing. My name's Lisa. Lisa Lochmere."

"Cassandra." She offered no more.

Lisa studied her. Did she know her from another place, another time? From school maybe? No, this Cassandra couldn't have been more than twenty-five, which gave Lisa a good twelve years on her.

"I'm a psychiatrist," Lisa said. "Maybe we've met in that function."

"Christ, no," Cassandra laughed.

"I didn't mean to imply—"

"No apology necessary."

"We were both probably mistaken."

"Of course." Something about her tone indicated she didn't believe that for a moment. "Anyway, since we're both in need of company, we'll keep each other entertained. Shall we?"

"Why not?"

Cassandra cleared her throat. "So what brings the eminent psychiatrist Dr. Lochmere to the city by the bay?"

"Business, I'm afraid. Nothing but business."

"That's a shame. What sort of business? Or am I being too nosy?"

"No, not at all. I'm seeking out a patient of mine. A former patient. I'm afraid he might do something . . . unpleasant."

"That's fascinating. Does he have a name?"

Lisa thought about it. What was the point of bothering with patient confidentiality? Maybe she would know something. "Eddy Zero. He was under my care some years ago and then released before I thought he was sufficiently rehabilitated."

"Is he dangerous?"

"I believe so, yes."

"Wow. What an interesting job it must be being a psychiatrist. Always something new, I'd bet. You must've had to study a long time, I imagine."

Lisa nodded. "Pre-med, med school, internship . . . it takes years."

"It wouldn't be interesting for me, though. Spending all those years in institutions. It would drive me crazy. If you'll excuse that word."

Lisa smiled. *You have no idea, my dear.* "And what about you?"

Cassandra laughed again at her own expense, as if her life was a great comedy she was playing out. Maybe it was. But there was tragedy here, too, a dark and glaring hurt just beneath the words. Lisa liked her immediately. It took a great person to laugh at their misfortune. So many live lives of pain and so few have the ability to laugh rather than cry.

It was an endearing quality.

"My life is beyond words," Cassandra said. "I wouldn't even know where to start. Let's just say I've had my share of hurts and heartbreaks. But I've never let it keep me down. I always get back up and start again. It's my philosophy, you might say: Never give in, never give up. I've risen up against odds that would've buried others."

"I don't doubt it a bit," Lisa said.

"And that's what it's about, right? Never give up the ghost until you've done all that has to be done."

Lisa smiled. She was so easy to like. So terribly easy, almost like they had been friends before. "What about now?" she asked. "Do you live here or are you visiting?"

"Visiting. I'm at a stage in my life where I don't have to work for a living any longer."

"I envy you."

"I envy myself."

They both started laughing. Cassandra excused herself and went to the ladies room. Someone walked up behind Lisa and she knew it was Fenn before she turned.

"I'd really like to talk you out of this," he said, sitting down. "It's too dangerous."

She just looked at him. Even though she knew what he was talking about, his habit of resuming conversations hours or even days old was somewhat irritating.

She sighed. "It has to be done and you know it."

"Sure I know it. I just don't want it to be you alone in that fucking house."

"I'll be okay."

"Yeah, you're pretty tough, I guess."

"Somebody has to do it, Mr. Fenn. And who better?"

There was no one better suited and he knew it. "Can't blame a guy for trying. Who was that you were talking with?"

Lisa grinned. "I honestly have no idea."

"I want to ask you about something," Fenn said. "I've been keeping something from you, I guess. I'm not sure why."

"Tell me."

"That P.I. you hired a few years ago to track Eddy—"

"Soames."

"I did some checking on him. He's in the psychiatric wing of San Fran General. Did you know that?"

Lisa shook her head. "No. I'm sorry to hear that. He was good at his job. He found Eddy, gave me addresses he was staying at. Very thorough. Then, one day, he called me, said he was onto something big."

"And?"

"And zilch. He never called again. I hounded him for months. He never would tell me what he found. He even returned the retainer. Go figure."

Fenn looked suspicious. "I've been to see him a few times. He's in a bad way."

"Is he?"

Fenn told her everything Dr. Luce had told him.

"He's a mystery, all right," Lisa said. "What do you make of it?"

Fenn shrugged. "Did you know he helped stop William Zero in the first place?"

"Yes. That's why he was my first choice. He's the source of most of our information concerning Zero and the others. Without him, most of it would be guesswork."

"He's delirious, paranoid as hell. Talks in riddles. I couldn't get much out of him." Fenn was drumming his fingers on the tabletop. "Have you ever heard of someone called Cherry Hill?"

Lisa went pale. "Yes, our paths have crossed. She was a patient at Coalinga and later an inmate at Chowchilla. Not my patient, but I remember her very well. A psychosexual killer. Very dangerous."

"A strangler."

"Yes, she liked to use a wire. Though she killed her family—her mother and brother—she was also suspected of murdering at least five other people. It was believed that her psychopathy was a result of a combination of biological and psychological factors. She was horribly abused as a child, both sexually and physically. She was typical of primary psychopaths in that she was egocentric, of high intelligence, anti-social, disenfranchised, and a pathological liar that would twist reality in order to substantiate her delusions. She was completely lacking in remorse for her crimes and had nothing that we might call a conscience. Essentially, an inhuman monster wearing the skin of an attractive young woman."

"I did some checking," Fenn said. "She escaped from the prison a year or so ago. Never figured out how. Never was seen again. Shortly afterwards, there was a string of unsolved homicides across San Francisco and Marin Counties. Some figured it was her. But, as I said, she was never caught."

"And what does this have to do with anything?"

Cherry. Oh good God.

"Maybe nothing. Soames mentioned her name."

"He's probably not even aware of what he's saying."

"You're probably right. But why would he mention that particular name?"

"Who can say? It really depends on the level of his psychosis. Maybe he was looking for her as part of his job before his collapse . . . .though, the fact that he's still alive means he probably didn't find her."

Fenn shook his head. "I don't think I'd want to meet our Cherry Hill in a dark alley."

"No, you wouldn't," Lisa said, a darkness passing over her eyes. "Cherry, as I said, was a very pretty girl and she knew how to use her looks. She easily manipulated men. She could be very sultry and flirtatious when it suited her needs or shy and innocent. The problem is that we tend to trust attractive people, thinking that because they are perfect on the outside they must be perfect on the inside. Cherry was good at role-playing and she could almost instinctively sense what was expected of her by others and act the part to perfection. If you did come across her, you would never suspect the monster that hides inside her. She had a need to possess her lovers one-hundred percent: she mated and then killed. A black widow."

"There's something else, though. What is it? I can hear it under your words."

Lisa swallowed. "Yes, there's something else. At Coalinga she developed a fixation for Eddy Zero. She believed she was in love with him."

"Was she?"

"No, it's impossible for her to love as such. Inside, she's very cold. She was infatuated, yes, but in the end it was only about possessing him."

"Quite a lady."

"You have no idea."

*   *   *

Later, when Lisa was alone, the whole idea of going into the House of Mirrors wearing a transmitter seemed wild and dangerous.

If not bloody stupid.

She couldn't believe that she'd volunteered for such a thing. Bravery had never been one of her strong suits. And this little adventure would take more than merely that, it would take nerves drop-forged from iron.

Did I really suggest this whole thing? she asked herself.

Yes, I believe you did.

But it was far too late to back out now. Oh, Fenn would've been very happy to call the whole thing off. He couldn't bear the idea and had argued through the night against it. In his eyes, she was a fragile doll of porcelain and lace. In the end, though, the policeman in him had succumbed to the logic of it. If Eddy was in the house or hiding nearby and he saw Lisa in the vicinity, his ego would necessitate that he pay her a visit.

And what kind of visit would that be?

One with gleaming knives and glaring hatred? One in which the patient got the chance to settle the score with some pretentious headshrinker who'd declared him unbalanced? Would it work out that way? It was hard to say and the criminally insane mind was a dark and bottomless pool to fathom. It was terribly difficult to second guess someone like Eddy. Expect only the unexpected, Lisa's abnormal psychology professor had once said. Never a truer statement had been made. But she didn't think Eddy would kill her. Even if his mind and its demented workings were an alien quarter to her, which they surely were not, she could still draw certain conclusions based upon the pattern of his crimes. All of his victims, save the woman in the house who was as yet unidentified, had been prostitutes. It was logical to assume he wouldn't change his MO this late in the game.

But that doesn't mean hookers are his prey of choice, a secret dread voice reminded her. He may have found them convenient as Jack the Ripper did once upon a time and countless other killers have since. Prostitutes are easy victims. They'll gladly follow a strange man into a dark and lonely place for the right price.

Fenn had already worked out the details with his superiors. They liked the idea. It was a terrible gamble and chances were nothing would come of it, but it was better than waiting for Eddy to strike. Anything was. There would be no cops in the house, just herself. But she would be wired and Fenn and his boys would be in their van a short distance away listening to everything. Other cops would be watching from across the street and still others would be at the corner, disguised as street people. It was an awful lot of manpower to sink on such a thin hope, but Eddy had to be stopped.

All Lisa had to do was engage him in a conversation and the moment he spoke, the house would be flooded with cops. And she would be carrying a small, snub-nosed .38 in case anything went wrong. She'd carry it in her coat pocket with her finger on the trigger and if anything went wrong, a simple tug would right things again.

It all seemed quite flawless in every respect. The only thing she worried about was Eddy springing at her out of the darkness. If that was the case, she'd be dead before the police even arrived. But they'd have their man. She didn't think that would happen, though. Eddy would want her to know who was going to take her life, he'd want to tease her with it. His inflated ego would accept nothing less.

It was all set to go down tomorrow night. In the meantime, as the police organized themselves, Lisa would start visiting the house. If Eddy was nearby, hopefully he'd see her and come calling. If not right away, then tomorrow night when she would be trapped in the house for the duration.

For these first visits, Fenn would be in the back seat of her car, communicating with the officers who were monitoring her. Gaines had suggested that she might want to take a piece of chalk along and leave a little message for Eddy. Scrawl something on a wall so he'd know it was her without leaving her name. Maybe drop the idea that she'd be waiting for him the next evening. It was worth a shot.

All the bases were covered now and with any luck she'd soon be meeting the man she'd come to meet. And the idea of that filled her with a black and nameless horror like nothing she'd ever before known.

ALONE IN THE HOUSE OF MIRRORS

Lisa stood silently at the precinct as two technicians—one male and one female—wired her. Her shirt was off and Fenn looked uneasy as they taped the transmitter to her belly and breasts, then she dressed and went out to her car. She drove about in traffic while the police van with the listening equipment trailed a block or two behind and made adjustments at their end. They told her to speak off and on in a normal tone of voice. It was strange talking to no one, so she recited a thesis she'd presented years ago on Erhard and the notion of Self. It was terribly boring and tedious and she never realized to what extent until she had to read it aloud from memory.

Afterwards, they returned to the precinct and the games ended.

It was time to do it for real.

The police van disguised with a Pacific Bell logo on its side parked well up the street and Lisa stopped at the house itself. Fenn was lying in the backseat with a walkie-talkie. He winked at her as she got out and went up the steps cut into the hill. The House of Mirrors brooded above her and for reasons unknown, the sight of it made her heart race and her palms sweat.

She was dressed in a London Fog knee-length raincoat. It was a big, roomy thing that hung on her and disguised the bulge of the gun in her pocket. The door was open and she went into the secret world of gloom. Despite the coolness of a November afternoon, the air was hot and pungent inside. It had an unpleasant, damp smell like the inside of a reptile house. Bits of peeling paint dropped from the walls. There were curled Autumn leaves scattered over the floor. They hadn't been here on her last visit, which led her to believe that the front door had been left open recently.

She waited and listened for footsteps that would give away Eddy's approach and heard nothing. The house was quiet and tomblike. Fenn had told her to stay on the ground floor and let Eddy come to her if he was there. It would be safer that way.

She swallowed and drew a deep breath. "Eddy?" she called out. "Are you here? It's Dr. Lochmere."

Her voice echoed up the stairwell and died like a memory.

She waited and there was no response. She hadn't expected one.

"I'm going up," she whispered.

Fenn was probably writhing, but no matter. She was on her own and she would follow her own instincts. She went up the stairs and moved slowly up the dusty, dank corridor. It was cooler up here for some crazy reason and a sort of frigid clamminess rained in the air. She didn't bother checking the rooms, instead she went directly to the attic door and started up.

The house was a study in contradictions. The bottom floor was hot and wet, the upstairs cool, and the attic like a freezer. It made no sense. In this damnable place, heat seemed to fall rather than rise. Everything here raged against physical laws. She zipped up her raincoat and hugged herself for warmth. Her breath frosted as it left her lips. A slight, frozen breeze skirted the floors. She tried to empty her mind of imagination, yet the place still seemed to swim with a glaring aura of hate.

The skeletal remains of the animal still rested on the floor. The dust was beginning to insinuate itself once again where it had been stripped clean by that unknown sucking wind.

She stared at the grime-covered mirror. Why had Zero been so obsessed with mirrors? There had to have been some psychological modus operandi to it, but no one had ever discovered what it was.

Her breath was coming quick and she felt an uncanny sense of impending disaster. But it was just her mind playing tricks and she had to keep it in check. But it wasn't easy; the attic was an envelope of suffering. Negativity and inhumanity oozed from every board and crevice.

She turned to leave and a cold, arctic wind enveloped her. She turned and there seemed to be no cause for it. Her nerves danced on edge, her hands trembled, and it felt like something thick and greasy was lodged in her throat. The building anxiety in the air made her want to collapse in a ball and cry.

"Just a room," she said aloud as if to verify the fact.

She took a stick of yellow chalk from her pocket and wrote the following on the wall:

Tomorrow midnight
Wait for me, Eddy
Dr. L.

She turned and left, moving quickly down the stairs into the corridor and not stopping until the front door was in sight. Only then did she feel somewhat at ease.

"Nobody home," she whispered to relieve Fenn and the others and herself, she supposed.

She grasped the doorknob and was struck by a sudden claustrophobic sensation that it wouldn't open at all, but it did. She felt almost as if she were being watched. The air smelled different, just a suggestion of an odor that hadn't been there before. She left the front door open and followed the scent. Tobacco smoke. In what had once been a sitting room, a cigarette smoldered on the floor.

Fenn?

"Is someone here?" she said in a dead, dry tone.

The wind rattled the eaves outside and the house seemed to shudder. She was rooted to the spot, paranoia raging in her brain. She wanted to put her hand in her pocket and touch the gun, but her fingers were unwilling to move.

A board creaked overhead.

The front door swung shut with a deafening slam.

She ran down the hall and threw it open, her heart slamming in her chest, her breath locked in her lungs.

"Just the wind," she said and looked down at the floor. The warped frame of the door had scraped a trail there. It was unlikely the wind could have sucked it close.

She shut it and left.

*   *   *

"It's crazy the way an empty house can prey on your imagination," she told Fenn later. She didn't mention the cigarette for fear he wouldn't let her come back and she knew she had to now.

"Don't I know it."

"I almost felt like I was being watched."

He looked concerned. "Maybe you were."

"No, I don't think so. It was just nervous tension, that's all. I heard a board creak and then the door slammed and I ran. I hadn't been so scared since I was a kid."

"Fear's okay," he told her. "It's a good thing. It can save your ass in some situations."

"I suppose you're right."

"Trust me, I am."

She winked at him and wondered who'd left the cigarette. It could've been Eddy, but something told her it was someone else entirely.

And that's what really scared her.

LETTERS FROM HELL (6)

Dear Eddy,

Once we were back on the road, I felt a lot safer. Remember how it started to rain when we hit the highway again? Practically a downpour.

I love storms.

I love driving in them, sleeping in them, fucking in them.

We figured it would be awhile before anyone looked in the trunk of my car and found that guy. Not that it mattered. That car wasn't registered in my name, anyway. It was just a rental. Too bad about that guy. He was so happy to help a woman in distress. Oh, well. Things happen, I guess.

The idea of the two of us cruising around together was like a dream come true for me. You have no idea how often I thought about that. The destination was never set in my mind. In my dreams, I only saw us driving away together, towards the future. Our future. As long as were together, it never mattered to me where we ended up.

The road was practically deserted. There were a few trucks, but not much else. The rain and the wind had scared all the lambs back into their holes. But that was okay. We owned the road that night of nights and what else really mattered? Just the two of us and miles and miles of emptiness.

It wasn't too long after we'd passed that turn off for Petaluma that you saw the lights behind us. Those flashing red lights. What a thrill that gave me. We had already discussed what to do in such a situation. You thought of everything, didn't you?

"You know what to do," you said.

And I did.

There was a rest stop ahead and you turned off into it. We were in luck: it was deserted. Not a soul in sight and given the conditions, it was unlikely anyone would show up. We pulled into the empty lot and you shut the engine off. The cop—a CHP trooper—slid in behind us, his lights flashing. He sat there for the longest time before coming over. Why do they always do that? Just sit and sit before coming over?

Finally, he approached us. He was a short man, solidly built. Gray hair. Tired-looking, though, as if he hadn't slept in some time.

He played a flashlight in through your window.

"In a hurry?" he asked.

"Yeah . . . my wife's hurt. There was an accident."

I moaned and acted woozy. He put the light on me and I made sure he saw the blood all over me.

"Christ, what happened?" He came around to my side of the car and opened the door. He checked me over real quick, looking for wounds.

"I better call a—"

His words died on his tongue. He must've seen a glint of steel as my razor opened his throat. Then he stumbled back, gagging on his own blood. His fingers were trying to find his gun, but they weren't fast enough.

Not as fast as the razor.

By the time he gave his last breath, the rain was hammering down again.

"We better make tracks," you said.

I knew you were right and we did. No doubt he'd already called in our plate number.

We ran.

Yours,

Cherry

VICTIM

Gulliver was learning to hate his life. Not what it was, as such, but what it had become: a joyless celebration of paranoia. There was nothing left in it that brought him even a moment's pleasure. Every act, every movement, every thoughtless mundane activity which he'd once went about with a self-hypnotic banality now had to be thought out carefully. The world, his world, was now fraught with dangers. Simple things that one rarely gives a moment of thought to like taking a walk or going into the bathroom, now had to be plotted carefully.

Eddy Zero was to blame.

Gulliver saw him in every dark alleyway, every shadowy alcove. And each time he did, which was painfully often, he drew in a sharp intake of trembling breath and waited for the knife to fall. He was no longer living, he was only existing in a world in which the rules were dictated by a homicidal maniac, ever changing.

He'd liked his life, such as it was. Barren of love and family, it was still good. It was still something he clung to with repetitious ferocity. He liked the normal, dull channels of his existence, each day resembling the one it replaced. It was boring. It was predictable. But he'd never been one to seek excitement, never one to live on the edge. He liked the monotonous grind of things. No surprises, just quiet living.

Gulliver had few close friends and dozens upon dozens of acquaintances. He'd never had a steady lover since he'd abandoned the ministry and his wife had left him. There was only a weekly fling that had lately become monthly with some stranger, sometimes male, sometimes female, occasionally both. It was enough to satisfy the animal urges.

Now even that had been shattered.

He didn't dare frequent the bars and clubs he'd once visited nightly. If Eddy was out hunting him, it would be the first place he'd look. He hadn't even gone to work since Eddy had stabbed him. His supervisor understood, thinking the reason was because of physical duress from the knifing. But that wasn't it at all. Gulliver was afraid to go anywhere or see anyone. His personal bogeyman was always near, he felt, waiting to strike and butcher. He missed his job. It was tedious, but he'd liked it. Work gave a man a sense of worth to himself and his fellow creatures. He was part of the art department of Macy's in Union Square, handling window displays. It gave him a chance to express his creativity and the pay wasn't bad.

Eddy Zero had taken that away from him, too.

He had learned, since the assault, to hate Eddy like he'd never thought he'd be able to hate another living soul. To injure someone was one thing, but to steal their life was quite another. He saw only one way of bringing things to an end and that was to find Eddy himself. He trusted Fenn, but he knew how the police worked. He'd always likened their methods of justice to that of a man circling a house and hoping he'd fall through the front door by accident, rather than just proceeding up the steps and letting himself in. It wasn't entirely their fault. Their hands were duly tied by laws that were set to protect the individual. Laws the criminal could work to his own advantage.

If Eddy was to be stopped, then Gulliver decided he would have to do it. He had no set procedures to follow. He could walk right into the front door, as it were. He wanted only to locate Eddy and he'd let the police handle the rest.

Fenn had come a long way in a matter of days, as far as Gulliver was concerned. He'd transformed from a cynical, bigoted cop into a real human being with an open and thinking mind. Yet, Fenn was still a cop and bound by rules. And he was also hopelessly distracted by his worship of Lisa Lochmere's face. And under the might of such infatuation, he saw only her.

His head wasn't clear enough to deal with the task at hand.

No, Gulliver would have to do it himself.

With this in mind, he took to the streets and took his chances. If he was going to put an end to this madness, he had to start somewhere. But first, he was going to buy a gun. The sort of weapon that could send Eddy spinning into hell to join his father.

The idea of this brought a smile to Gulliver's lips.

ALONE IN THE HOUSE OF MIRRORS (2)

It was the night of nights.

Lisa had spent the previous day visiting the house and now it was time for her all-night vigil. If Eddy had seen her message, then she was sure he would come. He wouldn't be able to help himself.

There were police everywhere nearby and all it would take was one word from her and they'd come running, yet she was terrified. Her head spun with a raw and ominous sense of dread. She couldn't stop thinking about the smoldering cigarette butt she'd seen and who had left it. She'd seen or heard nothing at the house after her first visit, although she hadn't dared go beyond the entry.

She brought a small flashlight, but it probably wouldn't be necessary to use it. Equal portions of moonlight and streetlight were spilling in through innumerable rents in the walls and the broken windows. She kept one hand in her pocket on the butt of the .38 and she had no intention of letting go of it. The safety was off and her finger sweated on the trigger. One slight tug was all it would take. It gave her a fleeting sense of security.

"I think I'll take a walk upstairs," she whispered into the microphone at her lapel. The thought that someone friendly was hearing her words was comforting.

She went directly to the attic door and found it standing open. Had she closed it? Probably not since she'd been in a bit of a hurry and closing doors hadn't been of primary importance.

There were great gaping holes in the roof, and the attic was positively glowing with light. It almost seemed luminous. She went in and immediately regretted it. There was another dead animal on the floor, possibly a rat, its flesh stripped clean, moonlight gleaming off its vertebrae. She turned on the flashlight and studied its denuded corpse. There was very little but polished bone and scraggly bits of dark fur. Again, she saw the floor was vacuumed clean of dust, meticulously robbed of anything but the wood itself. And again, the motion of the sucking disturbance indicated that it had started with the rat and ended with a vortex near the wall. At the foot of the full-length mirror.

"My God," she said and then remembered she was being listened to. "Just a dead rat."

She went over to the mirror and touched its surface.

It was warm. Terribly so.

And what exactly did that mean?

She turned and studied the message she had left. A black insanity itched in the back of her mind. No other message had been left, but hers was smeared as if by a passing hand.

A board creaked somewhere. She spun around, playing the light about.

Nothing. She was quite alone, her eyes told her, yet her other senses disagreed. There was something here out of the ordinary. She just couldn't put a finger on what it was.

"Is someone here?" she asked in a weak voice. There was no answer to her query and she was glad of it. "Guess not."

There was a clicking in the wall: slow, insistent. The result of some nocturnal insect worrying at the plaster, she reasoned. A deathwatch beetle, as they were known. As she listened, it stopped. Then stillness: heavy and sullen.

She heard something else suddenly, a dragging sound down in the hallway below. With her heart in her throat, she turned off the flashlight and tightened her sweaty grip on the .38. The sound had died now. She started down the stairs, running her free hand along the wall of the narrow passage. Then she was at the door and there was nothing to do but open it. And she did, knowing a fear that was absolute.

The corridor was empty.

But there was an odor again, of tobacco—strong, pungent, and exotic. It barely masked something worse beneath. She wasn't alone. Whoever had been here yesterday was back again. Probably the same person who had rubbed out her message.

Much as she wanted to run from the house and never return, she couldn't allow herself, but her instinct demanded she do just that. It was the safest of possible courses. Flight or fight, it told her. There are no other choices. She chose the latter and stood her ground on uneasy legs.

Another sound now, this one from the attic. If she had imagined the others, there was no possibility her mind had conjured this one up. There was a huge din coming from up there, as if the place was rattling itself apart. Timbers were groaning, floor boards straining against the nails that held them in place.

She threw open the door and it stopped.

She clicked on the flashlight and the passage was filled with swirling dust. There was an odor present as she started up, something like the sharp tang of ozone after lightning has struck. A reek of ammonia followed in its wake. She played the light around, the beam barely penetrating through clouds of dust pounded from the rafters. A frozen wind was blowing, nearly sucking the breath from her lungs and the warmth from her skin. Everything had changed, even the very pressure of the air seemed heavier, thicker, like moving through ocean depths.

She paused at the top of the steps, once again ignoring the voice in her head that told her to run while there was time. Panic was surging in her guts, her skin tight like leather. The flashlight beam cut only a few feet into the dark and died. It wasn't possible, but then none of this was. There was no moonlight or streetlight coming in now, just an even inky blackness that had swallowed the room in a bleak completeness. She couldn't see the roof overhead nor the gaping holes that had shown the stars earlier. The light bounced and jigged in her trembling hand.

"Something's happening here," she said aloud, hoping they'd hear.

She checked her watch. Was it midnight yet?

Fresh panic assailed her. Her watch was running backwards, counting the seconds in reverse.

She heard the sound of a woman crying and it seemed to come from a great distance. The attic was a polluted abyss. The air seemed inundated with grit, and sandy ash lodged between her teeth as she drew in a gasping breath. The light revealed a form and she started. She wasn't afraid, really; shocked, if anything.

The form was standing before the full-length mirror . . . or was it reflected in it?

Thoughts tumbled wildly in her head.

It was a cadaver, her brain told her, standing there on frozen legs. A cadaver dressed in a ragged black overcoat. It could have been one of Eddy's victims, save that it was male. It appeared to have been carved and divided on an anatomist's table and hastily reassembled in a gruesome patchwork of humanity. A lurching suture ran from the crown of its bald skull to its disjointed jaw, several others dividing the face into grim quarters of gray, necrotic hide that were held together by black thongs of catgut and what appeared to be metal surgical staples. The result was a visage that was distorted and stretched and horribly scarred, the nose a skullish triangular cavity, a ragged stitching pulling the corner of its mouth up into a sneering grimace. It was a Frankensteinian monstrosity, one eye a juicy gelid green, the other the diseased yellow of leprosy.

But it was no cadaver, for she heard it breathing with a clotted, pulpous hissing and it leered out at her with an intense craving, an appetite for suffering and sadism that made her bowels fill with ice water. Yet, for all its maimed disfigurement, there was something terribly familiar about it.

If there was ever a time to run, it was now. But she didn't. For some insane, unexplainable reason, her curiosity demanded she stay and see this lunatic episode to a close. A stink of corruption came from the figure, and it was no single odor, but a veritable bouquet of many. Her mind reeled as it tried to attach names to them all. It started with human excrement and ended with old blood and mucid decay.

As she watched, it moved, stepping in her direction with an uneasy, pained gait as if one of its legs was longer than the other. Its leprous, pitted lips formed a grin of something that might have been recognition. It reached out a skeletal claw with abundant stitchwork.

In a scraping voice, it said, "I knew you'd come eventually, Lisa. I knew you wouldn't be able to stay away . . ."

*   *   *

Fenn was in the police van down the street. He was trembling inside with nervous agitation. This was all a bad idea, a reckless and stupid idea and he couldn't believe he'd gone along with it. He should have known better.

"I don't like this at all," he said to Gaines. "She hasn't said a thing in twenty minutes."

"Give her time, just give her time. If she walks around in there talking to herself, it'll tip Zero off. If he's even around."

Both of them, along with a technician who monitored the equipment, were wearing headsets. They heard nothing but silence.

"We should've put a man in there with her," Fenn said for not the first time that night. He was worried and rightfully so, but he had to remain impartial. Anything less and he would lose his professional edge.

"She's probably bored," Gaines told him.

"Or scared to death."

Fenn took his headset off and poured a cup of coffee from his Thermos. Lisa had been in the house since before ten, which was over two hours now. If Eddy got her message and didn't scent a trap, he'd be showing up anytime, if he hadn't already. And that's what was really eating at Fenn. That Eddy had already gutted her and slipped away. But he couldn't let himself think that. If he did, he'd go running over there right now and ruin everything. Besides, she was wearing a wire and the transmitter was a very sensitive piece of equipment. If there'd been a struggle or even if she'd been struck or fallen, they would've heard it.

"I don't know," the technician said. His name was Avery and he was a thin, sensitive black youth. He had intense, intelligent eyes that seemed to look right inside you, as if he was trying to see what sort of mechanism made you tick. Fenn had already decided he was probably the sort of guy who spent his free time taking electronic components apart and then reassembling them.

"What do you mean?" Gaines asked.

Avery shook his head. "We should be picking up something. Her footsteps, her breathing—something. I think . . . I think we're getting dead air."

Fenn dropped his coffee cup. "Are you sure?"

"Yeah, something's not right here."

"Move 'em in," he told Gaines and leapt out the door.

He was the first one in the house, but he could hear the sound of approaching feet. Lisa was sitting on the bottom step, her head in her hands.

"Lisa?" he said, his voice high with panic. "Are you all right?" He went to her side and she was still warm, still breathing. He thanked God for this.

"I'm okay," she said in a low tone. "You don't have to call in the Calvary."

But it was too late. Five or six heavily armed cops in ballistic vests kicked through the door, scanning the dimness with automatic weapons.

"Search the place," Fenn told them and they scattered in all directions.

"He never showed," she told him. Her voice had a strange lilt to it and he didn't care for it in the least.

"What happened?"

"Nothing." She studied the floor. "Nothing at all. I think this place is getting to me. It makes you imagine things."

"What sort of things?"

But she just shook her head and he wasn't about to push matters. He helped her out to the van and they drove back to her hotel. He came up and she sat in a chair, falling asleep almost immediately. He lifted her into bed and covered her.

He kissed her cheek. "Sleep tight," he said and let himself out.

When the door closed, she opened her eyes.

*   *   *

She was awake most of the night. Sleep was something for people with peaceful minds and easy hearts, not for those who feared they couldn't distinguish between reality and nightmare.

What happened in the attic was a mindless plunge into blackness. It couldn't have happened, not in any sane world, yet she knew it had. She knew all the symptoms of obsessive mania and hallucinatory delusion and suffered from not a one. Although she was feeling what Kierkegaard had deemed angst, an undefined anxiety, she was very much in command of her faculties.

As much as she'd suspected an underlying truth in what Spider had said, the confirmation of such was maddening. Some things were best left in a theoretical phase. But she had seen it. She had seen William Zero . . .

or the hideous monster he'd become. He'd come back now, ripped asunder in some alien chasm and pieced back together to come calling. But it *was* him. There was no getting around that. He'd slipped away from the police some twenty years before and plunged head first into a private hell she knew only as the Territories.

And now he was back.

I knew you'd come eventually, Lisa.

He hadn't threatened her, nor even attempted to reach out to her with his cancerous fingers. He smiled and asked only one thing: "Where is my son?" And that was enough of a question to rob the air from her lungs and drop her to her knees.

There'd been no other intercourse between them and if there had been, she feared her mind would've snapped like a stick of dry kindling and left her there, babbling and sobbing. He had departed the real then in a screaming rush of vacuum wind that shook the attic and nearly pounded the fillings from her teeth. He'd stepped *into* the mirror. Dust and dirt and splintered wood had rained down on her and then the attic was just the attic again, save for a sharp reek of ozone and death. The Territories had closed their loathsome gates with a huge, ripping sound and a reverberation of human screams. She'd found her way downstairs then. She couldn't even remember exactly how, only a vague half-memory of crawling like a baby and weeping. The next thing she remembered was the door opening and Fenn coming to her rescue. The only evidence that it had happened at all was that her watch had stopped at exactly midnight.

She'd told Fenn nothing. She couldn't bring herself to. Maybe later she would.

No, never, she told herself. *I saw a man step through a mirror. I must be crazy . . . I have to be crazy . . .*

Yet, she knew she would have to tell Fenn. Eventually.

And even then, what would she tell him? That reality had gashed open, its very unstable material had ruptured and no blood had seeped from the wound, only a black portion of some impossible, grotesque world between worlds? Some quasi-dimension of insanity had poked out and Dr. Blood-and-Bones had paid his respects? What would he say to that? And if she had the mettle to bring that to her lips, shouldn't she tell the rest, too? That William Zero, the very demented father of the very man they sought, had preyed upon her when she was an insecure, naïve teenager? That she had loved him even as he used her? Had harbored romantic visions of him even as he beat and sodomized her? That even if she had known, she might not have cared that he was off cutting up women when he wasn't abusing her? What would he say then? *I understand why you chose psychiatry, Lisa, because you're one screwed-up bitch.* And he wouldn't have been far from the truth. Because she had chose it for that very reason. She'd hoped that understanding the human mind in general would help her understand her own tormented psyche in particular. Understand why she did what she did, why she chose the men she chose, why her desires were a direct contradiction to all she held sacred. And most importantly, once she'd discovered her old lover's true identity, why she still held him in awe, still missed his perversions. And why she'd had something quite close to a sexual infatuation for his equally unstable son.

No, she could never tell him. He'd hate her if he knew what she was, who she was. Because no normal woman you could love felt the things she did, wanted the things she did. William Zero might have corrupted her impressionable mind at a very painful period in her life, but he'd eventually gone his own way and she'd been lost without him. And could she really point the finger at him for her inability to enjoy a healthy romantic or sexual relationship?

Her training told her no, not entirely. Every person is still their own master, still able to make their own decisions and choices.

It wasn't a puzzle she could hope to solve. Her own mind was every bit as complex as any other. And she lacked the needed objectivity to approach it as a therapist.

And what about Cherry Hill?

What would Fenn say when she unloaded that little gem on him?

You let a psychopath free into the world and you never reported it?

Oh, Christ.

Yeah, Cherry was here, too, now. If things hadn't been complicated or terrible enough before, now they were definitely worse. Lisa's past mistakes were about to gang up on her. Fenn already had suspicions about Cherry and eventually she'd have to tell him about that, if nothing else. Which brought up an interesting point. When Soames was working for her, he never once mentioned anything about Cherry Hill. But now he had, to Fenn. What did that mean? Was that mysterious lead he was working on something about Cherry?

If Fenn or anyone else ever find out about the illegal drug trials on Cherry, you'll not only lose your license but be charged with criminal negligence.

It was getting so complicated.

For now, certain questions remained. Mainly, why had Zero returned for his son? What was the purpose? Had he learned of Eddy's desire to enter the darker realms of the Territories and was he now ready to unzip the bowels of the chasm, walking hand in hand into a living nightmare with his son? Was that it? It couldn't be sheer coincidence that he'd chosen this particular time to reappear.

Before dawn she collapsed back in bed, exhausted from self-analysis and too many questions without sane answers. She closed her eyes and began to dream that Fenn was making love to her, sketching out his emotions and desires to her in a flurry of infantile kisses. There was no arousal for her, not until his face melted away and was replaced by that of William Zero.

Then there was no limit.

FRIEND TO THE FRIENDLESS

In the house he was renting, Eddy Zero was drinking and plotting out his next move. Spider was dead now, but his body was in the next room. Eddy had all the necessary materials to resurrect him now that he'd looted his flat, but actually going about it was another matter entirely. Spider's notebooks spelled out in detail how it had to be done. But, of course, it was madness.

And Eddy wasn't mad.

Just as corpses never live again.

The Shadows were mulling around him, excited at the prospect of a dead body rising up.

(bring him back eddy then we'll have a place to call our own)

"It's rubbish."

(try it try it anyway)

"Not bloody likely. I've better things to do."

(you promised him we heard you promise him you'd do it if he died)

"Leave me alone."

(you promised)

"Fuck off."

He started to pour himself another drink when he heard the front door open and close. He set his bottle down and sat silently. A thief? A looter? His fingers closed on the knife in his pocket and he turned off the lights. No one knew about this place but Spider and he. No one alive, that was.

The door to the living room swung open.

He saw a shape in the doorway.

"What do you want here?" he asked calmly.

There was no answer. The shape stood its ground.

"Well?"

There was a whisper of motion as the shape stepped into the room. "Turn on the light," it said. "I'm a friend."

That voice, that voice—

He turned on the light.

Cassandra stood there dressed in a skirt and blazer. His heart skipped a beat and for a moment he wasn't sure whether he'd laugh or scream. He did neither. He just stared. She'd come back to him . . . not in cerements stained with grave dirt, but in skirt and blazer. Like a woman on her way to the office. There was something damnably funny about that—walking dead, business elite class.

"Don't ogle me, Eddy. I'm not here to haunt you."

"Then why . . . how?" He could barely speak. The words seem to rattle on his tongue.

"Unfinished business," she said, sitting on the sofa and crossing her legs. "It's rather irresponsible to die before your affairs are put in order."

"I murdered you."

"You did."

"But you were dead, I saw—"

"Yes, yes, I'm dead, all right. Quit making a scene about it for God's sake, will you?"

"I'm must be going crazy." Feeling light-headed, he sank into a ratty chair. "Yes, that's it. I'm a fucking lunatic."

Cassandra laughed. "Of course you are. Like father, like son."

"Maybe it's really taking hold now."

She laughed with a throaty croaking sort of sound. "Oh, I'm real enough, Eddy. Dead as a bag of drowned kittens, but real enough."

His face was hanging, slack and sallow. "But how . . . how did you do it?"

"It's a long and dreary story. Suffice to say I'm here and I forgive you for killing me."

"It wasn't my fault, the Shadows made me kill you."

(you killed her because you wanted to we only unlocked your desires)

"You made me do it! You didn't give me a choice!"

(don't be such a baby be man enough to take responsibility for your actions your father ALWAYS took responsibility for his actions)

"I'm not my father!"

(pale imitation)

"Shut up!"

(The apple doesn't fall far from the tree but this one has a worm in it)

Eddy clutched his hands to the side of his head. "Sometimes they won't fucking shut up."

"That's some baggage you carry, darling," Cassandra said. "Daddy's pets, are they?"

"Yes, I'm afraid so. They won't leave."

(give us spider's body and we'll leave you alone)

"It makes perfect sense, doesn't it?" Cassandra said. "Give them the carcass and they'll be happy."

Eddy looked up at her. "You . . . you can hear them?"

She nodded. "Of course. The dead can hear the dead just fine. Now tell me about Spider's cabalism and alchemy. There's nothing like a good resurrection for laughs."

Eddy outlined the plan to her and showed her Spider's books and notes. It was very detailed stuff. She studied them over for a time as she pulled off a cigarette and he wondered how it was she looked so good. Why, he could barely see a hack mark on her anywhere. Amazing, is what it was.

"Bright boy, our Spider," Cassandra said. "Let's give it a whirl. Where is he?"

Eddy brought her into the next room. She set to work, handling his cadaver with the sort of respect only the dead have for their own. It was a lengthy, gruesome process opening him up and replacing his vitals with bags of herbs and salts and spices, injecting odd chemicals in certain locations. It took some time.

Eddy watched her as she worked. "Why did you come back?" he asked.

"For you. Who but me can take care of you? And you need looking after, you know. You're making a real mess of things."

Eddy didn't contest the fact.

No man is an island.

THE LADY IN BLACK

Two days after Lisa had her run-in with William Zero, a visitor paid her a call at her hotel. She was a thin, dark beauty dressed in a black leather skirt and jacket. Her name was Cherry Hill.

Cherry had decided it was time they meet face to face again and talk. As she saw it, things were reaching critical mass, and it was in Lisa's best interest to back off while there was still time. She planned only to convince her of this in the politest manner possible. And if the good doctor wouldn't listen to reason, there were always alternate methods.

The desk clerk smiled at Cherry as she came in. He was a younger man, probably in his twenties, she thought, and as such, putty in her hands. As she made her way to the desk, she could feel his eyes running up and down her legs. She could sense his hunger and it was very much to her advantage.

"Good evening, miss," he said. "May I help you with something?"

"I hope so. Is Dr. Lochmere in?"

"Yes, I believe so. But she left strict orders not to be disturbed."

Cherry smiled. "Did she now?"

"Yes . . . well . . . she . . ."

Cherry was leaning over the desk now, giving him a good view of her cleavage. Her breasts weren't large, but ample and firm. The clerk couldn't help himself. He was no longer looking in her eyes. Cherry's lacquered nails were drumming on the registration book.

"What's your name?" she asked.

"Richard." His voice was barely audible.

"Richard," she said, rolling it off her tongue. "Dr. Lochmere left orders not to be disturbed, you say?"

"Well . . . actually it was Mr. Fenn who did and he's, you know, a cop and all."

"Really?"

"Yeah, homicide."

"Nasty business. You couldn't just bend the rules a bit and tell her Cherry Hill is here, could you? We're old friends. She'd want to see me."

"No . . . no, I could get in trouble."

Cherry licked her lips. "Is this Mr. Fenn with her now?"

"No, not right now," Richard told her. "But he's in and out all the time. I'm sure he'll be back before long . . . and if I was to disturb her . . . you know how cops get . . . he'd probably get me fired."

Cherry put her hand on his. He started slightly. "I wouldn't want that to happen. Does she spend a lot of time with Fenn?"

"Yeah . . . I only work nights, but he's up there a lot. They came in pretty late last night. Well after midnight. God knows what they're up to, a cop and a psychiatrist."

Cherry was stroking his middle finger now. "I think I know what they're doing," she said in a husky voice. "Probably fucking."

Richard was trembling now.

"I don't suppose there's any way I could convince you, so I won't try . . ."

"Well . . ."

"You just tell Dr. Lochmere that Cherry was here. Not the cop, only Lochmere, you understand?"

"Yes."

"And maybe I'll stop by tomorrow night and see if I can make you break some rules."

Cherry ran fingers over his lips and left. She felt, rather than saw, him slump down in his chair. It would've been easy enough to seduce Richard and get up to Lisa's room, but there was time. Tomorrow night, if she indeed came back, he'd be begging to give her a key. Men were like that.

Cherry winked at the doorman on her way out and disappeared into the night.

MEMOIRS OF THE TEMPLAR SOCIETY (6)

This night, only Stadtler and Zero showed up for the meeting. Zero made them drinks and said, "I'm afraid we have trouble."

Stadtler's hand shook as he gulped his whiskey. "How so?"

"Mr. Grimes."

"Where is he? Has he done something?"

"He's told someone of our activities."

Stadtler lost what color he had left. "Shit! I knew it."

"He told our man Soames everything."

"That fucking pimp?"

Zero nodded. "I'm afraid so."

"Why for chrissake?"

"Blackmail, I would guess. Our association with Soames predates that of ours with you. Grimes and I spoke on the phone. He said Soames had photographs of him and . . . others. Items his wife wouldn't approve of. Soames wanted to know what was happening to the girls he'd gotten for us."

"Bastard."

"I'm afraid so. You shouldn't worry, though. He's never seen your face."

"But he knows my fucking name. Shit, this is just great."

"I don't think he'll go to the police. I have incriminating evidence on him."

Stadtler was trembling. "It can't be anything like he has on us."

"No, but—"

"But, nothing, Zero. If he goes to the fucking cops, they'll probably cut him a deal. Give him immunity from prosecution to testify against us."

"I hadn't considered that."

Sweat was boiling from Stadtler's face. "Shit, use your head man. We have to get outta town."

"Calm down."

"You fucking calm down."

"Please, we have time yet. There's more."

Stadtler shook his head. "Great."

Zero refreshed his drink. "Our Mr. Grimes has unfortunately taken his life. The scandal, guilt, perhaps."

"Killed himself?"

"Yes."

"Then it's only you and me. You can . . ." He stopped and rubbed his eyes. "You can do what you want, but I'm getting out of town. That girl upstairs . . ."

"She knows nothing. Her mind is blank."

"Yeah . . . but . . . she . . ." Stadtler's head was swimming. "I have to go . . . I don't . . . I don't feel well . . ."

"I think you'll stay."

Stadtler rose up, but he had no strength. Zero pushed him back down. "You'll stay and in time, you won't remember a thing."

He looked into Zero's eyes and the world went dark and he slumped unconscious. It never even occurred to him that he'd been drugged.

Zero brought him upstairs. "Goodbye, Mr. Stadtler," he said. "Next stop, a whole new you."

PEARL IN THE ROUGH

Sometimes it surprised Eddy the lengths he was willing to go to for a friend. It wasn't enough that he'd robbed Spider's apartment of books and other oddities. It wasn't enough that he'd stolen his corpse—and no easy task it was. Now he was getting meat for the bastard.

And he'd always thought such devotion was beyond him.

He put a gold loop earring in his right ear and wore a black longshoremen's chook and pea coat. His long, dark hair was now cut shoulder-length and he'd put on a false mustache and sideburns. He decided no one would recognize him. He wanted to look just like another fag fresh off the boats.

He chose a club named Smiley's that he knew was frequented by gays and pulled up a stool at the bar. It being just after noon, there were few people in there as yet. Less than a dozen older, unsightly queens dropped him rakish winks, but he ignored them. He found them sickening in their gowns and lace and crudely applied make-up, little of which did anything to hide the mileage under their garish hoods.

Eddy had a special type in mind.

Young, meaty, easy to control. A few swarthy young bucks tight with muscle and smooth asses propositioned him, but he declined. They whispered juvenile obscenities in his ears, trying to lure him into the lavatory for a quick round of buggery. But he didn't have time for fun and games, he was here on business. Any other time such simple amusement would've been acceptable, but not now. After some thirty minutes of laboring over a weak Bacardi and Coke, the right one sat down next to him. Plump with a shaven head and no gaudy attire. He looked rather like a businessman on lunch break with his somber gray suit and tie.

"Could I buy you a drink?" he asked meekly. "Friends call me Pearl."

Eddy smiled. Yes, this was the one. The subservient air about him was ideal. "Sure," he replied. "That'll do for starters."

Pearl blushed and placed the orders.

Eddy knew this one would do just as he was instructed and that was the way it had to be. Pearl, as he called himself, was a newcomer to the stage of rough trade. And that was something more in his favor. Eddy would play the part of the veteran queer and lead his young and eager quarry into what he thought were the secret realms of his own closet fantasy world. And Eddy himself, the seasoned maritime degenerate, would even indulge in a bit of dirty play with him before the knives came out and the messy work began.

They chatted for a time, Eddy and Pearl, but it was mostly a one-sided conversation in which Pearl spoke of the miseries of heterosexual relationships. And the more he drank, Eddy noted, the worse those miseries became. Soon enough, misery wasn't adequately descriptive of the hell he'd endured. Words like *atrocious, barbarous,* and *criminal* soon came into play. Pearl had suffered at the hands of women. As all men have, Eddy told him, suppressing a smile.

"That's women for you, mate," he said. "Every time they spread their legs, their meters are running. Gets so an honest swab like myself can't break off a piece of fun without paying the tab."

"Yes!" Pearl said. "Exactly."

"That's why a couple of shipmates like you and I can understand each other."

"And then some."

"Shall we take a walk?" Eddy offered in a lecherous voice.

"Where?"

"A little place I know. Not far," he said, then: "As the crow flies, mate." He was laying the sailor business on a bit thick, but he couldn't seem to stop. It was all endlessly amusing. It was all he could do to not burst out laughing with his own hammy performance, most of which was borrowed from bad movies, but Pearl didn't seem to notice.

They walked arm in arm, talking and laughing like two old friends thrown together by chance. They only paused once when Pearl said he could wait no longer. Alcohol had made him quite bold, so Eddy led him into an alley and Pearl unzipped him while he counted the bricks on the opposite wall.

"What do we have here?" Pearl said playfully, pulling Eddy's pants beyond his knees.

"A little treat," Eddy assured him.

Pearl went down on him with drunken abandon.

"Was that good?" Pearl inquired, flushed and wiping seed from his lips.

"Lovely."

"Want to do me?"

"Later."

Pearl nodded. "But it was good?"

"Yes."

"You're so much easier to please than my wife was. I'm glad you liked it."

Eddy moaned. "Oh, that was wonderful, mate. You'll have to ship out with me one day. Life on the water suits our kind."

"Is there many . . . with our tastes?" Pearl needed to know.

"More than not."

Eddy took a roundabout route to the house where Spider waited, in case they were being followed. On the way he told of his mythical adventures on the high seas. Of the intimacy men share in close quarters and the carefree days of sodomy and indulgence on a ship of fools. Pearl was beginning to talk as ludicrously as he before they reached their destination, spouting like some swabby from an old Warner Brothers picture.

Finally, the house: old, dark, decaying.

"This it, captain?" Pearl giggled.

"Aye, this be me lodgings," Eddy told him.

Pearl pushed drunkenly through the door. "Yo ho ho and a bottle of rum," he shouted in the black interior.

Eddy smiled. "And dead men tell no tales," he whispered under his breath. It was all so terribly easy, so effortless. Some things were just meant to be.

"Got anything to drink, captain?" Pearl asked when they were together in the living room. "Just one more would suit me fine."

The living room had no furnishings save for a sofa with a nasty lilt and a set of insect-ravaged curtains. There was a bottle of whiskey in the kitchen and Eddy fetched it, along with some ice and two glasses.

"You definitely need a woman's touch here," Pearl laughed.

"I only live here when I'm not on the boats."

"Still . . ."

It was a charmless old house and Eddy liked it that way. The Realtor had handed it over, as is, for a song. Given the neighborhood and the bad plumbing and ancient wiring, it was a fair deal. The place hadn't been lived in for two years. It was dusty, dirty, and decaying, just short of being condemned by the city. But it was home.

Eddy and Pearl sat on the sofa and drank. Pearl was quite intoxicated and whatever inhibitions he'd formerly held had long ago been washed away by the booze. He'd stripped himself down to his pants now and a word from Eddy and they'd go, too.

Pearl leaned against him and brushed his lips with his own. His eyes were rheumy and unfocused. One good blow would put him out for the night and so much the better. His fingers played at Eddy's crotch.

"Again?" he asked.

"Something better," Eddy told him and helped him up. "Follow me."

Pearl did, holding onto Eddy's hand and nibbling drunkenly at his neck. Eddy brought him across the room to a set of oak sliding doors. They might have been grand things at one time, but now they were defaced with names and initials and crude drawings. A reek of cat piss hung in the air.

"Have you a pussy about?" Pearl asked.

They both laughed.

Eddy opened the doors.

"What's in here, captain? Is this where you bury your treasure?" Pearl giggled.

"Yes, my treasure, it is."

They went in and Eddy closed the doors. He turned on the light, a single bare bulb protruding from an ancient fixture on the wall.

"Dim in here, captain." Pearl looked around. He pointed to a mattress shoved in the corner. "Is that where you sleep?"

"No, not me. Take off your pants."

"I never disobey an order," Pearl told him and begin to slip from his pants and underwear. He dropped them to the floor in a heap and fondled his length. He seemed quite impressed with himself.

There was movement behind him, a shuffling of feet. He turned and stared at the shape shambling out to meet him. He didn't scream or even gasp, he just swayed on his bit of floor and wondered if he was seeing this at all.

"Nice," Spider said, "very nice. We like it."

Pearl made a gagging noise and stumbled to one knee. Spider took a step forward and Pearl stared, his erection gone limp. What was it he was even looking at? A man? A man with skin the color of gray ash, his slashed open throat stitched crudely shut like a second disobedient mouth? His hair like a nest of serpents, braided, beaded, hanging in wild filthy strands that crawled with insect life? Was he even seeing this? And despite the intoxication that swam with a low, maddening hum in his brain, he knew he was. This thing was real, it lived . . . or had at some point. A stink of rot and pungent sweetness enveloped it in an appalling cloud. And its eyes, black, loveless holes drilled into the tombstone face, held no hint of humanity or compassion. They were miasmic alien dreams suffused with a glaring, ugly hunger.

"My God," Pearl managed.

When the nightmare spoke, its pitted lips cracked open like sores and a vicious tongue tasted the air. "Where did you find this?" it asked in the voice of a woman. And answered itself in the voice of a child: "Somewhere special, I think."

Eddy grinned like a cat. This was a special moment and he savored its depravity as one must do with all such moments. The fear, the total hopelessness in Pearl's rolling eyes gave him a lust that was boundless.

"What in the name of Christ is this?" Pearl cried. His voice was kept from total hysteria by the alcohol that deadened his senses.

"It's a game," Eddy said.

"Yes, a game," the ghoul said, gliding forward. "See all the pretty work?" It opened the ragged overcoat it wore. The exposed, graying torso had been slit from belly to ribs and stitched neatly back up. Patches of fungus clung to the chest. "Would you like to see the secrets inside?"

Pearl said nothing. Tears began to run from his eyes. He looked this way and that and saw no escape route.

Eddy slid a knife from his pocket. "You're meat," he said.

Pearl screamed and jumped to his feet. Spider put one cold, stiff hand over his mouth and drew a razor over his throat. Pearl went back to his knees, gulping for air and drawing only blood. Eddy came forward and opened his belly with an expert thrust of his knife.

The blood seemed to be everywhere within moments, spreading over the floor in a glistening pool. An electricity crackled in the air.

Eddy watched as Pearl died. There was a beauty in death, an art in gruesome slaughter and, he supposed, he wasn't the first to know this. The history of mankind was written in red and described in suffering. It was the only absolute of existence, that death would come and often it wasn't pleasant.

Spider grasped Pearl's head and ran his fingers over it. He seemed to be checking it over very closely, as he'd done with others they'd made sacrifice of.

"What now?" Eddy asked.

"A little taste," Spider told him. "And then some more."

Eddy watched him, watched the Shadows crawl over and through him. Spider was their vessel now. They had a place to call home and he supposed that's all they ever really wanted. If it hadn't been for them and the secrets Cassandra had gleaned from the books, Spider wouldn't be walking at all now. Regardless, he was a horror to behold.

He placed an arrangement of knives around the body and set to work with a scalpel, opening vertical slashes and humming to himself as he did so. He didn't remove anything, he seemed only concerned with opening up the skin and exposing the bounty which lay beneath.

Eddy grew bored after a time and gathered up Pearl's clothes and took them into the other room. He put all the dead man's belongings in the hearth and soaked them with lighter fluid and watched them burn. He fed logs and shredded newspaper to the flames to keep the blaze going. Soon, there was nothing but ash left of the garments. He lit a cigarette and went back to see how Spider was doing.

Spider was slitting his sutures and opening himself like a book. He squatted over the carved body and looked up as Eddy came in.

"What are you doing?"

Spider grinned. "What do you think I'm doing?" he asked. "Did you think I was going to eat him with my mouth? I have no internals."

Eddy nodded. He'd watched Cassandra remove Spider's viscera himself and replace it with the things the books had alluded to: salts, spices, powders, and knotted sacs of herb, cat gut, grave dirt. All the things Spider had stored in his refrigerator. He supposed all things living, and even those pretending to live, had to gather sustenance somehow. And ways had to be invented.

It started with a moaning wind and a shriek of discarnate voices that sent eddies of dust swirling around the cadaver. The floor boards began to rattle, the ceiling seemed to bow and groan. Eddy looked on, fascinated. He could feel it in himself, the hungry pull that emanated from Spider's body cavity. His own flesh trembled on his bones. And if that's what it was doing to him, what it did to Pearl's cadaver was something else entirely. His body trembled and thumped on the floor, the skin shuddering madly as if there were rivers of ants moving just beneath it. It came apart with a sodden ripping, atomizing into a viscid mist that was sucked free and absorbed into Spider's body. A channel was dug in the torso and its matter vacuumed free, muscle and organ and connective tissue disintegrating into a spray. Eddy studied the proceedings with gaping eyes as blood steamed in the air and meat was boiled into gas. Pearl was effortlessly stripped down to hissing bone and even that shattered and came apart as marrow was ingested. The great sucking wind yanked at the boards beneath and withdrew nails and splinters of wood and only then did it stop.

Spider stood and a variety of things spilled from his fluttering, stormy innards: fingernails and crushed bits of bone and then teeth. There was no meat left on the corpse, even the skeleton had been pitted and dehydrated to withered deadwood.

It had all taken only a few moments.

"Incredible," Eddy found himself saying.

"Pretty, isn't it?"

There were laughter and screams that died out as Spider stitched himself back up with nimble fingers. The Shadows were rejoicing now, carrying on with wild abandon as they fought like mad dogs over Pearl's soul in the vacuous spaces of Spider's flesh.

Eddy lit another cigarette. "How soon will you need another?"

"Not for a few days."

"Good. There's work to be done tonight."

Spider smiled and desiccated rents in his lips tore open. "Bring the whores back here, so I can help. It wouldn't be good for me to go out just yet."

"Right."

"Don't leave me out, Eddy. I want to go too, when the time comes. If it wasn't for me, you'd never have gotten this close. Remember that."

"Of course."

Spider didn't seem reassured. "And remember I can do to you what I did to that," he warned, pointing at the husk at his feet.

Eddy laughed. "And if you try, I'll cut you apart and put you back where I found you."

Spider took a step back.

Eddy went to the doors. "And don't come out unless I tell you to. You smell really bad." He closed the doors and locked them and settled down on the sofa for a drink.

It wouldn't be long now.

*　　*　　*

"It was quite a sight," Eddy told Cassandra when she'd returned from her dinner. "Quite disgusting."

"All things have to eat, Eddy. It's a law of nature."

"Even dead things?" he put to her. "What about you?"

"I have a very healthy appetite."

"I'd like you to come to the Territories with me," he told her. "You wouldn't really be dead there anymore than I'd be alive."

"Maybe."

"You and I, Spider, perhaps another."

"Who?"

He grinned secretly. "You don't know her. Name's Lisa Lochmere. A fucking psychiatrist. She played some head games on me once and I'd like to repay the debt. We could have fun with her. She's in town now, looking for me, so I hear. She's got a hot, hungry little slit between her legs and all the goodies to go with it."

Cassandra wasn't paying any attention. Her hand was busy working him to erection. Her touch still filled him with desire.

"I've been thinking about this for some time," she said. "Let's go in the bedroom."

As he sat on the bed, she stood and slipped from her dress. She was beautiful as ever, though somewhat pale. Even the autopsy stitching up her torso was enticing somehow. Eddy buried his face between her breasts. They were cool, but powdered and perfumed just so. Her nipples tasted sweet.

"Death suits you," he whispered.

She kissed him and freed him from his pants, pushing him back on the bed and mounting him.

"By God," she said. "You're warm."

She rode him fiercely until he came, sucking his warmth and seed up into herself where it lit fireworks inside. It was only then that she rocked and moaned with orgasm.

He closed his eyes and dozed. As he slept, she stroked his hair and cooed a sweet song in his ear.

Life was good.

* * *

He woke sometime later and she was still there, holding him like a babe.

"I must've nodded off," he said.

"For several hours," she informed him.

"I have to go out tonight. A few more and off we'll go into the Territories."

"Can I help?"

"No, I'd best do this alone. But there is something you can do."

"Yes?"

"Do you remember who our enemy is? The nosy one always prying into other's affairs?"

"Who could forget?"

"Pay him a visit."

Cassandra decided she would. If a life had to be taken, then it best be someone who had no reason to live.

DELIVERANCE

"Soames."

He'd heard his name spoken, hadn't he? He opened his eyes and looked around. There was someone standing in the doorway. A woman.

He felt he could barely breathe because this was the moment he'd been waiting for.

"Who are you?" he asked.

"My name isn't important."

"No, why would it be?" he found himself saying. This woman was his assassin and did he really need to know who she was? The other patients in the ward were sleeping, drugged and still. Nothing would wake them. Not even his screams, if and when they came. Whoever this person was, she was slick. Getting in here like this and choosing a time of night when no one could be woken.

But why did I wake?

Because, he knew, even full of drugs, he rarely slept. His mind was constantly on edge, waiting for this moment.

"What do you want?"

"I've come for you."

"Who sent you? The doctor? Was it the doctor?"

She laughed. "I'm afraid not. Another."

He wanted to laugh, too, and he didn't know why. Maybe it was because his life was such a dark and dreary mistake, such a comedy of errors. Only laughter seemed appropriate in this final hour.

"Another, you say." He laughed again. "Yeah, why not?"

"It's only fair."

"So get on with it."

She stepped forward, no malice in her actions, only necessity. Light was spilling in from the doorway, illuminating her. She was a lovely girl, this one . . . or was she? He was staring at her and knowing something was dreadfully wrong, but not what. Then he saw. It was her face. The very appearance of it. The flesh was wrong, discolored a bit, and the way it lay over the bones beneath . . . uneven, pitted. Make-up, he decided. She was wearing latex and paint and putty to conceal her identity.

If nothing more, he'd see that face before she snuffed out his life.

"Let's see who and what you are," he said under his breath. She leaned over him, not hearing a word. His hands were free now. They'd taken the restraints off this morning. His fingers hooked into claws and went at her face.

The woman uttered a mild gasp as his fingertips found seams and pulled strips of latex and globs of wax free. Oh, now that was a mistake, wasn't it? Her skin—what there was of it—was leathery and shredded, sliced and gouged. The mutilated musculature beneath was stretched taut and bloodless over a finely proportioned skull. A living anatomy print.

"You shouldn't have done that," she said. "There's nothing to be gained."

"Dead," he moaned. "You're dead. Make me as you are. It's all I've wanted. For so long, it's all I've dreamed about."

"Yes. No more pain. I won't allow it."

Her cold hands were on his shoulders now, tightening with grave rictus. He felt bones snap but there was no true pain, only release. Tears were falling from his eyes now and whimpers from his lips.

"It would've been easier dying at the hands of a pretty girl," the skull said, an odor of heavy perfumes and sweet powders masking something terrible beneath.

Soames gaped and never really understood.

"But you chose this," she cooed in his face, her tattered lips inches from his own, her breath sour and sweet and sickening. "A kiss before dying."

Her decayed mouth pressed against his own and a strip of flesh ripped free and stayed on his lips. He never screamed; he was way beyond that. She suctioned her mouth over his and sucked the breath from his lungs until his eyes rolled back and his face was blue-tinged. Then it was over.

*   *   *

It was less than an hour before they found his body. The nurse never thought anything at first. In the dim light, he was a man sleeping in peace. Upon closer examination, his face gave the game away.

The nurse looked him over quickly and sought out her superior to announce a death on the ward.

She did this all very calmly.

For death was nothing new here.

*   *   *

After Cassandra had fixed her face, she returned to Eddy.

"It's done," she said.

"After all this time, he's at peace."

Eddy looked content, truly content. It was as if a great burden had been lifted from his shoulders. He closed his eyes and allowed himself the self-indulgence of a satisfied smirk.

"Did he take it well?"

"He didn't fight. There was no violence. Just an end. He was anxious for it, the poor thing."

"He'll rest now."

Eddy kissed her and they sat together for some time, contemplating the future. That and what it might bring.

Life was rich.

BOOK OF HELL

Lisa wasn't sure why she'd come back to the house. There was curiosity, of course, and lots of it. But she'd thought the fear that had eaten her up since Fenn had dragged her away the last time would be enough to keep her away. Regardless, she was back, sitting in her car just up the street. Watching the house. Waiting, perhaps, for it to rise up and give chase.

She didn't have the nerve to go in.

She only wanted to study it from afar and see if she could make sense of any of it. But there was no sense to be had and she abandoned such naïve ideas moments after pulling up to the curb.

It hadn't been easy getting away.

The past two days since the incident at the House of Mirrors had been aggravating ones. Fenn had been with her every moment when he wasn't on duty, feeding her soup and stroking her hair and lording over her like a big brother. And when he was gone, he seemed to call every thirty minutes to see if she was okay. She was beginning to find his constant doting as hard to take as the return of William Zero.

His heart was in the right place, but his constant vigilance was stifling. There was just too much to be done to be a prisoner of his affections. He knew nothing of what she'd experienced. The transmitter had failed due to mechanical difficulty just as her watch had when the Territories opened up. Her scientific bent of mind told her that two dimensions interfacing must have produced a prodigious amount of electromagnetic energy, forces that contemporary physics were probably ignorant of.

Fenn. Poor, dear, sweet Fenn. He was in love with her, his head filled with dreams of bright and happy domesticity. He saw a future for them. A house. Lives intertwined. Maybe even children. But it would never come to pass. She knew that just as she knew she did not love him. A simple tranquil existence was beyond her. Twisted desires and obscene appetites were wrestling for possession of her soul like dogs fighting over a juicy bone. There was no denying them. If she let him get closer, there would only be heartbreak for him.

If he discovered who she really was it would destroy him.

His attentions were flattering, but stifling and suffocating.

When he went back to the station after spending his lunch with her, she made her move. Even as she drove off into the afternoon traffic, she wondered if she was being followed by some of his men. It was the sort of thing he'd do, blinded by infatuation and burning with protective instincts. She saw no cars that seemed to be tailing her, but then, she doubted that she would have seen them.

She'd been parked for nearly an hour now and only one or two cars had passed. Fenn was probably worrying and ready to send out the Calvary now that she wasn't there to answer his calls.

If he was half as smart as he pretends to be, he'd know exactly where you went. How you couldn't keep away.

There was no denying what had happened at the house. She'd seen William Zero and what appeared to be the threshold of the Territories. She knew what purpose the mirrors served—they were doorways of a sort. Such things shouldn't be and yet they were. Fine. She accepted that man's knowledge of reality was rather limited. The thing she wanted to know was *why* Zero had returned. What did he want? Was it his son or was he back to start on a fresh binge of crimes? If that was the case, she would tell Fenn the truth and they would stop him. But could he be stopped? Something that appeared to have been dissected and yet lived? If being taken apart and reassembled hadn't deadened the life in him, what good would police and bullets do?

The answers to these questions wouldn't be gathered hiding in a car. She stepped out and kept her hand on the .38 in her pocket. She was going in, God help her. If she didn't lose her mind this time, then maybe there wasn't one to lose at all.

She marched up the steps and went in, leaving the door open for a hasty retreat. It was silent within, as she knew it must be. Her mind relived her last visit and she quickly shrugged it aside. She looked around downstairs, unable to go up just yet. Her breath came quick, her skin cool and clammy. She was afraid and it wasn't a bad thing, it kept her vigilant.

Finally, she climbed the stairs, her heart filling her throat.

It seemed to take an eternity to reach the second floor landing and another to find the attic door. It was closed. Again, she wondered if she'd shut it or someone else had. Not that it mattered. She opened it and started up.

She knew she wasn't alone long before she reached the top. It was a dread feeling that started in her belly and spread through her limbs. By the time she reached the landing, her legs threatened to collapse beneath her. A stink of death filled her nostrils and she soon saw why: there was a body lying mere feet from her. It reminded her of the animal bodies she'd seen—horribly wasted and stripped of flesh. But this one had been human. Man or woman, she couldn't say. There was precious little left but ravaged bone and withered bits of clothing. She fought back an urge to vomit. It was something she needed to do, but she couldn't allow it, not until she'd spoken with the man who did this.

The attic wasn't swallowed by the Territories as before, perhaps the sunlight feeding in through the broken shutters and the fissures in the roof was keeping it at bay. It occupied only the full-length mirror now, a shifting curtain of black that was hypnotic in its very insane texture and promise. She could hear what it must be like in that awful place—screams, sobbings, cold laughter, a discordant singing of many suffering voices. That and the constant shriek of some demon wind that set her nerves on edge.

"Are you here?" she managed, moving no further into the room, afraid that the hungry vortex would suck her in.

"Yes." A voice from the darkness beyond the glass.

"Show yourself."

"Come and find me." A peal of cruel laughter.

"No."

She saw him now, walking towards the mirror, polluted mists the color of leaden ash swirling about him. He seemed very far away, despite how near his voice had sounded. It took him scant seconds to reach the attic. The physical laws were apparently quite different in that terrible place. He passed through the glass, the breach of worlds, with a subtle ripping sound as if two blankets charged with static electricity were suddenly separated. The good doctor was no more attractive than before, just a pieced together thing pretending humanity. He was wasted and festering, numerous incisions beginning to bleed now that he'd left the chasm where certain laws were suspended.

"You've come to see me, Lisa, and here I am," he said.

"What," she began, her lungs devoid of breath, "do you want here?"

Zero took a few steps forward, but no more. Drops of blood struck the floor at his feet. He smiled and she heard sutures, both within and without, popping their dusty seams. His eyes fixed her own. There was a cold and malignant appetite in them, particularly the yellow one which was like the eye of a rabid wolf.

He looked down at the leeched body. "A transient," he explained, "looking for shelter."

"You murdered him?"

"I was hungry," he told her and said no more, as if that was explanation enough. And it was; she had no interest in the details.

Zero shook his head, as if mourning the bones before her or perhaps his own blighted soul. "A pity," he said.

She felt nothing but hatred for him now, as she supposed she always had since learning of his true calling.

"My love for you never diminished," he told her. "I kept it here." He pressed two waxy fingers to his chest. The nails were dirty and ragged as if he'd been digging in the dirt. "I've kept it safe."

Madness tickled her brain at the idea of this monstrosity pining away for her. Was this the reason he'd returned? *For her?*

"I watched you each time you came to this house. Through the mirror I saw you. Your beauty still takes my breath away. I'd almost forgotten how much I loved you."

The impulse to retch was almost overpowering. How could such a thing know of love? The idea of this horror from a dissection table loving her was enough to make her sanity bleed and run.

"You . . . toyed with me that day, didn't you? You left the cigarette burning downstairs."

"A reminder. I thought then you'd know I'd come back."

"Why did you come back?"

"For you, my love."

No, she couldn't accept that. She couldn't accept him loving her or even thinking about her. It made her feel filthy, drained of hope and life. Her head reeled with dizziness and her stomach convulsed with nausea.

Her legs decided to run, but it was too late. He was already on her, Dr. Blood-and-Bones, the butcher of butchers. His left hand seized her arm and his right stroked her cheek with leathery fingers. The sutured, disjointed face closed in on her own, his gashed lips seeking a kiss. His teeth were like yellow nubs. She screamed and fought in his grip.

"There's plenty of time for romance," he promised, his breath like old meat.

He was terribly strong, stronger than anyone had the right to be. Her struggles were nearly useless. He dragged her effortlessly towards the chasm, whispering obscenities under his sour breath that she didn't dare listen to. Her fingers lost their instinctive repulsion of him and saw only survival. They scratched over his mummified face and loosened flaps of skin and broke stitches. He shook his head frantically to keep her nails away, but she kept on, tearing and clawing until he dropped her at his feet with a cry of anger. She was preciously close to the mouth of the chasm and she could feel its pull drawing her over the dusty floor. Her foot was sucked into the mirror and she could feel the Territories crawling in infectious waves. The other side was freezing. She fought free and crawled out of harm's way.

Dr. Blood-and-Bones was repairing the damage she'd done to his face, nimbly stitching himself back up. "You are full of life," he said with some-thing like joy. "Just as I remembered."

Lisa found herself unable to move. The strength had been tapped from her limbs and she could only lay there and wait for his attentions. She recognized the physical and psychological signs, knowing she was either in shock or quite near to it. The sight of the peeled cadaver and the stink of its wormy decay made her stomach heave. The knowledge of what Zero said and what he intended to do completed the process. She vomited and the very action of it freed both her mind and her stillborn limbs.

She stood and faced her tormentor, her fingers pulling the gun from her pocket. It might not kill him, but it would definitely make getting her a difficult proposition.

"Come now, Lisa," the ghoul said. "You've waited just as I have."

"Get away from me."

Zero took one defiant step toward her. He was maimed and bleeding from innumerable holes in his ruptured carcass. His desire was evident, it twisted in the air between them.

"Don't you recall how it was?" he asked.

"Yes," she said, not sure if she was lying or telling the truth, "it was a living hell."

"Hell?" he spat. "You don't know what hell is. But you'll learn soon enough."

Visions were swimming in her mind. Of the afternoons they'd spent chatting and viewing old movies. Of the secret tryst they'd shared. Of the love she'd freely and desperately given and he'd taken. Of the way he really was and the way she thought he would be. Of the perversions he'd inflicted on her, twisting her susceptible psyche into one that could know no real love, only abuse and debased yearnings.

"You sicken me," she told him point blank. "You used a naïve teenager, exploiting her at her weakest moment. You made me hate myself."

He licked his lips with a leprous tongue. "I made you into the woman you are."

"You made me become what I am. I studied the mind because I was so disgusted by my own. And then I found out about you, who you really were. A weak little man with a mind of filth, a butcher, a mur—"

"An artist."

"Butcher. Nothing more," she said. "I hated the memory of you then."

"And now?"

"Pity. I only feel pity for you. You're pathetic."

"In time," he said, edging closer, "you'll feel differently."

And now the time had come, her mind let her know. He was blocking the stairs and the chasm was directly behind her. He was working himself forward, by mere inches, hoping she'd retreat and be swallowed in the black throat of his world. But it wouldn't happen. She stood her ground and prepared to fire. It wasn't an easy thing to shoot another, surely not as easy as it appeared on television where bullet-ridden bodies fell with no remorse. This was reality and her sense of morality, of civilization, stayed her finger.

He held his hands out before him, clutching, ready to squeeze the swell of her breasts.

She began to squeeze the trigger. If he didn't fall, then she'd press the muzzle to her own temple. Better suicide than those withered fingers stroking her flesh.

"Don't be afraid," he cooed, standing directly before her. His fingers found the cones of her breasts and pressed into them. She felt a breath of heat rise from memory, but present reality dissolved it into revulsion. "Nice, very nice."

She pulled the trigger with a jerk of disgust. The explosion was deafening and the impact pushed him away. But he was still smiling like a lecherous zombie.

"Pain," he said almost tenderly. "Nothing new to me. It seems more real here, more desperate." He fingered the hole in his belly as if it were a woman's sex.

"Bastard . . ." The word slipped free with a hissing sibilance. She hadn't thought it, it was only a truth set free.

"I used to dream of this moment. But I thought it would never come. As they broke and destroyed me, I never forgot about our times together. Even when they made me like them, I still thought of you." He looked almost sad for a moment, a glint of despair blazing in his eye like that of a lost child. It died quickly. "I never thought we'd meet again. But the fates want us together, I think. And who are we to deny them?"

He wasn't lying. She knew that now. It wasn't a simple threat, an abomination to wave before her bulging eyes. It was true. He had thought of her, dreamed of her. All the while she built up her life and tried to forget, pretend that it hadn't happened, she was in his thoughts. As his new masters plied their profane crafts to his flesh, he thought of her and what they'd done together. If there'd been anything left in her stomach, this would have purged it.

He reached out for her again.

Her sanity had endured this long and she wouldn't forfeit it now. She would protect it like a helpless child.

She pulled the trigger again. And then, two more times after that. Zero jerked back like a puppet with clipped strings. His face mangled into a mask of anger. The bullets had bored through him as if he were made of dry wood, spilling blood and decay to his feet. She ran then, slipping out of his grasp and tumbling down the stairs. The gun was still in her hand when she found her feet and kicked through the door.

She stumbled up the hallway, knowing that it was far from over. But if she could just reach the stairs and throw herself down them, surely he wouldn't follow out into the light where the real world would rend apart a thing like him. But she never made it to the stairs. The wall directly before her began to creak and moan, unlocking itself and rearranging its atoms. Zero was slipping through, oozing forth in a tide of corruption like maggots from rotten pork. He shifted and shuddered and reassembled his mass in time to stop her.

"It won't be that easy," he promised. "No more games, my sweet. I saw the note you scribbled on the wall. You left it for me."

No, no, he didn't understand at all and she didn't have the strength to explain.

He came on and she emptied the remaining bullets into his noisome hide and he shrugged them off. The slugs fell from his gaping wounds and dropped to the floor. Lisa screamed and hammered at his face with the butt of the gun to no avail. His fists came down and she collapsed on her back.

"Now, I'll take what I want," he assured her in a vile tone.

And she knew what he intended. It was lunacy, sheer and utter, but she could expect nothing less in this hopping ground between two worlds. Through the ages, countless women had been overpowered and raped by men. It was a testament to their resilience that most survived this indignity of indignities. But Lisa knew there would be no surviving this, no possibility her sanity could endure something so totally decadent and loathsome. If Zero had his way with her, life and laughter were things of the past.

A carnal grin played over his mouth. "Just like it used to be," he told her, advancing. "I'll show you things you never dreamed of."

She was lying on the floor and Zero was crouched over her now. She could smell the hideous musk of his sex, feel the bloated bulge in his trousers. Waves of reeking heat came from the cuts and gashes of his skin. It made her positively giddy with disgust. She pushed against him, but he was irresistible. His fingers parted her coat, tore open her blouse and bra, roughly kneading her nipples. She felt something under her hand, a weight in his pocket. As he poured his attentions on her, she dug it out. It was a book.

"That's not for you," he said, making a grab for it.

She tucked and rolled, cradling the book in her arms. There was fear in his eyes now. There was no mistaking it.

It was a smallish volume, bound in greasy, pale skin. She had a good idea what kind. There seemed to be diary entries within. That and something like mathematical symbols scrawled over the pages. But it was no math of this world.

He came on, slowly, afraid she'd bolt. "Give the book to me," he said. "It has no use for you."

"No." The answer was flat, decisive. She had power in her hands, but of what sort?

"I want it."

She grasped a page between her thumb and first finger. It was damp, pungent paper and it seemed to crawl beneath her touch as if it were infested with tiny parasites. She started to tear it.

"NO!" he howled. "Don't do that! The passage . . ."

She stepped around him and started down the stairs, her eyes never off him, her fingers ready to shred the rancid pages. He followed her down, but at a safe distance.

"Please," he begged when she was at the door, "the book. Give it to me."

She opened the door and said, "No," and fled into the light. She raced down the steps and into the street. Zero didn't follow as she suspected he wouldn't. When she was in the car and the book was lying on the passenger seat, bathed by sunlight, she noticed what was happening to it. A stinking vapor was beginning to rise from it as if it were decomposing. She covered it with her coat and the dissolution ceased.

She raced back to her hotel with her bounty, realizing for the first time in her life she had the upper hand.

But what to do with it?

That was the question.

LETTERS FROM HELL (7)

Dear Eddy,

I don't suppose we should've killed that cop.

But what choice did we have? Our romance would have ended there and then had we tried to talk our way out of it. You know how cops are. Always asking questions, nosing into things that don't concern them.

He bled all over me after I cut his throat. I didn't mind the blood so much, but it got all over the seats. That was the bad thing. I remember we dumped him in the parking lot and danced together as the rain washed us clean.

"We'd better go," you finally said.

I knew you were right. He'd probably radioed in our plates and the dispatcher was waiting for a reply.

We got back out on the highway and I knew our time was limited now. Soon, they'd be hunting us. They were already after me. Now they'd be after you, too. Oh, how the bastards would have loved to get us back in a hospital where they could pick at the locks of our skulls for secrets. But they'd get none. Because they weren't going to get us. I decided that there and then as we cruised up the highway and I studied your pale face as we drove. We didn't talk much, you and I. We didn't need to. Communication wasn't a spoken thing for us, but something far beyond that, an exchange of thoughts and ideas. That's the way it is with real lovers, you know. They just know what the other thinks and feels.

And our love was pure.

Completely.

Those bastards wouldn't get us. I'd decided I'd kill you first and then myself if necessary.

"Let's stop," I said.

You nodded and pulled off the highway into a country lane. The trees were huge and the rain was coming down in sheets. You drove in until we were invisible from the highway.

I remember looking at the map I found in the glove compartment. I knew in a moment where we had to go.

It was perfect. We didn't leave then, though.

"Let's do it here," I said.

And you loved me while the rain pounded on the roof.

Beautiful.

Yours,

Cherry

MEMOIRS OF THE TEMPLAR SOCIETY (7)

When Stadtler woke, he was in darkness.

It took him some time to orient himself and remember exactly what had happened. His head was throbbing. Zero had drugged him. He knew that much. And now he was chained-up in one of the rooms upstairs. He was about to become a guinea pig. Zero wanted to cleanse his mind of identity and memory. But why? None of it made sense.

Stadtler was a reasoning man.

He wouldn't beg.

He wouldn't be broken.

Every cage had a hole and he'd find it and press himself through.

But how long might that take to find said hole? Hours? Weeks? Months? And in the meantime, what of his sanity? Would it begin to come apart? Like a house of cards would it slowly weaken and finally collapse, unable to endure its own uneasy weight?

Alone.

He was alone and would be for some time. He'd never really been alone before with just his thoughts and memories for companionship. Few people ever were, he figured. There's always the sounds of life nearby: the blaring of a TV, the passing of a car, voices shouting in the distance, birds singing in the trees . . . but where he was there was nothing but silence and utter darkness. No sensory input, no distractions whatsoever. Only silence and thinking and nothing to get in the way of either.

Stadtler began to panic.

He was naked and chained to the floor. He began to pull at his leash, straining against it with all his might while his tongue betrayed him and began to shout and curse. He hammered at the mirrors on the wall and called Zero's name until his throat was hoarse.

Stop it, he told himself, this is exactly what he wants you to do.

But he couldn't help himself. He'd seen the indignities Gina had suffered first hand. The cloying, terrible loneliness; the barbarity of living like a caged animal; the scraps of food tossed to her as if she were a mad dog. And although he'd told himself he would never, under the same circumstances, lower himself to begging or crying, he was doing just that now.

And the most infuriating part of it all was that Zero was watching it all. And soon, the bastard would flip the switch and the light overhead—a single bulb painted red—would begin to flash on and off without end. Then there'd be days of darkness. Then would come the starvation, days upon days of it. And when a few scraps of meat were tossed to him, they would be full of psychotropic drugs that would further unhinge his already weakening mind. Gina had refused the meat at first . . . but eventually hunger had gotten the best of her as it would get the best of him.

Everything carefully calculated to break his will.

To wipe his mind clean.

After a week or so of nothing but the bulb flashing, Zero would begin playing the first recording. It was nothing but dead air recorded from the radio. Mindless static. And that would be played softly for days, gradually the volume would be increased until . . . until . . . until—

Until I go mad.

Stadtler couldn't accept the possibility of that. He started fighting at the chains anew and bashing at the walls with his fists and finally his head until the mirrors shattered and he fell broken and bloody to the floor.

And lost consciousness.

And time dragged on and on and on.

LITTLE GIRL LOST

Some hours after Lisa had left the House of Mirrors, she had a visitor. She was huddled in her bed, studying Zero's book, when she heard a key card slip into the door slot and the door was opened. Fenn? No, she knew—somehow—it wasn't him.

She was right.

It was Cherry Hill.

"No, don't get up," Cherry said as she stepped into the bedroom. "Lie quiet and relax. Isn't that how it used to go? Just lie quiet."

"Cherry." Lisa said this and nothing more. There was nothing else to say. Somehow, even before the phone call, she'd suspected this was going to happen. Inside, she was shriveled white because she knew very well the sort of lunatic her visitor was and exactly what she was capable of. Outwardly, she maintained her demeanor—calm, cool, non-threatening. If Cherry sensed fear, she would exploit it.

"You look tired, Dr. Lisa. Have you been getting enough rest?" She laughed. "No, I don't suppose you have. Still chasing Eddy Zero. Tsk. Tsk."

"What do you want, Cherry?"

"To talk."

"How did you get a key card to my suite?"

Cherry sat on the edge of the bed. "That was easy enough. You'd be surprised what a little flirtation can get you, Dr. Lisa."

Dr. Lisa. Once upon a time, it was Cherry's pet name for her. It had seemed almost cute once. Now it was oddly disturbing. "So say what you came to say, Cherry. I have work to do."

"In time."

"Say what you have to say, Cherry. Then you need to leave."

Cherry's eyes narrowed. "Don't push me, Dr. Lisa. I don't like being backed into corners. I react in the worst possible ways."

Lisa sat up. "You're still a fugitive from justice. Need I remind you of that?"

"If you turn me in, you turn yourself in." Cherry didn't seem concerned. She was studying her nails and polishing them against her skirt. "You don't want that, do you?"

Lisa knew she was right. The police wouldn't think highly of what she'd done. "I'm willing to take that chance, are you?"

Cherry was filing her nails with a silver emery board now. It was long and quite sharp. "So, call the police, Doctor. Only remember that I'm very dangerous and you never know what might set off a psychotic episode in me."

Again, Cherry was right. Lisa knew her all too well. She was prone to violent outbursts at the drop of hat. It was important to remember she was dealing with a criminally insane mind. "Say what you came to say, Cherry. I'm listening."

"That's better. I always liked you best when you were cooperative."

Lisa tried to remain calm. She wanted to shout at Cherry, to scream, but that wouldn't do at all. Her past had come back to haunt her and in Cherry she saw the physical embodiment of that little fact. Watch what you're doing, she cautioned herself. She didn't take out that nail file just to do her nails. There's a warning implied by it.

"I want you to stop, Lisa. I want you to get the hell out of this town right now before it's too late," Cherry told her. "If you like living at all, get out before you lose your breath."

"Is this a threat?"

"Yes."

"You know where Eddy is, don't you?"

She smiled, cocking her head to the side. "He's quite close, I think. Only I stand between the two of you. Only I keep him from doing something very nasty to you. I cared for you once, Lisa. Despite the fact that you used me like a guinea pig, I did care for you. So, please go away."

Lisa didn't know what to think. Cherry looked to be near tears. She sensed a certain honesty in them. But it was too late to run now. William Zero was back and his presence paled all other dangers. Cherry and Eddy seemed almost comical in comparison.

"I can't, Cherry. I have to stop Eddy."

"I'm sorry, then. I really am."

"Why?"

"Because you're going to die."

"If you know where he is—"

"He's worked very long and very hard for what's going to happen next. And he doesn't want you messing it up. Your appearance here, at this time, is very bad."

"What *is* going to happen next?"

Cherry regained her composure. Gone was the sincerity, gone was the humanity, the concern. Her eyes had gone flat and predatory now. They were cold and reptilian. "He's near and before long he'll come for you."

"You'd better leave."

"Save yourself, Lisa. It's not too late."

Cherry left and Lisa wanted to cry, but tears were beyond her now.

*   *   *

That night, for Lisa, there was no sleep. Each time she closed her eyes, she saw him, she saw her personal bogeyman drifting in for a kiss. She could feel his swollen lips pressing against her own, the tongue jutting from his crooked mouth as it licked her face.

Sleep was something she'd always taken for granted, like reality. But when one is shattered, the other stands no possibility of survival. She was sitting in her hotel room, trembling, wondering if even now Dr. Blood-and-Bones was calculating some fresh mode of portal that would carry him into her sanctuary for the love so long denied. Given time, she felt certain he would find a way to her. He was nothing if not patient, if not infinitely clever. He'd been sucked into the abyss some twenty years before and now, according to his little notebook, he had solved the riddle of escape. He could come and go as he pleased, all through the operation of some alien mathematical theorem. And that was no doubt why he wanted the book so badly: those cryptic symbols and configurations were the key. Without them, his door was either permanently open or he was trapped in this sphere of existence. Perhaps both.

Mirrors now made her uneasy. She could barely stand being near one, always fearing a stitched and seamed hand might reach out for her.

But, despite this, her thoughts were centered on the book.

She'd considered more than once of bringing the book and its mysteries to some mathematician or theorist and letting them have a look. Chances were, it would take them time to divine its operations and variables. And to what end? To place dangerous, forbidden knowledge in the hands of misguided intellectuals who might sever the fabric of reality or of time itself? No. The book had to be destroyed. But not until William Zero was exiled back into the Territories.

Reading entries and pouring over the computations with her own limited knowledge of differential equations, she was struck by the fact that there was nothing supernatural whatsoever involved here. Hadn't she once read that certain spells and conjurations of witchcraft bore an unsettling resemblance to certain operations of theoretical physics? Zero kept referring to the Territories as a world between worlds and that got her to thinking that it was perhaps a loop in time and space between dimensions—this one and the next. Thusly, there was nothing supernatural about any of it. Zero had spent his last twenty years in some quarter where the physical laws of the third dimension were negligible to some degree. This loop, as it were, was probably a neutral ground between dimensions, a place ruled by laws of both dimensions and neither. But none of this set about explaining why pain and perversion were the norm there. Unless it was because it was peopled by individuals like Zero and a host of unfortunates brought for amusement. But it did make her speculate as to what the true origin of Christian hell was.

She was probably making a mistake by not bringing Fenn in on this. But in doing so, other less palatable matters would have to be brought up, such as her affair—if you could call it that—with Zero. She'd never discussed it with anyone and she really doubted that she could even now.

She was keeping the book hidden in her bureau, wrapped in pillow cases. It was degenerating rapidly as it was bound in some type of skin she took to be human. Already, this skin was drying out, loosing its original greasy texture and beginning to flake. The pages were becoming brittle, the edges beginning to crumble. If only it would last until she'd divined its secrets.

For the moment there was nothing to do but wait and think. Time was slipping away and each moment, she knew, Zero was plotting against her, devising some new route to his heart's desire—her and the book. If she wasn't careful, he'd get both.

Towards dawn, a rain began to fall and Lisa curled in bed shivering, and shedding some tears of her own.

The world seemed out of control.

THE CONFESSIONS OF DR. BLOOD-AND-BONES (4)

I didn't go seeking the Territories, they sought me.

The Sisters had been watching me, or so they said, studying my craft, taking great pains to observe the development of my art. I suppose others have sought out the Sisters, desperate men bored of the limitations of their world. I was not one of these. My world offered endless pleasure and experimentation. I was content with it.

But a man in my particular line of work has a short span of creativity. The police are everywhere, digging, probing, searching, and their informants mass in the shadows, always watching. It would have only been a matter of time before they would have found me and dragged me away to some prison or asylum. I knew this. When the Sisters made their offer, how could I not accept? They were giving me complete escape. No one could follow. They were taking me to a plane of existence where a man with my particular passions would be revered as a god, they said. Although there was a hint of truth in this, it was mostly a lie. And I found out soon enough how clever they were, how effortlessly they had deceived me, a child led into a dark lane with the promise of forbidden sweets. And I went, lamb to slaughter.

As I languished in that zone of dread between worlds, I spent a great deal of time dreaming. And what did I dream of? I dreamed not of my wife or son, or the world I left behind, but of Lisa. I remembered the two of us together and her infatuation with me and my own infatuation with her young and ripe body. I never grew tired of fantasizing about our times together. The act took on a new and vital urgency with her. This had little to do with taking her maidenhead on our first encounter, there was more involved here. Perhaps it was her age, her youth, her willingness to shrug off the complacent attitudes of her parents and engage in the forbidden fruits of desire.

I often wondered what sort of woman she had become. Even had I remained in that city, events would have necessitated that I move on. I would never have experienced the bliss of her blossoming into a woman of experience and texture. And had that avenue been open to me, no doubt I would have bored of her and she of me.

Such are the politics of life.

Before the Sisters came into my life, my plans were to push on to another sphere of influence. The world was full of cities to be conquered. I had planned on devoting my life to these dominations of sorts. But that all changed when I was taken away.

It seemed that ages passed while I was tormented and tortured. The Sisters told me it was my period of initiation and as such, it would pass. Regardless, it lingered for what seemed years if not centuries. But there is no time in that place, no limitations, no restraints. When I was told of what waited for me on the other side, it was too late to turn back. I envisioned being broken on racks and languishing in the stock. Perhaps, if they were especially creative, I decided they'd have me drawn and quartered or endure Caligula's Death of a Thousand Cuts. I overlooked their primary creativity.

But let me start at the beginning. The physical transposition from this universe to the next required preparation. No one may make the journey as a whole; you must be broken down and reassembled on the other side. It is a grisly experience.

After I was divorced of my skin—an agony beyond agony—I was dissected with infinite slowness, disassembled completely. My nerve networking was stripped free and secured to stiff boards with pins. Each anatomical system—vascular, muscular, lymphatic, and so on—were removed in due course and displayed in the same fashion until there were only bones and then these were separated and spread over tables sticky with the fluids of my victims. As I had done to others, it was now done to me. Yet, through it all, I lived, I experienced the agony, the inhumanity, the desecration of my being. My eyes, secured by hooks, watched and, divorced of their ducts, were robbed even of tears.

My cries, my pleading, my endless suffering was ignored. The Sisters, I think, believed that they were bestowing a great honor on me. Once I was completely broken down and taken apart, they brought me over to the other side. I remember little of it beyond screaming black spheres and crawling oblong shapes. During the passage, I blacked out. When I woke again, I was in what resembled a nineteenth century dissection room. I came to call it the House of Pain. An anatomy theater. It was only the beginning.

Assisted by other sadists and surgeons of lore and legend, boundlessly amused by my mechanics, the games increased in intensity. I was refitted and sewn back up, only to be dismembered and stripped of my biology a dozen times. Eons seemed to pass while I waited in extremis to be fitted together again like a lunatic's puzzle. Soon, they grew bored and left me to move on to fresh conquests.

Finally, I was free to roam my new world at will. I traveled for years and never found an end to the Territories. I passed through urban graveyards and villages of despair. I learned to live in a place where there was only darkness and polluted mists and agony.

I learned that death didn't exist here. I encountered dozens who'd hung themselves, cut off limbs, slashed their own throats, carved free their entrails, all in hopes of escape.

But suicide was impossible in this place. Getting out is much harder than getting in. It was a great playground of the damned, but without victims to torment it was altogether boring. There was nothing to despoil, no innocent flesh to violate, no bodies to desecrate. For a creative individual, it was dull.

The cities were shrouded, evil places of cyclopean buildings and crumbling streets that were mazes leading everywhere and nowhere. There were rivers and stagnant pools of refuse and broken bodies. The shadows had textures, a physical presence; colors had odors; the ground heaved tears and flame; the sky rained blood and filth. There were no limitations here as the Sisters had promised. Every depravity and perversity mankind had flirted with through the ages was available and many never imagined. There were great empty spaces, blackened and blasted, dismembered bodies spread in every direction as if some terrible battle had taken place. The lanes were flanked with crucified children and adults impaled on stakes and set aflame. The flickering illumination intended to guide strangers to valleys of punishment they were better off not seeing. And everywhere, the hot, nauseating stench of cremated flesh and the cries of the damned.

I wondered if I was in hell. But I met no Devil, no grand master that lorded over this zoo of atrocity. I learned things slowly. Just bits of gossip gathered from faceless prostitutes and weeping clergymen and bored sadists. In arenas where the young and the old were set aflame, broken, mutilated, dismembered and staked to the muddy ground, I heard more. In medieval torture yards and gallows and gibbets, I was told there was a way out. A system of mathematical logic that could rend the seal of eternity and release one into the realm they'd been snatched from. If this system was mastered, one could come and go as it pleased them.

It took time, but I was patient. I copied arcane symbols and alien equations from the walls of black alleys and the floors of crypts. I found answers carved into tombstone and flesh alike. I wrote it all down. I showed them to intellectuals and nobles on the guillotine. I found answers and fitted them into a coherent pattern.

It took time, but I had nothing else at my disposal.

And always, I dreamed of Lisa as I plodded through the human carnage and jagged shadows. I was no longer human as such; more a thing of lust and depravity as those that had imprisoned me in the chasm. Yet, I clung to whatever vestige of sanity that still remained and I dreamed of Lisa. I sometimes could feel her dreaming of me.

It was then that I began to think of what I might do once the puzzle was solved and freedom was at my disposal. I would need to bring innocents back with me. I would need playthings.

That's when I realized only one plaything would do.

I needed Lisa.

I had to seek out my lover.

DECEPTION

The storm had abated by the next afternoon. Lisa slept perhaps four or five hours and it was enough. She woke around eleven and told the front desk to keep holding her calls. Fenn was probably going mad and sooner or later he would just flash his badge and demand to be brought to her room. It wasn't something she looked forward to.

She showered quickly and threw herself together and left the building via the back entrance. If he was going to come, then she just wouldn't be there. Better to hide out until she could think this all through. She caught a cab to the Financial District and took lunch at a Greek restaurant, losing herself in the spring lamb for a time. She ate and drank wine and did not think. Above all, she did not think.

But eventually it had to come to an end. She went back to the hotel around three and Fenn was waiting in the lobby. She supposed he would've waited weeks if that's what it would've taken.

He rode up to her suite with her on the elevator, not saying anything, not knowing whether to smile or frown and deciding on the latter. They went in and sat on the sofa and she made them drinks.

"You wanna tell me about it," he said. "Or should we just sit here and pretend we don't know one another."

"Everything's fine."

"Really?"

She nodded and drew away when he touched her hand.

"You've been acting odd ever since that night in the house," he said to her flatly. "Something happened and I want to know what."

"No you don't."

"Tell me."

"Nothing happened."

"You're lying," he said.

"I got scared. I was alone in house with a bad history. My imagination got the best of me." She couldn't even look him in the eye.

"And that's all?"

"What else could have happened?"

"I thought maybe you'd tell me." He was moving in close now, his concern genuine, as was his lust. She could smell it all over him.

"There's nothing to tell."

His arm was around her, his lips at her ear. He whispered things that she didn't hear, had no interest in hearing. His hand casually fell to her breast.

"Don't," she said.

"Why not?" He kissed her neck and ran fingers along her thigh.

"Stop it." She pushed away. "I don't want that."

"What's wrong? What did I do for chrissake?"

"You didn't do anything," she told him, hugging herself. "Nothing at all. It's just me."

"Tell me what's wrong."

"Would you stop interrogating me like one of your criminals? I don't need it right now."

His eyes narrowed. "Oh, is that what I was doing? I thought I was showing concern for the woman I love."

She shivered. Why did he have to say things like that? He didn't even know her. He was in love with her face, her body, the sex they'd shared. That and some pristine image of her he'd developed. There was no truth in it. He didn't even know the person he pretended to love and if he did, his love would wither like an October rose.

"C'mon, Lisa," he pleaded. "Stop this and tell me."

But she couldn't. She just couldn't tell him the truth. The fear that he'd abandon her then and there was terrifying. She couldn't stand being alone, with no friends in this awful city. She'd lie first. She'd swindle, cheat, deceive, but she wouldn't be left alone. Not now. If there was no love for him, she'd invent it.

"Tell me what you're thinking," he said.

"Nothing. Just daydreaming."

"I bet."

She ignored that. "Anything going on with the case?"

"One little item. Maybe unconnected."

"Which is?"

"Remember Soames? Your P.I.? He's dead. He asphyxiated. But as to the how or why, we don't know yet."

"My God."

"Interesting, I'd say. But not as interesting as what's on your mind."

"There's nothing on my mind."

"Christ." He left her and went to make himself a whiskey sour and drank it down. Then another. He brought this one back. The phone shrilled almost immediately and Lisa went in the bedroom to answer it.

"Who the fuck can that be?" she heard Fenn say. "If it's Gaines, you don't know where the hell I am."

"Of course not," she said.

She sat on the bed and sighed, picking up the cordless. "Hello?"

Breathing. Heavy, insistent.

"Who is this?" she asked, a tickle of fear at the back of her neck.

Fenn was at the door. "For me?"

She shook her head and he stalked off.

"Who's there?"

There was a peal of laughter and she knew all too well who it was. She wondered briefly why he'd waited so long to begin his campaign of terror. "Who is this?" she asked again, trying to show no fear. It was important that the bastard not suspect that she indeed knew, that he was burned on her memory.

"You know who this is," the voice taunted. "You've never forgotten me. You never could."

"Eddy . . ."

"Now you're using that analytical brain of yours, Doc," he said happily. "I'm the reason you're in town, aren't I?"

"Eddy, please—" she began and realized that she wasn't alone. Fenn was in the doorway again. He had a sour look on his face and his drink was almost gone. He looked suspicious, jealous even. She knew he hadn't heard her speak Eddy's name. If he had, he'd have snatched the phone from her grip. No, he was worrying that some lover, old or new, was on the line, whispering of seduction, alluding to some private rendezvous.

She held the phone against her bosom. "It's a colleague," she lied. "From the hospital."

Fenn said nothing, he just stared at her a moment and then left. She heard him make another drink and sit on the sofa.

"What do you want?" She was polite, painfully so. Good sense told her not to be, to slam the phone down and tell Fenn. At the very least, call him in and let him know what was happening here. But she did neither. She asked her question as if she didn't really know the answer and displayed no fear. After her encounter with the elder Zero, Eddy seemed almost harmless. She'd almost forgotten she'd come to stop him.

"Have we company?" Eddy asked.

"Yes." Why lie to him?

"Your cop friend, I'll bet."

She bit down on her lip, wondering why she didn't terminate this conversation. She told herself that if she could find out where he was or arrange what he thought was a secret meeting, Fenn could do the rest. But was that the real reason? "Why are you calling?"

"I heard you were looking for me."

"Yes and you know why."

"I know why," Eddy said covertly. "But do you? Do you know the real reason yourself? Is it law and order or something more personal?"

Lisa felt as if the breath had been sucked from her lungs. He was so like his father, so cunning, so confident. Perceptive to the point of sixth sense.

"I don't know what you mean."

"Don't you?"

She was the psychiatrist here, the trained therapist, and here was Eddy pummeling her with suggestive questions and she couldn't seem to stop him. He'd gotten into her mind more than once when she'd left her guard down. And he was doing it again. So effortlessly, knowing exactly how to orchestrate his attack. Alfred Adler would've called Eddy Zero a classic high dominance male personality, Lisa thought. And a very rare one at that. He had a great deal of skill in mastering people, particularly those who thought they were mastering him. She likened him to Franz Walter, a German confidence man who'd also been of high dominance. A fiend who'd turned a woman into a prostitute and made her attempt to murder her husband merely through hypnotic suggestion. Eddy seemed to possess those same skills. Very few had them, but it ran in his family.

"I don't have time for your games, Eddy. Why don't you tell me where you are and we can help you."

"I'm near," he said, "and far."

"Please, Eddy."

"Yes, do beg, dear Doctor. When the time comes, I'll have you begging and you won't be able to help yourself."

He hung up and the phone slid from her grip. What did he mean by that? *What do you think he meant by that?*

"Trouble?" Fenn was in the doorway.

"No," she said in a shaky voice.

It was a clever lie and Fenn seem to buy it. He was showing the signs of drink and looked unkept and worn. He sat on the edge of the bed and sipped his whiskey, not bothering with sour this time.

There was a sound from the living room, almost like the door knob was being jiggled.

"What the fuck?" Fenn said.

He pulled himself slowly to his feet and went out there. Lisa couldn't follow. There was no strength in her legs. She waited, listening for the sound of a knife arcing through the air and plunging into Fenn's chest. The door was opened and then closed.

He returned. "Nothing. Must've been my imagination."

Mine, too? she wondered in a panic.

"I'd better be going," he said in a defeated tone.

"You're too drunk to drive."

"Not as drunk as I'm going to get," he promised.

Like a little boy, she thought, a pouty little boy. "Stay here," she told him.

"Do you want me to?"

"Yes." And she did. The idea of being alone with Eddy lurking so near . . . or far for that matter . . . was unnerving. Let Fenn stay. Even if she didn't love him, she could pretend for one night that she did. It was something. The desire he'd displayed to her before sounded intriguing now. Sex would be the perfect prescription for taking her mind off the terror of the night.

"Stay with me," she entreated him. Her fingers loosened his tie and unbuttoned his shirt. He closed his eyes and teetered drunkenly in rapture as she undressed him and took his cock in her mouth. It was engorged and ready within seconds, and seemed to need little prompting from her lips. She took his length completely, feeling him push against the back of her throat, and she held him there, sucking, biting tenderly. He gasped and nearly fell.

"I love you," he managed as she pushed him onto the bed and slipped out of her blouse. "I do love you."

He said it almost as if he were trying to convince himself of the fact. But she understood. He respected her and liked her as a human being, but he didn't love her. Not really. He loved her cunt, her mouth, any of the secret places he could push into and spill his seed. It had never been any different for her. Men never got close enough to love her because her looks got in the way. They were ensnared in the web of her physical charms, transfixed by her eyes, her face. They worshipped her body and all the things she could do with it. But the real Lisa was hid away in a back room of her mind where no one ever went. And this person, the one that needed love, never got anything but infatuation and that was a constant. Her looks were a curse.

She worked his cock as these thoughts tumbled through her mind and she wondered if any of it—from her teen-age affair with a psychopath to her inability to crave anything but rough sex—was really her fault. The thoughts faded as she released his cock and let him push it in the valley between her breasts.

As he dropped her down onto the bed and stripped her, she knew he didn't love her. She'd wondered before, but the truth had come now. He, like the others, saw only her face and body and nothing more. He could never be made to realize that it was nothing more. But in the years to come, when his head wasn't dizzy with heat, he'd come to know the truth.

He pushed himself roughly into her and she managed a moan. It was the best to hope for under the circumstances. Fenn seemed to enjoy himself and if nothing else, this did her heart some good. It seemed to take a long time, but finally it was over and Fenn fell away and passed out, satisfied with both himself and the weak passion he'd spurred from her.

Some time later, she put on a robe and went into the living room, staring at the TV. When the phone rang, the sound of it went through her like a knife. She ran in the bedroom and snatched it from the cradle.

It was Eddy again.

"You call that fucking?" he asked bluntly.

She couldn't speak. How had he known? Had he guessed? Or had he been in the suite, watching them?

"You work wonders with your mouth," he said.

"Fuck you," she said. "How did you get in?"

He laughed. "I have my ways."

"What do you want?"

"You know what I want. The same thing you do."

"Fuck you," she said again. There was nothing else to say.

"I could've killed him while he mounted you, but I didn't."

"Why?"

"I have my reasons," he said. "See you soon, Doc."

He hung up and she had a drink. The door was unlocked and she fastened it again for all the good it would do.

The phone rang again about three, but this time it was for Fenn. There'd been another murder. Eddy had been busy again.

*   *   *

About an hour after Fenn left, Lisa sat on the sofa and waited for Eddy Zero. He was coming; she had no doubt of this. It was only a matter of when. She sipped cognac from a tumbler until her nerves stopped jangling, keeping her right hand underneath a pillow and in it was the .38.

About 4:30 the doorknob rattled and opened. Eddy walked in, knowing he was expected: confident, cool, in control. He knew he wasn't being set-up and this was just an additional comment on his arrogance.

He wore a black leather jacket, a bulky, greased and glimmering thing that hung down to his knees. His hair was long and dark and he wore mirrored sunglasses over his eyes. She understood now how Gulliver hadn't recognized his photos, he looked completely different.

"It's been a long time, Doc," he said. "I suppose we should've got together before this. But there wasn't time."

Lisa said nothing. She didn't feel afraid really, just a little tense. She had the gun and all she had to do was pull the trigger.

Eddy took off his coat and laid it across a chair. "Very clever of me, wasn't it?" he said.

"What?"

"Killing that whore so I could get your boyfriend out of here."

She was shocked, but she didn't show it. "You took a life just to get me alone?"

"Yes."

"I would have met with you any time. It wasn't necessary to do that." Her professional demeanor was intact. It slid into place like an oiled mechanism. "Murder isn't an answer to anything."

"Oh, I'm not a cold-blooded maniac," he assured her, sitting down. "I had to kill another one for the Sisters. Otherwise, I wouldn't have bothered. It's terribly strenuous and fatiguing stuff taking apart a body like that. And messy."

"How many do you have to kill before they'll let you cross?"

"A few more. It's all getting very boring by now, you know. I wish they'd take me already and we could dispense with this slaughter." He reclined and locked his fingers behind his head. "Oh well, they're bound by traditions, I suppose, as we all are."

"And what are yours?" Her voice was even, clinical.

"You know what mine are. I'm following in the footsteps of a great man, my father." He smiled as if some enchanting memory had struck him. Then: "Why don't you bring your gun out into the open? Aim it at me directly, if you like. Hell, I'm not here to hurt you, Doc. I don't kill for kicks, just out of necessity. Besides, we've got some unfinished business."

She shook her head. "We don't have any business."

"You're wrong. I slipped from your hands and now you want me back, right? Back in a little cell where you can get into my head."

Lisa avoided his eyes. "You know this can't go on. You'll be caught before long."

"It's a chance I take. But you're avoiding the subject, aren't you?"

"I don't know what you mean." Her hand was beginning to sweat on the butt of the gun. It felt greasy, ready to slide from her fingers.

Eddy smiled. "Why don't you drop the facade? Isn't it all getting a little tiresome? Pretending all this professional, moral interest in me when the real reason is lust?"

"Bastard."

"Have I touched a nerve, Doc? Have I peeled away your defenses so easily?" He looked pleased. She was squirming and it gave him no end of joy. "All this time, you've been thinking about me, haven't you? And you probably told yourself it was out of scientific curiosity and nothing more. You probably saw the whole episode, the whole situation of hunting me down, as meat for some book or paper you wanted to write. Am I correct?

But that's a lie. You're subconscious knows the truth and I can see right into it. I know what you're about."

Her hands were trembling, her reserve falling free like ice from a roof. "And what's that?" she asked with some effort.

Eddy laughed. "You know that as well as I do. You wanted me to rape you that night at Coalinga. You were aggravated that I didn't. You still are."

"You're crazy." She couldn't even look at him now, not even for a moment. She could feel his dark eyes staring at her from behind the mirrored lenses. They were so intense, so hungry, it made her skin crawl. She felt violated.

He stood up, stroking his crotch, his erection straining against the material of his jeans. "So are you." He captured and held her eyes with his own lecherous gaze. "Don't pretend to be offended. I know you too well."

"You need help, Eddy."

"Your kind of help?"

"Fuck you."

"Exactly what I had in mind."

He went to the door and returned with a large white package he'd left outside, pulled a knife out of his coat and slit it open. There were a dozen red roses inside. He said: "You like flowers, don't you? No, don't answer. I know you do."

He began dropping them to the floor. He took the last few and brought them to her, pressing them into her face, forcing her to drink in their sweet odor. The petals fell like rain down her face and into her robe. Eddy grasped the belt and threw it open. He wasn't surprised that she was naked beneath it.

"Don't," she said weakly as he took a handful of petals and rubbed them violently between her breasts.

The sweet, almost sickly smell of roses filled her nose, overloading her senses with a pungent intoxication. Her head felt giddy, her heart hammered. Hot blood rushed through her limbs.

He grasped her hair in one fist and jerked her head forward. She gasped, but did not fight. Not even when he dragged a rose stem across her throat and drew blood. She was trembling and her heart felt like it would pound right out of her chest.

Fight this . . . fight it . . . don't let him dominate you, don't let him give you what you want . . . don't weaken . . . don't . . . don't . . .

But she was beyond self-control. She wanted him like she'd never wanted anything before in her life. He pressed a finger into her mouth and she took it, tasting the salty flesh, biting it, licking it. He put petals in her mouth and she chewed and swallowed them. And then his lips came in for a kiss. But it was no mere kiss, not the sort of tender, intimate brush of the lips or tongue that she'd shared with Fenn. He took her head in his strong hands and pulled her up roughly, covering her lips with his own, his tongue pushing into her, dancing a primal rhythm in her mouth that she joined in on. She was not merely being kissed, but devoured. His lips were smashed into her own, his tongue and hers wildly loving each other as he grasped her chin with one hand and a handful of her hair with the other. Then he pulled his tongue out and bit down on her lower lip. She gasped, but did not fight him off.

No, she couldn't fight her heart's desire, the twisted machinations of her libido. The exchange between them had all the subtlety of rape and she wanted it even as part of her brain screamed for it to stop.

Eddy threw her to the floor and chewed her ear, whispering crude obscenities into her ear that made her blood boil. He went after her breasts with the same almost vengeful ferocity, licking and eating the uplifted cones with a hot-blooded animal need that was frightening. As he worked her from head to toe, she said things she wouldn't remember later, begged and pleaded with him never to stop. Or never to begin.

She never forgot he had the knife, but in her racing, reeling mind it was only another symbol of his appetite. He brought it into view and ran the blade between her breasts, tracing a line of blood to her crotch. She thought for one dizzying, delightful moment that he was going to kill her, take her life with the blade and all she was concerned with was that he enter her first. He took up her robe and shredded it with his blade as her body rocked beneath him, anxious for any and all indignities he would press upon it.

He tied her wrists tightly with strips of the robe, nearly cutting off her circulation. He fastened the strips to the legs of a chair and then gagged her with the belt.

"Can't have you screaming on me, my darling. Not yet."

He shed his pants and pushed himself into her with a violence that urged a cry from her throat. Words crossed through her mind, things like *desire* and *lust* and *lovemaking*. If the former was adequately descriptive, the latter certainly was not. This was animal fucking, completely devoid of love or tenderness or sensitivity. Eddy fucked her with a vengeance, trying to kill her with each thrust, to burst her from the bonds of reason and it was all she could do not to explode free of her confining skin with each shuddering orgasm that rocketed through her body. He unlocked something in her, a starving beast kept behind lock and key for far too long. Her teeth tore at the gag, biting and shredding it until her gums ached and her lips bled. Her hands were forced into contorted fists by his incessant pounding, the knuckles strained white, nails digging into her palms. She knew sex as her ancestors had, not as an overly-festive and civilized affair, but as something approaching hatred. She was being raped and liked the feeling of being used, abused, and degraded. She hated Eddy and if her hands and teeth had been free, she would've slashed him to ribbons. An atavistic mania was erupting in her cells as her body arched and slammed into the carpet, as muscles tensed and released. Uncounted millenia of breeding and evolution and civilized behavior were washing away in a thundering tide of bestial hunger. Her brain and body were out of contact with present reality, instinct was surging up and releasing suppressed urges forgotten since the time man violated the mate of his choice in a damp and dark cave. Her head was raging with race memory, her nose drowning in odors of an ancient time: pungent smoke, raw meat, hot musk, sweaty muscle . . . as orgasm after orgasm ripped through her like tumultuous waves crashing on a foreign, primal beach.

She lost track of what happened then. Half-memories struck her later and vanished as quickly as they'd come: the lunatic, chemical frenzy that muddled and mastered her thoughts; the raw and real eruptions of racial memory that reduced her to an animal in heat and let her glimpse a moment buried in time; the wrists and bloodied fingers pulling free of their bonds and scratching and clawing at her lover; the evil, triumphant grin on Eddy's features as he fucked her and she drew blood; the sharp explosion of pain as he sodomized her and struck her again and again; her own thundering need; the sight of his huge member spitting seed over her bruised breasts as he straddled her and tried to choke the life from her, finally forcing his cock into her mouth where she greedily sucked it. The memories came and went.

In the end, only one fact remained: Eddy had taken her farther than any man had before. Fenn and the others had merely incited a violent appetite in her; William Zero had taken her to the edge of the carnal abyss and dangled her above its hot mouth, but it was Eddy who threw her in, kicking and screaming.

*   *   *

When she woke later, she was alone.

She couldn't remember Eddy leaving, but he must have. The suite was empty and she knew this from the breathing silence that pervaded the rooms. She was lying naked on the floor, her lips tender and caked with dried blood. Her insides hurt from the punishment he'd inflicted. Her throat felt swollen and raw from his mock strangulation. He'd had his fun, leaving his whore senseless on the floor.

The memories struck her one after the other and dissipated just as quickly. She knew vaguely what had happened. They'd gone beyond the reasonable limits of sensuality, broke the bonds so to speak, and had journeyed physically and mentally back to a time when humans mated only once or twice a year like the beasts of the forest they were. She'd experienced animal heat.

Eddy had shown her things she'd never dreamed of.

And did she love him for this?

No, she hated him and was disgusted by herself as she supposed her female ancestors were when the time of ritual mating had come to an end.

She pulled herself off the floor and her entire body ached. Walking was a chore and it took some time to reach the bathroom. She was shocked by her appearance in the full length mirror. She was bruised and battered from throat to crotch. There were red, hurting finger indentations in her ass, and her throat was discolored from being throttled. There were cuts and teeth marks on her breasts. Her nails were nearly all broken off, her palms ragged and bleeding. Dried blood was smeared over her face like warpaint and her teeth were stained pink. She looked, if nothing else, like the end result of a very abusive rape.

And she supposed there was a glaring truth to that.

She wondered if his father was watching her now from beyond the mirror's glass.

She showered slowly, cleansing herself of both Eddy and the act. Afterwards, her head reeling with anger and self-disgust, she went to bed and slept.

*   *   *

She opened her eyes some time later, feeling sore and raw, but not too bad despite the punishment she'd endured. It was after six and she realized she'd been sleeping for some ten hours. She wondered why Fenn hadn't called and could only hope he was beginning to see her for what she was. She checked her cell. Nothing.

Eddy had raped her, but he could have done worse.

Rape?

You wanted it.

No.

You asked for it and now you got it. Did it feel good? Did it feel good enough to throw away your dignity, your professionalism, and your ethics?

She shook her head to clear these thoughts. There was no time for self-recriminations. No time at all.

Then the phone rang and she wondered if it was Fenn and if she'd have the strength to lie to him. She couldn't tell him about this, not yet—

She answered it and it wasn't Fenn at all.

"Sleep well, dove?" Eddy asked, sarcasm tainting his words.

She bit her lip and started to tremble. "Better than in ages."

He was silent for a moment, perhaps expecting a string of expletives to be shouted in his ear, cries of hatred, accusations of assault. He got none and was at a loss for words. "Really?"

"Why shouldn't I have?" It was painful to be so kind and unaffected towards him. She despised him beyond words, almost as much as herself. But there were ideas in her head now, dark and plotting. She held the upper hand now and they both knew it. In the back of her mind, a web was being spun and she was drawing him into it.

"You're not angry?"

Lisa grimaced. "Angry? Why would I be angry?"

"You liked it?"

"You know I did. My feelings go way beyond like."

One word was all he could afford. "Really?"

She laughed. "Why are you so surprised? You said you knew me."

"I don't know," he told her. "I don't understand you."

"No," she said. "I don't suppose you do." And he didn't, she knew, no more than he understood himself or what was happening here. "Are you going hunting tonight?"

"Hunting?"

"Don't be an idiot, Eddy. You know what I mean."

She could almost feel him pale over the phone. "Yeah, I'm going. Just a few more and it's done with. Then me and Spider are lighting out of this place."

Spider was dead. What did he mean by that? Was he going to drag a corpse along with him? There was no time to ask such things. "Maybe I'll come along for the ride," she told him.

"You'd like that?"

"Why not? You think you're the only one bored of the limitations of this place?"

"I never suspected." She could hear him breathing on the line as if the prospect excited him. "Maybe it could be arranged. Maybe."

"Think about it."

"I will. Yes, I will."

"Keep in touch," she said and hung up. She raced into the bathroom and vomited in the toilet. But even as she did, her mind still plotted. As disgusted as she was by him and herself and the secret they shared now, it all might just prove to be a means to an end. If she was exceptionally lucky, she might just get rid of Eddy, his father, and the book in one fell swoop.

And maybe yourself in the bargain.

So be it.

It was a risk worth taking.

MEMOIRS OF THE TEMPLAR SOCIETY (8)

Stadtler was awake for some time before he realized that he indeed was. Sleep. Awake. Dream. Reality. They were all the same, weren't they? All segments of common cloth? Cloth? For a moment he couldn't remember what cloth was.

It's something you wear, silly boy.

He laughed under his breath. No, no, no, that's clothes . . . not cloth. Cloth is something you make clothes of. You can make many things out of cloth. Yes, yes, that was right. Ha, ha, Zero, he thought, you can't drive me mad. See, I remember everything. I remember that mama makes things out of cloth and she uses her sewing machine. I'm perfectly fine.

Don't you dare go outside in your new clothes.

No, Mama, I won't. I promise.

He felt his body and started to giggle. Why, he was naked! He didn't have any clothes on! What was she thinking of? Poor Mama.

I'm not wearing any clothes!

He moved and his ankle throbbed with pain. Ouch. Oh God, oh Jeezus, that hurt. Mama, please take this chain off me, it hurts so. A terrible, terrible hurt. Please take it off.

Not until you're broken.

Mama? No, it was the bad man. What was his name? A number name, wasn't it? One? Two? Three? Three? Two? One? Zero? *Zero?* Yes, Zero! I haven't forgotten who you are, you bastard, you bad man you rotten terrible—

Noise.

Oh, that ugly noise and the light flashing on and off.

That voice speaking over and over. A man's voice. Not Zero. Someone else. A man telling about his life over and over again. Every meaningless detail.

I won't listen to your life! I don't care about your life! I won't be you! I won't!

The voice ended sometime later. Hours? Days?

The badman was talking now.

What's your name?

I won't tell you that.

What's your name?

I know my name, I know who I am. But I won't tell you because it's a secret, a private personal secret and I won't tell you!

Your name?

I know it! Stennbetter! Starling! Studlater! Those are my names!

Name.

I know who I am I know who I am I know . . .

And he did and he didn't. If he could only remember. Just think and you'll remember, he told himself, it'll come to you. Just think.

That other voice started again, telling about his life.

I won't listen!

He curled up and started to cry, sucking his thumb.

I know my name, I know my name, it's . . . it's . . . it's—

But he did not know anymore.

He knew very little.

It had been seven weeks.

THE CONDEMNED MAN

"Lisa? This is Gulliver."

She'd been expecting Fenn again. "Oh, how are you doing?" she asked. "I've been meaning to come and see you. Things have been so busy lately."

"Yeah," he said, as if he didn't believe her.

She felt a momentary pang of guilt. If it hadn't been for him, they wouldn't have even known what Spider and Eddy had been doing, let alone that Eddy was in the city at all. Conversely, if it hadn't been for him, none of the shit that had rained down on her would've happened at all. But it wasn't his fault. Eddy had a knife on him, so he'd had to tell about her. He'd risked his neck to help and had been stabbed as a result. Both Fenn and she owed him for that. And how had they repaid their debt? By not so much as visiting the man while he recuperated.

There was just too much going on.

And that was increasing by the day, it seemed.

"Is Fenn there with you?"

"No . . . I don't know where he is." And she didn't. It was nearly eight and, as yet, he hadn't stopped by or even called. Thank God.

"Is there anything going on?" he asked. "With Eddy and that?"

Where should I start? she thought. "No, not much. Spider killed himself and we think Eddy snatched the body. But you know that. There's been a few more murders . . ."

Tell him about the rape and how you liked it.

"Yeah, I read about that."

"I don't think Fenn and his men are any closer than they were before," she admitted and wondered if he sensed the cynicism in her voice.

"He knows what he's doing," Gulliver said, almost as if he were making excuses for the man. "Eddy's slick, though. He won't be caught unless he wants to be. It's a game to him."

"Yes, isn't it, though?" she said under her breath, ugly memories blackening her thoughts.

"What?"

"Nothing." She was silent for a moment. She needed to talk to someone, so why not Gulliver? If there was anyone in the world that wouldn't judge her, it was him. "Why don't you come by? I could use someone to talk to. Maybe we could have a late supper in the lounge."

"I can't."

"Oh?"

"I have something to do tonight," he said.

She didn't like the tone in his voice. It sounded ominous. "Well, if you change your mind."

"Maybe you should talk to Fenn," he said, his words heavy with suggestion. "I'll see you."

He hung up and Lisa set the phone down and brooded. What had that meant? Talk to Fenn? Was it all that apparent that she was keeping something from him? No, there was no way Gulliver could suspect anything. She'd told him she needed to talk to someone and he'd just put two and two together. That was it. But, then again, maybe it wasn't. Gulliver was self-admittedly a bisexual, someone who could see both the good and bad in both sexes. Not the sort of man who would be deceived by female beauty. He wasn't like heterosexual men who were so blinded by physical looks that they saw nothing else. He probably saw her for what she really was and she didn't like that at all.

But all that was minor. The thing that really bothered her was his insistence that he couldn't come over, that he had something better to do. She was certain she hadn't imagined the dread lurking behind his words. Was he going to do something foolish? Seek revenge against the man who had attacked him? She hoped not. He had no idea what he was getting into. Regardless, if Fenn and his cops couldn't bring Eddy in, how could Gulliver hope to locate him? But the answer to that was grim: because Gulliver knew the streets, he knew the underworld and where a man could hide. The police did not.

She went down to the lounge for a light supper and a drink. Her mind was racing, heading for a crash.

THROUGH THE GATES OF HELL

If a man was truly dedicated and had a bit of money to flash about, there was no one he couldn't find in time. And if you weren't a cop or didn't act like one, so much the better. Gulliver decided he knew how Eddy thought and once you had that going for you, the rest was only a matter of legwork and asking the right questions to the right people. That and biding your time.

His theory would've worked in time. It was logical, he knew, from start to finish. Once again he began frequenting the various leather bars and gay clubs. And much to his surprise, he was propositioned by dozens of men and a few women. It just went to show that you can't find love; it has to find you. And all the thankless, frustrating hours he'd spent doing just that. Had it been any other time, he would've been flattered, but he found himself only irritated. He saw only business and that business was locating Eddy Zero.

In the few days since he'd returned from the hospital, he'd done nothing but scheme and plot. After he'd forced himself out of hiding and taken the offensive, he felt much better. It was a pleasant change of pace being the hunter and not the hunted. He asked a lot of questions and flashed a picture of his quarry around that he'd clipped from the newspaper. But that was only part of his strategy. Eddy was going to show up at some tavern or stroke parlor and Gulliver was going to be there when he did. He spent his days hanging around dozens and dozens of these places, making discreet inquiries and showing the photo about. Sooner or later, he would've spotted Eddy.

But as it turned out, Eddy—crafty devil that he was—spotted him first.

Gulliver was urinating in the men's room of a place called Sonny's and reading the graffiti on the wall. He heard someone come in and thought nothing of it. Not until the stranger came up right behind him and slid the gun from his coat with the ease of a pickpocket.

"Everyone in the place knows you're carrying," Eddy told him, prodding Gulliver in the back with his own little .22 pistol.

Gulliver hadn't finished pissing, but his penis had shriveled up on him and that was the end of it. "Eddy?" he asked.

"Who else?" Eddy said, not letting him turn around. "So tell me now, why is it you're looking for me? I was going to let you go after our last little run-in. I thought to myself: Well, the impotent little fag knows I mean business, he'll back off like a good boy now, climb back into his hole and keep his nose clean . . . but you couldn't do that, could you, Gully?"

Gulliver was trembling, words of defense simply weren't available. "I . . ."

he began and decided there was no use in pleading a case that didn't exist.

"I've seen you off and on for the past two days," Eddy told him. "Didn't you know? You walked right past me more than once."

Gulliver felt weak inside, his guts gone to stew. He chanced a sideward glance into the mirrors over the sink and knew Eddy was right. He had seen him and more than once. Eddy's little disguise was perfect. Gulliver hadn't thought Eddy would try anything quite so dramatic. He'd thought the man's inflated ego would necessitate going as himself. Even if he had been looking for a disguise, he doubted he would've spotted him. The pea coat and longshoreman's cap and sunglasses were perfect. As was the long black mustache and sideburns he sported. He looked exactly like one of hundreds of men fresh off the docks. In a port city like Frisco, the bars and clubs were always full of that type.

"Clever, ain't I?" Eddy giggled.

"What now?" Gulliver asked. "Are you going to kill me?"

"I don't know. I was thinking of raping you in the old naval tradition, but you'd probably like that too much, wouldn't you?"

"Asshole," Gulliver grumbled.

"Walk with me," Eddy said, giving him a shove towards the door. "And don't cry for help, Gully, or I'll shoot you in the head. I don't give a fuck how many people see me do it."

Gulliver zipped himself and did as he was told. Eddy pocketed the gun and out they went. Gulliver started towards the bar room, but Eddy told him otherwise. "I think we'll go out the back way. I wouldn't want to lose you to another man." They went down a short hall and through a door marked private that led into a stock room. Then they were in the alley.

"Where?" Gulliver asked.

"Just walk. I'll point you home, don't worry."

"Are you going to kill me?"

Eddy sighed. "No, not me."

Gulliver wasn't exactly relieved.

*   *   *

Eddy steered him to a bleak, crumbling neighborhood not far from the Excelsior District. Crowds of nasty youths littered the sidewalks. Whores and criminal types of both sexes skulked in doorways and cul-de-sacs. It was a fearsome, depraved little stretch of real estate. It took them well over an hour to reach it and all the while Eddy spoke of things Gulliver refused to hear.

They went into a ramshackle house with a slouched roof, boarded-over windows, and a yard strewn with refuse and stunted trees. Eddy pushed him inside and turned on the lights. It stunk of dampness and old meat in there.

"Take off your coat," Eddy told him, shedding his own.

Gulliver did as he was told. He was too tired to fight. This had been coming for a long time and he was accepting it now. If only it would be quick.

"Now the rest of your things."

"You want me to strip?"

"That's right. Hurry on, now."

Eddy watched him, grinning the whole time. He took a certain interest in watching someone remove their clothes. There was something immensely exciting about it all.

"Well, what now?" Gulliver asked him. He sounded irritated, almost impatient with it all. "If you're going to kill me, why don't you just get it over with."

"I said I wasn't going to kill you," Eddy insisted. He crossed the room and opened a set of doors. "In here."

It was totally black in the room when Eddy closed the doors. Not a sliver of light found its way in.

"There," he said, turning on a lamp.

It wasn't much but it was something. Still, the room was dim and depressing. A dampness hung in the air, a stink of rotting wood and something worse.

"If you're not going to kill me, then what's the point of this?" Gulliver chanced. He was naked and defenseless. He didn't believe for one moment that he wasn't going to die. Nothing good could come of this.

"You'll see."

Gulliver heard a shiver of motion behind him. He turned and a figure clawed out of the shadows, something out of a nightmare.

"What the hell . . ." he managed, and saw the glimmer of a knife in the things gnarled paw. He had no time for recognition, only for pain. The knife slashed out at him and opened a gash in his chest. He went down with a cry and held his hand out in protection but the blade danced again and freed him of two fingers, leaving a third dangling by a grizzled thread. Blood flowed from the wound in his chest and spurted from the stumps of his fingers. A screaming, sobbing sound spilled wetly from his mouth in a mist of red.

"You said . . ." he began and then his attacker was close again and he realized for the first time who this night haunter was.

Eddy had done more than steal Spider's body, he had breathed a sort of life into it. Spider was a desiccated and withered thing, stitched and stapled, a living wraith. "Gulliver," he said, his shredded lips mocking a smile. "Fancy meeting you here."

Gulliver stared and saw the dead man walk and had no trouble believing it. Nothing was impossible, he'd long knew, where Eddy Zero and Spider were concerned. He saw and accepted and concerned himself only with the blood that was vacating his body in red rivers. He knew enough about first aid to know that his wounds weren't fatal. If he received attention and soon, he'd live to tell the tale.

"I said I wouldn't kill you," Eddy told him, "and I won't. Spider will take care of that. Won't you, my gutted lovely?"

"Fuck you," Spider said.

What was this? Dissension among the damned? Spider was surely no innocent in all of this, yet was he beginning to learn what sort of abusive monster he was being used by? It was something.

"Kill him," Eddy said softly. "Get it over with."

"There's no hurry," Spider insisted. "I've got all night."

"I want it done."

"In my own way," Spider insisted.

"Now."

"Who fucking left you in charge?"

Gulliver watched the two demons arguing over his life. It was, all in all, the worst possible situation he could've imagined himself in. Nothing was even remotely comparable.

"Do you have to make a fucking drama out of everything?" Eddy asked.

Spider ran a skeletal hand through his filthy, braided locks. He brushed a few beetles loose and stepped on them. "That's your problem, Eddy. You're in too much of a damn hurry all the time. Moments like this have to be savored. Do you think the Sisters would have paid us any mind had we rushed through our other works? Quick and brutal killers with no imagination are a dime a dozen."

"I can't wait all night."

"So go on."

"Shit," Eddy said and left, slamming the doors.

Spider laughed with a sound like ripping paper. "He's in for a nasty surprise, you know, in the Territories. They'll destroy him. He thinks he's wise and experienced because he killed a few whores. He's a veritable babe in the woods, a punk."

"Please," Gulliver gasped. "Let me go. He'll never know. I won't say a thing, I won't—"

Spider polished his knife against his coat, ignoring him. "Without me, that boy would never be nothing but a cheap, murderous hood. Oh, he'll learn, though."

Gulliver began crawling towards the door.

"When they get him," Spider continued, "he'll sing a different tune."

Gulliver was reaching for the door knob. Spider walked up behind him and dragged him back. "Dying is such a good thing, Gulliver. I'm sure you'll appreciate it. Death frees one of the excesses of life." He fingered the blade of his knife. "It's only now that I can truly realize what fools living men are. Rushing about, accumulating money, building little secure lives that will fall to ash with Death's inevitable breath. Such a waste. You'll understand, I think. In time."

Gulliver was weeping now, from his eyes, from his wounds. Desperation and hopelessness were raining from him. Spider almost felt sorry for him.

"I'll be quick and humane," he promised. "But first we'll chat. I think you deserve to know everything we've done, you little fag, and everything we're going to do."

*   *   *

Eddy returned about an hour or so later. He'd spent his time drinking at a bar a few streets over. The alcohol had relaxed him to the point where he felt human again. Sometimes, all this work and preparation just wore a body down. He went into Spider's lair and almost tripped over Gulliver.

"Please," Gulliver said.

Eddy ignored him. "I told you to take care of him."

"I didn't feel like it."

Eddy lit a cigarette and sat on the floor. "I risk my freedom bringing that bastard here and you don't even want him?"

"I didn't say that. Just not right now."

"See if you get anything else," Eddy threatened. "You can do your own fucking hunting from now on. I'm sick of it."

"Quit pouting," Spider said.

"Oh, I'm pouting now?"

"You are."

Eddy sighed. "I should've left your ass in the morgue."

Gulliver tried to crawl towards him. He was growing pale from the loss of blood and his voice was weak as he begged for mercy.

"You're losing sight of what we're doing, Eddy. This complaining is only complicating things. Our aim is to get into the Territories, not to live a life of ease and splendor," Spider explained like an impatient father. "Everything we've done has been dangerous, has involved risks. It won't be long now. Just do what has to be done and quit acting like a spoiled child."

"Fuck you."

"You know what you need?" Spider said. "You need death. It'll free you of all your petty worries and wants. You'll see only what matters."

Eddy laughed. "You think I want to be a stinking decayed carcass like you? Hiding in the shadows, eating dead things? Guess again."

Spider glared at him with bleached, lifeless eyes. "You see only the external of the matter," he said, anger rising in him. "A body is just a shell, my boy. When we get to where we're going, I'll find a better one."

"Yeah, I bet."

Spider broke into a bout of ghoulish laughter. It sculpted his raw and wrecked face into a thing of true horror, splitting and snapping as dried muscle and ligament strained beneath the mummified skin. "Maybe yours will do."

"Try it."

"In time."

Gulliver was sobbing now. But like a whining dog, he was ignored by both.

"This all better be worth it," Eddy said in a whisper.

"It will be."

"I'll get one more whore, maybe two, then I'm done. This is all getting a little boring."

There was a strange, almost magnetic humming in the air, a vague and vibrant electricity. A glow of sickly phosphorescence flickered from the other room. A reflection of mirrored light. A sound of weeping and distant screaming. They both knew what it meant.

"Boring?" said Haggis Sardonicus in a silvery voice that sounded like fine surgical cutlery scraped over bone. She stepped into the room with a blast of freezing air and a few dust devils of whirling bone ash. *"Boring?* Did you hear what he said, Sister?"

Haggis Umbilicus remained indifferent. She/it floated there, a swollen flesh sack, a dozen peeled hides stitched together, blackened and overlapping, sliding over each other with the sound of nails scratching on windowpanes. Hundreds of carrion-fattened meatflies lit from her blowhole mouth each time she exhaled. Her single bleary eye watched from beneath coiling tangles of wormy red hair greased with human fat. Her flesh was constantly in motion, a flyblown circus of unspeakable rhythm.

If she had an opinion, she did not voice it.

Eddy felt ice water in his bowels. "I didn't mean it like that, I only meant—"

Haggis Sardonicus drifted towards him, the stink of a thousand bloody seductions seeping from her breathing pores and overwhelming him like a noxious gas. His cock filled with life and demanded to be put to proper use. There was no denying the sensual, ominous charm she possessed. It got beneath his skin, a mutiny of sensations both carnal and repellent. Eddy knew she smelled his musk, wanting it, but her seductions ended only in death and he wasn't ready for that yet. Physically, she was caught in her transitional phase where she was neither huge and porcine fat or skeletal and machine-like. She stood before him, heaving and voluptuous, her pores gasping like tiny mouths. Her breasts were huge and round and shining with oil, swollen with milk. As he stared at them, droplets dripped from her dark nipples, which were like hazelnuts, yet sharp as pins. Even the minute suturing on them made him tremble with carnal appetite. He wanted to slide his cock between them and tit-fuck her violently until cream gushed from them.

She seemed to know it, too. Her coppery, metallic eyes gleamed with lust, her teeth pressed against her full, juicy lips were red-stained and hungry. She reached long pink fingers down between her legs to the hairless vulva that was engorged and throbbing. It was like a juicy rind of star fruit, fizzing and fermenting with dark human wine. It would be petal soft against his lips, sweet on his tongue.

"I understand your impatience," she told him. She took his hand and her touch was like ice, yet her fingers were so hot they steamed. She pulled his trembling hand to one heaving, glistening breast and held it there, her bloated, undulating flesh seeming to suck the heat from his skin. Her nipple was smooth as onyx between his shaking fingers.

"The end is near," she told him in a motherly tone. "We're nearly satisfied with all that you've done. But it can't end now, you can't let it."

He tried to pull his hand away, but it was affixed to her. Her flesh was hot wax and his hand was sinking into her magma. "No," he promised, "we'll do whatever it takes."

She released him. "Very good."

"It will be soon?" Spider asked.

Haggis Sardonicus nodded. "Very."

"There's a woman who says she wants to come," Eddy said.

"Her name?"

"Lisa Lochmere."

"It's unfamiliar."

Eddy rubbed his cold hand against his leg, trying to put warmth back into it. "She hasn't done anything to get your attention, she's—"

" . . . an innocent?" Sister Sardonicus said with an appetite that was frightening.

"Yes, but she's eager."

"Why not? We'll see that she's kept amused." She looked over at Gulliver's trembling form. "Ah, you've brought him back for us. How very kind. He is so pretty."

She went over to his quivering form. Only the loss of blood and his weakened state saved him from the true horror of what was about to happen. Sister Sardonicus stood before him in her transitional phase, legs spread wide so he could see her sex which was starving for him. At first, he smelled jasmine, wild roses, and jungle orchids. This made him dreamy and relaxed, but soon there was another smell, of rank carcasses and decomposition. He let out a cry when he saw the gash between her legs, which was like an infected mouth filled with fly eggs hatching like popping bubbles. She pulled his face in closer so he could taste her. Flies crawled over him, silverfish and squirming blood flukes filled his mouth.

By this time, he was insane, of course, and quite oblivious to everything.

He stared at her vulva, a red exotic jewel, pulsating and swelling, until the gash beneath it became crimson-dripping jaws that seized his head and cracked it like the shell of a peanut, sucking free his scalp and peeling his skin. By then, Sister Umbilicus had moved in like a black tornado, vacuuming Gulliver's corpse right down to the lattice of bones beneath.

Sometime later, the Sisters departed.

As Spider picked at the bones, Eddy felt his desire for Haggis Sardonicus begin to wilt.

*   *   *

"Cassandra."

I'm here, Eddy, she thought, and I will be until you are no more. I'll watch over you and protect you until that time comes. Until your end.

"I didn't hear you come in."

She wanted to laugh. The dead are nothing if not stealthy. Poor, sweet, demented Eddy. Taking life with no remorse, fashioning a private world of insanity and nightmare that even now threatened to crush him. Such a poor, pitiable, deranged little thing.

"I'm glad you've come," he said. "I feel . . . safe when you're here. I suppose that sounds ridiculous coming from someone like me." He was standing before an oval mirror leaning in the corner. He fingered its surface.

"Of course not. Our histories are knotted together."

"They are, aren't they?"

You have no idea, she thought, sitting by him on the sofa. "Where's Spider?"

"In his hole."

"Poor thing."

"You pity that?"

"Yes." I pity him no less than I pity you and your twisted ambitions, she wanted to tell him. *But I won't stand in the way. The place you're going is where you belong, God help you.*

"He's one of your own, I suppose."

"In a way."

"Where have you been?"

"Here and there. Miss me?"

"Always."

"Tell me what happens now, Eddy."

"What do you mean?"

"You know what I mean."

He grinned. "The Sisters came tonight. We go soon."

"And it's what you want?"

"Of course it is," he snapped. "What else is there for me? I've worked too hard and too long to accept anything else. It's my destiny."

"I suppose it is."

"I have no choice now. If I stay, what kind of life will I have? They'll hunt me down and stick me in some hospital."

"There's always death."

"What do you mean?"

"If you're dead, they couldn't follow."

"Kill myself?"

"Why not? Death sets one free."

"I couldn't kill myself."

"I could do it for you."

"Murder me?"

She laughed. "Don't be so dramatic. Death is death, regardless of how you obtain it. I'll do for you what you did for me."

"No."

"Are you afraid?"

"No."

"Yes, I think you are. Don't be. I've been there. I can show you the way."

"It's out of the question."

Too bad, she thought. Death frees the mind and body of all its illnesses. "It's up to you."

"The Territories. That's where I'm going."

She smiled, trying to show some enthusiasm for his choice. There was none to be had. Eddy didn't notice: he was totally consumed by his ambitions. That and madness.

"To my father," he said.

God help you, she thought.

LETTERS FROM HELL (8)

Dear Eddy,

I think these letters are at an end. This is the final installment. I'll say what's left to say and we'll leave it at that.

After we killed that cop, half of the state was organized against us. I assumed they were, anyway. The only problem with our law enforcement agencies is their lack of organization, their lack of cooperation with one another. Had things been different with them, they would have have pieced together our trail and followed.

Thank God for their ineptitude.

We had places to go.

Do you remember where we went next?

We drove the car down to the end of that dirt road and left on foot. Hand in hand, we set out through the woods together. Through fields and thickets. It was nearly dawn and the rain had subsided.

"Where to?" you asked.

I led on and we bounded up a hill. The grass was yellow and wilted. I turned and kissed you. I saw love in your eyes. You saw it in mine. There was a stone wall and we climbed over it. The air was cool, still. Overhead, the dark sky was heavy with bloated clouds pregnant with rain. Thunder rumbled in the distance.

It was perfect.

A cemetery.

I don't remember the name of it. I'd been there many times before and still the name eludes me. My family was buried there. In the damp, black earth they were waiting for me. I thought I could almost hear them weeping. I brought you to the back of the cemetery. Where the graves are old, the weeds long, the trees crooked and thick-limbed. You picked up a bouquet of wilted flowers along the way and gave them to me. I loved you so much then it hurt.

I led you to the vault.

It was overgrown with skeletal creepers. We had to hack our way through. The door was open, it was always open. I used to go there to be alone, to think, when I was a girl before the trouble started. It was as I remembered it. Frozen in time.

Our honeymoon cottage.

It was cold inside. A rush of dry, October wind greeted us. Your hand was in mine. My heart belonged to you. There were dead autumn leaves carpeting the floor and they crunched underfoot.

"Here?" you said.

"Yes."

I started to laugh and I couldn't seem to stop.

You were trembling.

When you closed the door behind us, it made a scratching sound. Sweet, dread music on this day of days. Tarnished bronze plaques were set into the cracked, mildewed walls. This was our place. There was a rotting bier and you broke it into kindling, lighting a fire with it. Flames licked orange and yellow. Huge, grotesque shadows played over the walls. We made love then amongst the dead and dreaming. There were ancient, mummified flowers and you threw their petals into the air. They drifted lazily down over my shuddering nakedness.

I was yours. You were mine.

You forgave me for what came next. I know you did.

In the dank, dusty confines of our tomb, I put the razor in your throat. You died quickly. There was little pain. Our moment was captured forever in that still, October place of time and memories. I laid with you all day while a frozen wind blew leaves and dead roses over us. While spiders spun webs and the dead became dust. Sometime later, a moon rose in the raging sky. It was huge and full and orange. Almost as huge as your dead, staring eyes.

When night came I was still there. I never left. In that vault of funereal charm and cold mourning my heart burns forever. A bleeding corpse-fat candle.

I still hear the wind, the thunder, the graveyard rats clawing in the walls. We'll always be together in our womb of dread and beauty.

Good-bye, Eddy. Good-bye dark heart.

My screams go on forever.

Yours,

Cherry

MEMOIRS OF THE TEMPLAR SOCIETY (9)

It had been three months now since Stadtler was put in the room, since Zero began destroying his mind, unmaking it and laying it bare as bones. Finally, the door opened and Zero went in.

"How are you, my boy?"

Who was this man? Was he a friend?

Zero unlocked his shackles and Stadtler crawled into the corner, hugging himself.

"You don't have to be afraid of me, my boy," Zero soothed. "I'm your friend. I've come to help you."

Stadtler looked at him. The place stunk of his own filth. His dark, quiet little hole was full of light now.

"Can you tell me your name?"

Stadtler shook his head. He couldn't remember. He could only remember the name of the man who told his life story over and over. He knew every detail of that man's life. But that wasn't his life, was it?

"You see what I have here, boy?"

He did. It was a coin. A pretty, shiny silver coin. It caught the light and glimmered.

"Look at it, boy. It's pretty, isn't it? The beautiful light shines and shines? No, don't look away. It's a game, you see? Just keep looking at it. Shining. Glittering. Lovely coin."

Stadtler watched it and it was so pretty. He saw so many things in the light that moved back and forth, back and forth. What a nice game this was. His eyelids slipped shut and he never even knew it.

"Can you hear me, boy?"

"Yes."

"Do you want to know who you are?"

"Yes."

"Good. First you'll have to remember the voice. Are you ready?"

"Yes."

Zero lit a cigarette and began the final stage of his little experiment.

PRETTY LITTLE LIAR

When Lisa woke the next morning, Fenn was already there. He was sitting in a chair, staring at her when she opened her eyes. Somehow, she'd suspected he would be. He hadn't contacted her at all the day before and it seemed logical that he would come calling bright and early. And he did.

"Sleep well?" he asked in a cool tone.

"Fine."

Her encounter with Eddy sprang into her mind and darkened her thoughts. The sheets were pulled up to her chin, so maybe Fenn hadn't noticed the bruises on her body. She hoped not. If he had, there would be no way to lie her way out of it.

"I was busy yesterday," he explained. "I should've called, but there just wasn't time."

"You don't have to explain. I'm not your master."

He lit a cigarette and there was anger in his eyes. Had it been the remark or was there something much worse eating at him? Oh, she'd know in time, but not until he was ready to tell her. She knew that much from experience.

"Something unusual came to light yesterday."

"Oh?"

He nodded. "There's a lot of crazy shit involved in this investigation, but this is the topper. This is a real good one. I don't know whether to laugh or cry or have myself committed."

"Tell me."

He looked pale, his eyes beady. "You remember me telling you about that undertaker name of Fish?"

"Yes. He disappeared along with our Jane Doe."

"We found him." Fenn smiled a rubbery grin. "His car was abandoned in an alley. He was in the trunk, cut up like a side of beef and stuffed in garbage bags. What was left of him, that is. Nice, eh?" Fenn laughed. "But here's the real good part. There was some blood and prints on the steering wheel. His blood. Guess whose prints?"

"Eddy?"

"Wrong. Our Jane Doe."

Lisa waited for the punch line, but none was forthcoming. "Must be a mistake."

"No mistake. I spent my day yesterday on this. I was on the boys at the lab like flies on shit. They checked and re-checked and re-re-checked. No mistake. Her prints, all right. If I didn't know the dead couldn't rise, I'd assume she killed him, cut him up, and stole his car."

"That's crazy."

He laughed again. "Tell me one thing about this case that isn't. His remains had been chewed on, Lisa. Something had been eating him. A great deal of him, in fact."

Lisa felt like she was going to be sick. This was all too much. Eddy Zero. Cherry Hill. Dr. Blood-and-Bones returning from some extra-dimensional dead zone. And now their Jane Doe stalking the streets like some goddamn zombie. She didn't want to believe this last bit—and she didn't, not yet—but it was only a matter of time and she knew it.

"There must be some rational explanation."

He ignored her. The subject was closed for the moment. "What did you do yesterday?" he inquired, a certain edge to his words.

"Nothing much."

"What exactly?"

"Is this a formal inquiry?"

"It can be."

She shifted herself up in bed. One of her arms was prickling, attempting to wake up. "I didn't do anything, if you must know. I was here all day."

"Nothing out of the ordinary happened?"

She wanted to choke him. "Nothing," she said curtly.

He didn't look satisfied. He looked, if anything, terribly suspicious, as if she weren't the woman he professed to love, but a suspect. His eyes never lost contact with her own. Even when she closed them or looked away, he was watching, studying. She could feel his gaze burning into her.

"You're in trouble, I know that much," he said. "I love you, Lisa. Just tell me what it is."

She shook her head. "You don't love me, Mr. Fenn. You've slept with me, you love my face, my body . . . but not me. You don't even know who or what I am. You can't love someone you don't even know. It's not logical."

He just stared at her, partly out of surprise, partly out of anger. "Since when does a man's heart know anything of logic?" he asked her. His face, which moments before had been etched with compassion, concern, and understanding, now became a cold mask. "I guess I shouldn't have said that. It was a waste of my time. You won't hear it again."

Lisa softened instantly. "Mr. Fenn, *Jim,* I—"

"I don't want to hear it."

She shut her mouth and hugged the blankets around herself. She felt like a child who was being scolded.

Fenn lit another cigarette. "Okay, now that the niceties are out of the way, let's get down to business, Doctor."

Something ugly was about to happen. She felt cold and helpless.

"Whether it was out of my feelings for you or just plain suspicion, I've been keeping tabs on you. No, you haven't been followed. Not yet. But the hotel staff was more than happy to inform me of your comings and goings and any visitors you had." He paused and dragged off his cigarette, fixing her with a steely glare. She felt like an insect impaled on a needle. "Up until today, nothing of interest came my way. But as I was coming in this morning, the night manager said he'd seen a man leaving yesterday morning. He didn't remember admitting him, so he asked this man who he was and what he was doing here. The man said not to worry, he was a friend of yours."

Lisa's throat felt constricted. She could barely draw a breath.

"You know," he said, "I'm just a dumb cop. I didn't spend thirteen or fourteen years in college like you, but I'm a crafty bastard all the same. I thought to myself: Now who might this man be? I thought it might be Gulliver, but the manager said my description didn't fit. So, on a crazy off chance, I showed him a photo of Eddy Zero. And guess what? He identified him positively."

Lisa had never expected any of this. She was completely caught off-guard, lies tumbling through her brain with no string of logic to knot them together. He had her and he knew it. She hated the sinister, amused look on his face. It was probably the same detached cynicism he used on his criminals. She supposed, at the moment, that's exactly what she was to him.

"You can start explaining any time now. I'm listening."

She felt sweat trickle down her back. "What do you want me to say?"

"Don't act like a dumb bitch, Doc. The truth and right now."

Lisa looked him in the eye. "All right, he was here. Satisfied?"

"Very. Now tell me why."

"He wanted to know why I was after him."

Fenn laughed. "Oh, come on. Our Eddy's a bright boy. He damn well knows *why* you're after him. Tell me the truth. Were you gathering a bit of background for your fucking book or what? An interview or two? Let's have it."

"I told you what he wanted."

Which was the same thing you wanted.

"And you're lying, aren't you?"

"Believe what you want," she said. "I told you why he was here. Whether you believe that or not is up to you."

He laughed again.

"That's funny?"

"No, you are. You're the shittiest liar I've ever come across and I've dealt with some dandies." He started laughing again and then a grim silence suddenly fell over him. "You're right, though, Doc. I don't really know you. Maybe I did think I loved you, but I was wrong. No one loves a liar. Especially one that protects a killer."

"I'm protecting no one."

"You know, if you would have only told me about this or at least come clean, I might have had some respect for you. You didn't have to love me, you just had to be my friend, to be honest with me. That's all I asked."

Lisa said nothing.

"Okay," he said, "let's try another angle here. The night manager is a young guy. He's been pretty cooperative, I guess, for the most part. I had to pry one thing from him, though. I could see he was keeping something else from me, so I kept at him until he told me about your other visitor."

Lisa waited. It was all she could do.

"He said she was beautiful, very sexy. Said her name was Cherry. Cherry Hill. Got anything to say about that?"

"Not much. She came here. She told me to stop looking for Eddy. That's the truth. She said her peace and left."

"I don't believe you, Doc. I don't know what the fuck you're up to, but I'll find out in time. I guarantee you that much. Cherry Hill's another psycho. Just like Eddy Zero. There's a connection here. Soames said I'd find out about him by starting with her. I think you know what that connection is. If you're smart, you'll tell me."

"I don't know."

He shook his head. "Like hell you don't. Your name keeps coming up here, Doc. You were at the nuthouse with Eddy and at the prison with Cherry. Now they've both visited you. I might be just a dumb cop, but I'd say you're hiding something big from me."

Lisa opened her mouth and shut it again.

"You're in deep shit, Doc. Very deep shit."

"Really?"

"If and when I tell my superiors about this, they'll be under the assumption that you are an accomplice in a homicide investigation. They may want you charged with aiding and abetting a known fugitive. Regardless, once I tell them, your life won't be your own. You'll be under constant scrutiny."

"So are you going to tell them?" she asked.

"In due time. I'll let you take the day to think out these lies of yours. I'll be back tonight for the truth. If I don't get it, your ass is in a sling. Then you can do your lying from a jail cell. Are we clear on that?"

"Yes," she replied.

"Oh," he said, rising to leave. "Don't try leaving town. It wouldn't be in your best interest."

"Am I being charged with something?" The sarcasm was thick in her voice.

"No, but that can change without notice."

He left and she heard him slam the door.

Her treachery and lies had bound her up good now. She supposed it was what she deserved. There was no more time now for planning and scheming. She had to act immediately. All she lacked was a plan. She dug out Dr. Zero's little book and began to read, praying for divine inspiration.

MEMOIRS OF THE TEMPLAR SOCIETY (10)

Stadtler was walking aimlessly up the streets.

The nice man had cleaned him up, dressed him and sent him out into the world. The city was a beautiful place. Full of bright lights and music and many, many staring faces. So many people tried to help him, but he wouldn't let them. He didn't need their help. Not tonight. Not in this wonderful loud, pretty town. He loved it here. He almost felt like he should know every street, every corner and cubbyhole, but he didn't. Not anymore.

He didn't know who he was.

He didn't know where he was.

He didn't even know what he was.

But the nice man told him not to worry. He'd know in time. When things were right, he'd remember it all. The nice man said he'd put a special word in his mind and when he heard it, he'd remember everything.

But who cared?

It was so wonderful walking and walking.

So many things to see.

As he walked, he saw that a car was following him up the street. He stopped and smiled. He waved. A man got out of the car. He was big and strong and wore a lovely blue uniform. But he didn't smile. There was a piece of metal on his coat. Shiny, silvery. It winked back light. Stadtler almost remembered something for a moment, something about shining, blinking light—

"What's your name, pal?" the man asked.

"I can't remember."

The man still didn't smile. "Give me your name."

"I don't have a name. Not yet—"

The man grabbed him and threw him up against the car. He was mean and rough and . . . brutal. Stadtler didn't even know what that word meant. *Brutal.* What a strange word.

"You know," the man said. "I really need this shit. Thirty years on the fucking force and I get all the hippies and freaks and weirdos."

The man was very terrible. He spread Stadtler's legs and forced his hands onto the hood of the sleek car.

"I want your name," he said.

Stadtler wanted to cry. This man was so mean and all because he had no name and this man thought he should have one. Was it important for all men to have names?

"Fucking freak," the man said and began searching Stadtler's clothes for something. He found it.

"This your wallet or did you steal it?"

"I—I don't know."

The man spat on the sidewalk. "Shit," he said. "Let's see here." He was looking through the wallet, never taking one powerful hand from his freak.

"I don't know my name. I don't know it," Stadtler kept saying, tears in his eyes.

The man shoved him against the car and stuffed the wallet in his pocket. He said, "Well, I know who you are. That's all that's important. I think you're stoned, boy. You need to dry out and I got just the place for ya."

"Who am I? Who am I?" Stadtler asked.

The man knew who he was and he wouldn't tell. I want to know who I am, Stadtler thought. I have to know. If only he'd say the special word, all would be right.

"Tell me," he said to the man. "Please tell me who I am."

The man sighed and Stadtler heard one word: "Fenn."

And then he knew.

THE CONFESSIONS OF DR. BLOOD-AND-BONES (5)

I knew about Hell.
  Because Hell was my city.
  I knew every stinking, squalid corner of it in detail. And like it, I knew about pain and death and blackness. Just as the city turned a great blind eye towards the daily atrocities that were committed in its twisted streets, so had I back in the world. I remember the young women pleading for their lives. Asking me for mercy and getting only misery. The city had no name in the Territories. It was just one of many spat out of my world or some alien plane. A place too wicked to exist in its original surroundings, so it was swallowed up and brought here. I heard it called the Nameless City or the Forbidden City, but it had no true name. Its history was extant. Even in the world its memory had been blotted out, I supposed, by those who preferred to pretend it never existed. Judging by the architecture, it was my guess that the city had existed somewhere in central Europe four or five centuries ago. But what horrid cataclysm had thrown it into this awful place, I never learned.
  Not that it mattered.
  The city was here and it was my home. We understood each other. We both suffered from black, loveless souls and morals adulterated well beyond mere corruption. We were intertwined, threads of a common cloth, in our peculiar dance of darkness, parasite and host, lovers of agony and inhumanity. I slaughtered innocents for amusement, to wile away the endless periods of boredom, and the city welcomed my actions. I never learned where the innocents came from exactly. Only that from time to time, numbers of them were sucked from the world to keep the fires of the Territories burning. I supposed it would explain the rash of missing persons back home or the entire populations that vanished from time to time.
  I was known as Dr. Razor in the Territories. Perhaps my other titles weren't adequately descriptive. Who can say? I picked up the name mainly because of my weapon of choice: a straight razor drawn expertly over the throat. The designation of doctor stuck for unknown reasons. I liked that. When asked, I said I was a doctor of anatomy. And that wasn't too far from the truth.
  I spent my time in the city pouring over the equations and symbols I had copied down. It took a great deal of time to work out the muddled logic behind them. It seemed to take months in the Territories, but in reality, years were passing in the world like sand trickling through a child's fingers. But I was very close, yet my equations and formulas lacked an underlying logic. My fascination

with mathematical analysis and differential calculus was finally becoming useful. Each day brought me closer to escape from the chasm.

When I was but one variable away from my heart's desire, my reputation had spread. Many wanted out and finally, here among them, was a man very close to solving the riddle of the ages. I was long gone when they closed in, eager to steal my work. It was my own fault. I had shown my equations to many and asked for their help. I got it, but I also got to be known as a man with a key. I suppose it was that and too many casual, incriminating boasts to the wrong people. But they would never know what I had spent years in formulating. I wouldn't let them. While they brooded and tried to destroy themselves and each other, I worked towards my goal.

I left my rooms at a decaying building called the Pretorious and was swallowed up by the city long before they moved in. I disappeared into the reeking bowels of the metropolis in search of a certain brothel where it was rumored that the prostitutes derived sensual pleasure from certain calculations of fourth dimensional physics. The brothel was located in a dark section of the city called the Zone. A place where few dared go. It was rumored by some that the physical realities of the place were demented and constantly in flux due to the prostitutes' experiments with alien geometries. One might go in and never find their way out again due to the bending and corruption of time and space the whores had set into motion.

I walked for hours and hours, darting into mulling shadow each time I heard the sound of approaching feet. Soon I was quite alone and I knew I had arrived. A cloak of damp fog had fallen over the city and a chill mist was raining from the starless sky. I was in a foreboding alien landscape, one equally as unnerving as my first night in the chasm. I wandered the streets in a hypnotic stupor, confused, and hopeless. The fog, a rich and enveloping blanket of dreams, had consumed everything and what it had discharged was an exotic, foreign place, more lunatic than the chasm itself. I heard voices in that fog, but saw no faces; I saw faces, but heard no voices; there was insane laughter and piteous sobbing. A pale, cloistral haze hung over streets and buildings alike, painting all in a dreary neutrality. I was avoiding the shadows now and their razored heaps. Spreading pools of them seemed to seek me out. The buildings towering above the deep cut street were ancient, shuddered mausoleums of drab gray stone crumbling into rubble. They were huge sleeping cyclopean monoliths with no use for light or cheer reaching high into the mist at impossible angles. Their uniform repetition left my nerves jangled.

I was lost, I thought, in this land of gloom and whispered dread.

Empty, plotting desolation greeted me from every sullen quarter.

I remember thinking: Dr. Razor, I fear you've made a grievous error. You've gotten yourself into something no man can ever free himself from.

Panic hit me then. I could suppress it no longer. I thought I was beyond fear, beyond the reach of any decent emotion. I was wrong. I broke into a stumbling run, sprinting wildly down the most promising avenues and avoiding those which courted feelings of solitary abandonment. But nothing changed. The thoroughfares and twisting lanes were bland replicas of each other—heavy with mist and melancholy—and the buildings were gray, charmless slabs of repeating stone.

Even as terrible as the other sections of the city were, there were always hiding places. But here, sanctuary was just a word, a thought lacking substance.

I tried re-tracing my steps, but the place was a maze and I was the performing rat for the evening, if not for eternity.

Then I saw a doorway.

Why I chose this one out of countless others, I can't say. I was drawn to it, a fly to decayed meat. I went in.

I didn't know what I was expecting. Perhaps an interior as wanting as the exterior, but that wasn't what I got. It was lavish inside. Great violet and vermilion tapestries adorned the walls. Brass candelabra dripped with coagulated wax and cast dancing, hazy shadows over everything. Underfed women lounged in shapeless chairs that were upholstered in hide the color of rubies. The women were dressed in moth-eaten leathers and zippered bondage masks or they wore nothing at all. This was the brothel, I knew then, for what else could it be?

A naked woman with white skin like flaking pastry emerged from a low doorway and approached me. She was wearing an oiled leather skirt and a leather bondage mask, but nothing else. Her breasts were small, boyish, her ribs rising in angry contrast from the emaciated flesh that housed them. Her hair, a dusky blond, was greased with what looked to be petroleum jelly. Someone had painted arcane symbols and inverted crosses over her chest and belly with red lipstick. Her mouth was invisible behind the slash in the mask, but her eyes peered, unblinking, through slits in the material. They were cold, dark things, lusterless stones at the bottom of an icy creek.

"Excuse me," I said to her. "I think I'm lost, I need direct—"

"You're not lost. We both know that," she said to me in a dry, deathly voice lacking inflection. "You came in out of the fog, looking for sanctuary, and you've found it."

"Yes."

"Not many come here. Only the desperate. This is the last court of appeals for the damned."

I liked her. She was mad. "I'm new to this part of the city," I explained. "I've heard there's knowledge to be had here."

She nodded as if it were a pack of lies twice told. "Why don't you look around and see if anything amuses you? Then we can get down to business."

I did as I was told. It was all very intriguing somehow. I decided to play along if that was her pleasure. I'd take a whore and use her and be done with it. But none of them interested me. They were all starved and wasted. They reminded me of pictures of Dachau survivors. Not that this disturbed me; I'd seen far worse things in the Territories. But the pickings were better out there than in here.

"How about you?" I suggested.

She shrugged. "So be it."

Her apparent boredom brought a smile to my lips and inwardly disturbed me beyond description.

"Let's be done with it then," she announced and led me away by the hand, the flesh of which was cool and moist like fungi.

I followed obediently, vaguely wondering if I cared to commit an act with her. It was of no consequence. We went down a series of corridors that were more a maze than the streets outside. We walked in silence. The floors were thick with settled dust. A well-worn path ran through it. Finally, she stopped before a drab and colorless door. A length of rusted chain hung from the hook above it. She took it down and pressed it between her breasts.

"We heard you would be coming," she said, working her nipples to erection with the rusted coils. "You would've ended up here regardless." Ocher dust stood out like fire against the white, pathetic mounds of her breasts. "Men like you who leave the world of their own choice, often want to go back. Very few make it."

I smiled and nodded.

"Let me see your calculations before we go any further."

I handed my little book to her.

"Nice," she said, looking them over. "You've done well. A few variables and you'll be through."

She pushed the door open.

I hesitated.

"Is something wrong?" she asked with concern. "It's too late to turn back, you know."

I hesitated. Questions were assailing my brain, but I didn't voice them. I found I couldn't. All of this was so very familiar, as if I'd been to this place before. All my life, like anyone else, I'd experienced déjà vu, tiny half-memories that burst into my brain at any given time, then disappeared before my mind had time to process and identify them. And there'd been dreams, too, mostly from when I was a child. Dreams so vivid that I never remembered and only caught glimpses of at odd times. Scenes that made no sense, yet were so familiar they were maddening. And now, it was all clear in my mind: This was the place

I'd dreamed of, had visited before, a place so familiar it was alien.

"Yes," the girl said. "We've all been here before."

I went in and I heard the door close behind us. The room was immense, beyond belief. I could see no walls, no ceiling, just darkness everywhere, rolling thundering silent darkness. There was a counter of sorts ahead. A counter of arid, warped wood, ancient and huge. I'd seen it so many times in dreams, in misty half-recollections.

"What does all this mean?" I asked her.

"The soul travels while we sleep, before we're born," was all she would say.

I turned and she was gone.

I took out my razor and opened the door.

Cautiously, atavistic animal sense guiding me, I moved down the corridor. I didn't see the girl anywhere. I moved quickly down the connecting passages and found the door we'd originally come through. I opened it carefully, almost hoping someone would try and stop me so I could intersect flesh with steel. There was no one. In fact, the room was gone. In its place, a set of steps leading down, down. How clever she was, trapping me in this place. It was her intention, I supposed.

On the top step, there was a cigarette smoldering. I didn't have to look too close to see that it was my brand, the kind I'd smoked back in the world. The filter was even slightly bent. It was a trademark of mine. But who had smoked it?

I heard a sudden, slow rustling of cloth coming up behind me. I turned and saw nothing but a glimmer of steel winking in the distance. I rushed down the steps. This room was huge, too. A spidery maze of shadows.

"All right," I said aloud. "I'm here to learn. So teach."

I waited. The person who'd been following me came down the steps, slowly, slowly, their footfalls almost inaudible. I found myself backing away, terror in my veins instead of blood. I bumped into something and turned around.

It was a table and on it was the girl. Her throat had been slit, bright scarlet rivers bathing her chest. She looked to be dead, but I wasn't sure. Death wasn't an absolute in the Territories. Her face was tight, stretched painfully over the architecture of her jutting skull. Her skin, no longer pale, was the livid color of a bruise. A fly lit on her nose, then buzzed away. A discolored tear slid from one staring eye. Between her lips, a cigarette with a bent filter smoldered.

"So, you've arrived, have you?" a voice asked.

I turned. A man stood there . . . or a caricature of one. He seemed to be two-dimensional, cut from black vellum. He had height, length, but no width. When he turned sideways, he no longer existed. Where his face should've been, there was an X for each eye and a slash of a mouth drawn in white chalk. He carried a straight razor in his papery fist.

"Who are you?" I inquired.

The man giggled. "The one who will instruct you. Look there." He motioned to the wall. All my calculations were scrawled on the wall in chalk. The missing ones had been added. I took out my little book and copied it all down.

"You should be proud," he said, his voice not seeming to come from that chalked-in mouth of his, but from above and behind me. "You're only one of few who've ever made it this far."

"What is this place called?"

"I call it home, nothing more. My own little subcellar of creation."

"I can leave now? Whenever I please?"

"Yes, if I let you." He brandished the razor.

I had my own out by then. He closed in and I lashed out, slitting a gaping hole in him. He was indeed made of something like paper. I could see through the wound, yet blood, red and real, flowed from it.

The man laughed. "Very good, Doctor. Very, very good."

He swung out with his own razor, but I side stepped his lunge. I opened his throat, then his belly. It was like slicing cardboard. He slumped to the floor, something which might have been his anatomy bulging from the openings I'd made.

"Nasty," he said. "I guess you can go now. No more time to play." He struggled vainly with his papery limbs and pulled himself into a corner. He stuffed his internals back in the wounds.

The wall was opening now, the one with the equations scribbled on it. It started as a thin aperture of light and soon yawned wide to admit me. An endless corridor revealed itself. I started in and the wall sealed behind me. It took me what seemed hours to reach its twisted end.

And then, before me, the world.

THE PIT OF THE CHERRY

Fenn was going to give Lisa the rest of the day to come clean, but no more. He was sick of her shit and if he had to arrest her, so be it. God knew he didn't want to. He wanted nothing less. He wasn't entirely sure if he loved her any longer, but he still liked her, and there was no getting around the fact that he lusted after her. *Like a dog in heat,* he reminded himself. She was a lovely woman, though. Maybe it wasn't love, but infatuation as she herself said. Fenn could live with that. If only he knew what she was up to, what she was keeping from him. This was the only thing that soured his feelings for her: the lies and deception. Gulliver had been right, the woman definitely had a hidden agenda and much as Fenn tried, he never really got to know her.

But soon, hopefully.

And speaking of Gulliver, where the hell was he?

Fenn was going over to Soames' apartment. He had a warrant and he was going in to have a look see. It took him about fifteen minutes to fight his way through traffic. He showed Soames' landlady the warrant and she gave him the key and a dirty look she probably reserved just for cops. The other cops assigned to Soames' murder hadn't been there yet. They were still following the possibility that he had been killed by someone inside the hospital. That was a good thing. Fenn wanted to be the first one.

It wasn't much of a place.

Bedroom, bathroom, kitchen, a little living area that had been transformed into an office of sorts. It smelled of must and dampness inside. Fenn tried the office first. There was nothing in the file cabinets about Eddy Zero or Cherry Hill. Nothing whatsoever to link Soames with Lisa Lochmere. He tried the desk next. Nothing too interesting. But the bottom drawer was locked. Fenn fished out the letter opener he'd seen and set to work on the lock. It wasn't much of one. For looks mainly, not practical security. He popped the mechanism within a few minutes.

There were three things inside. A box of Giants baseball cards from the fifties in mint condition. Probably worth a small fortune. A deck of pornographic playing cards and a small, spiral-bound notebook. Fenn took up the notebook. The first section of pages were covered with tight scribbling concerning the numbers and whereabouts of bank accounts, life insurance policies, and assorted phone numbers and addresses. Nothing much of interest there. The second section was more revealing. There were diary entries here dating back twenty years. Fenn lit a cigarette and started to read.

Twenty minutes later he'd gone through them.

And in the process had learned a great deal about Mr. Soames. His connection with William Zero was quite apparent. Apparently Soames had been a cop once upon a time and had been dismissed for some shadowy dealings concerning a pornography ring. Fenn pieced this together mainly from references Soames made of his former business dealings. The most interesting thing he discovered was that Soames had been practically an accomplice in Zero's murders. He had been a pimp of sorts and had gotten women for Zero and his associates, known collectively as the Templar Society. Soames wrote that he had been unconcerned with what these degenerates did with the girls until they turned up missing. He became very concerned when two of them were identified as murder victims of Dr. Blood-and-Bones. They'd been found in the brewery, the same one Gulliver had seen Eddy and Spider do their nasty work at. Everything was starting to fit into place. But he still knew nothing of Cherry Hill or Eddy Zero. The rest of the notebook was blank. He searched the apartment and turned up nothing.

But there had to be something. Some record of his affiliation with Lisa Lochmere and Eddy Zero.

But where?

He picked up the notebook again. There was an Irene Soames listed amongst the phone numbers. Sister? Wife? He dialed the number.

"Is this Irene Soames?" he asked.

"Yes." The voice sounded old, weary.

He told her who he was and what he was doing. "I wonder if I could have a word or two with you?"

She sighed. "I was wondering when you boys would get around to me."

"I'm sorry to hear about your—" Brother? Husband? He never had a chance to wonder. She cut him off.

"Brother, Lieutenant. And don't be sorry. He's better off dead."

This was getting good. "I wonder if I might drop by and ask you a few questions."

"No. I have to catch a plane. If you have questions, ask them now and make it quick."

She wasn't even going to be around for the funeral. There was hate here, deep-set and real. "Ah, okay. First off, we learned that your brother was involved with a pornography racket. You wouldn't happen to know the names of anyone he associated with then, would you?"

"No and I don't want to. I only know it destroyed his family. That's all I need to know. It turned his daughter into a monster."

"Come again?"

"That bastard would've swung by a rope if I had my way."

Oh yes, this was getting good. "What do you mean it turned his daughter into a monster?"

"Just what I said."

"Could you be more specific?"

She was silent for a time. "I guess it couldn't hurt to tell now. He sexually abused her, Lieutenant. His own daughter. He used to dress up like a clown and rape her. He forced her into making those damn movies. Those filthy, terrible movies."

"Pornographic films?"

"Yes, that sick sonofabitch. He should've been locked up."

Fenn agreed with that. No wonder Soames was trying to kill himself. The guilt must've been eating him alive. Pathetic bastard. It was appalling. "The daughter's name was—"

"Cherry."

Bingo. "Cherry Hill?"

"Yes." She sounded on the verge of tears now. "He destroyed that poor child. His own goddamn daughter. Later, Cherry became . . . ill. She attacked her mother and her brother. She killed them both . . . with a wire. She took their heads off it with it."

He knew about that part. "Is there any more you can tell me?"

"What else could there be? Cherry was sent to an institution. Later on, they decided she was fit to stand trial. She pleaded guilty. Showed no remorse. She was sent to prison. She escaped. After that, I don't even like to speculate."

"You've been very helpful."

"I hope you wrote that down, Lieutenant. I never plan to speak about this again to another living soul."

Fenn thanked her and she gave him a grunt and hung up.

He lit another cigarette and leaned back in Soames' chair. He knew about a lot of things now. About Soames. About Cherry Hill. All he needed was the link between her and Eddy. According to Lisa, Cherry had been infatuated with Eddy at Coalinga. Later, she'd escaped from prison and now both she and Eddy had visited Lisa, who was their former psychiatrist. Lisa no doubt knew what was going on here, but it wasn't going to be easy cutting through her lies.

He took Soames' notebook with him and jotted down what Irene Soames had told him. He went out to his car and drove until he came upon a row of adult video stores and stroke parlors. He went in the first video place he saw.

He flashed his badge and the proprietor looked nervous.

"I'm looking for a film with a girl named Cherry Hill in it. Got anything like that?"

"Hill? No, we got Cherry Divine, Cherry Wild, Cherry Pie, Cherry Road. We even got Cherry Kiss. No Hill that I can think of."

"Dig me out the others then."

The man did and showed Fenn into a private showing booth. It took him the better part of two hours, but he found what he was looking for. Cherry Hill had a stage name. It was Cherry Wild. She was a young thing at the time. A teenager, maybe fifteen or sixteen. It was hard to believe a father could let his kid get involved in something like that. Regardless, she was a beauty. He couldn't help but get aroused by the sight of her doing her thing. No wonder the night manager at Lisa's hotel was so taken with her. She must've blossomed into quite a woman.

Quite a dangerous woman, he reminded himself.

For Cherry Hill was a homicidal maniac.

And she was on the loose.

REVELATIONS IN BLACK

There was a knock on Lisa's door that afternoon. She expected Fenn or Eddy or Cherry and dreaded them all in their own way. But it was none of these people. It was Cassandra. The girl she'd met downstairs in the lounge. She was wearing a dark business suit with matching skirt and a veiled hat. She looked ready for a funeral.

"I'm really sorry to intrude," she said. "But I think we should talk."

Lisa said nothing. Words were beyond her. Now what could Cassandra have on her mind? Her guest pushed past her and Lisa was struck by an overpowering scent of perfume. It was sickening.

"Could I get you a drink or something?" Lisa asked.

Cassandra shook her head. "No, I never drink anymore. It doesn't agree with me. I'm not keeping you from anything, am I?"

"No, of course not."

"It's important that we talk."

Lisa sat down. "About what?"

"Eddy Zero."

Lisa felt a headache coming on. Eddy again. Cassandra was involved in this, too? Christ, what next? She'd been secretly hoping this would be about some personal problem. Anything to distract her mind for a while.

"You're tracking him down. You told me that much the other day. I'm afraid I wasn't totally honest with you then. I do know who he is and what he is. I probably know better than anyone else."

Lisa chewed her lip. "I'm listening."

"This is really hard to say. I wouldn't have come forward unless I felt it was necessary. And it is."

"Tell me," Lisa urged her. "Nothing you could say would surprise me."

Cassandra laughed softly. "Don't be so sure, lady."

"I'm waiting." Lisa realized there was an edge to her voice, but she didn't really give a damn if she was being rude or not.

"The other day you remarked that I was familiar, that you thought you knew me from somewhere. You do. I said you were familiar, too. And you are. I knew from where. I sought you out that day. I wanted to talk to you, to feel you out as it were."

"Why? Where do you know me from?"

"The first girl Eddy murdered in this town was at his fa- ther's old house." She stopped and let that sink in. "But what you don't know is that I was there when it happened."

"You witnessed it?" Lisa asked.

"I was the victim."

Lisa just stared. "What do you mean?"

"Just what I said. The body that was found in the house was never identified, was it?"

"No, but—"

"But it turned up missing from the funeral home along with a certain undertaker named Fish. Right?"

"Yes."

"I'm afraid I'm the missing cadaver."

Lisa sat up. She could say only one thing: "You're crazy."

"No, not at all. I'm probably one of the few sane voices in this entire mess. Look, I'll prove it," she said, taking a tissue from her purse and holding up her right hand. As Lisa watched, she began rubbing at it with the tissue. It took only a moment and when she was done, the tissue was stained with dark make-up and her hand was stripped of color. The revealed flesh was gray and mottled.

Lisa was on her feet now. "This . . . can't . . . be . . ." her voice was saying.

But it was.

She'd been in enough dissecting rooms and morgues to know dead flesh when she saw it. There was no life in that mottled gray skin. Cassandra was either dead or this was an elaborate joke. But she knew better. Once upon a time people returned from the grave on occasion. Back in the days before embalming. They were usually victims of catalepsy, but that was rare. Usually, they expired in their coffins, waking six feet under the earth. But that sort of thing didn't happen anymore. And Cassandra definitely didn't fit into that category anyway. She'd been murdered. There was no doubt about that. Slashed to ribbons. And even if some freak occurrence had allowed a bit of life to languish in her body, the following autopsy would've taken care of that. Yet, this person before her who claimed to be their Jane Doe, was very much alive.

But the flesh of her hand . . . it was dead.

"This is insane," Lisa muttered to herself.

"The world is insane," Cassandra told her.

Yes, it was. Lisa had no reason to doubt that any longer. The very fact that William Zero had returned from some awful, impossible place as a zombie was evidence enough. And with that firmly in mind, was the idea of a dead woman walking about so far-fetched?

"I know this is hard to take, but you have to accept it. Eddy killed me and I never really died. Physically, yes; psychologically, no. This body moves because I make it move."

"You're a medical impossibility," Lisa said.

Cassandra shrugged. "So I am. What of it?"

"I guess I'd want to know how you did it."

"That's not important." She threw back the veil. She was lovely . . . yet, there was definitely something wrong about her face. "Wax and latex rubber," she explained. "I was involved in the theater in high school. Make-up. It came in handy."

My God, Lisa thought, I'm talking to a dead woman who fixed her face with cosmetics. She felt a tickle of laughter in her throat and she didn't like it at all.

"I didn't die because I chose not to. There were things that needed looking after."

"Eddy?"

"Yes."

"Did he help you . . . escape from the funeral home?"

"If by that you mean did he help with my resurrection, no. Nor did he have anything to do with the murder of Mr. Fish. I did that myself and enjoyed it."

Lisa was speechless.

"Don't look that way. I had to kill him. He violated me." She grinned. "Besides, I was hungry."

Lisa swallowed down her nausea. "You say you came back to look after Eddy?"

"Exactly. The fact that he's killing people doesn't concern me too much. Death has a way of opening your eyes to life."

Lisa massaged her temples. "Either I'm crazy or you are."

Cassandra laughed. "You're fine, dear."

"I wish I could believe that."

"Please do. As I said, I'm not concerned with Eddy's killing. It's his plans for you that bother me."

"Which are?"

"He wants to take you into the Territories with him."

"That's my own fault. I suggested it."

"You'd better explain."

Lisa did. She started with her affair with William Zero and talked of everything since: her infatuation of sorts with Eddy, their time together in the asylum, her study of Cherry Hill . . . everything. Right up to William Zero's reappearance and Cherry's visit and the rape . . . if that's what it was at all. And she didn't forget Jim Fenn. He was very much a player in this twisted tragedy now.

"It seems your life is intertwined with that of the Zeros," Cassandra commented. "I don't think you should blame yourself for your feelings and desires. As a psychiatrist you must understand that your . . . *involvement* with Eddy's father at such a young age is the cause of what has come since."

"I'm learning that. After what Eddy did, it's finally come full circle. I liked it at the time, God help me. Or some part of me did. But I think that part's dead now. I'm starting to see things the way they really are. I only want to put the past behind me and to do that, I have to deal with Eddy and his father."

Cassandra nodded. "The Territories are the perfect place for them. If you can seal them in there permanently, you can close that chapter in your life. Which is why I'm here, Lisa."

"You'll help?"

"I'll be indispensable. First, I want you to do something." She handed Lisa a slip of paper with an address on it. "This is where Cherry Hill is staying. I want you to visit her. I can't tell you why. When you go there, you'll discover the last missing piece of the connection between her and Eddy."

"You know Cherry, too?"

"Very well." She stood and started to leave. "Go see Cherry. She won't harm you any more than Eddy would. Prepare yourself for a revelation. Make sure your Mr. Fenn isn't following. The police could make a terrible mess of everything. I'll be in touch."

Lisa watched her leave. She would go. This was a day of revelations, what would one more hurt?

LITTLE MISS CHERRY

The apartment Cherry Hill was occupying was the upper floor of a cozy and clean little house. Lisa went up the stairs prepared for just about anything. *Revelations.* That word was beginning to lose its impact, she'd had so many surprises in the last few weeks. She set to knock and then tried the door. It was open.

She went in.

It was well-furnished inside and paneled in dark woods. Everything was dim and subdued. The shades were pulled over the windows and there were subtle odors of powders, perfumes, and cigarette smoke. Exotic, foreign brands all. Cherry always had exquisite taste.

She found her quarry sitting in a recliner, studying her face with a handheld mirror. She wore a satin robe and probably nothing else.

"Somehow I knew it would be you," Cherry said. "I wondered when you'd track me down."

"I think we'd better talk."

"You start."

"A mutual acquaintance visited me today. She knows both you and Eddy. Her name's Cassandra."

"Nosy bitch," Cherry said. Her features were darkening. They looked ready to slide off the bone that housed them.

"I want to know what your part is in this, Cherry. Are you working with Eddy? I find the chance of you both descending on me at the same time a little coincidental."

"We both belong to you in our own ways, don't we, Dr. Lisa? I don't know about Eddy, but I know you made me into what I am."

"How so?"

"Do you remember the night I escaped from prison? The night you found me in your car?"

Lisa grunted. "How could I forget. You nearly strangled me."

"But you took care of me. You hid me in your house. All so you could get inside my head and pick at my brain."

"I studied you, yes. I wanted to do a book—"

Cherry glared at her. "It was more than a study and you know it."

Lisa felt weak. She sat down. Yes, it was more than that. It had started out as a study of a psychopathic personality under controlled conditions, but their relationship took a major change when they went to bed together. Lisa wasn't sure even now how it had happened or why it continued happening for some time. Cherry was beautiful, yes, but she'd never been attracted to women before or since. The memories of those times still contained a certain amount of heat. She marked that down as still further evidence of her own sexual obsessions.

"Yes, it was. For a time. But that didn't last and you know it."

"And what happened then? Shall I tell you? Should we talk about Hypothalamine?"

Lisa felt something drop inside her. "I never realized you even knew about that."

"I'm not stupid, Doctor. I never thought for a moment those were tranquilizers you were injecting me with. You were experimenting on me."

"You weren't a guinea pig. HT was a new drug, experimental yes, but it had been thoroughly tested at the time."

Cherry was grinning now. "Is that why it was never put on the market? Why it's illegal now?"

Lisa was squirming. "There were unforeseen side effects."

"You have no idea," Cherry said.

Lisa wondered what she was getting at. Hypothalamine was a new antipsychotic drug that hadn't completely passed the FDA at the time she'd used it on Cherry. Yet, it was considered safe and had been successfully used at Stanford and Johns Hopkins. It was pulled from the experimental market some time later when it was found to cause irreversible organic damage to the brain's limbic system. Was Cherry suffering from this herself? It was possible.

Cherry rose and took Lisa by the shoulders. "I think Hypothalamine made me into the person I am today. I should thank you for that, Doctor."

"Cherry, there was no way of knowing—"

"I don't blame you. Not really. You were trying to help. No one could have imagined at the time what that stuff could do."

What? What had it done? She had a terrible feeling she was about to find out.

"I never stopped desiring you," Cherry whispered and pressed her lips against Lisa's own.

Lisa pulled back. "Stop it, Cherry. That's in the past."

But she wasn't stopping and her hands were everywhere—on Lisa's breasts, between her legs, searching out territory that was still bruised and sore from Eddy Zero's touch.

"Stop it!" Lisa shouted and fought in her grip as Cherry's lips and hands played over her. She wasn't about to be overpowered by this crazy bitch. She slapped her and shoved her away, knowing very well how dangerous it could be to stir Cherry's primal passions.

Cherry was laughing uncontrollably. "You think you can fight me off so easily?" She took Lisa in her arms again and this time, there was no struggling free.

As bad as that was, there was something much worse afoot. Earlier, she'd thought Cherry's features looked like they were about to slide free from the bone, and now they actually *were*. Cherry's face was moving like wax, flowing, rippling, raging. The flesh was in fluid motion, sculpting itself into—

Into Eddy Zero, of course.

Into a perfect physical replica of the man who'd violated her. The shift, as it were, took no time at all. Cherry's skin flowed and flexed with a mutinous plasticity that was more than merely alarming, but shocking. And the transformation was not merely concerned with her face, it took her entire body along for the ride. Cherry Hill no longer existed, there was only Eddy now.

"Fancy meeting you here, dove," he cackled.

Whether it was fear or desperation that gave her the strength to break free, she could never say. All that mattered was that she did. She broke his grip and stumbled back, her mind reeling with confusion. "HT did this," she muttered, more to herself than him.

He grinned and took a step in her direction. "What are you whispering about, Doc? Playing games with Eddy, are we?"

"The drug," she gasped, "it did this. It did this to you."

"What drug?"

"Hypothalamine."

"What the fuck are you talking about?"

Lisa's legs were ready to fold up. Her heart was hammering, her brain aching in its attempt to process and explain this new information. HT caused permanent organic damage to the brain, yes, but from what she'd read that was mainly damage to the hypothalamus which caused hormonal imbalances that resulted in fragmented circadian rhythms, sleep patterns, and sexual drive . . . but nothing like this. Unless, maybe, it had affected Cherry differently. Perhaps her brain chemistry was not ordinary to begin with or her insanity played a hand in things. Maybe all three of these things in concert. Cherry decided she was Eddy, hence, she *was*—physically and psychologically. The interesting and perplexing thing was that he was acting like he didn't even know what HT was. And maybe he didn't. Maybe only Cherry knew and this wasn't Cherry. She'd been obsessed with Eddy and HT had given her brain some god-awful power of externalizing him in the flesh. Total and complete mastery over her molecular biology. A shapeshifter. And in the process her mind had splintered so that Eddy was very much a real entity, not just Cherry hiding behind a mask.

Lisa fought to get control of herself. "Eddy," she said, forcing her lungs to quit sucking air like a beached fish, "where is Cherry?"

Eddy looked confused. "Cherry?"

"Cherry Hill."

"How the fuck should I know? Haven't seen her in years."

"Is she inside you?"

He smiled and then frowned, a look of utter bewilderment crossing his features. "Cherry is . . . I don't know where she is."

Lisa swallowed down her unease. This, of course, explained the connection between them. How they happened to appear in town at about the same time. But if Eddy was only another face of Cherry's, then where the hell was the real Eddy Zero?

"I want to talk to Cherry, Eddy. Can I talk to her?"

He swayed drunkenly on his feet. He started to shake his head and for a split second his features started to run like wax. "Cherry's . . . not here."

"You're Cherry."

"I am not! I am . . . I am . . . I—"

"You are."

His features went all the way this time, sliding and sculpting into Cherry's face. His body became hers.

"Bitch," Cherry pouted, "you'll ruin everything."

"I want to help you."

"Keep away from me."

"Please, Cherry—"

Cherry was glaring at her now. She was angry and Lisa knew she was in very dangerous territory right now. Cherry shrieked at her, then turned and ran into the bedroom, slamming the door behind her. Lisa heard a key in the lock and then the sound of weeping.

Lisa stood there, feeling useless and ignorant at this new and puzzling phenomena. She didn't know what to do or what to say or who to call. Maybe Fenn. Maybe the only thing to do was to call Fenn and let him have a good look into the face of insanity and see what he thought. But no, she couldn't do that. Not yet. This was the revelation Cassandra had promised her. It was the final piece of the puzzle. She looked for a place to sit down and gather her racing thoughts. There was a Queen Anne style writing desk shoved under a window and she sat there. Tucked away with a variety of stationary supplies were a stack of letters tied with red ribbon. She undid the ribbon and looked them over. They were all written to Eddy.

She started to read.

By the time she had finished, it was quiet in Cherry's bedroom. Lisa was stunned. Literally, completely stunned. Her body felt heavy and weak. Yes, this certainly was a day of revelations. For unless Cherry was writing fiction in the letters, Eddy Zero was dead and had been for nearly a year.

She tucked the letters into her coat and got out while the getting was good. In the bedroom, Cherry began to sing a lullabye.

THE HOUSE OF SKIN

"It ends tonight," Eddy said later that day. He said this to the rotting and ruined thing that had once been Spider. He said it with the confidence of a craftsman who knows a difficult task is near completion. "We'll go and never look back, you and I."

"And what about that bitch?" Spider asked with no little concern. "Do you really intend to bring her with us?"

Eddy smiled haughtily, his arrogance on display. "Definitely. Tonight we'll do our last bit of work where my father did his—in the old house. I'll have her meet us there."

"It's a trick," Spider moaned. "I know it is. She'll bring that cop and ruin everything."

"He can come, too."

"Leave her out of this," Spider demanded.

"Why? The Sisters said they'd be more than happy to have her along. If she brings the cop, we'll deal with him."

Spider shook his flayed head. "You're taking too many chances," he said. "If that cop brings more, they could ruin everything. I have to go, can't you see that? You can afford to play games, but I can't. I won't last another week in this damn place. I'm falling apart."

"Trust me."

"It's not a matter of trust," Spider told him. "It's a matter of reality. If I don't get through and soon, there might not be enough of me left to make the journey."

"Don't worry so."

Spider attempted a laugh but it came out as a hiss. His face was hanging from the bone in flaking loops, his festering skin jumped with lice and vermin, a stink of dampness and decay oozing from him. "Easy for you to say."

"Relax."

"Yeah, right." The Shadows crawled up and out of him, vacating his mouth, his nose, his innumerable wounds. Wherever they found an opening, they slipped free.

(we don't want to take chances eddy we can't afford to)

"I have everyone's best interests in mind," Eddy assured them.

(see that you do)

The voices died out and the Shadows filed back into their holes.

"Be careful," was all Spider would say when they were quiet.

Eddy lit a cigarette and dropped him a wink. "The way will open tonight and there's nothing the police can do to stop it."

"I hope not. You have no idea what it's like being this." He rubbed his temples and strands of flesh rained down. "Or having them inside you all the time."

"I know what that's like very well. Soon everyone will be free."

"I hope so."

Eddy smiled. "Keep it together, old boy. You can't be coming apart at the seams now."

*   *   *

It was out of desperation that Lisa did what she did. She needed to take her mind off of the inevitable confrontation in which she would be forced to tell Fenn everything. So, it was with this in mind that she took out her calculator and a pad of paper and began to decipher the code of the Territories.

It had been years since she'd dabbled in any higher mathematics. Not since her trig and calculus classes in pre-med had she been confronted by anything like this and it all came back to her as she copied down the theorems from the crumbling book. It was good, she decided, doing this. It gave her something to focus on.

If nothing else now, she understood everything. She knew about William Zero. She knew about the Territories . . . or as much as she wanted to. She knew what happened to Fenn's Jane Doe. She knew the dead could walk if it pleased them to do so. And most importantly, she knew that Eddy Zero was dead. That she'd been chasing a phantom for some time. Eddy was Cherry now and vise versa. Cassandra was right: the world was insane. Lisa was no stranger to guilt, but it was only now that she really understood what guilt was. And it had little to do with her personal life, this was totally professional. First off, after Cherry had escaped from prison, it was Lisa who hid her, studied her—all in direct violation to the professional principles and moral codes that went with being a physician. That was the first bad thing. Then she'd used HT on her, a more or less experimental drug. She'd gotten it from the prison infirmary where it was being used as part of a test group by the FDA. Countless other institutions were involved in the program. What it had done to Cherry wasn't her fault . . . not totally. She blamed the FDA for that. But the fact still remained that she'd violated professional principles by helping and studying Cherry and by using the drug on her in the first place.

In her own way, Lisa had created this entire ugly scenario. HT was partly responsible, of course, but it was Lisa who administered it to Cherry. And after Cherry had fled from her house that night, she went on a murder spree with the real Eddy Zero that resulted in her taking his life in more ways than one. So, all things considered, Lisa knew what guilt was. If she hadn't helped Cherry, if she hadn't given her the drug to fulfill some twisted ambition of writing a book, a lot of people might now be alive. Everyone from those Cherry and Eddy had murdered on their little cross-state run, to Eddy himself, and all the other bodies that were piling up in the city now.

I'm responsible, Lisa thought, for nearly all of this mess and maybe for *all* of it. But I'm going to make amends. I'm going to take care of Eddy and Cherry and William Zero at the same time. If this goes right, they're all going to be taking a trip somewhere they'll never return from.

With the help of the book and Cassandra, she was determined to do just that.

When Fenn came, things would get ugly. He probably despised her by now and, although this pained her, she knew his hatred would multiply geometrically once the truth was out. But he would demand to be told. And she would tell him and leave nothing out. And for the first time in his life, she knew, he'd curse his policeman's curiosity for all and everything. His image of her as an innocent dove would change dramatically. Oh, she was tarnished in his eyes right now, but it was nothing compared to what was coming. And when she told him, what then? Would he just walk out disgusted, or would he throw her in jail as an accessory? Or, was she misjudging the man completely? Would he want to help her after all?

It was no simple feat trying to make sense of the equations and symbols in the book. They were written in no particular order and she'd copied them down as such. First, it was a matter of forming them into some logical order, if that was even possible. She spent the better part of an hour trying one combination after another and all to no avail. Her background in math was too limited to make sense of these jumbled configurations. William Zero understood them and maybe you had to be insane like him to understand any of it. The idea of a mathematical system of logic only lunatics could solve was amusing. But it didn't seem too far off the mark.

She kept at it out of lack of anything better to do. After a time, whether it was her jangled nerves or simply exhaustion, it all started to make sense. Once she'd linked two or three equations together, the rest seemed to fall into place. She likened herself to an ignorant savage who, although he can press the keys of a computer and make it work, has no true idea of what he's doing. And she definitely had no idea. Zero had arranged the equations in random order on purpose, she supposed, so that even if someone found them, they'd never glean his secrets. Everything seemed to fit now, yet she was certain there was still an error somewhere. On a whim she began rearranging everything and finally reversing the very order of what she saw as the logic of the equation.

And that's when she heard the sobbing from the other room.

She was alone; she knew that much. Yet, she heard a sustained, muted crying from the next room. She rose slightly on the bed and peered through the doorway. The room was dimming as if the sun had slipped behind a cloud. But it was more than that. If blankets had been thrust over the windows, it wouldn't have explained what was coming down. The light was being chased away, the room becoming enveloped in murky gloom. She could see the shadows, black, swirling clouds of coal dust, swimming out of the corners and blackening the air like ink dropped in water. She knew then what was happening. She knew what was coming from the antique mirror in the living room.

The Territories.

She thought: *I've done it. Jesus Christ, I've opened the chasm.*

And she had.

Beyond the doorway, the living room was a fathomless, dark abyss. Fingers of ebony shadow were creeping into the bedroom. A pungent, hot wind with a texture like ash blew the sheets up around her. The sobbing was louder now and she could hear screams and whispers. A singular bleak desolation settled in her heart.

William Zero came walking through the mist, looking every bit Dr. Blood-and-Bones. He was stitched and scarred and wasted, his clothing hanging in fluttering rags . . . or was it his flesh? It was hard to say where one ended and the other began. He was a walking hide, a sutured human pelt, a stuffed and stitched monstrosity barely holding his shape.

"I'm very much impressed," he told her with envy in his voice. "It isn't just anyone who can solve the mystery of the equation."

Behind him, there seemed to be other maimed and skullish faces flitting in the mists, anxious to cross over, but not daring.

"It was an accident," she found herself saying.

"Nonetheless, through accident comes revelation. You called me and I am here." His sutured face attempted a smile. It was horrible, a cadaver's grin. "Now, the book. Give it to me along with your calculations. You have no idea how dangerous they can be in the hands of the ignorant."

"And if I don't?"

"Your cooperation isn't necessary," he promised her. "I'll have it one way or another. There's nowhere to run this time."

She stuffed her pages of work into the book and threw it to him. It was an awkward toss, yet it landed in his seamed palm, driven there by the stinking wind. He slid it into his pocket.

"Very good of you," he said, taking a step forward. "And now how should I reward the trouble you've caused me?"

"Just leave," she said. "I won't tell anyone."

He laughed. "Tell anyone you like. But first, we started something the other day. It's high time we finished it."

Her lips trembled, trying to speak, but words of supplication were beyond her. His appetite made her bowels turn to ice. "Don't touch me," she finally said. "Please don't touch me."

"Now, now, quit your squirming," he said. "We have places to go, things to see." He held out his hand to her. "Come with me. You'll find the journey painful, but the rewards are beyond words."

She crawled away until her back was against the headboard. "Why me? Why do you have to take me? What we had was a lifetime ago."

He came alongside the bed with a straight razor in his hand, its blade stained brown. His stink made bile squirt into her mouth. He was grinning . . . if you could call it that . . . the abundant scar tissue and stitched seams of his face pulling up the corner of his lips into a toothy cadaveric grimace.

"Why don't you take your son?" she gasped, barely able to breathe.

This stopped him. "My son?"

"Yes, Eddy. Your boy."

"Is he near?"

"No, but I can bring him to you," she bartered. "It won't take long. Tonight maybe."

"I had almost forgotten the boy."

"He never forgot you. He's recreating your crimes in detail."

"Really?"

"Yes! He and another are trying to get into the Territories to see you. The Sisters have told them it will be soon."

"I had no idea. Communication is lacking in the chasm."

"Just take him instead of me. He'd be better company."

Dr. Blood-and-Bones was grinding his yellowed, pitted teeth in indecision. "But it's you I've dreamed of, my love. It's you I wanted to spend eternity with."

"You wouldn't enjoy me. I'd scream and cry. I'd hate it."

He grinned. "You're teasing me." He rolled his eyes in ecstasy. "How I've longed to see you in blissful torment."

"But Eddy . . . he's your flesh and blood . . ."

"The Sisters will be bringing him over anyway. I'll see him soon enough."

Her mind was racing, trying to think of something. "The Sisters brought you through, didn't they? Wouldn't you rather bring your son through personally?"

He cackled dryly. "It would be delicious, cheating them of him . . ."

"I can arrange it. He wants me to go with him. I can get him to the old house and you can take him there."

"No tricks?"

"None. I promise. He's just like you. You'll be proud." She opened her robe, exposing her bruises and cuts. "He raped me."

Zero practically beamed with pride. "My, my, what a mischievous thing he is."

"I'll get him for you."

"Very well. Bring Eddy to me and make it soon."

"It will be."

"If I'm pleased, I'll let you stay in this depressing place," he promised her. "If not, your picked bones will warm our marriage bed on the other side."

He stepped back through the door, humming something under his breath. The darkness and mist followed in his wake and disappeared completely. There was something like a sigh as the chasm closed back up and a great wind raced through the suite, pulling pictures from their hooks and scattering newspapers.

Then she was alone again.

* * *

Fenn let himself in around six. He fixed himself a drink and waited for the woman he loved to begin. And as he did, he wondered silently what he'd get from her. Would it be the truth or just more lies? Or even a clever mix of both? Love could be a blinding thing and maybe he'd been deceiving himself for too long. She never said she'd loved him; she never even pretended such. Yet, he'd been certain that she had in her own way. But maybe it was all just a dream and nothing more. The possibility was ominous. All the nights he'd whiled away dreaming of their lives. The times he'd watched her sleeping beside him and thought it would never end. Had it all been just a delusion? He'd never been an emotional man nor a compassionate one. Love didn't come easy to him as it did to some. But when it came, it took him completely and there was no going back. And if this all turned out to be nothing more than a delusive dream, he knew it would destroy him.

Watching her now, sitting across from him like a stranger, it was hard to remember not having doubts. Everything she did—flicking a strand of hair from her eyes or meeting his gaze and then looking away—seemed to be a confession from her that they'd shared nothing but a few amusing sexual interludes.

The possibility was frightening.

There was nothing about her that suggested there was anything more between them. There was no electricity in her eyes, no magic in her face when her eyes found his, only something that might have been guilt or indifference.

"I'm waiting," he said. But was it for the truth? He almost hoped she'd lie and save his heart agony. "Or do you want me to begin?"

She shrugged.

"I've been doing a little research today. Let me tell you about it."

He did. About Soames pimping for William Zero and the Templar Society, about him being Cherry Hill's father. His abuse of her, forcing her into pornographic films. The murder of her family. He stopped there. He assumed Lisa knew the rest.

"Incredible," she said. "It explains a lot. When I hired Soames, I never imagined how involved he really was in this."

"Yeah, the puzzle is fitting together. I think you know the rest. Enlighten me."

"I don't have a choice now."

"No, you don't."

She hugged herself. "There's no easy way to begin this."

"Just do it." His heart was sinking in a pit of despair.

She looked away. "The truth. About me. About all of this. Are you sure it's what you want?"

"Tell me," he managed, wanting to tell her to forget it right then and there, not wanting his sand castles to be washed out into the cold sea of reality.

She looked sad beyond words. And he knew then, if he hadn't before, that it was going to be bad, worse than he could imagine. Her beauty was marred by the dark circles under her eyes and the worry lines around her mouth. He wanted to take her in his arms, but he couldn't. Not just yet. Maybe not again.

"Just tell me," he said, his voice distressed.

"It starts when I was a teenager and my parents got divorced. My mother moved us to Sausalito . . ."

*   *   *

None of it was any better or worse than he'd suspected. During the telling, his mind ran the gamut of emotions from sympathy to dread to disgust. He squirmed and wriggled at times, like a worm in the sun; at other times, he sat completely still, drained of emotion. He wasn't sure what was the worse part of it all, William Zero taking advantage of her vulnerability or Eddy raping her or the bit about Zero returning from the Territories. When she was done and silent, he felt compassionate . . . mainly because he thought her mind had become unhinged.

"Lisa," he said, "you could've told me about this before. I would've understood."

"Would you?" she asked. "I've never told anyone what's inside my head. It's ugly and twisted."

"Don't say that. None of it is your fault." And it wasn't, he'd decided. Zero had messed up her head and she wasn't to blame for that, for any of the confusion that had dogged her since.

"You're wrong," she said briskly. "It is my fault. Eddy came here knowing he could take me if he wanted and that I was too screwed up to stop him."

"You're alive, that's what counts. If you had fought, he would've killed you. I think we both know that."

"Don't lower yourself into feeling pity for something like me," she said evenly. "I'm not worth it. I got exactly what I deserved. I've been deluded and dangerous for years. I formed him into his father in my mind. A man I despise but love at the same time. He saw this in his own way. Saw how easy it would be to toy with me."

"He's a monster," Fenn said, going to her.

She pushed away. "You know the truth of it all now. You know what sort of person you pretend to love. Why don't you just admit I disgust you? That you hate everything that I am?"

"I love you."

"Don't say that!" she screamed. "Don't you ever say that! Can't you see what kind of thing I am? What kind of freak I am?"

He wanted to hold her, but she'd have none of it. He wanted nothing more than to help her, ease her mind. "You're no freak. You have problems, even I can see that, but we can work them out."

"Don't be too sure. What I'm going to tell you now is going to change your mind. I'm going to tell you about Cherry's part in all this."

He looked pale, but he listened. He listened to her tell him about Cherry's escape from prison. The study she made of her. The Hypothalamine. What it had done to her. About Eddy being dead. And lastly, about Cassandra, their Jane Doe. When she was finished, he said nothing. The bit about William Zero returning from the Territories was hard enough to swallow, but this . . . this was madness.

"This is a little hard to take, Lisa. Cherry shapeshifting into Eddy? The walking dead?"

"I know it all sounds ridiculous. But it's the truth. Do you think I'm deranged enough to make up a tale like that?"

"No, of course not, but . . ." But this was too much. He wanted very much to give her the benefit of the doubt, but it wasn't easy.

"You'll have to trust me, Mr. F—*Jim*. I'm afraid it's all you can do, unless you want to throw me in jail."

Fenn lit a cigarette. Of course, that's what it came down to. Either trust her and give her the chance to prove what she was saying or throw her in jail for aiding and abetting. The police were no closer to stopping Eddy Zero than they were a week ago. Trusting Lisa was the only possible choice if he called himself a cop.

"I'm not sure if I believe any of this or not," he grumbled, "but I'm going to give you a chance to prove it all. I guess I owe you that much."

"That's all I ask for." She brought him a stack of letters. "Read these. They'll confirm a few things."

"Cherry's?"

She nodded.

When he was finished, he said, "I'll help you. I'll do everything I can."

"Will you?"

"Yes. And I'll do it for you, not for the sake of the law."

"Everything is coming full circle now, Jim. It started with William Zero and that's where it will end. Eddy's going to call and I'm going to lead him to his father and if I die in the process, then it serves me right, doesn't it? I belong that way." She started to cry and he held her now.

Poor deluded thing, he thought. "Don't worry, it'll be all right."

She pulled away. "All right? My God, you're humoring me, aren't you?"

He couldn't deny it. "Lisa, Eddy is very real. But the Territories . . . they don't exist. It's all nonsense. You have to see that. And the rest of this . . . it just can't be."

The phone rang.

She wiped the tears from her eyes and answered it.

"Do you still want to come along?" Eddy asked.

The emotion left her. "Yes, you know I do."

"Tonight's the night, my dear. Listen very carefully."

"Yes?"

"Do you know the house my father did his work in?"

"I know it."

"Go there tonight if you want to come along. Midnight."

It was too good to be true. Eddy was working right into her hands. "I'll be there."

The line went dead.

"Looks like you'll get your chance to see if I'm crazy or not," she said to Fenn.

"Eddy?" He looked pale.

"Yeah. Tonight we cross over."

Before he could comment on this, the phone rang again.

Lisa answered it. Fenn was on the extension.

"Did you pay a visit to Cherry?" Cassandra inquired.

"I did."

"Good. Then you know her secret."

Lisa said, "Yes. Eddy just called. He said tonight at midnight."

"Good. The sooner the better. I'm getting a little stiff." She laughed quietly. "Go there and make sure your Mr. Fenn is with you. We may need someone with official connections to explain it all away when it's done."

"Will you be there?"

"Yes. I'll be there. The witching hour. How fitting."

The line went dead.

*   *   *

It was raining when Fenn and Lisa reached the old house. Neither said much on the journey over. Lisa had no idea what Fenn was thinking, but she could pretty much imagine what he thought of her and this whole mess. Right now, however, none of that mattered. Within a few hours, she hoped, Zero, Cherry, Eddy and possibly herself would be no more. She wasn't afraid of this. The memories of Eddy and Dr. Blood-and-Bones had to be exorcised and if this meant her death, then it wasn't too great a price to pay to be free of what had haunted her for years now.

She started all this and only she could end it.

She knew Fenn wasn't taking anything about William Zero or the Territories too seriously. They were delusions, he'd decided with his cop's pragmatism, dementias shared by Eddy and Spider and now by her. He didn't give a damn what Gulliver had professed to see, there were no Sisters or alternate worlds of experience. Regardless, he took Eddy very seriously. In his thinking, Eddy was luring her there to rape and possibly kill her, under the guise of making an impossible journey. But what Eddy didn't know was that Fenn was coming along to break up his little party. And as far as Cherry and Cassandra went . . . well, they'd just see, wouldn't they?

Lisa only hoped he was right, that they did indeed take Eddy by surprise. But she had her doubts. She'd have felt better if a dozen cops were waiting in the wings for back-up, but Fenn didn't want it that way. He could take care of Eddy, he insisted. And she wondered if a usually careful man like him was motivated into this thinking by sheer confidence or the macho need to punish Eddy Zero for molesting her. She'd have felt worlds better if he believed her implicitly and went into this nightmare scenario armed with the knowledge that a garden variety psychotic was the least of their worries.

They parked up the street and he said, "Just give me a minute to get around back and then you start slowly walking to the house. Take your time. I want to be in position when he shows himself."

She nodded. "Are you sure we shouldn't call Gaines and have him bring more men?"

"No," Fenn growled. "This is my party."

She didn't like this at all. "You're making a mistake," she told him.

"We'll see. Besides, Cassandra doesn't want a mob of cops, now does she?"

"We're playing with fire."

He ignored her. "Don't take any chances. Once he shows himself, get him talking. Do just as we said: Tell him you have a confession to make and spill it about his old man. That'll keep him busy. I'll do the rest."

"You just won't believe any of what I told you?" Lisa asked one last time.

"Be careful," he said as if he hadn't heard her and slipped off into the storm.

Despite the rain, she did as Fenn asked and walked slowly up to the house. He was going to ruin everything, she knew. He would come busting in with his gun blazing and Dr. Blood-and-Bones would be robbed of what she'd promised him: his son. And what would be the penalty for this? For surely there would be one. Would he be content in dragging her off to his marriage bed or would he want more, like maybe Fenn as well? Another soul to amuse him as the wheels of hellish eternity ground on? She knew only to expect the unexpected and clawed to a dangling thread of hope that told her Zero and Eddy would go their way and Fenn and she theirs.

And that just might happen, she told herself, if you're really lucky and if Cherry wears Eddy's face and not her own.

As she worried over this, she wondered what Cassandra was up to and what her part would be in all this.

Christ, what a mess. What an ugly, awful, horrible mess.

By the time she reached the top of the frost-heaved steps and stood before the threshold, she was soaking wet and taking an almost childish delight in being so. She savored it, for delight was something she feared she'd never know again. Once upon a time, she'd been frightened of storms. Now they gave her a sense of security, of reality.

She went in, intersecting her nightmares.

Gray, uneven light spilled in through broken windows and worm-eaten shutters. There was plaster dust heaped along the baseboards and a stink far worse than mere wood rot or animal droppings. It was like being in some monolithic sarcophagus, it occurred to her, trapped in a crypt as night approached. A miasmic stench of death and blackness crept from the dehydrated walls.

"Eddy?" she sang out. The darkness was silent like a vacuum. Her voice echoed and went stillborn with the dust.

She stepped in further. "Eddy, it's Dr. Lochmere . . . Lisa . . ." The sound of her voice in this awful catacomb was the most frightening thing she could imagine. "Eddy? Are you here?"

"Yes."

Her heart galloped in her chest. The reply came from off to her right. She followed it into a filthy, deserted parlor. Wallpaper was peeling from the walls in arid strips, cobwebs were tangled in the chandelier overhead. "Where are you?" she asked in a wispy voice. Meager illumination flitted in through dusty, stained windows. The smell of death was worse in here and she pictured dry, pitted bones wrapped in a wormy shroud.

"Where?" she tried again.

He stepped from a low alcove. "Here." A light was switched on. A single bulb in the chandelier provided dim light.

"I've come as I said I would," she told him, wondering when the power had been turned back on and deciding it didn't matter. She had light to die by. It was enough.

"Are you ready?"

She nodded. "Yes."

He took her left hand in his. His fingers were cold, the skin parched. His touch induced neither lust nor hatred now, only indifference. He ran his thumb in circles over her palm. "You won't regret this," he told her.

"No . . ."

A suggestion of chill brushed against her, an icy ambience. But it wasn't coming from Eddy, but the alcove.

"No tricks," he said. "And no head games like today."

"No."

"There'll be no going back."

"I know," she lied.

"You don't look well. Are you ill?"

"No, I'm fine. Just out of sorts, I guess. The last few days have been strange ones."

"But pleasurable?" he inquired.

"Yes."

"The Sisters will be here soon, then we'll get started." He looked upward. "They'll arrive up there."

There was a subtle creak of a board and Fenn stepped into the parlor with his gun out.

"Eddy Zero at last," he said.

Eddy didn't look too surprised. "I should've known. Lieutenant Fenn, I presume?"

"In the flesh," Fenn said, his finger tickling the trigger. "Step away from him, Lisa."

She looked from Fenn to Eddy.

Eddy shrugged. "Do as he says. It won't matter now."

"You're done, Eddy," Fenn said, almost casually, as if the game was at an end. "I should kill you, but life behind bars for you will suit me."

Eddy backed away.

Fenn followed him. "It's too late for that."

"Much later than you can imagine," Eddy tittered.

Lisa realized too late what Eddy was doing. He had maneuvered Fenn so that his back was to the alcove. She heard a dry rustling in there and she opened her mouth to shout a warning, but before words could flee her lips, a black impossible shape swam up and took Fenn from behind, throwing him against the wall where his head resounded with a dull crack. He slid senseless to the floor.

"Well done, old boy," Eddy cried.

Even more than the horrid, cadaverous appearance of the thing from the alcove, Lisa was aware of its hideous stink, a reek that made her knees go to rubber and her stomach want to heave. It was Spider. She knew that from the filthy braids that swung like whips from his rotting head.

"My God . . ." she said, not really all that surprised at such things since Cassandra.

"Let's get down to business," Eddy said in a relaxed, almost bored tone. "Spider, truss him up for later. Use the handcuffs I'm sure he's carrying. That's a good wretch."

Spider bared his yellowed teeth, but did as he was told. "And his gun?"

"Put it back in his holster. He may want it later."

Spider did as he was told.

"Don't look so concerned," Eddy said to her. "He's harmless."

She could only say: "He's alive."

"In a manner of speaking."

"How?"

"It's terribly complex. The method exists, that's all you have to know."

That's what she wanted to hear, what she was fishing for. Her scientist's mind had to know that there was a method, a system of rules by which the dead could walk. Cassandra had inferred the dead could live through sheer willpower and Lisa's brain had raged against the idea. But, Eddy now said there was a method. It was something. It soothed her logic to hear it.

A month ago, the knowledge of such a blasphemy against natural laws would have unhinged her completely. It went in direct defiance of everything she knew of physiology and medical science. Yet, she now accepted it with a cool indifference. There was nothing else she *could* do. Her faith in science and physical statutes had been nearly destroyed in the past few weeks and now her years of training were likewise falling to dust at her feet.

"I'm proof of that," Spider said, a certain species of remorse in his voice, almost as if he wished it weren't true.

"Incredible." And it was.

Spider looked up at her as he fastened Fenn with the cuffs and then looked away quickly, as if he didn't like being looked at. And who could blame him? He was little more than a decomposing human scarecrow now, his face gone to leather, his tangled hair alive with crawling things. There was no hope or happiness left in his foul, withered hide, only a bleak desperation.

She motioned to Fenn. "What are you going to do to him?"

"We'll let the Sisters decide," Eddy explained in a whisper. "If they want him, they can have him. If not, we'll leave him be. Would you like that?"

"Yes," she said. She stooped over and ran a hand through Fenn's hair. There was blood on his scalp, but not much. She made a cursory exam and decided he'd wake with an awful headache, but he'd be no worse for wear. She kissed his forehead and, a tear in her eye, wished she'd never involved him in this.

Eddy was watching her. "How touching."

"Fuck you," she said.

"Ha, ha," Eddy laughed. "That's all you ever think of."

*　　*　　*

Cassandra was running a bit behind schedule.

She was out at a cemetery just beyond the city limits. It was here the dead of all denominations and races were buried side by side. It was also here that the city fathers planted their charity cases, like the prostitutes Eddy had murdered. Their graves were lined up one next to the other. None of these nameless women had families or friends. They only had each other and the streets. And now they had this bleak burial yard. It was a terrible place for the dead to dream away eternity. The grounds were ill-tended. Weeds and blighted grasses were left unchecked, save by family members. Dead flowers were tangled in the dirt. Youths frequented the place and left graffiti and beer bottles in their passing. Tombstones had been tumbled over and defaced.

The chapel was scrawled with obscene writings.

Cassandra was alone here this night.

Beneath a pale moon and a mist of rain, she stood on the muddy ground, a pain in her heart at the sight of this place. There were no teenaged, tattooed toughs lurking amongst sepulchers and overgrown vaults, singing vulgar songs and drinking and drugging themselves stupid. It was a good thing. What she had to do, must be done in secret. Death is a mystery; resurrection only for the eyes of the dead or insane. When Cassandra began to call them up from their beds of mold and memory, she wanted no witnesses. She wanted no prying eyes to observe their rebirth but her own. The dead deserved that much. They deserved the dignity of not becoming a tourist attraction.

When she started to sing the song of resurrection, the earth heaved and gave up its buried secrets. The victims of Eddy Zero, not sleeping too well in their lace and silk, swam up from their pits. Fingers broke the dank, dripping soil, followed by hands and flyblown faces. Yellowed and ruined eyes studied the night. Lungs filled with dust and insects gulped in the cool wind. The victims rose and chatted in arid voices, helping the weaker from their beds of dirt. When the gossip and commotion was at an end, they looked upon Cassandra and knew.

Whispering of decay and disillusionment, they followed her into the world of men. Faces robbed of beauty, life, and flesh made their way to the House of Mirrors where a special party was being held in their honor. And who were they, that courted worms and time, to refuse such an invitation?

*   *   *

Eddy came up behind Lisa as she gazed down at Fenn who was hand-cuffed to a furnace grating. He kissed her neck and she shuddered. "I can't begin to tell you how disappointed I am in you bringing a cop here. Not that I didn't suspect your sudden turn of mind, but I had hoped . . ."

"Hoped what?" she asked. "That I'd want to spend eternity with a man as deranged as his father?"

"You know nothing of my father," Eddy said. "Keep a civil tongue in your head or I'll have Spider bite it out."

Spider looked disinterested.

"I knew William Zero better than you ever will," she said.

"Oh really? Do tell."

"Let's get up to the attic," Spider said. "They'll be coming soon."

"No, I have to hear this."

It had the expected result on him. So she told him, leaving out nothing, save his father's reappearance.

Eddy was amused by it. "So, dad and I have shared more than genes and common interests, have we?" He laughed. "The family whore."

She said nothing.

"Did you think any of that would matter?" he asked. "Did you think that I'd let you walk off as a friend of the family? I could care less. He used you, I used you. You like being used. It's your way. You were born to please men of peculiar tastes. It's your calling in life."

She felt raw hatred in her stomach. Was Dr. Blood-and-Bones near? Was he listening right now to this exchange and smiling with fatherly pride at the monster he had created? She was tempted to play head games with Eddy and force Cherry out of hiding. But no. Not just yet. Not unless she had to.

Eddy took her by the hand. "The Sisters were excited by the prospect of you coming along. They'll have endless amusements lined up to keep you busy. You'll never be bored." He squeezed her fingers. "It's time to go."

She allowed herself to be led up the stairs. She was running out of time and knew it with a heavy heart. Would Zero be waiting up there to take custody of his charges? Or would it be the Sisters, anxious not only at having Eddy and Spider, but her as well?

Where the hell was Cassandra?

"It's too bad you'll never write that book about dad and I," Eddy said. "What a read that would make. I wonder if it would've sold."

"Of course. People like reading about monsters, didn't you know that?"

He gave her hand a painful squeeze. "Monsters. You have no idea."

It was all funny somehow, she found herself thinking. It was like the fates were behind Eddy one-hundred percent. Dozens of men looking for him and they couldn't catch him. Yet, he wasn't in hiding, he was merely roaming about town, picking up whores to kill and murdering anyone who got in his way. God must love the damned and deranged. There was no other explanation. Even the fact that he was hiding in Cherry some of the time was no excuse.

"Are you ready?" Eddy asked at the door to the attic.

"Why not?"

Spider opened the door and they followed slowly in his putrescent wake. The end was drawing near and if Zero and Cassandra didn't show soon, she'd spend eternity damning the day she'd ever decided to hunt Eddy Zero down.

The attic looked much like the blurry crime photos taken twenty years before. The walls were quilted in human skins. Each had been fastidiously and carefully removed in whole, then tacked to the wall. Her stomach jumped as she looked upon them . . . the dangling arms and eyeless death masks staring out at her.

The air was warm and reeked of death and hot blood. Two butchered women hung by the feet from hooks set in the roof beams. They were raw and bleeding, slit, plucked, and eviscerated. Their skins and entrails were deposited in the corner along with a black raincoat and a collection of knives.

Lisa turned away, wanting to vomit.

"The final offering," Eddy said, pleased with himself.

Lisa couldn't bear to be in the same room with such butchery, this human slaughterhouse. Her sanity seemed to flutter, wanting to take flight. She held it down. Just for a bit longer.

"You should consider yourself lucky," Eddy told her. "If Spider had had his way, it would've been you hanging there."

Spider gave him a caustic look.

It was quick, but she caught it. Was there some animosity between the two of them? Something she could exploit? She remembered interviewing Spider before his death and thinking that he wasn't particularly dangerous, just driven by personal mania.

"They're coming," Spider said.

And they were.

The mirror flanked by drying hides was darkening, bulging as if some force was pushing from the other side. It rippled like water and lost its physical density.

Lisa gasped.

The air was growing thick with sinister import. The molecules surrounding her seemed to sense a certain profanity of physical laws and were racing about wildly, trying to seal the wound that was already beginning to open. A rush of scorching, stinking air filled the attic and oily shadows crept from the corners. There was a weeping in the distance.

Though she'd never be able to account for it later, a surprising cool confidence settled into her. She saw exactly what had to be done and she did it without hesitation. Eddy was no longer holding her hand. She turned to him as if for a kiss and planted her knee in his groin. He went down with a hissing cry and she was already galloping down the stairs.

"Get the bitch!" Eddy cried, his features fluttering.

She stumbled down the stairs and landed in a heap at the bottom, quickly pulling herself to her feet. The door to the Territories was swinging wide now and she could feel it eating at her back with a baleful anxiety. It was pulling at her, reaching out to claim what it had been promised, unimaginable debaucheries at the ready. She could feel it in her head, too, like needles piercing her thoughts, visions of atrocities swimming in her mind, muddling her jumbled reasoning.

She could feel Dr. Blood-and-Bones, too, knowing he was close, somewhere. It was this knowledge as much as Spider's dragging feet on the stairs that got her going again.

"Wait," he called out.

She stopped, not knowing why.

"It's no good," he explained. "They want you, Lisa. You can't get away. If they don't get you here, it will be somewhere else."

She ran regardless. Something was happening to the house now, it was swallowed in a pale luminosity. The walls were breathing, groaning, the floor trembling, the ceiling shuddering. The rolling contortion of the foundation spilled her to her feet. Spider wasn't in pursuit just yet; he, too, was mesmerized by what was happening. She knew without a doubt that the Sisters were taking the house, ingesting it into the Territories. If she didn't escape and soon, she'd emerge from the house not into freedom, but into hell itself.

Spider was behind her, shambling in her direction. He had a knife in one blighted, stringy paw. He was doing what he thought best for her and himself, she realized. Apparently, she'd been promised to the Sisters and they intended to have her. And Spider was taking no chances: if she wouldn't come of her own accord, he would drag her bleeding body to them. He had worked too long for this moment and he wouldn't be denied passage into the other world because of her fear.

She started down the steps, grasping the bannister for dear life. The house was swaying and teetering madly beneath her. The floors were moving like water, flowing and undulating, making escape no mean feat. She ascended with desperate slowness, the stairs compressing and rippling even as her feet sought solid footing. Zero was close, yet he didn't show himself. What was he waiting for? Only he could end this nightmare for her and she was longing to see his mutilated face. She had no other hope. She had already decided that Cassandra wasn't coming.

She tumbled onto the landing and crawled feverishly towards Fenn. He was floating in midair, carried aloft by unseen forces. The far wall of the parlor was flaking away and beyond an absolute blackness was inserting itself. Fingers of misty teleplasm were drifting into the room, snaking through the roiling air like strands of ghostly flesh.

"Fenn!" she shouted.

He either didn't or couldn't hear her in the thundering commotion of two worlds meeting on a common, blasted ground.

Not that it mattered. All was lost and Spider was at her back.

"You see?" he said. "It's too late."

His ghoulish face was running like wax from the bone beneath. His flesh was hanging in shredded strips of decay, one eye sunk deep into its housing. He was degenerating even as she watched. His pursuit of her had apparently been costly in terms of his strength.

"Come with me now," he managed.

She looked from him to the hole in reality that was rapidly expanding.

She was the cause of all of this. In her own way, she had been. Her insistence on finding Eddy and conquering him and her own confused psychology had started this all into motion in the first place. Eddy Zero was dead, but a much more degenerate and vicious version of him lived on in Cherry and this, too, was her doing. Everything begins somewhere, with some random act, and she had set this terrible wheel of fate into motion. She tried to convince herself it wasn't true, but there was no getting around the cold and cruel facts. Her lust, her desires, her memories of something too horrible to remember, too wonderful to forget, had been her undoing and that of countless innocents. She had unearthed this nightmare, freed it from its noxious grave of aspiration and now she was about to be swallowed alive and screaming by it.

Spider was getting close now.

She opened her mouth to protest, to scream perhaps, and then she saw Eddy bearing down on his dead compatriot. When Spider was a few feet from her, the blade of Eddy's knife exploded from his throat and sawed his bobbing head nearly free. Spider went down in a heap of dust and fragmented flesh. Eddy began hacking at him, stealing the life he had given, slicing him apart like a moth-eaten rag doll. It was all done quite effortlessly. There was little holding Spider together by that point, save spit and determination. When Eddy was done, all that remained was a filthy pile of something that looked more like parched, slashed rags than a thing that had once boasted flesh and blood.

"I should've done that a long time ago," Eddy told her.

There was a sudden hissing, howling eruption of black steam from Spider's remains. The Shadows that had hidden in his putrid folds were oozing forth now, looking for a new home. She could see their faces as they departed the shredded cadaver in undulating, twisting balloons of murk. And such faces. They were men, women, and children, these faces, victims all of gruesome deaths and ghastly survival. There were tales to be told in their rolling black eyes, atrocities to be recorded. Bits of pain and madness and sheer horror; fragments of laughter, love, and loneliness. They were a livid, vaporous catalog of humanity and inhumanity, a parade of mankind and its multitude of sufferings.

She watched them light into the air like flies and they watched her.

There was nothing even remotely human left in them now. Those things had long ago been dispersed like ash in the wind and only a reflection of it remained in their hollow, searching eyes. These were beast of hate and lust and depravity, killers and victims all, bound by psychotic aspiration into one loathsome volume of excessive wants.

And what did they want? Why, a place to hide.

But none was offered.

They pressed in around Lisa in a polluted mass, sniffing and tasting and teasing her flesh and thoughts. They quickly abandoned her and sought Eddy like a train seeking a tunnel, punching right into him.

He wasn't alarmed, only irritated.

"And now for you," he said.

He seemed to glide in her direction, the knife describing elaborate arcs in the screaming, tattered wind. She had no weapon, no hope of salvation. He was going to cut her wide so the Shadows would have a new home to brood and scheme in and he would have a lover to carry into the chasm.

He brought the knife up to strike, but a voice stayed it.

"She is lovely. So very pretty."

The voice of a woman, but scratching and dry and inhuman. Lisa smelled a sharp, almost violent odor of skinned minks and rancid pelts.

Dear God, she thought, *The Sisters.*

At least, one of them. It was something from a freak show, a grotesque sculpture of rolling meat scarified by a surgeon's knife, a grisly anatomy display sewn together from a dozen separate corpses. A woman, yes, but obscenely bloated, discolored oil oozing from her pores with a sweet, revolting stink of musk. Her breasts were immense, perfectly round and hard-nippled, absolutely succulent with life. As Lisa stared at her with barely concealed horror, she saw her body was really a mass of writhing, porcine flesh horribly intersected by dozens of converging sutures that were almost artistically patterned in her skin like intricate tattooing. There was a dark beauty to it *and* her, from the blood-oiled hair to the flawless bubble gum pink of her rounded hips.

Haggis Sardonicus, a voice like a tolling funeral bell said in the back of Lisa's brain. Yes, that was her name. And all who looked upon her knew it.

"You didn't lie, Eddy. She is exquisite," the Sister said, grinning like a scythe. She studied her prey with glossy purple-red eyes like a dog appraising a shank of bloody meat. They seemed to bulge from their flayed sockets.

Lisa tried crawl away until her back ran into the wall. Oh no, she would not escape this. There was no way this horror would let her slip through its ensanguined fingers. Just no way.

As Sister Sardonicus approached her, Lisa saw that her body was roiling with fleshy pulsations as if there was boiling lava beneath it. It moved and shuddered and shivered and she saw faces, dozens of tiny plum-sized embryonic faces pushing from the mass against the veneer of skin like the faces of dolls pressed against a sheet of Saran Wrap.

Lisa screamed.

And as she did, Haggis Sardonicus seemed to deflate until she was skeletal and machined-looking, her face like some carven fetish mask with ruby eyes set in gouged, upturned slits. The skull beneath had the appearance of something whittled and pared from bone, the skin covering it looking braided and beaded and ritualistically slit with tribal cicatrisation. Her lipless mouth revealed gums like raw meat and yellow tusklike teeth.

"I told you you would like her," Eddy said. "She likes to squirm, she likes to squeal, and she likes to scream."

The Sister smiled like death, her sutured face moving uneasily over muscle and sinew, a fluid jigsaw puzzle. "Don't quiver with fear," she said to Lisa. "I can smell the heat between your legs. I can taste your need. You're *our* kind. You're hungry."

She turned to Eddy. "Come here, Eddy," she said.

He dropped the knife and did as he was told, stumbling into her enclosing arms as she bloated to impossible dimensions. His fingers, long denied the mysteries of her flesh, explored freely now, teasing and twisting her pendulant breasts which expunged droplets of milk like shimmering pearls, his fingers disappearing beneath the skin and locating treats that hid below. He was drawn into her, his flesh bisecting her own, drawn in, erection and body alike. For a moment they seemed to be nothing but a tangle of limbs and blubber and then Eddy was cast away, seed running from his cock.

Lisa was whimpering now and not because of what she had seen, but what was seeing her: Haggis Umbilicus. She came out of the darkness, the birth cord connecting her to her sister like a flaccid fireman's hose. Lisa could barely take in what she was seeing: an immense bag of leathery flyblown skins and stretched hides that flapped like sails caught in a high wind. A semi-human monster composed of living witch skirts stitched together with thongs of gut that burst their seams randomly to reveal ropes of creeping entrails within. Its head was a mop of writhing scarlet ribbon worms that crawled free of a puckered corpse face, the mouth suckering like that of a leech. It had one bleached, yolky eye darting in a shriveled socket.

Haggis Umbilicus, Lisa heard in the back of her mind.

This was the end. It had to be. Zero had lied to her. He had set her up for this great fall into insanity. Cassandra had betrayed her. There was nothing left now. Nothing at all.

She screamed again as Sister Sardonicus plied her hair with distended, oily fingers, orgasmic moans making her swollen lips tremble.

Lisa pulled away. Sardonicus looked unhappy, as if Lisa really were her only child.

"Where are you, you bastard?" she screeched into the void as her mind began to come apart. *"We had a deal! You wanted your son and he's here! Take him for God's sake! Stop this!"*

Sardonicus snatched Lisa's ankle as she tried to crawl away, pulling her back. Her eyes were huge and red like arterial blood, her tongue shuddering in the air in a perverse simulation of cunnilingus.

"Zero!" Lisa cried out, her sanity sinking fast. "If you ever cared for me, if you ever pretended to, stop this! For the love of Christ, *stop this!"*

The Sister's swollen tongue was tasting her calf now, drawing upwards, upwards in a burning wake.

"Edward," a voice said, almost playfully.

The Sister's stopped, as did Eddy.

Dr. Blood-and-Bones stepped into this arena of lunacy and his blanched eyes swept the room. His disfigured face literally cracked into a lewd mockery of a smile and his maimed anatomy pulsed through rents in his clothing and the threadbare stitching that held him together.

"Are we playing?" he inquired.

Haggis Sardonicus looked guilty as if she'd been caught at a naughty game.

"Father?" Eddy said, his features unstable.

Lisa could see bits of Cherry trying to insinuate themselves. Not now, she thought in desperation, for the love of God.

"Yes, my boy," the good doctor said. "I've come to take you home."

"He's ours," Sardonicus purred. "You can't have him. We've worked very hard for this one."

"There'll be others," Zero assured them.

"No . . ."

He held up his book. They fell silent at the sight of it, knowing what he could do with it. "But you can help," he promised.

Lisa remembered Fenn and went to him. He was drifting in the air like a man in a hammock. She pulled him to her and they stumbled to the floor. His eyes flickered open.

"What the hell is this?" he asked, looking around.

"And who is this?" Zero asked, stepping in their direction and stroking his withered chin. "Who is this, exactly?" He stepped even closer. "What's your name, friend. Tell me."

Fenn's eyes were staring, confused. Everything Lisa said was true, he now knew, and the revelation of this was staggering. He couldn't seem to find his voice.

Zero started to laugh. "Your name is Fenn."

"Yes."

"And how are the headaches, dear sir? Do they plague you often?"

"How did you . . ."

"You're haunted by memories you do not understand, a déjà vu that torments you continually . . . am I correct?"

Fenn looked shocked. The headache was back and he grimaced in pain. This was the big one he'd been waiting for. The final attack that would destroy him.

Zero was grinning now. "The seeds one plants," he mused. "You never know what sort of fruit they'll blossom."

Fenn looked at Lisa. "What the fuck is he talking about?"

But Lisa didn't know. The Sister's didn't know. And Eddy didn't know. But they were all waiting to find out.

"The Templar Society," Zero said. "Do you remember any of it?"

Fenn just stared.

"When things were coming to a close, when our Mr. Soames was beginning to ask too many questions, things had to be done. Grimes committed suicide, weak and soft thing that he was," Zero told them. "That left only Stadtler and myself. Something had to be done with him. He couldn't be trusted."

"You have Eddy," Lisa said. "Let us go."

Zero continued undaunted. "Something had to be done. I had mastered a technique of personality transference. After a period of deprivation and harassment and the use of psychotropic drugs and hallucinogenic reinforcement, it was possible to destroy a person's psyche . . . wipe it clean. I didn't want to kill Stadtler, so I decided to give him a new personality. I had already selected individuals of the exact physical make-up as Grimes and Stadtler, in case I wanted to toy with their minds. The rest was simple."

Fenn was quiet; he had no words to say.

Lisa wasn't sure what this was about, but the possibility of what he was saying was professionally fascinating.

"It took some months to break down Stadtler, but I did it. After which, I had him listen to recordings of the life of the man he was to become. He listened and listened and listened. Soon, he knew nothing else. With the use of hypnosis and drug therapy, I completed the transference."

"What're you talking about?" Eddy asked.

"I'm talking about my friend Stadtler and who he became."

But Lisa was way ahead of him. She knew. She knew everything now. Fenn just stared.

"Stadtler became Mr. Fenn. And he's been hiding in that guise for some years."

Fenn was on his feet, one hand clutched to his exploding head, the other waving his gun about. "You . . . lie," he said between clenched teeth. "You . . . lying sonofabitch . . . I know who I am . . ."

"Jim! Jim, just wait," Lisa said. "What kind of game is this, Zero? If he's not Fenn, then where—"

"You'll find the real James Fenn in a shallow grave at the rear of the house." He almost seemed pained that it had to come out. "Fenn was selected because of his uncanny resemblance to Stadtler and the fact that he had no family, no friends. He was clay waiting to be formed. A body waiting for a life."

Fenn screamed something, struggling with the handcuffs that held him. He jerked and twisted, his face contorted with hatred. Zero stepped over to him, then his coat fluttered open and his disfigured anatomy was revealed. As Lisa watched, it opened, it unzipped, and a terrible wind began. Fenn screamed once before the flesh left his bones in a noisome vapor and was sucked into Zero's body cavity. All that was left were bones.

Lisa started to scream and she might never have stopped, if it weren't for a voice.

"What a display." Cassandra's voice.

They all turned to see her troop in with a collection of women fresh from their graves.

"A party," one said.

"Such a party," said another.

They began to clap and shout at Zero's handiwork, jumping and screeching, losing bits of themselves in the process.

Cassandra went to Lisa and pulled her to her feet. "It's all right now, dear," she said. "Eddy wanted some friends to come along and I've brought just the ones."

Eddy began to tremble, his features contorting and running. He became Cherry, then himself, then Cherry, then himself once again.

This brought fresh applause from his admirers and they danced about him in a circle as his flesh played its mutinous tricks. The Shadows got in on the act, invading the dead women and finding new homes.

"What a spectacle," Zero tittered. "What an absolute delight."

He didn't seem to mind that his son was a shapeshifter. He didn't seem to mind at all. "Don't fret, my dear," he told Cherry, "there's always room for a lovely creature like you."

Cherry gave way to Eddy and took a doddering step back. His/her circle of friends let Zero through.

"Time to go, boy. It's what you wanted, isn't it?"

"Yes . . ."

Zero grinned. "Excellent, blood of my blood. But you can't go like this, now can you?" he cackled. "You'll have to go into the chasm as I did—in pieces."

Haggis Sardonicus grinned with mirth. "Now comes the time of the rending and the remaking," she said.

Her sister made a slithering sound of acquiescence.

They set to work on Eddy immediately, peeling his skin free with their fingernails which were like surgical blades. As he screamed, his hide was separated from muscle and connective tissues, organs and bones removed. He was dissected, dismembered, taken carefully apart, what was inside him neatly stacked in orderly piles. But the real horror, the real agony came when his nervous system was plucked free. The Sisters enjoyed this part the most, plucking his nerve endings like the strings of a lyre and picking at his ganglia until they reverberated with a white-hot humming agony as if they'd been scraped with a cello bow.

Though he couldn't possibly be alive, he shrieked and begged for mercy . . . even though his lungs and mouth were on opposite side of the room from one another.

"You can go now," Dr. Blood-and-Bones told Lisa. "There's nothing more for you here."

She stood her ground, unable to move or even think of doing so. Like a child with her eye to a keyhole, she could do nothing but watch the carnage taking place before her. The whores Eddy had strung up as offerings were beginning to dance and shudder on their ropes, their fleshless faces attempting grins that were mere muscular contractions. The first fell, then the second. They crawled in Lisa's direction and she ran, Cassandra coming behind her but most casually.

She made it down to the second floor landing before darkness welled up in her brain and she lost consciousness. She might've been out for a minute or a day when she woke and she came to slowly, like a dreamer awakening. Cassandra was stroking her hair.

"It's over now, Lisa. But you'd better run and fast," she said.

Lisa scrambled to her feet and made it downstairs.

The house was beginning to come apart completely. Great rents and slits were gashed in its floors and walls, darkness pooling up from them like blood. She made a frantic run into the parlor, but most of it was gone.

Fenn was dead, she kept reminding herself. He's dead and he wasn't even himself this whole time no more than Eddy is himself or I'm myself and—

"I told you to leave."

She turned and Zero was blocking her escape route. He snatched her by the wrist and forced a wormy kiss on her lips. He shoved his book into her hand.

"Take this," he said. "I don't need it now. Call me anytime. You know I'll be home. I'm *always* home."

Cassandra looked at him and said, "You're terribly dramatic, aren't you?"

He laughed. "Would you like to come along, my pet?"

"Not likely."

He shrugged. "Pity."

Lisa fought from his grip and they fled through the door and into the night.

"We better get clear," Cassandra said.

A sudden, horrendous explosion threw them down the steps and onto the sidewalk. The house seemed to fold in on itself, becoming insubstantial and finally vaporizing into a black mist that faded in the wind. Nothing remained but a smoking, blackened area to mark its passing into another world. Lisa thought she heard a peel of laughter from somewhere distant.

But maybe not.

ESCAPE

"Let's go," Cassandra said. "I haven't much time." She led Lisa to her car and gave her a few minutes to collect herself. "Can you drive?"

She nodded. She knew she was in a state somewhere near shock, but it would pass. Cassandra slid a cigarette between her lips and lit it. Lisa took great drags and began to cough. "My God," she whimpered, "my God."

When the tears had subsided, she drove them away.

"You know where I have to go, don't you?" Cassandra asked.

Lisa did. Somehow she knew exactly where she had to go.

"We'll be a long time in making sense of this," Cassandra said. "But, time will pass as it always does, and reflection will soothe our souls."

Lisa looked at her in disbelief.

"It will. In time, even the most horrible of events makes a certain sense."

"Fenn's dead. I don't know how that makes sense."

"He was tied up in this, too. His identity would've surfaced eventually. You didn't kill him. The knowledge of who and what he really was did. Remember: he was Stadtler. He was a monster like Zero. And now you've put your past to rest. In the process you've healed a wound in this city that's been open for far too long."

"I suppose you're right."

"I am. In time you'll really believe that. The guilt will ease."

Lisa slowed and pulled through the gates of the cemetery. "Good-bye," she said.

Cassandra got out of the car. "Till we meet again," she called out as Lisa drove off.

Lisa was alone again.

Just like at the beginning.

She cradled Zero's book in her arms and went back to the hotel. She'd wanted to write about father and son, but now she had a more important task in life: keeping the book out of the hands of the unwary and driven. Maybe in time it would fall to dust, but until then she was its guardian. She had only tears now and black memories that would haunt her to the grave. She was alive and that was something. The whimsical turn of the wheel of fortune had spared her. She would watch and wait now, guard against their return. Because they would open the chasm again. It was only a matter of time.

But it wouldn't be tonight and that was enough for now.

Comet Press is an independent publisher
of horror and dark crime.

Visit us on the web at:
www.cometpress.us

and follow us on twitter and facebook:

twitter.com/cometpress
facebook.com/cometpress

Made in the USA
Lexington, KY
31 January 2014